Sugar & Spice

The Army Cadets

Also By
CHRISTOPHER CUMMINGS

Sugar & Spice

The Army Cadets

C.R. Cummings

DoctorZed
Publishing
www.doctorzed.com

This edition Published 2021 by DoctorZed Publishing

DoctorZed Publishing books may be ordered through booksellers or by contacting:

DoctorZed Publishing
10 Vista Ave
Skye, South Australia 5072
www.doctorzed.com

ISBN: 978-0-6454665-6-0 (hc)
ISBN: 978-0-6454665-5-3 (sc)
ISBN: 978-0-6454665-4-6 (ebk)

National Library of Australia Cataloguing-in-Publication entry

Author: Cummings, C. R., author.

Title: Suger & Spice / Christopher Cummings.

ISBN: 9780645466560 (hardcover)

Series: Cummings, C. R. The army cadets.

Target Audience: For young adults.

Subjects: Adventure stories, Australian.

Military cadets--Queensland--Fiction.

Cover image © Ekays | Dreamstime.com
Cover design © Scott Zarcinas

Printed in Australia, UK & USA

DoctorZed Publishing rev. date: 25/04/2022

Dedication

This book is dedicated to the teachers of my youth who provided inspiration and help at a critical time in my life, and in particular the Principal of Cairns State High School, Mr Norm Croswell, Deputy, Mr Fitzgerald and Mr Charles Reich. They, and the other teachers were a most professional and dedicated band and a credit to their profession. Their inspiration and leadership produced classes of high achievers who have mostly done very well in life and provided Australia with a group of valuable citizens.

Chapter 1

SECRET LOVE

Declin Riley, 19 and a worker at the Caster Sugar Mill, walked slowly along the footpath of the little town, his mind clouded with dark thoughts about the 'accidental' death at the mill the day before. One of the long-time mill workers, Jack Henley, a middle-aged father of four, had fallen into the slashers at the start of the milling train and had been killed, the upper half of his body mutilated beyond recognition by the steel cutters.

And Declin had been a witness. His workstation was in the computer control room and it was he who had stopped the mill. He had been routinely scanning the dozen closed-circuit TV monitor screens when, out of the corner of his eye, he had glimpsed sudden unusual movement on the top left screen. Glancing at it he had seen what could only be a man's legs and body among the latest load of cane billets. To his credit he had acted almost instantly to hit the stop button. But it had been too late and already Jack's head and upper half had been slashed to scarlet ribbons by the rapidly revolving steel cutters.

Sick with anxiety, Declin had hit the alarm button and then run to the scene. For him it wasn't far, the control room being just up a flight of steel steps from the start of the milling train. Here the rail wagons of freshly cut sugar cane were tipped into a steel pit. The short lengths of sugar cane, the billets, were then slashed into tiny pieces and shreds of fibre by the slashers before being passed through the huge steel rollers of the actual mill. Human flesh and bone had been no match for the toughened steel blades.

The mill chief engineer, Mr Battersby, had arrived at almost the same time and joined Declin as he leaned over the steel railings to look down into the pit. The sight was so ghastly that Declin had at once thrown up, then turned away to spew again just outside. By then the shift foreman, Frank Carmody, had also arrived and several other workers. They had all stood and stared, aghast. It was instantly obvious that no First Aid was needed. Mr Battersby and the foreman had quickly made the decision to rope the area off and to leave the body where it was. At the very least it was a death that would have to be investigated by the Health and Safety people and by the police.

But was it an accident? That was what was bothering Declin as he made his way towards the mill. *Jack had worked at the mill for nearly thirty years. He was very aware of the dangers,* Declin mused. *And there are plenty of dangers in a sugar mill.*

The mills were huge factories full of large, heavy, moving machinery. Water and grease made the concrete floors and steel walkways and ladders slippery, and there were steam pipes and hot vats and lots of electrical circuits.

But how did Jack come to fall in? Declin puzzled.

Jack's place of work was a few paces back at the controls to the rotating tipper that up-ended the cane bins from the light railway to empty the billets into the pit. Not that the operator had much to do now. The whole process was controlled by the computer and he was only there to see that it was all working normally. If there was a problem, he also had a stop button to bring the slashers to a stop.

And there is a steel safety rail between the control position and the pit. Was Jack leaning over to look at something? Declin wondered. That steel safety rail was almost chest high.

But what was really bothering him, apart from his conscience, was a fleeting, blurry image on the CCTV. *Was that a hand? Did someone push Jack?* he thought. *Was it murder?*

That notion set his heart hammering with anxiety and added to the gnawing feelings of guilt that chewed at his conscience. *If I had seen him sooner, I might have stopped the mill in time,* Declin fretted. It was sickening thought.

As he passed the last house he glanced to his right to watch one of the sugar trains go clanking past hauling cane to the mill. The mill was served by a rail network of light railway lines, 2-foot gauge (Well, 610mm really, but nobody called it that, preferring to use the old Imperial measure that had been in use when the lines were laid a hundred and forty years before). The trains were hauled by small diesel locomotives which usually had forty or fifty 'bins' behind. Each bin was a small rail wagon with a wire mesh cage on it that held about 4 tonnes of cane billets.

As the end of the train rattled and squeaked past him Declin reached the end of the town and he then crossed the main North Coast railway, the 3-foot 6-inch Queensland Government line. He paused here to look both ways along the clearing of the railway and then turned his attention on the mill. It now loomed up, towering over the trees in the park ahead of him, the gigantic steel sheds and huge steel chimneys dominating the landscape. It was a sight that always impressed Declin and he marvelled that he was lucky enough to work in such a place.

He walked on fifty paces to the bitumen ring road which enclosed the park which lay between him and the mill offices and mill. Now he was in the 'Mill Estate', which was counted separate from the town. The town of Caster was laid out in a T-shape. The head of the T was a kilometre behind him and was straggled on both sides of the Bruce Highway, the main highway from Cairns to Townsville. That part of town on the other side of the Bruce Highway had the petrol station, mechanic's workshop, a shop and the school and police station. It also contained the better of the two hotels.

The old main street of the town on this side of the highway made up the stem of the T. Unusually it had buildings on only one side. The other side was the light railway and then fields of sugar cane. The buildings were a straggle of different styles and ages, most of them old weatherboard 'bungalow' type houses dating from more than hundred years before. There was one shop and the second hotel, the Caster, which was where Declin boarded. The whole place had a sleepy, decrepit air. 'Quaint' some people called it, but to Declin, who came from Bundaberg, it had the feel of being a rundown dump. Many of the old buildings badly needed a new coat of paint and many had mildew and even moss growing on the walls, a result of the extremely hot and humid tropical climate.

And it was hot and humid now and Declin wiped perspiration from his brow as he crossed over into the park and walked past the old steam locomotive that stood there as a monument to past glories. The 'sugar' crushing season is the six months from June to November and even now, in early October, there were hints that the wet season might be starting early in Far North Queensland. Usually 'The Wet' started in December but there had already been a few unseasonal showers to warn that this year things might be different. Everyone hoped it would hold off for a few more weeks so that the harvest could be completed. If the ground was too wet, the mechanical harvesters could not operate in the cane fields without bogging so there was no cane for the mill to crush. That affected the whole community, so they did not want rain. Every day that the crushing stopped cost the mill thousands of dollars and also cost the farmers and workers money, and then the shopkeepers, hoteliers and so on.

As he walked Declin kept glancing to his left and he paused at a park bench to retie a shoelace, for he was fastidious in his dress and somewhat old-fashioned as he wore polished leather shoes, a relic of his boarding school upbringing in Brisbane. His gaze roved around the Mill Estate and he could not help smiling and shaking his head at the antiquated nature of the whole layout. The 'Estate' had been set up back in the early pioneering days of North Queensland in the 19th Century and the layout reflected the social mores and values of the time. On his left were four very large and graceful old bungalows, mansions almost, set in well-kept gardens. These were the homes of the mill manager, bursar (They still didn't call the job title something modern like 'finance officer'!), the superintendent of the rail system, and the chief mechanical engineer.

On the other side of the park was a row of ten houses and these were the homes of the foremen, under-managers and skilled technical people, the houses provided by the mill as part of the job package. The ordinary workers like Declin either lived in the town or in the nearby city of Cairns or the neighbouring towns of Innisfail and Babinda, all less than an hour's drive away.

Then Declin's heart skipped a beat. What he had been hoping for happened. *There she is!* he thought.

'She' was Carol, the 15-year-old daughter of Mr Battersby, the Mill Engineer. Declin was aware that Carol was no beauty in the fashionable sense. He had to admit that she had a plain face liberally sprinkled with freckles and her hair was a mousy brown cut short and she had only a teenage girl's slim figure. But none of that mattered. To him she was a beautiful person and he had found her to be kind and friendly and as a result he was in love.

But Declin was also hotly aware that she was four years younger and still at school. Quite apart from any social stigma at being possibly accused of 'cradle snatching', Declin was a profoundly moral young man and his conscience determined his actions. That age difference really worried him, and he was determined not to let his urges and desires harm her in any way. Not that she knew about them. At no time had he let his thoughts be obvious to anyone, let alone her. He had very little experience with girls and was extremely shy in their presence. So he had only ever spoken to her in group social situations and admired her from afar, dreaming of what the future might hold.

At that moment, Carol, dressed in the uniform of Cairns State High School, was placing her school bag on the back seat of her mother's car. As she closed the door, Declin again briefly wondered why Carol attended an ordinary state high school when her parents could obviously afford to send her to the best of private schools. Wistfully admiring, he watched as she then turned and kissed her father goodbye before climbing into the passenger seat.

As the car began moving, her father glanced up and his eyes met Declin's across the hundred paces of open lawn. For a moment a frown crossed Mr Battersby's face and Declin forced a smile and resumed walking, his heart hammering. The trivial incident reminded him very forcibly of the social and employment gulf between him and the Chief Engineer.

I am just the lowest cog in the machine, he thought despondently. *The boss won't take kindly to me courting his under-age daughter.*

So far Declin had avoided any trouble during the four months he had worked at the mill, and he believed that Mr Battersby was happy with his performance. Certainly he had praised his quick reactions the day before and that had helped.

As he resumed walking across the park Declin's eyes followed the car as it drove around the one-way ring road. It went past the front of the mill offices and then the massive steel sheds of the mill before coming back around past the worker's houses. As the car came around Declin noted that Carol was looking in his direction and he was surprised when she raised a hand and smiled.

Is she waving to me? he wondered, hardly daring to hope she even knew he existed.

As the car was 50 metres away, he was not sure if she was waving to him or to her father. He was unsure if her father was still at the front of their house, which was now behind Declin, and he did not dare turn to look. All he could manage was a sickly grin and a brief wave, flushing with embarrassment as he did.

To his relief, she flashed a smile in return, and then he was sure the greeting had been for him and his heart thudded with hope. To his relief, her mother did not even glance in his direction and the car vanished off behind him along the main street of the town.

So it was with very mixed emotions that Declin arrived at the mill. Part of him was uplifted by hope and what he thought was love and the other was depressed by the tragedy of the day before. He had experienced a terrible night of guilt and despondency, oppressed by thoughts of death and grief, and had woken feeling ill and emotionally drained.

And he knew there would be more stress. *The police said they would be back again today,* he thought.

As he walked past the first of the crushers, he saw that the police tape had been removed from the steel uprights and posts around the tipper and pit and that steam was billowing from the mill chimney.

The police have done all their forensic stuff, and they have taken away Mr Henley's body he decided. *So we will be restarting the mill.*

Ghastly images of that mangled body flashed across his mind and his whole being quivered with revulsion and he almost threw up again. He had not been able to manage breakfast and now half regretted that as he felt nauseous but had nothing to bring up.

Standing at the pit were four of his co-workers dressed in their grey overalls and 'Hi Vis' vests and they all looked gloomy and despondent and had obviously been discussing the accident. They greeted Declin and he managed a greeting in return. One of them, Paul Walsh, clapped him on the shoulder and said, "Good job yesterday, young Declin."

That made him feel better but moved him so much he nearly burst into tears. For a moment all he could do was nod. Another man then said, "How did you know to stop the crushers?" he asked.

Bill Pascoe, Declin remembered. *Works with the centrifuges.*

"I saw the accident on a TV monitor," he answered.

"Quick work then," Bill replied.

"Not quick enough," Declin replied, unable to keep the regret out of his voice. Then he swallowed and shrugged. "We starting the mill today?" he queried.

"Yep, soon as the cops have finished interviewing us again," Paul replied, gesturing to where the loaded train of sugar wagons stood on the rail line leading into the mill.

"I'd better make sure everything is set to start," Declin replied. With that he turned and made his way up the steel steps that led up to the control room.

As he did, one of the four turned and followed him. Beyond noting that it was a big man named Rossiter, Declin did not pay him any attention. At the top of the steps Declin walked along the steel landing in front of the air-conditioned Control Room and opened the door to go in.

As he did, Rossiter caught him up and grabbed at his sleeve. "Just a minute Declin me boy," he said.

Declin was surprised and turned to look at Rossiter. But Rossiter just pushed the door open and looked in. He then stepped inside and gestured for Declin to follow. Mystified, Declin stepped into the Control Room, noting that his work mate Alfred was not there yet.

Rossiter looked around and then closed the door firmly. Giving Declin a hard look he snarled, "Did anything show up on the CCTV about how the accident happened yesterday?"

Realization burst in Declin's brain like an exploding bomb. *It was murder! Rossiter knows something,* he thought, his heart rate shooting up with fear and anxiety. For a moment he hesitated about what to say and then nodded. "A bit," he admitted.

"Show me," Rossiter said, his facial expression and body language threatening.

"But the police will want to see it," Declin objected.

"And so do I. Now show me," Rossiter snarled, any pretence of friendliness gone.

Declin glanced towards the door and window, hoping that someone else might come along. Fear began to prickle the hair up the back of his neck and he started to breather faster and to perspire. "I ... I don't know if I should," he stammered.

"You bloody well show me and now, or you will regret it!" Rossiter snarled, shaking a fist under his nose.

Blushing with shame at his own weakness Declin nodded. He was now so scared he had to swallow before answering. "OK," he agreed. He moved to his seat and sat down, then switched on the computers and monitors. While waiting for them to boot up his mind raced, wondering how he could get out of the situation.

Worse still he now realised he had made a tactical mistake as he was seated with Rossiter standing close behind his right shoulder, placing him at a real disadvantage. But there seemed nothing for it but to comply, so he started the CCTV recording, speeding it up to get quickly to near the time of the accident. *4:25 that was,* he remembered.

Slowing the images to normal speed two minutes before that time Declin stared at the screen. Rossiter leaned close over his shoulder, also staring hard, his breath coming in deep exhalations that smelt so foul that Declin wrinkled his nose in distaste.

And there it was.

A hand and arm pushing and then Mr Henley's face, surprise turning rapidly to terror. In a moment he was tumbled over into the pit, and then the arm flicked back and the view was blotted out by the cane bin rotating up into view and the load of billets tumbling down onto the frantically struggling man.

That's what I saw, Declin thought, sick from the memory and now from the anxiety induced by Rossiter's close and threatening proximity.

Then the screen registered the system stopping and Declin shuddered.

Rossiter nudged him. "Is that it? Is that when it stopped?"

"Y... Yes," Declin stammered. "I... I saw Mr Henley down there and hit the stop button. But I wasn't in time."

"Who else has seen this video?" Rossiter asked.

"No-one," Declin replied, then realised he had made another mistake. "But I told them about it."

"Told who what?" Rossiter demanded to know, his angry face now close beside Declin's.

"Mr... Mr Battersby and the police sergeant," Declin replied. He was sweating now and shivering with stress and nausea.

"Told them what exactly?"

Declin was now so scared he had to swallow several more times and gulp some air before replying. "I told them I had seen Mr Henley down in the pit and had then stopped the crushers."

"What about the bit before that, when he fell in?"

"No," Declin replied.

"Then wipe the tape," Rossiter ordered.

Declin was aghast. "I can't do that! That would get me into real trouble," he replied.

Rossiter leaned even closer and fixed him with an angry glare. "You are already in real trouble boy! You do as we say or you might have a bad accident too," he said with a silky hiss.

Declin was appalled and almost paralysed by fear. "But I could lose my job!" he wailed.

"You'll lose more than your bloody job if you don't!" was the snarled retort.

Nausea swirled in Declin as the terrifying reality of the situation hit him. He found himself gasping for breath and struggling to think of what to do. "But... But they will know I did it," he protested.

"How?"

That question surprised Declin and he let the astonishment show on his face, to Rossiter's obvious annoyance. "Because the computer guys can trace who was logged on to do any task," he explained.

"So just get rid of that little bit where my... where someone's arm is pushing Henley," Rossiter said.

"They will still know that the tape has been tampered with and that I probably did it," Declin objected.

"Too bad! Now, do as I say," Rossiter growled.

Declin hesitated and Rossiter grabbed his shoulder and dug his fingers in. "Do it! And don't tell anyone, or you will be next."

For a few seconds Declin hesitated, his mind racing with fears and possible consequences. Rossiter helped him to act by leaning close.

"Don't worry about your job boyo! Worry about staying alive. Do as I say, or you might be next."

Fear swirled in Declin like a paralysing fog and all he could do was nod and shake. Rossiter gestured to the computer.

"Well, get on and do it! Be quick before someone comes."

By then Declin's emotions were almost swamped by terror and he had trouble making his limbs function. But his mind was still racing, filled with conflicting ideas and emotions. Reluctantly he began to tap at the keyboard.

"Check that nobody is coming please," he managed to mutter.

Rossiter nodded and moved to the door. He opened it and leaned out. As he did, Declin clicked on several icons and then on the 'save as' button. Terrified that Rossiter might suspect he had made a copy of the tape he changed screens even as the man stepped back and closed the door.

"Nobody coming. Now get on with it."

Rossiter now leaned close to watch and Declin step by step explained what he was doing, clicking on the 'edit' and 'partial delete' and then carefully winding and rewinding to select the shortest possible cut before hitting the 'start' and 'end'. Inside he was so upset he wanted to throw up and his hands were trembling, but he managed to keep functioning.

"There. Done," he said.

"Show me. Replay the tape," Rossiter insisted.

Declin did, relieved that the cut was barely noticeable, even to him. Rossiter grunted with apparent satisfaction. "Good," he muttered.

Suddenly the door opened, and to Declin's intense relief the Control Manager, Mr Parsons, came in. He started to give a friendly greeting, then frowned.

"What are you doing, Declin?" he asked.

"Just getting the system ready, Mr Parsons," Declin replied.

"Don't touch it. Just leave it. I'll do anything that's needed when the police get here," Mr Parsons ordered. He then turned to Rossiter who had taken his hand off Declin's shoulder and stepped back. "What are you doing here, Rossiter?"

"I just wanted to see what happened," Rossiter answered.

"Leave it for the cops. Now get to your workstation," Mr Parsons snapped.

"Yes, Mr Parsons," Rossiter replied, a meek and respectful tone. "Okay Declin lad, you have a good day. See you later," he added in a bright and friendly voice.

Then, as Mr Parsons went to his desk, Rossiter suddenly leaned close to Declin and hissed softly in his ear. "And don't you say a word about me kid, or you are dead. And telling the cops won't save you because there are more than just me and they will make sure of you. Got it?"

Declin could only nod as Rossiter moved away. As the door closed behind the man Declin shuddered and began to tremble, terror coursing through him. But the threat was so effective that he realised he had to hide his fear.

Oh my God! What will I do? he thought.

Chapter 2

GRAHAM

Tuesday. October. Day 2 of the new school term.

Graham Kirk, 15, sat under 'F' Block nursing his injured leg and feeling pleased with himself. Around him sat a group of girls, all wanting to know the details of his holiday adventures. Among them were his little sister, Kylie, and her best friend, Margaret. And it was Margaret who was the most interested. As she gazed into Graham's eyes, he inwardly sighed and wished she wouldn't.

The problem was that she was two years younger, and only in Year 8. Graham was in Year 10 and was concerned about being seen talking to her.

Other kids will get the wrong idea, he thought.

And by other kids he didn't just mean boys. He was deeply concerned that the girls in his own class, or some of the prettier Year 9s, might draw the wrong conclusions from seeing them together.

They will think we are an item and that will cruel my chances, he thought.

For Graham was at that age when he was very interested in girls. Driven by romantic and natural urges he hungered to have a proper 'boyfriend-girlfriend' relationship with one of the really attractive and desirable girls.

Like Rowena, Ailsa or Rosemary, he thought wistfully.

Over the last few years he had developed intense 'crushes' on them and tried hard to get them to like him but while he had some success with Rosemary and Rowena Ailsa seemed not to have even noticed him.

And they were beautiful. Rowena had a heartbreakingly pretty face framed by glistening black hair. Her figure was very curvy and made her look years older than she was.

And Ailsa's bosom! he thought, staring with mute adolescent yearning at the out-thrust front of her blouse.

To make matters worse, Margaret made no secret of being in love with him. "She follows me around like a pet dog!" he had unkindly said to his friend Stephen.

"She says she's going to marry you," Stephen had replied.

It was an idea which secretly massaged his male ego and made him feel special but which he publicly derided.

"Fat chance!" had been his retort.

Not well-chosen words, Graham thought later because Margaret was quite a tubby little girl with no real figure.

Nor was she really pretty. She had a nice but plain face with freckles. Her main assets were in her personality. She had a cheerful and very determined character. And it wasn't as though Graham didn't like her. Several times over the last few years he had even thought he was in love with her. He certainly admired her for her courage and loyalty.

So he chatted to her and tried to hide his concern until the bell for classes went. As he picked up the crutches he had been loaned by the hospital, she pointed at them and asked anxiously, "Will you be able to walk properly again?"

"Yes. It is a greenstick fracture and I can already hobble about on it okay. I walked fourteen kilometres during the night along a dirt road last Friday when I went to get help at Stannary Hills," he answered.

He had actually spent Saturday in hospital in Atherton and Sunday and Monday in bed at home. As both Kylie and Margaret had seen him then most of the conversation was just filling in details of the week's adventures.[1]

Margaret looked concerned. "Was it very dangerous?"

Graham shook his head. "Not really, not once I had given the first crook the slip," he answered.

"I think you are a real hero," Margaret said.

Graham shook his head. "Not me. All I did was walk to get help. Roger was the real hero. He saved Peter and Stephen from being burnt to death. Anyway, there's the bell. Got to go," he said.

With that he hoisted himself to his feet, cradled the crutches under his armpits. Taking care not to bump his plaster encased ankle, he began crutching towards his classroom. Margaret gave him a wistful, yearning look and then she and Kylie hurried off in the opposite direction.

Graham found himself beside Joseph Chandler, a big youth from

---

1   Read *Stannary Hills* by C. R. Cummings

10A. Joseph glanced at his crutches and plaster cast and then said in a sneering tone, "Trying to make out you are the big hero again are you, Kirk?"

The comment annoyed Graham and he resented it because he had in fact done just that, not once but twice during the holidays. A spurt of resentment sparked a flash of temper. With difficulty he restrained himself and managed to bite back an angry retort.

"No, just talking," he answered in as mild a tone as he could manage.

"Looked like you were showing off to the little girls, trying to impress them with what a big man you think are," Joseph said.

"No."

Joseph curled his lip. "I suppose if you can't win with girls your own age you have to pick up the little ones."

"I wasn't trying to pick up anyone," Graham retorted through clenched teeth.

"Are you a cradle snatcher?" Joseph added, his tone insulting.

Being on crutches put Graham at a severe disadvantage. Several times during the last few years he had been involved in fights and had stood up to bullies but even though his blood was now up he kept his temper in check.

He's just jealous, he told himself. *And anyway, he's not worth the grief that would result from punching him in the mouth.*

So he gritted his teeth and turned away, then hobbled off, burning at the comments. *That was exactly what I didn't want people thinking,* he thought. *But I do wish I had a girlfriend my own age.*

That thought returned to him a few minutes later when he was seated in his classroom ready for Geography. While he waited, he scanned the room, noting the girls in the class. He was still engaged in this pleasant diversion when the teacher arrived. Mr Conkey was Graham's hero. Of all the people he held in high regard his teacher was the one he admired most. The previous year he had helped save Graham from going bad and it was a debt of gratitude that Graham would never forget.

Graham had been in real trouble over serious misbehaviour with a girl. The girl's father, a regular army warrant officer, had caught them at it and Graham had found himself facing both the parent's wrath and possible police and court involvement. That was when Mr Conkey, or Captain Conkey as Graham always thought of him, had arranged with the warrant officer and the school principal for Graham to be taken under his wing. Graham had been given the unofficial option of joining the school's army cadet unit or facing the legal consequences.[2]

Capt Conkey was not only a teacher but was the Officer Commanding the school's army cadet unit, a part time volunteer job. In his younger days he had been a regular soldier and had seen active service in the Makassang Campaign. Later he had served in the part-time Army Reserve. Now he was a tubby man in middle age with a growing family and he was Graham's teacher for both History and Geography. He was the one teacher Graham never gave any trouble to as he both admired and respected him and was determined to repay the debt.

Graham had found the army cadet experience a revelation. It had helped turn his behaviour and attitudes around, and being an army cadet was now the most important thing in Graham's life. This had been reinforced ten days earlier during the unit's annual camp. Graham had been a section commander with the rank of corporal. His patrol had been the only one to succeed during a big field exercise. He had also helped save a cadet from committing suicide and Capt Conkey had obviously been impressed as he had promoted him to temporary sergeant and asked him if he wanted to be the Company Sergeant Major next year.[3]

As the CSM was one of the most important postings in the unit, and also one of the jobs with the most power and prestige, it was a huge boost to Graham's status. The rapid elevation and the promise of going to Cadet Warrant Officer Class 2 the following year had won him instant envy and made him some enemies. Graham knew that being selected to be the next CSM was a great vote of confidence in him, and he was determined to do the job to the best of his ability.

But Capt Conkey knew nothing of his mishap during the hiking trip to Stannary Hills a few days before. As soon as he came into the room and replied to the 'good morning' of the class his eyes noted the plaster on Graham's lower leg and the crutches leaning against the windowsill.

"Hello, what this, Graham?" he asked. "Been in the wars?"

Graham gave a wry grin and nodded. "Yes sir. We got involved with a gang of crooks during our hike last week and I broke a bone in my leg while trying to get away," he explained.

---

[2] Read *Fourteen* by C. R. Cummings

[3] Read *The Cadet Corporal* by C. R. Cummings

Capt Conkey shook his head and looked at Stephen Bell who sat next to Graham and said, "You and your friends seem to attract trouble like magnets. You were all there I take it?"

Stephen pushed his glasses up his freckled nose and nodded. "Yes sir. We were all there."

Graham smiled. He knew what Capt Conkey meant. He and his friends Stephen, Peter and Roger formed a group nicknamed 'The Hiking Team' and they had several times become involved in quite desperate adventures.

Capt Conkey turned back to Graham. "The injury, is it serious?"

"No sir. I can hobble along alright," Graham answered.

Capt Conkey frowned. "Will it cause you any permanent injury?"

Graham shook his head. "I don't think so sir. The doctor said it was only a greenstick fracture and should mend without any problems," he explained.

"That's good. Will you be alright for cadets?"

"Yes sir, as long as I take it easy for a couple of weeks," Graham assured him.

Capt Conkey nodded and looked relieved. "Good. And do you think you will be up to our field trip to the sugar mill next week?"

"Yes sir. The plaster comes off next Monday and as long as I take it steady and use the crutches there shouldn't be a problem," Graham replied.

Capt Conkey looked concerned. "There are a lot of steel steps and walkways. The mill people might not be too keen for you to be limping around the place in case you slip. We will have to check," he said. He then faced the class. "Now class, I want you to get out your notebooks and a pencil and follow me. We are going to Ten 'A's' room for a briefing session for the field trip."

Graham did as he was told and then waited until everyone else had left the room before standing up and using the crutches to make his way along the veranda to the next room. Once there he edged in through the door and looked for somewhere to sit. His friend Peter waved to him and moved to help him through the milling throng.

"Here Graham, sit here," he said, indicating an empty chair.

Graham said thanks and eased himself down onto the chair. As he looked for somewhere to lean the crutches, his eyes met those of the girl seated at the next desk to his left. Her name was Carol Battersby and he had often seen her, had known her for years, but she had never attracted his attention in any particular way before. Now suddenly their gaze locked and it was as though an electric current passed between them.

Carol gave him a sympathetic smile and said, "Does it hurt much?"

Not wanting to tarnish his 'tough' image, he replied, "Not really."

Once again, he met her eyes and a second spark of electricity seemed to jump across. *Gee, she is nice,* he thought.

But his attention was drawn away by questions from other friends in 10A, particularly from his friendly rivals who were in the Navy Cadets. There were two of them: Andrew Collins and Arthur Blake. Andrew had once been Graham's best friend, when Graham had been a navy cadet two years earlier, but that relationship had cooled.

Sitting at the next desk to Andrew was another navy cadet, tubby and very busty Tina Babcock, and seeing her caused Graham a little stab of envy. Earlier in the year he had tried to win Tina away from Andrew. There had been a couple of dates and few steamy clinches, but in the end Tina had chosen Andrew. Ever since, the pair had enjoyed the type of relationship that Graham yearned to have.[4]

Their conversation was ended by Mrs Westacott calling for silence. Both classes were going on the field trip so they were to be briefed together. Mrs Westacott explained, "We are going to visit a sugar mill. The one we have arranged to visit is the Caster Mill. It is about an hour's drive away. Has anyone here been to the Caster Mill before?"

Graham had visited the mills as Gordonvale and Mossman but had only ever seen the Caster Mill from a distance while travelling south along the Bruce Highway. He looked around to see if anyone else had been there. To his surprise only one hand went up: Carol Battersby's.

Mrs Westacott also looked around and then said, "So you are the only one to visit Caster Mill Carol. When was that?"

Carol smiled and looked a bit embarrassed. "I live there Miss. My dad is the Chief Mechanical Engineer for the mill."

"Is he now! That's interesting. So why don't you go to high school in Babinda or Innisfail, or even Gordonvale?" Mrs Westacott queried.

"My mum is a university lecturer here in Cairns, so we drive up every day," Carol answered.

---

[4] Read *Cockatoo* by C. R. Cummings

"That must take you a while."

"Not really, Miss. We leave home at about seven thirty each day and I am usually here on time. It depends on the traffic on Mulgrave Road," Carol answered.

The mention of traffic on Mulgrave Road brought a chorus of moans and murmurs from the students and Graham, even though he lived in the middle of the city, knew what she meant. It was the road works as much as the density of traffic. But he was glad he didn't have to waste more than two hours every day just getting to and from school.

The briefing then began. Capt Conkey handed out information sheets and permission forms then reminded them to have their permission forms and money back by the following Friday.

"So we can confirm the bus booking," he explained.

This was all fairly normal stuff for Graham as they usually did several class excursions each year. This one was combining a Geography study for his class with a science study for 10A. It was a trip he was looking forward to. Sugar mills were places he found fascinating and impressive, and which also had a real railway focus. Being a keen railway modeller, he wanted to study the layout at the mill.

During the briefing, Graham took the opportunity to study the 10A girls. Several he knew well. There was Gwen Copeland, a beautiful and classy blonde who was also a corporal in the army cadets, as was the tall and athletic Harriet Harris. Lynn was a really pretty English girl with a very sweet nature and a nice figure. His gaze roved over Helen (very nice) Judy (lovely figure and shiny black hair), Jessica and Fleur (both nice girls who were starting to blossom into womanhood). There was Donna who was huge and fat and was the school vigoro champion and several 'Plain Janes' like Laurel and Jessica.

Graham then gave Carol a surreptitious scrutiny. She had nice hazel eyes, straight mousy fair hair cut to collar length and what looked to be nice legs and a trim figure. While he was studying her, she suddenly turned and looked at him. Before Graham could turn his head away their eyes met. A quizzical little smile crossed her face and then she turned back to face the teachers. Graham did the same, hot with embarrassment at having been caught looking.

She is nice, he decided.

But he had no chance to study her again until the end of the session.

Only then, as he waited for the room to empty, did he glance at her again as she stood up. Once again, she turned and their eyes met. This time she gave a little smile as she went past. That allowed Graham a back view and he liked what he saw.

He was then taken up with hobbling back to his own room for an English lesson. During the remainder of the morning session Graham found that images of Carol would flit across his mind from time to time and he decided to try to get a better look at her during the morning break.

However he failed in this as she was nowhere to be seen and because of his injured leg he could not hurry around the school looking for her. Instead he found himself seated with a group of friends who were all busy discussing the holidays and cadet activities. They were chatting happily away, with Graham secretly fuming and wishing he could go and look for Carol, when a boy and girl came strolling by. The boy was in Year 9 and the girl in Year 8.

Noddy Parker, a Navy Cadet in 10C, looked at the pair and called, "Hey Willy, how's yer willy?"

The boy, Willy Williams, the school's 'mad scientist', stopped and glared. "Better than yours!" he retorted, obviously embarrassed.

The girl with him, Marjorie Morton, also looked embarrassed and Graham felt ashamed at the sexual comments in the hearing of a girl.

Stephen now chimed in. "How are the 'Space Cadets' Willy?" he called.

Willy was an Air Cadet and the Air Cadets were often the target of jealous teasing and jokes from the other services. The inter-service rivalry was strong.

"Good!" he replied. "Better than the Army Cadets."

That drew snorts and jeers of disagreement and disbelief from the group. Willy faced them and grinned. "Don't forget we have the interservice field exercise in two weeks. That will prove it once and for all."

Again there were jeers and laughter. Graham joined in but doubts flashed across his mind. *Oh! I'd forgotten about that,* he thought.

The exercise was a grudge rematch after the Army Cadets had convincingly beaten the Air Cadets in a field exercise back in June. It was to be a tri-service activity with the Army Cadets against the Air Cadets and the Navy Cadets providing umpires and communications.

Graham glanced down at his leg. *I wonder if my leg will be healed by then?* he fretted.

He had no idea how long bones took to knit and knew that the officers would not allow him to take part if there was any risk of causing further injury.

Mention of the exercise caused more jeers and teasing comments. "You haven't got a hope! You airy fairies aren't good enough," Stephen said.

Marjorie bristled indignantly. "Oh yes we are! We will beat you. Willy will use his secret weapons," she snapped.

The comment caused another outburst of laughter and comments. Graham noted Willy frown and give Marjorie an annoyed glance. *Secret weapons* he thought, glancing at Peter. Peter grinned back but it was Noddy who again called loudly.

"Secret weapon! There's nothing secret about Willy's weapon," he said jeering.

"That's right," Stephen agreed, leering at Marjorie. "You should know all about Willy's weapon by now," he added.

Graham was both shocked and embarrassed at the rude comment. He was a little surprised at Stephen, but a glance showed a glint of malice in Stephen's eyes and Graham remembered that Stephen had tried to win Marjorie earlier in the year but had lost to Willy.

Marjorie turned up her nose and her mouth curled. "Don't be gross, Stephen Bell!" she retorted.

But Graham noted that she was annoyed at Stephen, rather than offended by his comment. The rumour around the school was that Willy and Marjorie weren't just an item but had been hard at it for a long time.

Willy looked annoyed and he now took Marjorie's hand. "Come on, Marj. Let's leave these rude people to contemplate their impending defeat."

With that he and Marjorie turned and resumed walking, holding hands in blatant defiance of the school rules.

More teasing comments were flung at their backs, but Graham now turned to Peter. "Secret weapons?" he said quietly, raising his eyebrows as he did.

Peter looked thoughtful and nodded. "Willy will be up to something," he commented.

"Up Marjorie," Noddy called.

That caused more laughter and Graham another spurt of annoyance. He did not want to discuss strategy or tactics in the hearing of the Navy Cadets and wasn't in the mood for crude sexual innuendos. But he was also well aware of Willy's reputation for mad schemes and dangerous gadgets.

"Another rocket to the moon," he said.

That caused more laughter, and the group quickly retailed the more famous incidents of Willy's career, the model Zeppelin that went down in flames, the model aircraft that had buzzed the Army Cadet Passing-Out Parade the previous year, the 'poison gas' scare during a Chemistry lesson.

"He will have aircraft with cameras for sure," Andrew suggested.

"Sure to have," Graham agreed, "And drones."

"Radio controlled UAVs," Blake added.

"He's a tricky bugger," Stephen said. "We need to watch him."

Graham again glanced at Peter, who gave a little smile and an even smaller nod. That cheered Graham up and he smiled in return.

Pete is a clever bugger too. He will think of ways to outsmart Willy and the Air Cadets, he thought. But the real question was, would he be allowed to take part in the exercise?

Even that worry was superseded when classes resumed, and Graham remembered his plan to try to get Carol to notice him. But she was not in any of his classes so he did not see her again that day.

As the bell for the end of school rang, he hurried downstairs, hobbling as fast as he could, to try to see her as she left. But he failed in that as well as there was no sign of her on the footpath outside or at the bike racks. He had remembered the comment about her mother driving her to school each day from Caster, but he had to admit he had no idea where she was picked up, or even when.

Oh well, never mind! I will see her tomorrow, he told himself.

Chapter 3

THWARTED AMBITIONS

The mill accident was on the Tuesday when Graham had gone back to school. But he only learned of it that night when he heard it on the news.

Caster Sugar Mill! Oh, I hope Carol isn't too upset, he thought.

But beyond that he did not give the accident much more thought. He had homework to do, and he was worried about how he might function at cadets, and the bad news soon slipped out of his thoughts.

The following day at school he made a point of seeking out Carol and asking her. "Are you alright Carol?"

"Yes, I am okay," she replied. "It was more upsetting for dad as he was one of the first on the scene and saw the...the body."

"It was in the crushers, wasn't it?" he asked.

Carol nodded. "The knives that chop the cane billets up and mash them before they go into the rollers," she agreed.

Remembered horrific images of a man being sprayed out of a wood chipping machine filled Graham's mind and he shuddered. The previous June he had helped rescue Willy Williams from a gang of crooks who were illegally logging the rainforest of valuable hardwoods and had seen the man slip and fall in.[5] The memory of the scarlet spray that had spewed out onto the woodchip pile made him shudder and feel slightly queasy.

"Will that stop our visit do you think?" he asked.

Obviously Carol had not thought about that as she now paused and frowned. "I don't know," she admitted. "I will ask Dad."

At that moment Lynne and Anne both arrived so Graham got no chance to have a more personal conversation. Feeling quite self-conscious, he nodded and said, "Oh well, stay safe," and then sauntered off, nodding a friendly greeting to the other two girls as he did.

And as he walked away, he heard Anne say, "What did Graham want?"

"Just asking about the accident at the mill yesterday," Carol replied.

---

[5] Read *Airship over Atherton* by C. R. Cummings

"What accident?" Lynne asked.

By then Graham was out of hearing so he shrugged and hobbled on, his mind working hard at possible strategies to get Carol's attention and then to ask her for a date.

But girls were not his top priority after lunch. Worry about being fit enough to take part in Cadets began to bother him. He still had his chest strapped and his right leg in plaster and he was using crutches. That worried him as he badly wanted to be able to walk normally and to march.

We will start practicing for the Passing-Out Parade today, he thought.

Having been promoted to Acting Sergeant on the second last day of the cadet unit's annual camp he was hopeful of having a sergeant's part to play on the parade. That got him thinking about the format of the previous year's parade. That had been as a 'Company in Line' with four platoons side by side with a Flag Party in the centre and he hoped he would be one of the platoon sergeants with scarlet sashes.

As soon as he had changed into his cadet uniform after the last class, he made his way to the Cadet HQ office under B Block. As the platoon sergeant of Number 3 Platoon he wanted to get the Platoon Roll Book.

Capt Conkey was there and frowned at the sight of Graham limping along on his crutches. "Will you be alright to go on parade Sgt Kirk?" he queried.

"Fine, sir. I just have to take it easy," Graham replied. He was deeply anxious he might be made to sit out and was determined to do his best.

Capt Conkey looked doubtful and shook his head. "No. We won't risk it. You sit out and I will get Sgt Crane to take Three Platoon."

Crane! That hurt. Sgt Crane was a Year 11 and was in HQ and Graham had a low opinion of him both as a person and as a sergeant. But his plea came to nothing and regretfully he had to sit at the side while the company admin parade was conducted.

Having done admin parades only twice before as a platoon sergeant Graham watched closely. *So that when I get a chance again I won't make a mistake*, he told himself, with the niggling worry that he might never get that chance.

To his secret satisfaction, Sgt Crane made several mistakes. And he did poor drill and kept looking around at the other sergeants to see what to do next.

Bloody drongo! It's not that hard to remember, Graham thought.

Having stood in the ranks for nearly two years, and thus having watched dozens of admin parades, he was confident about what to do.

The CSM was practicing the admin parade in 'Close Column of Platoons', that is with each platoon in line in three ranks but with the platoons one behind the other. He was also practicing them at 'Moving on Parade'.

"That is to practice the fifteen paces for the Advance in Review Order during the Passing-Out Parade," he explained.

So the markers were called and marched out 15 paces, halted and did a left turn before standing at ease. Then the company was called on parade and carried out the same movement.

The Roll was then marked and the CSM took the reports and then called the company to attention and handed over to Capt Conkey. The OC ordered the officers to fall in so Sgt Crane did a right turn and moved out past the Right Marker and waited for CUO Anastasia Mitrovitch, a very attractive Year 12 girl, to march across to face him.

As Anastasia marched on, Graham could only admire her. By almost unanimous consensus she was voted the sexiest girl in the entire school and was the secret fantasy heartthrob of many of the boys (Including Graham!). But he knew he had no chance of winning with a Year 12 girl and could only gaze in lustful admiration at the way her long legs moved with a lithe grace that even the baggy camouflage uniform could not obscure.

Salutes were exchanged and Sgt Crane and the CUO stepped around each other to the left and Crane made his way to the rear of the platoon. Both then turned to face the front.

Capt Conkey faced the company. "Company, Stand at…. Ease! Now cadets, today we start practicing for our main ceremonial event of the year, the annual Passing-Out Parade. But before that we have some important admin and information to do. So I want you seated in section lines for a briefing. Officers! Fall out!"

The company was moved by the CSM to sit in a compact mass in lines behind their section commanders. Graham limped over and found a spot to sit behind 3 Platoon. That put him next to Crane, but he did not mind that as he had a notion that he needed to remind Crane that he was only there for the day.

The CSM then called them to attention and handed back to Capt Conkey who explained that they were now deciding who would go on promotion courses at the end of the year.

That got Graham quite anxious as he remembered what he believed was the understanding with Capt Conkey. *He specifically asked me if I would be CSM,* he thought. *But he might have changed his mind,* he fretted.

All cadets were given a small questionnaire to which they added their name and then filled them in. Graham saw that the headings to the questions were: What grade will you be in at school next year (Year 11); are you staying in cadets next year (An emphatic YES); what rank would you like to be? (Warrant Officer Class 2); what posting or job would you like? (CSM).

The questionnaires were collected by the sergeants and passed to the CSM. He handed them to Lt Maclaren, the Coy 2ic, and Capt Conkey moved on to the next topic. "In a week and a half we are taking part in a field exercise. As you know we don't usually do a field activity this late in the year, but the Air Cadets have issued us with a challenge after we beat them back in June. After our experiences on annual camp we should be ready for this. It will be in two parts. On the Friday night and Saturday we are the raiders. We then swap over and on the Saturday night and Sunday morning we become the defenders. Full orders will be issued next week but for now here is the Joining Instruction. CSM, get the sergeants to hand these out."

Sgt Crane moved to the front to collect a bundle of Joining Instructions and then divided the bundle into three and handed them to the corporals. He then moved back out of the way.

As Crane made no attempt to give him one, Graham had to put up his hand and attract his attention. "I need one," he said.

Sgt Crane curled his lip. "Don't know if we want cripples in the bush," he retorted. But he reluctantly handed him one from the remnants of a bundle at the back of 7 Section.

"Make sure CUO Mitrovitch gets one," Graham added.

That caused Crane to shrug and curl his lip but he did so. As he did, Graham noted the Officers of Cadets and CUOs looking through the questionnaires. Seeing Lt Hamilton read one and shake his head set Graham's anxiety level shooting up.

I hope that wasn't mine he just read! he thought.

And there was more anxiety when he noted the OOCs shaking their heads and smiling at another questionnaire. But there was also some anticipation and worry over the field exercise. Graham had known about it for months, ever since Willy Williams had told them about it, but now it dawned on him that he was no longer a section commander.

And with my gammy leg I am unlikely to be allowed to lead a patrol, he reasoned.

It was a sharp disappointment but one that was swept aside a few minutes later by anxiety when the unit marched down to the school oval to begin the practice for the Passing-Out Parade. The reason was simple, it had to do with glory, status and ego. Capt Conkey allocated jobs for the parade. A CUO was required to be parade commander and another to have the honour of carrying the Australian Flag on the parade. Because the platoons were all about twenty strong and had done well at Annual Camp, he had decided to parade them as four platoons in line with HQ used to equal up the numbers. Graham thought that was wise choice as the platoon identities were very strong.

But as there were only four CUOs two platoons would be commanded by CUOs and the other two by sergeants. Other sergeants would be in the flag party

The choice of parade commander was always a tense one for the CUOs and Graham was glad he didn't have to choose. *They are all really good this year, well, maybe not CUO Mitrovitch,* he thought. He thought she was a nice person but was a bit weak and her platoon had done badly all Annual Camp.

It was CUO Grey, commander of 4 Platoon, who got the top job. Graham shrugged at that and shook his head. He thought that CUO Masters, his old platoon commander from 2 Platoon, was better. But he did concede that CUO Grey was really competent and really looked the part. CUO Masters got the honour of carrying the flag.

There was then more tenseness as the sergeant's jobs were allocated. Graham did not think he had much chance for anything special as he was the newest sergeant, so he had reconciled himself to standing behind 3 Platoon. That turned out to be the case.

At least I get to do a bit as a sergeant and get to wear a red sash, he consoled himself.

The escorts to the flag were named as Sgt Loretta Gayney, the HQ Signals sergeant, and Sgt Vince Crane, the HQ Recon sergeant. Graham shook his head at that and as he did he noted Capt Conkey looking at him. He immediately stopped the gesture and made his face go neutral.

Capt Conkey kept looking at him, a slight frown on his face which worried Graham. *I've questioned his judgement and he resents it,* he thought.

Capt Conkey then looked at Sgt Crane. "Sgt Crane," he said, "You will have to do two jobs during this practice, act as Three Platoon sergeant and as soon as the officers are fallen in move to join the Flag Party."

That was a bit of blow to Graham as it meant he could only sit and watch the practice.

A talk through practice was then commenced. The first part of the parade would be a Guard of Honour to receive the VIPs and that was formed by 4 Platoon, the 'Senior' platoon, made up of older cadets and 2nd Years. After that there would be displays and these were all at section level.

When the company moved to the side to prepare for the main parade Graham watched with envy as CUO Masters and Sgt Gayney moved to the far side of the parade ground. Lt Hamilton joined them and began talking them through the manoeuvres required of a Flag Party on a ceremonial parade.

Capt Conkey had driven small, coloured flags into the turf as markers and the company now marched on to these under command of the CSM and the talk-through began. While this went on the Flag party practiced off to the side, turning on the march and doing left forms and left wheels. All Graham could do was sit and feel left out.

As the Flag Party marched on Graham was concerned to note that all three of them seemed unable to stay in step. *Sgt Gayney is swinging her arm too high and Crane can't even keep in step or do proper turns on the march,* Graham fretted. He knew he could do better and could only lament his leg.

It got worse. Twice Sgt Crane turned the wrong way and he seemed to be out of step more than he was in it. *And he needs to swing his arms higher,* Graham criticised. But there was nothing he could. But he did note Capt Conkey frowning as he watched.

The practice went on but they only got as far as the Inspection before it was dismissal time. It was only when he got home that Graham remembered Carol.

I will make a big effort to be nice to her tomorrow and will ask her for a date, he told himself.

But that did not happen. Next day at school he could not find her, and he did not dare ask anyone as he did not want to be teased. During both breaks he hobbled quickly around the school in a fruitless search for her. As a result he sulked and felt thwarted and his leg throbbed and hurt. School just ground on in its usual boring grind and instead Graham worried about his cadet career. Anxiety about possibly not being the CSM the following year gnawed at him.

Carol was there on Friday. Graham saw her as soon as he limped up to his classroom. She was with her friends outside the next room, busy unpacking her bag. But what to do? He did not want to make a fool of himself or get a public rejection.

Not with that toad Chandler standing next to her, he thought.

Hot shame at past failures with girls and the resultant humiliation caused him to stop outside his own room. While pretending to unpack his bag he tried to think of a strategy to get to 'casually' talk to her so that it did not appear he was making a pass. But again his plans were thwarted by the arrival of Stephen who immediately pushed in and began chatting about an incident in a Year 8 class the day before.

Graham's chance to chat to Carol did not happen until the lunch break when he met her in the tuckshop queue. Summoning up his courage he met her eyes and then smiled. "Hi!" he said.

"Hello," Carol answered in a friendly tone.

"How are things at the mill?" Graham asked, thinking that was a suitably common topic.

He was astonished at her reaction. Her face clouded with anxiety and tears formed in her eyes. She shook her head.

"Not good. The workers are pretty upset over the accident the other day. My dad has had a few troublemakers grumbling to him and he is very upset by it all."

"Sorry to hear that," Graham replied, now anxious to move the topic on to a more favourable topic for his plans.

But Carol would not let it go. "Some of the men are talking about going on strike until safety at the mill is improved. Dad and the management team have been busy trying to talk them out of that. The mill can't really afford stoppages," she explained.

"Is there a safety problem?" Graham asked, more out of politeness than interest.

Carol shook her head but looked worried. "There hasn't been. There hasn't been a worker injured in more than ten years and it was a very friendly place to work. But now they have had two deaths in a month," she explained.

"Two?" Graham cried in surprise.

Carol nodded. "Yes. There was another man who was electrocuted a few weeks ago. That caused a lot of worry. Now things are not going well."

"Sorry to hear that. Do you think our Mill Tour will be allowed?" Graham asked.

Carol nodded again. "Dad says so. But there will be lots of extra staff to supervise and a lot of places we won't be allowed to go."

Graham was pleased to hear that as he liked visiting sugar mills. But his plan to ask Carol for a date did not get any further as he turned to be served and then said a fairly neutral 'goodbye' as she walked off with her friends.

Graham was left feeling frustrated and thwarted and wondering what to do. And that is how he stayed all weekend and into Monday. During the weekend he stayed home and rested his leg, wanting it to heal as quickly as he could. But when he tested his weight on the injured leg he was dismayed to get sharp twinges at certain angles and he knew he had to wait longer.

If I still have this plaster on and need crutches I may not be allowed on the tour, he fretted.

And that was his big worry when his mother took him to the doctor's on Monday afternoon. Graham tried to bluff and pretend his leg was healed but the doctor obviously noted a few grimaces as he walked across the room and decreed that the plaster stay on another week.

Oh no! I may not be able to go to the mill tomorrow! Graham thought.

And then anxiety about not being allowed to attend the cadet field exercise added to his sense of grievance.

And he still hadn't asked Carol for a date!

Chapter 4

MILL TOUR

A s Declin walked to work on Tuesday morning, he was aware of very mixed emotions. There was anxiety about happenings at the mill; and there was the knowledge that he would get a chance to see Carol for at least some of the day. The previous afternoon he and a dozen others had been briefed by the manager on the school tour. The tour had come as no surprise to Declin as he had learned about it from Carol the previous Friday. He had met her as he was walking across the park near the old steam locomotive while on his way back to his hotel. Carol had been playing with her little sister and baby brother and had greeted him with a very friendly smile.

With his heart beating fast at the chance to speak to her, Declin had stopped to chat. It was then she had told him. And now another chance had come. His hopes went up and he smiled.

As he crossed the mill park on his way to work, Declin glanced at her house, hoping to see her. But he did it surreptitiously, not wanting anyone to suspect he was at all interested. However he saw no sign of her or her family. He did not even know if she had gone all the way to Cairns to school.

Declin started his work shift at 8am and he settled into the Control Room to check all the systems. Satisfied everything was working normally he handed over to Mr Jordan at 10:15am and made his way to the Conference Room at the rear of the nearby office building.

The manager, Mr Connors, was there with Carol's father and a dozen other workers. When all those rostered to help with the tour had arrived the manager spoke to them again.

"Normally we would only have one or two of you as guides for school groups but because of the problems we have experienced I am allocating you all on the basis of one worker to five school students. You are to watch them like hawks to make sure nobody does anything foolish. No horseplay or tomfoolery. No childish pranks or bullying and nobody wandering off into restricted areas. Safety is our absolute priority.

Any problems, stop the tour and fix the problem. Remember, no safety problems."

At that moment, Rossiter, who was sitting at the back, sat forward and put his hand up. "We should stop school groups coming at all. They are a risk and a nuisance. If some kid gets hurt that will cause real trouble," he grumbled.

Up until then Rossiter's presence had barely registered with Declin. Now a sharp stab of concern caused Declin to glance at the man.

Should I be worried about him? he thought.

Since the previous week he had tried to push the ghastly images out of his conscious thoughts but now they flooded back. A niggling suspicion wormed its way in.

Rossiter wants the mill to keep stopping for some reason. A school kid being mangled would certainly bring it to a halt!

Declin decided to keep a very close eye on Rossiter and on any students near him. The thought of the man deliberately pushing a child into one of the big machines was too appalling to really think about. But think about it Declin did, with Carol's face as the main image.

And there it was! Hers was the first face he saw as the students filed off their coach twenty minutes later. The school group was ushered aside as they debussed, to stand on the lawn in the shade of a nearby tree.

Jeff the Welder, one of the younger mill workers, nudged Declin as the students waited. "Some very pretty young things there," he whispered.

"There are," Declin agreed, briefly scanning the group.

But really he only had eyes for Carol. And what he saw caused him a little spurt of annoyance. One of the male students, a big good-looking lad with his right lower leg in plaster, was chatting to her, and she was smiling and giggling back.

Then Carol looked across and saw him. Her face lit up and she smiled and gave a little wave. That instantly filled Declin with a swirl of emotions: delight that she had seen him and obviously thought he was nice; and worry that the other mill workers or her dad might have noticed and might guess his secret love.

These concerns were heightened as the group was ushered into the Conference Room. As Carol filed through the door, she passed close to Declin. Again she smiled.

"Hi Declin," she said.

"Hello Carol," Declin replied, hotly aware of a look from Jeff.

"How do you know her?" Jeff hissed as the group settled in rows of chair set up for a briefing.

Declin was astonished. "She's Mr Battersby's daughter. She lives here on the estate. Surely you've seen her around?"

Jeff peered at Carol and then nodded. "Oh yeah. I think I have. But I've never seen her in school uniform," he said.

To Declin's relief, the topic was dropped as Mr Battersby began to brief the group on the layout of the mill and the processes they would see. As he talked, Declin kept glancing at Carol and was irritated to note that she was sitting next to the lad with the plaster cast who was continually turning to whisper to her, making her nod and giggle.

One of the boy's jokes must have been good as Carol let out an audible chuckle, drawing a pause and a frown from her father. The boy desisted for a while but then began whispering again.

That toad of a Mister Smoothy is trying to win on, Declin thought, aware that he was both surprised and jealous. *I don't know why I am surprised,* he told himself. *Carol is a good looking girl. Of course the boys will try to hit on her.*

And that notion got him worrying some more. Did she have a boyfriend? Was Mr Plaster Cast Smoothy her boyfriend?

The briefing over, the students were shown a short film on how sugar was processed. That meant sitting for 20 more minutes in the air conditioning in the dark. Declin was happy enough with that but was still irritated by the way the boy with the plaster cast was sitting close beside Carol and obviously whispering to her. Declin learned his name when the male teacher called, "Graham, stop talking!"

From the Conference Room the students and their two accompanying teachers were led out and then formed into groups. Declin badly wanted to be with the group Carol was in but to his disappointment she ended up with Jeff the Welder. Noting that Rossiter was with another group well away from her gave him a small spurt of relief.

After another safety warning by Harold the Foreman, they made their way along the side of the mill to the northern end where the trains came in. Here there was a large marshalling yard with a dozen train tracks side by side, most now crowded with loaded sugar wagons. Even as the group arrived at the end of the mill a train came in from the other direction. The small diesel locomotive was uncoupled and went on along a siding to where it was able to reverse back along another track. It vanished out of sight towards where Declin knew the Engine Shed was.

Declin also noted that the boy with the plaster cast, Graham he now heard Carol call him, seemed to be more interested in the trains than in her. Graham certainly did a careful study of the track layout and of the arrangement for moving the loaded 'bins' to where they were emptied.

He must like trains, Declin decided.

The group then moved to the pit where the bins were unloaded. As they approached the pit two bins were rotated in the gigantic circular cradle used for the purpose and a load of 8 tons of cane 'billets' tumbled out and down into the slashing blades that began to shred them. Declin glanced down and experienced a searing flashback that almost paralysed him with horror and fear. For a moment he was quite unable to move and could only stand and stare.

His emotions were further added to by the boy, Graham, who loudly asked Carol if that was where the man had been killed the other day. Declin glanced at Carol and saw that she had gone so pale that her freckles stood out like dark dots on bleached linen. She swallowed and nodded before croaking the answer.

"Yes," she said. Then she gestured to Declin. "Declin here saw the man fall in and... and tried to stop the machine but... but he wasn't in time."

Declin was aware that everyone was now staring at him but his mind was again flooded with the ghastly images and he found he was almost gasping for breath and could only shake his head. He was dimly aware that the students were all staring morbidly at the pit and that they were all discussing the incident, some with an evident ghoulish relish that disgusted him and others with fascinated horror.

Mr Connors now spoke. "Let's not dwell on it please. It was a terrible accident and we still don't know how it happened."

I do! Declin thought.

That caused him to glance up and he immediately locked eyes with Rossiter who glared back at him from across the pit until the rotating bins, now empty, was dropped back upright onto the tracks and pushed on out of the way. The machinery clanked and whirred, and the next two rail bins were hauled forward into the rotating tipper.

Mr Connors pointed to it and explained how it worked, shouting above the noise of the machinery. "This is a very dangerous place so always watch what is going on and keep away from any moving machinery. Never lean across or try to climb over any of these safety rails."

Declin glanced down and his eyes scanned the shiny steel safety rails which kept people clear of the tipper. His mind formed another horrible image, and this was instantly reinforced by Graham again speaking.

"How could you fall into the pit with this railing here?" he commented.

Declin had wondered the same thing the previous week and now his mind again came up with the images of Jack Henley being grabbed from behind and pushed.

It was murder alright! he thought.

He found he was gripping the railing and that his hands and arms were shaking. Hoping that nobody had noticed (Carol!) he hastily let go and stepped back, breathing deeply to try to regain his composure.

The group was moved inside and led up the steel steps to the platform outside the Control Room. Harold the Foreman, who was now in charge, pointed in through the half-opened door and explained that the computers inside controlled the whole mill.

"Young Declin here is one of the operators. He makes the whole show go," he explained.

That made Declin glow with pride as everyone turned to look at him. He was particularly pleased by the way Carol's eyebrows shot up with surprise and by the new look of respect she gave him.

"Sorry, you are not allowed in there," Declin said, gesturing in and then waving to Marty, who was his normal relief and was swivelled around in his chair to see.

Marty gave a friendly grin and a wave and then spun back to face the rows of screens and keyboards.

Declin closed the door and gave a halting explanation of how the computers controlled all operations in the rail yard and milling train. He had to shout above the roar and rattle of machinery and was embarrassed to find he was tongue-tied and felt he wasn't impressing Carol. He was also mentally thrown off his balance by noting that the students and workers stood in a tight bunch with their backs to the safety railing below which the bins were being tipped into the pit.

When Declin indicated he was finished Harold the Foreman pointed along a steel walkway. "We go that way. Stay in your groups and be very careful. Hold on and make sure you don't lose your footing or slip," he said.

He then led the way past and onto the long sloping steel ramp which led up into the very heart of the mill buildings. The ramp had handrails on both sides and stood on the left of the Milling Train.

Declin gestured to the five students in his care and had them follow him. Jeff the Welder and his group followed. As they moved along the ramp Declin noted that the other staff had placed themselves in among the students for safety and supervision.

Declin had been impressed by the milling train from the first moment he saw it but, like all big machines, he treated it with wary respect. There were four giant rollers, each greater in diameter than a standing man. These were the actual 'mills', and they were matched by another four below them so that the grinding flanges on each ground together. They were all connected by a series of huge conveyor belts in a line going upwards. Each roller was turned slowly by what looked like a gigantic bicycle chain and as it turned it crushed the shredded billets of sugar cane. In the process the sharp little ridges on the outside of each mill squeezed the juice from the cane. This was drained away and led off to be processed.

The huge conveyor at the base of the milling train carried the crushed fibres up to go through another mill where more juice was extracted. Declin had seen it many times but had also been told horrible stories of people falling into the milling train in the 'old days' and of being crushed to death.

As that old story flitted across his mind, he stared down at the gigantic drums of the next mill and his imagination conjured up images of a desperate man screaming as he was dragged into the crushers.

They are so big and so strong you would have no chance, he thought, shuddering at the images of bones splintering, blood vessels bursting and flesh being pulped.

And that got him to look back and what he saw sent a spurt of alarm through him, Rossiter was now standing directly behind Carol and very close to her! Rossiter's comment about a child being killed flashed across his mind and Declin found he was gasping with anxiety.

He wouldn't surely! he thought.

But the smirk on Rossiter's face and the knowledge that he was probably a murderer caused Declin to feel paralysed with fear. He saw that Carol was staring down into the slowly moving milling train with fascinated interest and that boyfriend Graham was grinning and gesturing down into it. He said something that caused Carol's face to curl up in disgust and horror and she turned and shook her head at him before thankfully moving on.

Declin urgently wanted to get back to be near Carol but there were so many people on the gangway that he couldn't. But his eyes met Rossiter's and Rossiter gave what he thought was an evil grin and made a pushing gesture towards Carol. Declin was appalled and deeply concerned.

"He won't, not with all these people here," he comforted himself by muttering.

Declin decided that Carol was safe while they were all together and was able to relax a bit. The group paused to watch a welder who was busy working on the ridges of the third roller. The man explained he was rebuilding the ridges which got very quickly worn down by the grinding action.

"That's what I do a lot of," Jeff the Welder explained, obviously trying to impress Carol and the other two girls in that group.

His actions also concerned Declin and he could only name the emotion as jealousy. *I shouldn't have told him Carol was Mr Battersby's daughter,* he thought.

At the top of end of the milling train the students were shown where the now fairly dry by-product, a fluffy mass of fibre called bagasse, was also taken away by conveyor belt. "It is used to fire our boilers to make the mill work and to generate electricity," Harold the Foreman explained.

They were now led across a deck that was four floors up into an area filled with the distillation vats, giant cylinders in which the cane juice was boiled and from which various by-products and waste liquids were drained off. It was an area of semi-darkness and full of small dribbles of water and several small outlets which emitted plumes of steamy vapour.

Harold the Foreman began an explanation, shouting above the noise of the steam and machines, of how the extracted juice was heated and then the molasses was skimmed off. The remaining juice was moved into the next row of giant cylinders where it was 'seeded' with sugar crystals and reheated so that the juice also began to form sugar crystals.

As the foreman talked, Declin studied the students, checking where Carol was. He had lost track of her for a minute while the long line of students and staff had filed off the walkway and onto the deck among the cylinders. But he could not see her.

Where is she? he worried.

Out of the corner of his eye Declin saw movement, and as he glanced that way he caught sight of one of the workers in his Hi Vis shirt move around behind one of the cylinders.

Was that Rossiter? Declin thought.

Another swift scan failed to show him Carol and sharp stabs of anxiety began to needle Declin. He edged out of the crowd and quickly walked across to the far side of the cylinder Rossiter had vanished around. And what he saw made him gasp with anxiety.

The cylinder was on the outside of the deck area with only a steel safety railing along its outer edge. Beyond it was a four story drop to a concrete floor cluttered with machines, steel frames and pipes. And Carol was standing looking over the edge!

And Rossiter was behind Carol and walking towards her! Declin gasped and felt his chest tighten with anxiety. He sucked in his breath to shout a warning as it was obvious Carol was not aware Rossiter was there.

What is Rossiter going to do? he thought.

Chapter 5

BIG, DANGEROUS PLACE

Graham stood in the semi-darkness on the deck four floors up and stared in wonder around the vast interior of the mill. He had visited several sugar mills over the years but was still awed and impressed by them.

Those old engineers back in Queen Victoria's time certainly thought big, he told himself.

He was well aware of the 19th Century origins of the Queensland sugar industry and marvelled at how such gigantic industrial complexes had been built in the middle of isolated rural districts way back in the early years of British settlement.

Turning to his friend Stephen he said, "I am amazed at the effort those old pioneers went to, to set all this up. Lugging all these giant machines for miles across cane fields must have been a mammoth job."

Stephen nodded and pointed to the huge distilling vat beside them. "They certainly thought big. And they must have been mighty engineers to make machines that still work so well a hundred and fifty years later."

Graham had thought of that but not being mechanically minded had not focused on it. But now his eyes travelled over the vast machines which were rotating or grinding or hissing steam and seeming to do it with a smoothness that belied their weight and size. The sight of gleaming smooth metal and glistening, oiled steel all shining in the numerous lights he found both fascinating and impressive.

And he was glad he had made the effort to come on the mill tour. This had only been achieved by persuading his mother he did not need the crutches for a few hours and by hiding the pain he felt at almost every step as he limped along.

He glanced around to make a comment to Carol but found she had walked away. *She probably knows all about this place if her dad is the mill engineer,* Graham thought.

He certainly knew enough to understand it all from his previous visits. He did not need the shouted explanation from the foreman.

Where is she going? he wondered as Carol vanished around the left side of the next huge cylinder.

Then the impish idea came to him that this might be a good chance to be alone with her for a few minutes. *I'll surprise her and go around the other way,* he thought as he edged out of the crowd and began hobbling towards the huge steel vat.

Limping past some gauges and past several huge pipes covered by thick lagging, Graham made his way to the right and around the giant cylinder. There was another one beyond it but the space between the two was large enough for people to walk through. Beyond it was a steel safety railing and then a huge empty space.

And there was Carol. She had come into view from the left and had stopped to face the empty space. Leaning on the railing with her back to him she stared down. Not wanting to scare her and aware she could not hear his limping footsteps because of all the machinery noise Graham sucked in a deep breath to call out.

But before he could speak a man in a bright yellow Hi Vis shirt suddenly appeared beside her and reached out to grab her arm. Carol started in fright and spun to half face the man. Seeing her fear Graham hurried forward, ignoring the pain in his leg, and did call out. "Hey!" he shouted.

Both the man and Carol spun to face him, the man still gripping Carol's arm. The man, a middle-aged, tough looking worker who Graham recognized as being one of those tasked with looking after the students, stared at Graham with a look he could not interpret, angry? Alarmed? Annoyed?

As Graham reached the pair another worker appeared behind the man, the young man named Declin who operated the control room. His face looked pale and white with shock or anxiety which changed to annoyance and relief as he saw Graham. For a moment their eyes met.

The middle-aged man tugged at Carol's sleeve. "Please don't wander away from the group," he called. "This place is dangerous. Stay with the group."

Carol snatched her arm free and looked annoyed. "Let go of me!"

"I am just making sure you are safe," the man replied, gesturing in the direction he wanted her to go. He then turned to Graham. "You too sonny, go back and stay with the group."

His whole manner annoyed Graham, who was also disappointed that his plan to be alone with Carol had been thwarted. For a fleeting moment his eyes met those of the man and then of the youth behind him.

The man turned to the youth and snapped, "What do you want, Riley?"

"Just making sure Car... er. everyone is safe," Declin replied, his eyes flicking to Carol and then angrily to Graham.

The man shrugged and snarled. "You just look after your group, Riley. Now you kids get back to the group."

"She's not in your group either Rossiter," Declin retorted, his eyes again seeking Carol's.

For a moment the two men faced each other in an obvious confrontation, which Rossiter ended by snapping, "We don't want anyone falling from up here. Let's all go back away from the edge."

At the mention of falling, Graham glanced down past the railings to the concrete floor far below and as he imagined a person landing on it he shuddered. Then he eyed the crisscross steel girders, pipes and machines and shuddered again. Rather than argue he turned and made his way back between the huge vats, Carol and the others following him.

As they rejoined the group and Carol came to stand beside him Graham nudged her arm with his elbow. "You okay, Carol?" he asked.

"Yes," Carol replied. "That man just gave me a fright."

"He's a mean looking brute," Graham added, glancing at Rossiter.

Then he looked down at Carol, noting the tiny hairs on her left arm and the gentle swelling of her school uniform top. He wished he had the courage to tell her he liked her and wondered how to proceed.

This romantic planning was interrupted by the group being moved on. They were led past the distillation vats to an area of deck outside a brightly lit cabin. It was explained that this was the process control room. Despite feeling some sharp twinges of pain in his leg Graham made the effort to keep up. Through the windows Graham could see two men seated facing computer screens and a large board with rows of coloured lights.

Carol turned to Declin, who stood on her other side. "I thought you did the controlling, Declin," she said.

Declin nodded. "I control the rail yard and the milling train. This control room is for the processes once the juice is extracted," he explained.

As he did, he smiled down at her. Then he glanced up and briefly his gaze met Graham's. He did not exactly frown but Graham decided it certainly wasn't a friendly look.

The group was led on along past a line of what looked like huge washtubs with lids on them. There were eight in a row and humming and whirring noises were coming from them. The foreman stopped one and opened the huge stainless-steel lid so they could see in.

"This is a centrifuge," he explained. "It works just like the spin drier in a washing machine."

He moved a lever and from a pipe near the top a gush of sticky brown sugar crystals flowed down to half-fill the metre wide bowl.

"We will now spin it at high speed and the extra juice will be spun out and forced through the holes in the sides. That will be further processed to make treacle and syrup."

Graham wondered what the difference was and turned to ask Carol, only to discover to his annoyance that the youth named Declin was standing between him and her!

Irritated he leaned forward. "Carol, what's the difference between syrup and treacle?" he asked.

Carol opened her mouth to answer but Declin beat her to it. "They are the same thing. Treacle is just a bit more viscous," he explained.

Graham had to scratch around in his mental thesaurus for the meaning of 'viscous' and that further irritated him. He managed a smile and then limped along with the others when they moved on.

Is that Declin joker trying to cut me out with Carol? he wondered.

This led to further worrying thoughts. Declin worked here with her father, and she lived nearby. And she had waved to him when they had got off the bus. The awful notion that Declin and Carol might be friends, or even more than friends sent little stabs of jealous anxiety darting through him.

For several minutes the group stood and peered into the tiny glass portholes in the lids through which they were able to watch the sugar rapidly change colour from dark brown to pale. The whole load of sugar crystals was then dropped through an opening in the bottom onto a conveyor belt under the deck to be taken away for storage. The centrifuge then automatically reloaded with more raw sugar.

Peter shook his head. "They certainly spin fast," he commented to the foreman.

The foreman nodded and pointed to the lid. "When I first started at the mill forty years ago none of these had lids and men had to lean in and use wooden paddles to free the crystals and make the load smooth, and that was while the centrifuge was spinning."

Peter was shocked. "My word! That must have been dangerous. Was anyone ever hurt?"

The foreman nodded. "A few men were killed. If you fell into that while it is spinning it would just drain you out before anyone could possibly stop it. That's why they are now a closed system and automated."

Graham had been staring in through a porthole as the centrifuge next to him spun at fantastic speed and he shuddered as his imagination tried to picture that. He opened his mouth to comment that it would be a horrible way to die, but his gaze settled on Declin's face. Declin was shaking his head and looking aghast.

Poor bugger! He saw a man slashed to bits the other day. I'd better not be a ghoul, he told himself.

The foreman obviously had similar thoughts as he called on them to keep moving. The group walked on past the centrifuges and descended several sets of steel steps to the concrete floor near the back of the mill. Here the foreman had a table set out with dishes and containers with samples of sugar and various liquids.

"This is what the mill produces," he explained.

He held up a bottle of dark, almost black liquid. "Molasses," he said. "Try some."

Graham did not want to. He was quite familiar with molasses. "Mum has some at home in the pantry," he explained when urged to pick up a wooden paddle-pop stick to sample it.

"I love it!" Carol said, spooning up as much as she could and placing it into her mouth. She then made mmm noises to show her appreciation. "And I love the smell."

"Only good for cattle feed," Stephen commented.

"And poo to you too Stephen!" Carol retorted.

Next, they were offered some syrup and Graham did sample it. "Tastes great on pancakes," he said as he lifted the stick to his mouth. But a thin thread dribbled off and swung onto his jaw and down onto his shirt.

"Serves you right for being a guts," Stephen commented as he leaned forward for his go.

Next, they were offered large light brown crystals of raw sugar. "People like these for their coffee," the foreman explained.

Graham did not particularly like them, but when a bowl of really dark brown sugar with much finer crystals was offered he moved forward to get some.

But before he could Carol held up a plastic teaspoon filled with the brown sugar. "Try this Graham," she said.

Graham did. He leaned forward and opened his mouth wide so Carol could put the spoonful in.

That brought a snort from Peter who grinned. "I thought Graham was just a big baby. Now I know," he commented.

Graham was unable to make a suitable rejoinder as Carol had placed the spoon in his mouth at that moment. Nor could he respond to Stephen's chuckled comments about needing a bib.

"He probably wears a nappy too!" added Vince Brookes.

That comment hurt but Graham held his temper and did not reply.

They moved along the table and this time Carol sampled some lighter brown sugar. She then scooped some up into the palm of her hand and held it up.

"Try this one Graham," she said, her eyes meeting his with what he interpreted to be a smiling 'come-on'.

With his heart beating suddenly faster at the unexpected invitation he reached up and gently held her hand with his and leaned forward to take a mouthful. Again their eyes met and this time he was sure she was giving him an invitation and not just teasing.

I might be winning, he mused hopefully.

Stephen shook his head. "Look, she's got Graham eating out of her hand already. You are sunk buster! You will now be her slave for life."

Once again, Graham could not reply as he tried to eat the mouthful of sugar. But he was hotly aware of all the eyes now focused on him. Among them was a hostile glare from Declin Riley.

He must fancy Carol and doesn't like me, he decided.

And Carol wasn't amused. "You keep your wicked thoughts to yourself, Stephen Bell!" she snapped.

There were a few moments of tension and Graham worried there might be a scene. Hastily he munched on the sugar, spilling some and trying to get the rest to turn to saliva in his mouth so he could intervene.

Then foreman commented, "These are all the products from the mill," he said.

Stephen spoke up. "What about the rum? Isn't rum a by-product of sugar?"

Mr Conkey, who had been listening closely, stepped forward. "You are too young to know about rum, Stephen. And yes, it is but I don't think they make it here?" He glanced at the foreman who nodded.

"That's right," the foreman answered. "We send raw sugar away to a rum distillery at Bundaberg. And your teacher is right. You are too young sonny. You watch the rum."

Stephen smirked and went to make a comment but then closed his mouth and Graham felt relief. He knew that Stephen sometimes drank alcohol without his parent's knowledge.

Once again, it was a change of scene that ended the situation. The group were ushered across to another building. This was the boiler house, and they were only allowed to stand in the doorway to look in. The place contained two gigantic cylindrical boilers mounted on massive concrete blocks. Huge steel pipes covered with lagging to insulate them took the steam to where it was required.

The place was hot, but not uncomfortably so to North Queenslanders, but it looked and felt unpleasant with hisses of steam and the grind of the machinery feeding the fireboxes. These were closed to viewing but there was a conveyor belt bringing dry bagasse in where it was mechanically loaded into the grate. The base of one of the massive steel chimneys led upwards through the high roof.

After a quick explanation, the foreman took them all out between the buildings and then along a concrete path to the back of the buildings. Here the stench of the bagasse and the sickly-sweet smell of molasses were almost overpowering, even to Graham.

The foreman pointed out a huge brick 'tank' with a sheet steel roof that was set against the wall.

"That is the molasses tank. It will be taken from there by rail along that railway line." he explained.

Graham was at once more interested. He noted that the railway line in question was not one of the mill's 2' gauge but was 3'6". "Is that a spur line from the main railway?" he asked.

The foreman nodded. "Yes. Trains can come into this end of the yard to load the raw sugar and the molasses. They load the sugar from those big hoppers," he said, pointing to a row of huge steel bins standing up on steel girder frames over the railway line.

Peter nudged Graham. "This place is huge, isn't it?"

Graham nodded and voiced an idea that had been growing in his mind. "It would be great to have a model sugar mill on our model railway."

"It would," Peter agreed, staring thoughtfully around.

Stephen had been listening to this and now grinned. "Graham just wants an excuse to go to that cane farm again, you know, the one beside Kanaka Creek where that pretty little farmer's daughter lives. What was her name? Sophie, was it?"

That annoyed Graham and made him worry in case Carol had overheard the comment. A quick glance revealed that she had not, but it drew him another unfriendly look from Declin.

Next, they were shown more big hoppers under which a tip truck was being loaded with black, gooey muck. The foreman pointed to it.

"That is mill mud. It is just dirt and soil that is washed off the cane billets during the milling process. It is very good fertilizer, and the farmers buy it from us," he explained.

The foreman next led them right to the back of the yard where huge piles of bagasse were stacked, some in open fronted steel sheds and some just on the ground.

"Sugar mills have been clean and green for hundreds of years," he boasted. "Long before the 'Greenies' began spouting about renewable energy we have been using our own by-products to power the mills. We also make our own electricity."

"How do you do that?" Fleur asked.

The foreman pointed back at the boiler room and then to shed beside it. "We burn the bagasse to boil water into steam. Some of the steam is used to turn a turbine which is connected to a generator. We can make enough electricity to power the whole mill and hundreds of houses."

"So why don't you use it for that?" Blake asked.

"We do, and have for many years," the foreman replied. "All the houses on the estate and on our farms use our power and we sell any surplus power to the state electricity grid."

Graham was impressed and it made him feel proud of the sugar industry which he knew had been the target for 'Green' politics for many years. He was about to comment on this to Carol and had even opened his mouth when the thought occurred to him that he knew nothing about her likes and dislikes or of her political opinions.

Maybe I'd better wait until I know her a bit better, he decided.

But he did look at her and she raised her eyebrows in a quizzical little smile in return. At that moment, Graham realised that most of the others had moved away, at least were out of earshot and, on an impulse, he decided to seize the moment.

"You are really nice," he whispered. "I'd like to have a date with you."

Carol stared at him in surprise and for a moment he thought he had made a major tactical blunder. But then she smiled and nodded and put her hand on his bare forearm before shaking her head.

"I think you are nice too," she replied. But then she shook her head. "But sorry. My parents think I am too young for dates."

Graham nodded and tried to hide his disappointment. Carol kept her hand on his arm and kept smiling.

"But you can come and visit if you like."

Graham's spirits soared, only to be brought back down to earth by Stephen calling from near the huge opening that led back into the main mill building.

"Come on you two! Save that for later."

Graham scowled but Carol laughed and he felt like taking her hand as they hurried across the gravel yard. Then Declin's face appeared at the doorway and he was scowling too. That got Graham worrying again.

Hmmm! I might have a bit of competition, he thought.

Chapter 6

PRESSURE APPLIED

For Declin, the whole visit by the school group was a stressful and unsettling experience. Right from the start when he had seen Graham trying to win on to Carol, he had been jealous and anxious. That anxiety had shot right up when he had found Carol alone on the high deck with Rossiter moving behind her.

Surely he wasn't planning to push her over? he thought, unable to credit that a person could be so callous and evil. Yet his rational mind told him that Rossiter probably was, that he was a killer.

"He certainly hinted at the possibility of a child being injured or killed," he muttered. But why?

There had been more emotional pain when the foreman had described an accident in a centrifuge. For a few searing seconds Declin had experienced vivid flashbacks to Jack Henley being slashed to bloody shreds down in the tipper pit. It had so shaken him he had been forced to grip a steel pipe to stop himself shaking. To his own dismay he had almost fainted. What had saved him had been the enquiring look on Graham's face as he had glanced at him. This had been replaced in Declin's mind by another stab of fear when he noted Rossiter staring thoughtfully into a centrifuge and nodding.

Surely that brute isn't thinking about pushing someone in to one the centrifuges? he worried. It was just too horrible to even contemplate.

Declin had been relieved when they had moved away. But then his emotions had been battered some more when he saw Carol hold up her cupped hand with sugar in it for Graham to taste. Seeing Graham reach up and hold her hand was a sort of agony for Declin.

That is what I want to do! Oh! How can I save her from that boastful lout?

For Declin had overheard Stephen's comment about the girl on the cane farm and from it he formed the impression that Graham was just a skirt chaser. To his own annoyance, he conceded that Graham was better looking than he was and that he had a really good physique.

The worst had been near the end when he had looked back and seen them alone and Carol had been smiling at Graham and had her hand on his arm. *Pity Mr Smoothy didn't have an accident!* he thought in a fit of jealous anger, which he instantly regretted.

Once again, he was tormented by the fact that he was four or five years older, that he was an adult and she was a child.

"I shouldn't be letting my feelings run away," he told himself bitterly.

But that was no help as he knew there was no logic to who a person was attracted to. But the notion that he was infatuated by a schoolgirl when he was a working adult bothered him and he made himself look into the dark corners of his personality to try to determine if he was actually a paedophile.

It was a jealous and upset young man who had watched the school group board their bus and drive away at midday. Feeling emotionally battered and down, Declin turned and started walking back across the lawn in front of the office building, only to find he had a man walking on either side.

Rossiter was on his right and an even bigger brute, a real hulking lump of man, was walking close on his left. Declin glanced at the man on his left and recognised him as one of the workers from the Boiler Room.

Marvin? Melvin? Marvin Kloste? he thought.

Rossiter nudged Declin's right arm. "Enjoy the school visit did ya Declin me boyo?" he said.

Declin could only nod and feel anxious.

Rossiter laughed and nudged him again. "Lucky there were no accidents, eh? We didn't want a kid mangled in one of those big machines."

"No," Declin croaked, anxiety turning to fear.

Rossiter gave a laugh that sounded to Declin like an evil chuckle. "Anyway, we managed to keep them all safe this time, eh?" Rossiter said.

Declin nodded. Fear began to seep in, clouding his thoughts. *What do these two want?* he wondered.

Rossiter chuckled again, fixing his eyes with a hard stare. "You need to be careful too, boy. We wouldn't want you to fall from a great height."

Then he gave another chuckle and turned away, Marvin going with him. Declin was terrified. He glanced after the pair but was careful not to stare.

Rossiter just threatened me! he thought. The meaning was obvious:

talk to the police and he would have an 'accident'. *What was that all about? What are they up to?* he wondered.

Back at the control room he took over his normal shift after lunch and the routine of the mill then took up most of his thoughts.

But the fear did not go away. *I am a witness to murder,* Declin thought. *It might be convenient to them if I am dead too.*

That was an absolutely chilling thought and left Declin agonising over what to do. He knew he should just go straight to the police but also knew he would then be in trouble because he had tampered with the computer records.

I will lose my job, he brooded.

After work, he walked slowly back to his lodgings in the Caster Hotel. As he made his way across the park, he glanced across at Carol's house, but he knew she would not be home yet.

Maybe I should leave, he thought. But where to? And to do what? That meant another job somewhere else, but what job? *And how can I make sure Rossiter doesn't track me down?* he worried.

The sickening realities of trying to get away from a murderer in the hope he would never find him suddenly bulked large in his mind.

The Caster Hotel was an old 19th Century timber building, two stories high. It was painted a ghastly 'baby-shit yellow' and dominated the street. Like the shops next to it, the hotel's upper story was built out over the concrete footpath to provide a sheltered veranda area. On the ground floor the public bar took up the left side of the downstairs front with a doorway from the footpath. Next was the main entrance which opened into a hallway that led through to the back and the stairway to the second floor. The ground floor front right of the hotel was the lounge where patrons could sit at small circular tables rather than on stools at the bar. Behind that was the dining room and kitchen.

Declin was not a great drinker, but this afternoon he really felt the need for one. So he went into the bar and ordered a beer and then sat in the corner staring out through the open windows facing the street. Two other mill workers were the only other patrons and Declin only knew them by sight as maintenance men in the rail yard. After a cursory greeting they ignored him and went on with their conversation.

"What do I do?" Declin muttered to himself. "Do I run away and try to hide, or do I go to the cops?"

But would going to the cops keep me safe? he pondered. *There are two of them for sure and there may be more.*

Declin had several times seen Rossiter with a group of four or five workers who now, when he thought about it, all appeared to be what might be termed 'hard men'.

The notion that even if he told the cops the men might be back out on bail very quickly, or might not even be arrested, came to bother Declin. Again he considered leaving town. But just running away home did not seem like an option.

And I don't want to leave Carol, he thought. And there she was! Through the front door and windows he saw her go past, a passenger in her mother's car. *Back from school,* he decided as she was still in her school uniform.

And that led to more jealous and anxious memories of the school visit and of the boy named Graham. Declin began to think about ways to get Carol's affection and to block Graham.

* * *

All of Declin's fears came swamping back the following morning when he made his way from clocking in at the office towards the Control Room. As he walked along the concrete path at the rear of the office, Rossiter suddenly stepped out of the main mill building and sauntered across to walk beside him.

"Mornin' Declin boyo. How's tricks this morning?"

Declin swallowed and tried to hide his fear. "Fine," he lied.

"And it will stay that way if you know what is good for you," Rossiter added.

Again Declin felt a wash of chill as the implied threat sank in. To his own shame all he could do was nod and mutter a 'yes'.

"You know, it would be a good thing for your health if this mill went a bit slower," Rossiter commented as they approached the tippler.

Declin was amazed. "You mean use the computer control to slow the process?" he queried.

"Somethin' like that," Rossiter agreed, grinning cheerfully.

Declin was shocked and shook his head. "I can't do that! It would cost me my job," he replied.

"But you could do it?"

"If... if I had to," Declin reluctantly agreed. "But they would know it was me. The system records all that stuff."

"I see. Well, just you don't see too much out in the yard today then," Rossiter replied, the grin vanishing and being replaced by a glare.

Declin was aghast. "You... you aren't...?"

He found he was so scared he could not even frame the question to imply that Rossiter was contemplating murdering someone else.

Rossiter gave him a sideways look and shook his head. "There might just be a few little things go wrong. Don't worry. Nobody will get hurt. We don't want to harm anyone, not even you. Not if we get what we want."

By then they were at the tippler and only a few paces from the bottom of the steps leading up to the Control Room. Declin swallowed and nodded. To add to his swirling emotions Rossiter gave a crocodile smile and patted his shoulder.

"See ya later, boyo," he said.

For Declin, the morning became a period of steadily increasing tension. *What are they going to do?* he fretted. *And why are they doing it?*

Hoping to prevent anyone being hurt and to forestall any plan to slow or stop the mill, Declin began to focus on every screen, his gaze darting from one to another.

But the morning went by and nothing happened. Tiredness came to sap his alertness and while he kept trouble at the front of his mind it was not with the same degree of awareness.

Thus it was Mr Parsons who cried out, "Oh bugger! What's gone wrong with Number Six?"

Declin immediately sat upright and stared at the TV screen to his right. This was from a camera out in the rail yards, and it was immediately apparent that Locomotive No6 had a problem. It had stopped and was leaning over at an odd angle.

"Has it derailed?" he suggested.

"Might have. Yeah, there's Colin getting out now and looking underneath and swearing." Mr Parsons reached across and picked up a phone. He buzzed it and then said, "Mr Battersby? I think there's a problem out in the main marshalling yard. Yes, here's a call coming in. Wait a moment."

Declin took the radio call. It was from Old Charlie Lennon, the driver of No6. "We've come off the tracks damn it!" Charlie called.

Declin relayed this and then looked up to study the layout of the rail yard. He saw at once that No6 was off at a set of points.

And those points will block any trains trying to get to the tippler, he thought.

He had no option but to call the second control room and then the main office and then the railway workshop. That brought Hoskins and the rail repair and breakdown crew hurrying to the scene. For the next two hours, Declin was busy helping to co-ordinate the situation. Despite the threat from Rossiter, he did his very best to get things moving again as quickly as he could.

Mr Parsons called in Steve Mullany to take over at the control panel and went out to the yard to learn what had happened. Declin watched on the CCTV and saw him talking to Mr Battersby, Charley Hoskins, the train crew, and a couple of people from the main office.

When he came back to the control room Mr Parsons held up his fingers to make a small circle. "It was a nut," he said. "Wedged in the points."

"How did it get there?" Declin asked.

Mr Parsons shrugged and shook his head. "We don't know. It isn't off any of the track work and Steve Mullany is definite it isn't off any of the wagons. We aren't sure if it fell off a locomotive. They will check that now."

Declin's mind raced. *Did someone put it there?* he wondered. The word 'sabotage' flitted across his mind, along with Rossiter's image. He resolved to check back over the CCTV records as soon as he could do it without anyone noticing. *Unless the office or Mr Parsons asks me to anyway,* he thought.

But he was also very reluctant to do that as the fact would be recorded in the system and questions might be asked as to why he was looking through the records. So he settled back to work, his mind and emotions filled with doubts and anxiety.

Maybe I should just resign and go somewhere else? he worried. But to where? And to do what job?

That he had cause to be worried was brought home to him forcibly that afternoon when he stopped in the bar of the hotel to have a drink after work. He had no sooner made himself comfortable and opened the paper to read it than Rossiter suddenly appeared at his side.

"Hello, young Declin. How's things goin'?" he queried in a voice that sounded full of utterly false goodwill to Declin.

"Good thanks," Declin replied in a neutral tone.

"Now don't be like that, young Declin!" Rossiter chided. "I was just tryin' ter be friendly."

Declin felt his insides squirm with what he knew was fear, but he managed to control his face.

"What do you want?" he was able to say without quavering.

"Well, if that's how you want it!" Rossiter replied. He leaned closer and hissed, "Have the bosses been asking to study the CCTV records at all?"

Declin swallowed and shook his head. "No," he replied, just managing to bite back saying that they hadn't thought of that yet.

"Is there anything on it that looks suspicious, you know, out in the railyard?"

Declin shrugged and tried to appear calm. "I don't know. I haven't looked. Should I?"

Rossiter fixed him with a glare. "You should. And if there is anything that might raise anyone's suspicions, wipe it like you done last time."

"They will know I did that," Declin replied. "The computer records everyone who logs on and what they do. All the footage has time and date information on it."

"Tough! That's for you to worry about. But you look after us and we will look after you," Rossiter replied. With that he moved away and vanished through the side door.

Declin sat and shuddered as the fear washed through him. He felt caught and knew he was very scared.

Maybe I had better leave town, he again thought.

Chapter 7

FAINT HEART NEVER WON FAIR LADY

All the way back to school after the mill tour Graham felt on top of the world. Carol sat next to him on the bus and chatted the whole way. She even laughed at his silly jokes. But, as always, there were worms in life's garden. While Graham was able to preen his ego at his masculine attractiveness, and note that he and Carol were obvious targets of gossip, he also noted Stephen giving him wry little smirks.

And, even though Carol had said he could visit, that raised a whole palisade of possible barriers. *I have to get permission from mum to do that,* Graham thought. But after some consideration he decided that might not be such a difficult obstacle.

There was also the not inconsiderable problem of travel. *How on earth can I get to Caster on a weekend?* he wondered.

He had no idea if there were busses, and he certainly did not think he could ask his mother to drive him. Nor did he consider riding his bike. The previous year he and Stephen had ridden their bicycles to visit girls in Kuranda, and memories of the dramas that resulted caused him a surge of very mixed emotions. He had nearly been killed while saving the girl and she had not even thanked him.

Sour memories of being dumped by her were mingled with sharp twinges in his right leg, both of which confirmed him in thinking that trying to travel that distance on a bike would not be a good idea.

And certainly not along the Bruce Highway! Mum wouldn't let me anyway. So busses it might have to be. I will look into it, he decided, knowing in his heart that he was putting off the biggest worry of them all: having to meet her parents.

Having no idea what they even looked like, Graham instantly conjured up images of dour, disapproving parents who strongly suspected his intentions of not being strictly honourable. To add to his concerns, there was the niggling notion that he did not even know what his intentions were, other than he was a young man who wanted a girlfriend, and he thought he was in love.

At home that evening Graham worried about being told no. All through dinner he kept thinking of when and how to ask and while cleaning up afterwards he kept trying to pluck up courage.

Finally, he told himself: *Come on coward! Faint heart never won fair lady. Move!*

But he waited until his brother Alex and sister Kylie were out of the kitchen before broaching the subject with his mother. He particularly did not want Kylie present as she would immediately suspect his motives and give him grief on Margaret's behalf. Just thinking of that made him feel guilty. Perversely that sparked anger and made him determined to go ahead.

Margaret doesn't own me! he told himself.

But it was still hard to raise the subject with his mother.

In the end he did it while washing up, saying in an off-hand tone, "Mum, can I go to Caster one weekend?"

"Caster? You were just there yesterday," his mother replied, frowning. "Why? And when? Do you mean this weekend? I thought you had a cadet bivouac."

"Not his weekend mum, the one after. Yes, there is a cadet exercise this weekend."

His mother frowned. "I am not sure if you should be going on cadet exercises. That leg of yours still isn't healed. You can't run around the bush on crutches," she said.

That worried Graham too. "It will be alright mum. Capt Conkey has me down to be in the CP... in the Command Post. I will just sit at a radio. I won't be walking around the bush."

"Oh alright. So this trip to Caster, do you mean the whole weekend?"

"No Mum, just one day, Saturday or Sunday," Graham answered, all the while listening in case either Kylie or Alex returned.

"Why?"

Faced with that Graham squirmed and shrugged. "Just... just to see a friend," he answered, knowing his answer sounded lame.

"Friend? Who?"

"Just a girl in Ten A," Graham muttered, blushing fiercely as he did.

"A girl! I might have known. Who is she? What's her name?" his mother asked.

"Carol... Carol Battersby. Her dad is the mill engineer," Graham said.

"Does she know? Are you invited?"

Graham shrugged and nodded. "She said I could visit," he answered.

"Do her parents know?"

"Not yet. She will tell them when I let her know if I can come," Graham answered.

"Is this some sort of date?"

Graham shook his head. "No Mum. Her parents think she is too young for dates," he answered.

"And they are quite right. So this is just to visit this Carol at her house?"

"Yes Mum."

"And how will you get there and back?"

Ah! That was the nub! Graham could only shrug. His mother looked at him hard and then nodded. "Alright. I will find out about busses and things. I certainly can't drive you. And you must be back before dark."

"Thank you, Mum," Graham answered, his spirits soaring.

"And any bus fares come out of your allowance," his mother added.

That now meant very little to an ecstatic Graham and he just nodded and grinned.

"And you will still do all your chores around the house," his mother added.

"Yes Mum."

"And you can start now. Finish your homework and then go and iron your cadet uniform ready for tomorrow," she ordered.

So Graham did.

That night he lay awake for hours, his mind filled with romantic fantasies.

At school the next day he immediately sought out Carol. To his relief, she gave him a smile when he saw her, and she even stood up and left her friends to come and meet him as he limped towards her on his crutches.

"How's the leg?" she queried.

"Good. Getting better," Graham replied, hotly conscious that all the other girls were looking and some were doing some behind-the-hand whispering.

"What did you want?" Carol asked.

That shocked Graham a bit. *No beating about the bush with this girl!* he thought.

"I just wanted to let you know my mum will let me come and visit you," he said.

"Oh that's nice! When, next weekend?" Carol answered.

That also shocked Graham more. "No... er... No. I've got an army cadet field exercise next weekend. It will have to be the weekend after that," he said.

He felt quite anxious as he did, hoping that Carol did not have a lot of negative opinions about cadets or the army.

To his relief, she grinned and said, "Is that the one where the Air Cadets are going to show the Army Cadets who is best?" she commented.

"No!" Graham cried. "We are the best."

How does she know about that? he wondered. For a few seconds dark suspicions flitted across his mind. But then he realised that Gwen Copeland was one of her friends.

"How can you go if you can't walk?" Carol queried.

Graham again explained how he would be in the Command Post. Nodding she led the way to an empty bench seat. They sat and chatted until class and after that the day went quickly, with Graham in a good mood and able to do his schoolwork with no difficulty. He even endured the pains that niggled in his leg when he wasn't careful.

* * *

After school was Cadets, and that meant more challenges. As usual, Graham changed into his cadet uniform, but not without difficulty as he had to tug the long trousers on over his plaster cast. Not being able to wear a boot bothered him and made him feel bad but he could only shrug philosophically and limp over to join the others at the side of the quadrangle.

As on the previous week, Capt Conkey queried if he was fit to go on parade. This time Graham was determined. "Yes sir. I walked all over the sugar mill the other day," he assured him.

"Alright. You go as Three Platoon sergeant for the company parade. Go to the CSM and get the roll book, but do not risk exacerbating that injury. You take it carefully and if you need to, you get someone else to do the parade and marching."

"It will be okay, sir," Graham assured him.

He found Cadet Warrant Officer Class 2 Cleland, the CSM and a Year 11, and collected the 3 Platoon Roll Book and then moved carefully to where 3 Platoon formed up on the side of the quadrangle beside C Block after school. For a few seconds he experimented with marching without the crutches, but the sharp twinges immediately told him that was not a good idea. So he regretfully used them to hobble out to the correct position on the lawn. Once there he leaned on the crutches with his left leg taking most of the weight and called one of the corporals as the Right Marker.

The CSM was again practicing the admin parade in 'Close Column of Platoons', that is with each platoon in line in three ranks but with the platoons one behind the other. He was also practicing them at 'Moving on Parade'.

To practice the 15 paces for the Advance in Review Order during the Passing-Out Parade, Graham thought.

So the markers were called and marched out 15 paces, halted and did a left turn before standing at ease. Then the company was called on parade and carried out the same movement. For Graham it meant swinging along on his crutches with his right foot held clear of the ground. He was quite unable to stay in step but could still keep a close eye on his platoon.

"Get in step Cadet Markwell!" he growled. "And count the timings you lot!"

There was a Right Dress and Graham had to hobble out to the side to line the ranks up. He had never done it on a parade ground before and felt a bit self-conscious. Worse still he could almost feel the animosity of some of the corporals and older cadets.

Understandable, he told himself. *I was only a corporal myself a few weeks ago.*

On the command 'Eyes front!' Graham limped back to his position at the front. The CSM then stood the company at ease and ordered rolls to be marked. That meant Graham had to do an About Turn, which he could not do correctly with his sore leg. He saw the grins (Or was it smirks?) on the faces of the cadets but gritted his teeth and kept acting as he thought a sergeant should.

After the roll had been marked the CSM took the reports and then called the company to attention and handed over to Capt Conkey. He ordered the officers to fall in, so Graham did a right turn and moved out past the Right Marker and waited for CUO Anastasia Mitrovitch to march across to face him. Salutes were exchanged and Graham met the CUO's eyes, noting that there was no warmth or friendliness in them.

She resents me being her platoon sergeant too, Graham thought.

That also was understandable as the previous sergeant had been the CUO's friend. But that sergeant had been removed for misbehaviour and the CUO really had no choice but to accept the OC's decision.

Graham saluted, stepped awkwardly to his left front to pass the CUO and then hobbled around to the rear of the platoon. There he leaned on his crutches, trying to stand as still and straight as he could.

The company was then marched down to the school oval. Graham managed to hobble along fast enough to keep up by swinging along on the crutches. Then he was able to sit on the grass near the platoon while the first activities were rehearsed: the Guard of Honour to greet the VIPs and the section displays of training activities.

Only when the whole company marched on for the main event did Graham stand and limp along with them. Despite a few twinges and stabs of pain he made a real effort to do as much correct drill as possible. He managed the 'Right Dress' procedure alright and could easily come to attention when the CSM handed over to the Parade Commander.

By then Graham's leg was definitely sore and he was relieved when the officers were called to 'Take Post' and he could do a right turn and make his way painfully around to the rear of the platoon.

Here he was met by Lt McEwen, who had noted him grimacing. "Sit down until the marching, Corporal… I mean Sergeant Kirk," she instructed.

So Graham did, feeling very self-conscious as he did, even though he was behind the company.

And he was then further upset by watching the Flag Party march on and noting how Sgt Crane and Sgt Gayney could not seem to get their drill right. Both were frequently out of step and Crane even changed step twice and then mucked up the left turn on the march and ended up behind the Flag instead of beside it. Graham could see that Capt Conkey was not happy about it but could only hope they got better and did not muck it up on the day.

But the Flag Party went wrong twice during the March Pasts. As the Flag Party were between 2 Platoon and 3 Platoon, Graham was behind them and watched Crane three times get the step wrong or end up in the wrong place on the Left Forms.

Finally Lt Hamilton, who was marching beside them, hissed angry words and when the company halted, he stepped close and spoke a few stronger words. All Graham could overhear was Crane replying that he was, "trying my best, sir, but I just can't seem to stay in step."

To which Lt Hamilton answered, "Then we might have to swap you with another sergeant. The Flag Party is the focus of everyone's eyes and has to look good. We can't have you mucking it up."

That gave Graham a malicious spurt of satisfaction and he began to speculate which of the other sergeants might get the job. There was then more speculation as Capt Conkey began a rehearsal for the prize giving. The previous year Graham had not expected to win any prize, being glad just to scrape onto the Junior Leaders Course nomination list as 2nd reserve but this year he thought he might get something.

Best Corporal? he thought.

But then he substituted Peter's name for that. To his annoyance he had not even got 'Best Shot' at the rifle range, being beaten by Sgt Grenfell. But he had forgotten the Best Attendance award. Capt Conkey explained it and read out a list of seven names of cadets who had not missed a single cadet activity all year. This included Peter but not Stephen or Roger, both of whom had missed a couple of parades.

So Graham limped out to join the line of prize winners for that award and then hobbled back. *At least I get an award for something,* he thought. But at the back of his mind was the niggling worry about who would be selected to attend the Warrant Officers Course in December.

After the Passing-Out Parade rehearsal, the company marched back up to the Q Store area and was then seated in section lines in the shade for a briefing on the Field Exercise that weekend.

And that field exercise turned out to be a memorable one for several reasons. To Graham's intense annoyance and chagrin, the Air Cadets were judged to have won and he knew they would crow about that for years to come.

Bloody Willy Williams and his gadgets! he fumed. *I warned Pete about them too.*

For the whole weekend Graham had sat with four other army cadets and two Officers of Cadets in a tent, talking on a radio, marking maps, and writing signals logs, and every time a report had come in of another Army Cadet patrol sighted or captured by the Air Cadets he had sworn, cursed and grumped.

It had not helped to have some Navy Cadets in the Exercise Control CP. Among them was AB Tina Babcock, now Andrew's girlfriend but earlier in the year a young lady he had nurtured high romantic hopes over.

The second phase of the exercise had been no better. During that the Air Cadets had switched from being the defending force protecting guided missile launchers and radar stations to being aircrew who had been shot down and who had to evade capture and escape from the area. More than half of them had succeeded, including Willy and his girlfriend Marjorie.

* * *

Back at school on Monday, Graham risked walking without his crutches. His leg still gave him a few twinges but by taking it easy he had no trouble. As a result he limped a bit but knew that was only temporary. And his romance with Carol prospered. They sat together during the breaks and Graham used all his wit and charm to try to impress her with stories and jokes. She seemed to like these and did a lot of laughing and giggling and his confidence went up.

They also agreed that a visit to Caster on Saturday would be the best time. "I will tell my mum and dad," Carol said, sending Graham's fears of meeting her parents shooting up. But his romantic hopes also went up and he thought he was very happy.

The fly in life's ointment for him was the fact that his sister and her friend Margaret both plainly did not approve and openly scowled when they walked past at lunch time. And when he got home, Kylie launched into an attack at once.

"You are so cruel, Graham!" she snapped.

"Why?" he queried while knowing very well what the reason was.

"You are hurting Margaret!" Kylie almost snarled.

"So? She doesn't own me," Graham retorted.

"She loves you, you blockhead!" Kylie almost screamed.

Graham squired uncomfortably, knowing that to be true. "I didn't ask her to!" he snapped in reply.

"You didn't have to! Love doesn't work that way, bonehead!"

That made him even more uncomfortable, and he did wonder if his attraction to Carol wasn't just a crush. Feeling quite torn emotionally he took himself to his room and worked on making a model ship, something he hadn't done for quite a while.

At school on Tuesday, his discomfiture was increased when he sat with Carol during the lunch break and Kylie and Margaret again walked past. Kylie glared at him, and Margaret managed to give a weak smile.

Carol saw them. "Who are they?" she asked.

"The one scowling at me is my little sister Kylie," Graham answered.

He invented a story as to why Kylie was annoyed with him. But he was careful not to mention Margaret and experienced quite a mix of emotions as a result: guilt, shame, doubt.

If I am with my one true love there should be no secrets, he thought. Which got him worrying and wondering.

Better still, his mother took him to the doctor after school and the plaster was removed. After a few checks it was agreed Graham should be alright, as long as he took it easy. He was able to ease on a shoe and limped out on his crutches and was taken home a much happier boy.

Wednesday was better. School was ordinary and Graham sat with Carol during the breaks and talked happily, assuring her he would visit on the next Saturday. During the day he was very careful with his leg and made sure he used the crutches.

It was after school when he went to Cadets that he got another boost. As he no longer had a plaster cast, he decided to risk not using the crutches. He was able to carefully ease on his army boot and to walk fairly normally when he went on parade. There were a few twinges, but he was able to do the drill and then could keep up with his platoon when he marched them down to the oval for Passing-Out Parade practice.

Capt Conkey noted this and nodded his approval. And then, when the Flag Party was told to get ready, it was discovered that Sgt Crane was absent. Frowning with annoyance Capt Conkey looked around and then beckoned Graham over. Graham immediately speculated that it might be about replacing Crane so he ignored the twinges of pain in his leg and marched over as though he was fully recovered.

Saluting he said, "Yes sir?"

"Do you think you are up to being in the Flag Party?"

Graham felt elation soar, just managing to hide a grin. "Yes sir."

"Then go over to them. I will get Sgt Bates to take the platoon."

"Sir!"

As the Flag Party was a very public job requiring good drill, he was instantly both pleased and anxious. He was also very conscious that he was now being trusted with a post of honour.

That the change was resented was also at once obvious when Sgt Sheila Sherry of 1 Platoon gave him a sharp look and curled her lip and so did Sgt White, the recon sergeant from HQ Platoon. The ill-will was offset by seeing grins on the faces of his friends.

A 'talk through' practice was then commenced. As the first part of the parade would be a Guard of Honour to receive the VIPs provided by 4 Platoon, followed by displays, all at section level Graham was able to just sit on the grass at the rear and watch. Only when the whole unit moved off to prepare to march on did he hobble over to where CUO Masters and Sgt Gayney stood on the far side of the parade ground.

Lt Hamilton joined them and began talking them through the manoeuvres required of a flag party on a ceremonial parade. Graham was placed on the left of the flag, which meant when the Flag Party was marching in file he was at the rear of the line of three. That way he did not upset the step of the other two while they practiced.

Capt Conkey had driven small, coloured flags into the turf and the company now marched on to these and the parade rehearsal began. While this went on the Flag party practiced off to the side, turning on the march and doing left forms and left wheels. Graham tried as hard as he could and several times experienced quiet sharp twinges from putting too much pressure on his ankle. Once he even cried out and Lt Hamilton asked if he wanted to sit out, but he shook his head.

"I'll be right, sir," he assured the OOC.

Then it was the turn of the Flag party to march on. The parade did a Present Arms (Even though they had no rifles, pretending they had) and the Flag Party was ordered to march on. Graham felt very self-conscious as he limped and hobbled along at the rear of the file as they marched right across the front of the parade. He was very conscious that some of the faces were showing disapproval and that there were curled lips on the faces of his enemies.

Left turn and then Left Form (with him as the marker) and then

Right Turn and Left Wheel and the Flag Party was in position between 2 Platoon and 3 Platoon. After a pretend Present Arms Graham was able to sit down and take the weight off a leg that had begun to throb annoyingly.

The welcome salute to the Reviewing Officer (played by Capt Conkey) and the inspection, by platoons followed. That was all they got done that day and as the company was given the command 'Move to the right in Column of Route, Right Turn!' ready for a march past practice Graham was told to fall out and make his own way back up to the school while the remainder of the unit marched around and gave Capt Conkey an 'Eyes Right!' before marching back to the quadrangle as a company.

By the time they got there, Graham had arrived. He rejoined the Flag Party just in time to practice marching off the flag. The company was then dismissed and Capt Conkey called him aside.

"Is your leg going to be healed, Sgt Kirk? You did alright but I can see you were struggling a bit. I don't want to make another change, but I can replace you if your leg is going to be a problem."

"The parade is weeks away, sir. It will have healed by then," Graham answered. *I hope!*

Capt Conkey looked doubtful. "Hmmm! You seemed to be limping quite badly out there. It has me worried."

"I will be very careful and make sure it heals, sir," Graham said. Now that he'd tasted the glory of the Flag Party, he really wanted that honour.

On Thursday at school, Carol sat with him again. "Are you still thinking of coming to see me at home on Saturday?"

"Yes," Graham said, anxious there was some reason why he couldn't.

"Good. What time will I tell mum and dad you'll arrive?"

Graham now had bus times and he had worked out that he could make it by about 9:30. He told Carol that and she smiled and nodded.

"Good. We can have morning tea. I will cook some scones. Do you like scones with jam and cream?"

That sounded very good to Graham, and he went off to his next class feeling even happier. He was anxious about meeting her parents but accepted that it was an ordeal he had to endure.

One of those life challenges a man has to face. Besides, none of my friends can come with me, he reasoned.

He had even hinted at it, but Roger and Peter had politely declined and Stephen had said maybe, "But not this weekend."

Chapter 8

TO THE LION'S DEN

That night Graham lay in bed and fantasised and anxiously tried to image the meeting with Carol's parents. He knew what her father looked like from the mill visit, but he had no idea what her mother was like. And he realised he knew nothing else about her family.

Has she got brothers and sisters? he wondered.

He began to dread the meeting with the family, fearing they would not approve of him. The meeting began to loom as a real ordeal.

On Friday at school the anxiety was intensified. Graham sat with Carol at every opportunity and chatted. He knew it would be good policy to ask about her family. Anxiety over possible siblings and their reactions to him grew. He conjured up an image of a disapproving younger sister meeting him and curling her lip. But he then shook his head and mentally flailed himself for being a weakling and a coward.

On Friday afternoon as he said goodbye to Carol after school, he was in a state of high anticipation. "See you tomorrow!" he cried.

As he did, he had to restrain himself from reaching out to hold her hands, to hug her. The urge to kiss her was very strong. It left him trembling as she smiled and walked away.

At home that afternoon he got no time to rest. His mother pointed downstairs. "Everything in life has a price," she said. "You need to do your home chores before you go gallivanting off."

"I don't have to when I go to Cadets on a weekend," he countered.

"That's because your father and I both approve of you learning to defend your country. Then you are doing a service. This trip tomorrow is just for pleasure. So pay for it. As I said, everything in life has a price. Nothing comes free."

"What about air? It doesn't cost anything," Graham retorted.

"Oh yes it does, Mister Smart Alec! You need to use energy to draw air into your lungs and that means food and that costs money. So stop being a bush lawyer and go and clean out that guinea pig cage!" his mother snapped, pointing to the backyard.

Reluctantly, Graham did as he was told. He was then directed to water his father's orchids before teatime. Mumbling under his breath, Graham did as he was told. But he was actually happy as with each passing minute the time to be with Carol came closer. But so did the moment of meeting her family and that was a nagging worry that increased by the hour.

By bedtime Graham was so anxious he had trouble sleeping. For hours he lay and worried, in between bouts of fantasising about wonderful romantic situations where he and Carol were in love.

But Saturday morning introduced a bit of life's grit into his affairs. To start with, Kylie kept scowling at him. He hadn't told her he was going to Caster but obviously their mother had. And Kylie clearly disapproved and let her feelings be known.

"You should stay and do your share of the chores," she snapped.

"I have!" Graham retorted.

"Have not!"

"Have! I cleaned the guinea pig cage, and I watered the orchids," Graham retorted.

"What about the lawn? Who's going to mow it?" Kylie cried.

Graham was astonished . He had never seen her so angry. "Alex can," he suggested.

Alex overheard this and snapped, "Pig's bum! You can do it when you get back."

Their mother now came into the room and intervened. "Stop that bickering! Get ready, Graham, so I can drive you to the bus depot."

"Yes Mum," Graham replied, glad to be given an excuse to escape the sniping. He fled to his room with Kylie scowling and poking her tongue at him.

After another shower, Graham dressed carefully in a casual shirt, long pants, and joggers. He fretted over what to wear, not wanting to appear overdressed but equally concerned that he not look, as his father often said, like an unemployed layabout.

Then it was down to the car, with Kylie still scowling and her face stiff with disapproval. It was a relief to escape her glares. But as the car backed out through the gate, anxiety came seeping back in.

Graham became so anxious that on the drive to the bus depot it overrode his romantic excitement and left him feeling a bit breathless and nauseous.

Oh! I hope they are alright, he worried. *And I hope they think I am alright too!*

Concern over his possible reception caused Graham to feel slightly upset all the way to Caster. The bus left on time, and he had a seat to himself. He had been along the Bruce Highway many times and hardly noticed most to the places, just mentally keeping track of progress: White Rock, Edmonton, Gordonvale. For a few minutes the sight of the steam billowing from the chimneys of the Gordonvale sugar mill held his interest and he was glad he had done the mill tour at Caster.

The sight of Walsh Pyramid, the triangular mountain that dominated the skyline, approached and then went past. He moved his thoughts to the Cadet exercise back in June.

That was a really good exercise, he thought as he looked down at the clear flowing Mulgrave River.

The exercise had run for 8 days and had started in Gordonvale. It had been run by 130 Army Cadet Unit from Heatley in Townsville but senior cadets from Cairns and Atherton had been invited, as well as Navy Cadets. It had ended at Tinaroo up on the Atherton Tablelands and by looking west along the Mulgrave Valley he could just make out the line of mountains that marked the eastern escarpment.

And that sight brought more memories: searching the jungle below Mt Bartle Frere for the family goldmine and then of the dramatic events of being trapped there by cyclonic flooding.[6]

The bus then travelled on south along the 'Coastal Corridor' the lush, wide valley between the coastal ranges and the rugged slopes of the Bellenden Ker Range. Staring up at the dense tropical rain forest that covered the entire mountain range, Graham could only speculate on what it might be like hiking up there.

We must try it one day, do some real exploring, he thought.

So he tried to divert his thoughts with memories rather than face the looming anxiety of meeting her parents. But now the coach was travelling through flat, open sugar cane fields, and as it rounded a curve to the left he looked out to the right and saw distant chimneys with white steam and smoke puffing out.

That smoke is from the Caster Mill, he thought. Then he corrected himself. *Steam. It is not smoke. Sugar mills make very little pollution.*

---

[6] Read *Below Bartle Frere* by C. R. Cummings

They burn the bagasse, the crushed cane fibre and use it to run giant steam boilers that turn the mill and also make their electricity.

But the sight sent his anxiety shooting up. *Soon be there,* he thought anxiously.

He began to fret over how he looked and how he would be received. For a minute or so the sight of a small yellow diesel locomotive hauling a long train of wire bins loaded with cane billets took his mind off the coming ordeal.

Then the coach rounded another curve to the right and he saw buildings ahead. *Oh bugger! This is it!* he thought.

His gaze took in a few sheds and houses on the left and then a petrol station and an old two-story hotel. There was a cane field on the right. It had been recently harvested.

The brakes hissed and came on and the coach pulled to a stop at the petrol station. For a moment Graham felt paralysed by what he didn't want to name as fear. Then he swallowed and pulled himself to his feet and made his way off the bus.

Almost as soon as he stepped down onto the concrete driveway of the petrol station, the door of the bus hissed shut behind him and the bus pulled back into the traffic flow and headed on south.

Graham swallowed and tried to pretend he wasn't nervous. Looking around he saw that the only person in sight, other than the drivers of the cars passing by along the main road, was a man who looked like a farmer over at the petrol pumps. He appeared to be refuelling a work vehicle.

Now Graham noted that a bitumen road went off to his left among the houses and that another bitumen road went left just past the hotel. Immediately beyond that was a light railway which crossed the highway at right angles. Graham's gaze followed this, noting that the other part of the town was one long line of buildings on the other side of the highway. These ran off at right angles along a bitumen road which ran parallel to the light railway. In the distance were a cluster of buildings and houses among a stand of very large trees, and beyond them the huge steel buildings and chimneys of the sugar mill. Looming a few kilometres beyond the mill was a jungle-covered range of mountains.

From his previous visit, Graham knew that Carol's house was among those distant buildings, and he felt another quaver of anxiety in his lower stomach.

Feeling like he was making his way into the lion's den, he began walking along the side of the highway towards the hotel. Within minutes he wished he had worn a hat as the sun was very hot. But the only hats he had were his old Scout hat he used for hiking and his Army Cadet KFF (Hat Khaki Fur Felt) which he knew he was not allowed to wear if it wasn't a Cadet activity. He had not felt like wearing his old Scout hat, thinking Carol would not be impressed.

And he quickly realised he had miscalculated the time and distance he would have to walk and the time it would take. The tropical sun was blazing down. Trickles of perspiration sprang out on his brow and between his shoulder blades.

Crossing the busy highway looked to be a bit of a challenge too, but he was saved from any real drama by the red warning lights at the light railway level crossing starting to flash. Bells began to ring, and the red and white boom gates came down, bringing the vehicles to a stop.

From the beyond the hotel came the blast of a locomotive's air horn and a few seconds later a yellow diesel engine rolled into view, hauling a line of full cane bins. Graham took the opportunity to cross the highway, and then stood near the boom gates waiting for the end of the cane train to pass. As it did, his nostrils were assailed by the odour of freshly cut sugar cane and he could not decide whether he really liked it or whether it made him nauseous.

The train seemed to go on for ever but was in fact only a minute or so. The yellow brake van at the end of the train rattled across the highway and on towards the mill. As it did, Graham looked that way and noted that the single railway track became a set of three sidings which seemed to extend the entire length of the town.

As soon as the train was past, Graham walked across the bitumen side road and turned right on the footpath. He began walking towards the mill, wishing that the sun was on the other side so that he might be in the shade of the few buildings that had awnings.

When he had passed through on the school trip, he had been so focused on impressing Carol that he had not looked out at the town except for a few casual glances and on family drives along the highway he had barely noticed the place. But now, as he walked slowly along favouring his sore leg, he had plenty of opportunity to study it in detail.

The layout was now clear. From right to left were a harvested cane field, the light railway lines, then the bitumen 'main street'. A concrete sidewalk extended most of the length and was lined with old buildings. These were mostly constructed of timber or corrugated iron. First was a service station with an old-fashioned garage in a big shed as the workshop. Next were a general store and then a newsagent. After that came a few houses. Some were low block houses set back in their own fenced-off yards with picket or wire fences and mostly nice gardens. Others were shops or sheds and halls and these nearly all had an awning over the sidewalk. Most of the buildings appeared to be in a poor state: peeling paint, moss and grime on walls, broken planks, and rusting corrugated iron. Behind the row of buildings were a gravel road and then a field of sugar cane.

The Caster Hotel came into view halfway along, two-story and with its veranda over the footpath. It was old and constructed of timber and corrugated iron and Graham saw it was painted a ghastly yellow and was the main landmark in the street. As Graham passed, he glanced nervously at the open front door and then at the open door of the public bar. A few sour looking old men sat in there and he quickly looked away, feeling very self-conscious and very much the outsider.

Immediately beyond the hotel a driveway led to the rear, and then there was a similar two-story building which turned out to be a shop with rooms on the top story. This building also extended out over the footpath.

As Graham approached the shop, a teenage girl of about his own age appeared at the door and she immediately got his attention. She had a round, plain face with a mischievous look about it. But her main attributes were a pair of very prominent boobs which stuck out and bobbled inside a very short pink T-shirt which was cut off to reveal her midriff and navel. Embroidered across the front of the bulging T-shirt was the logo: 'Betty the Babe'.

To Graham her breasts looked like they had been pumped up. He glanced through the shop door and noted it was some sort of hardware and general goods store. As he did, the girl studied him and then her face split into a cheeky grin.

"Hi!" she called, "Hot isn't it?"

Graham was so surprised that for a moment he could only give a vacuous grin in return. "Yes," he managed to say.

The girl changed her position, leaning on the doorpost and wiggling her bottom and jiggling her boobs. "Are you alright? Are you looking for someone?" she asked.

Graham stopped and wiped perspiration off his brow. "Er... Er, no. I am just going to visit a friend," he replied, his eyes taking in her curves and the legs that extended all the way up to her very tight shorts.

She moved again and her grin widened. "Oh yeah? Who's that then?" she asked.

What a nosy little minx! Graham thought. But he lacked the courage or wit just to ignore her question or to deflect it politely. "Carol Battersby. Her dad's the mill engineer," he replied.

The girl's eyebrows shot up and she nodded. "Oh yeah? How do you know here?"

"She's in my class at school," Graham answered lamely.

"I'm Betty. What's your name?" the girl asked.

Graham was surprised at her forwardness and could only goggle and gabble for a second, trying to work out how to break off the conversation without being rude.

At that moment, a gruff male voice called from inside, "Betty! Get in here and stop maggin' on the footpath. You clean up that storeroom, girl."

Betty giggled and winked. "See ya!" she muttered as she turned and scuttled inside. Feeling quite relieved and even more stressed, Graham resumed walking.

That took him back out into the bright sunlight again and he squinted against the glare. He noted that the concrete sidewalk had ended and that from there on the area between the concrete kerbing and the fences of the houses was just mowed grass. This was crossed at every allotment by a driveway, sometimes just two wheel-rut indentations and sometimes concrete or pebble. There were more houses and a derelict looking shire hall and a few sheds plus a couple of vacant blocks all overgrown with long grass and weeds.

As he approached the last house, Graham glanced at his watch. He had gotten off the bus at 9:15 and saw it was now 9:45.

His anxiety shooting up another notch, he hurried on, distracted by another sugar train coming from behind him and heading for the mill. As the end of the train rattled and squeaked past him, Graham reached the main North Coast railway line. He paused here to look both ways along the clearing of the railway and then turned his attention to the mill.

The mill now loomed up, towering over the trees in the park ahead of him, the gigantic steel sheds and huge steel chimneys dominating the landscape. It was a sight that always impressed him and he marvelled that the early pioneers had the foresight and skill to construct such a place.

He walked on 50 paces to the bitumen ring road which enclosed the park which lay between him and the mill offices and mill.

This is the 'Mill Estate', he thought, having learned that it was counted separate from the town during the Mill Tour.

Again regretting not having a hat, he wiped more perspiration from his brow and turned left towards the four large colonial style houses set among trees and gardens.

Carol's house is the one closest to the mill, he thought.

The sight of those houses brought thoughts of the social class divisions of the time when they were built to bother him. They had been built when there was a wider gulf between the 'manager's and the 'workers' and he felt a sudden stab of emotional insecurity. A glance across the park past the old steam locomotive added to this, as he noted the row of ten much smaller low-set houses which he knew were the homes of the foremen, under-managers and skilled technical people, the houses provided by the mill as part of the job package.

Then Graham shook his head. *Why am I feeling like this? My dad is a Master Mariner and owns four ships. We aren't some low-class family of peasants!*

But he still knew he was anxious and shy and a niggling worry about getting into trouble for trespassing or of not being socially acceptable gripped him.

Then Graham's heart skipped a beat. *There she is!* he thought.

Walking towards him from the gate of the last house was Carol. The sight set his heart hammering with hope and fear, and he noted a younger girl behind her at the gate.

Her sister? he wondered. Then he shrugged and walked faster. *Oh well, let's get it over with,* he told himself.

Chapter 9

FAMILY

"Hi Graham! You made it," Carol cried as he got closer. She hurried to meet him.

Seeing how welcoming she was sent Graham's spirits shooting up. He grinned in relief and had to resist an urge to take her hands and hug her. They met and Carol turned and walked beside him.

"I was starting to worry you weren't coming," she said.

Graham shook his head. "Sorry. I just miscalculated how long it would take to walk from the highway," he replied.

"Yes, it is a fair walk," Carol agreed as they strode past the first big house.

Glancing at that got Graham all anxious too. *That is the Big Boss's house,* he thought.

Into his mind flitted an image from an old historical photograph of a white plantation owner sitting on the front steps of his mansion surrounded by his family, white staff and a large group of black 'Kanakas', the Pacific Islanders used as indentured labour in the 19th Century. He knew the image was now quite ridiculous but that was when the house had been built and some of its aura of social class seemed to cling.

The pair walked on to the fourth house, a slightly smaller but still quite grand high-set house in the old style with a wide veranda to the upper story and a lattice screen or timber palings around the ground floor. The garden was lush with green lawns, palm trees, garden beds full of crotons and flowers. There was a large mango tree in the back yard.

Standing at the gate was a skinny, freckle-faced girl of about 12 who could not have been anyone else but a sister. That was how Carol introduced her.

"This is my little sister Kirsty, she's in Year 7," she said.

Kirsty smiled and gave Graham a thorough appraisal. Carol ignored her and pushed her way in through the gateway. Graham smiled at the little sister and followed Carol along the concrete path to the rather grand staircase that led up to the front door, only to get a shock.

Standing at the top of the steps was a naked little boy. Graham blushed with embarrassment and did not know where to look, hotly conscious of Carol ahead of him and Kirsty just behind.

Carol just looked up and called, "Billy! Go and get some pants on. We have a visitor."

As Billy scuttled off, Carol looked back over her shoulder and said, "Sorry, he can be a rude little monster at times."

Carol led Graham through the doorway and across a wide veranda then along a cool, dark corridor that ran straight through the house. There were rooms on either side and there was no floor covering, the smooth timber boards shining in the reflected light.

They went all the way through to a kitchen and small dining room at the back. Graham noted that there was a formal dining room on his right near the front, so assumed the kitchen was where the family normally ate. He half expected there to be servants but instead a middle-aged lady with mousy hair tied back in a bun and a face covered with freckles was at the stove. She wore old jeans and a loose cotton top. She turned from the stove and greeted him.

"Hi! You're Graham, are you? Nice to meet you. I'm Mrs Battersby, Carol's mum."

Graham blushed with shyness and returned the handshake but immediately relaxed. Her mum was just a normal person!

Mrs Battersby gestured to the table and chairs. "Would you like some morning tea? You look a bit hot after your walk."

She began to chatter about the bus and the trip while ushering Graham to a chair. As he seated himself, Mrs Battersby said, "Harry is over at the mill. You just missed him. He was looking forward to meeting you."

At that, Kirsty, who was sliding into a seat on the other side of Graham, piped up. "That's not what daddy said mummy. He said he would like to meet the poor fellow who had fallen under Carol's wicked spell."

"Oh he did not!" Carol cried as she walked to a side table.

There was sharp sisterly exchange until their mother told them to stop it. During this Billy appeared, now clad in a pair of shorts. He made his way to a chair at the end and climbed up to lean on the table.

Carol and her mother brought over scones and jam drops and Graham was asked if he wanted a hot drink or a cold. He opted for cold and was offered cordial or soft drink.

Billy beat him to answer. "I'll have lemonade, please," he cried.

Carol turned and snapped at him, "You wait your turn, you greedy little monster! I was asking Graham."

Billy gave a big grin and did not appear abashed at all. Graham began to relax and decided he liked Billy. He then happily sat and chatted with Mrs Battersby while he had a cup of tea and two scones with butter and raspberry jam. She asked questions about what his father and mother did and whether he had any brothers and sisters.

Graham was able to keep talking, describing his brother Alex and sister Kylie and then their many pets. This kept the conversation going until nearly 11:00 when Mr Battersby returned. To Graham's initial surprise, he saw that Mr Battersby wore a worker's 'High Vis' shirt and had a 'hard hat'. He had expected him, as one of the bosses, to wear a white shirt and tie.

As Carol's father came into the kitchen after hanging up the safety helmet, Graham stood up. He recognised him immediately and, to his relief, Mr Battersby stuck out his hand and said, "You must be Graham. My, you're keen to come all this way."

Graham could only mumble and nod and then say, "I came here a few weeks ago on a school trip."

"Oh yes, I remember that. Thanks dear," (This to Mrs Battersby who had placed a cup of tea on the table for him).

As Mr Battersby took a sip of tea, Graham surreptitiously studied him. He was an ordinary looking man of about 40, he decided, but he had that air about of him of a man who could make things happen and get things done. It was the same air of confidence and competence that his own father displayed.

Graham then had to answer again many of the same questions about his family and then how he had come to have plaster on his leg during the mill tour. He found it a bit of a test but, as it was partly what he had been expecting, he was able to answer easily. At the front of his mind was the notion that he was being vetted as to whether he was socially acceptable or not.

Mr Battersby finished a second cup and then stood up. "Well, I've got a bit of work to do, unfortunately," he said.

Mrs Battersby looked worried. "Was there much trouble?"

Mr Battersby shook his head but also looked worried. "Bit of bother with a couple of the men. I think it's settled but I need to write a report," he said.

As he left the room, Mrs Battersby turned to the group at the table. "Well children, why don't you show our guest around. What about the guinea pigs?"

"Oh yes!" Kirsty cried, earning a scowl from Carol.

Graham did not like being called a child but was happy to follow Kirsty down the back steps. Carol and Billy followed. The notion of guinea pigs he liked as there had been pet guinea pigs at his place for years and he liked the little creatures.

For the next half hour he sat on the back lawn with the two girls and Billy and fed, cuddled and played with the six guinea pigs. A game of shuttle cock was then played, a net being strung between the house and a palm tree at the side lawn. They were still in the middle of this when Mrs Battersby called them to come and have lunch.

Graham was a bit diffident about this, but was shown the bathroom and stood with Billy to wash his face and hands before being again seated at the table. Mr Battersby joined them, now dressed in shorts and casual shirt and the meal was very relaxed. Sandwiches with cold meat and, in Graham's case, peanut butter and honey, filled him and helped him to relax even more.

After the meal, Mr Battersby again left them and went off to a different room. Graham wondered if he should be helping with the washing up, not that there was much, but it was quickly evident he would be interfering as each of the siblings had a job: Carol washed, Kirsty wiped, and Billy put away. It was all done quickly.

There was then a discussion over what to do next. Carol led the way into the lounge room beside the kitchen and began to play music, some sort of string music. Now Graham wasn't a big one on music. Some he really liked, but his knowledge of the different types and genres was limited, and he was quickly made hotly aware of his ignorance when Carol began asking questions about what type of music and what composers, singers, bands, or groups he liked.

This had only been going for a few minutes when Mrs Battersby came in and shook her head. "Can you children do something quieter please," she asked. She looked at Carol. "Your dad is having a sleep. He was up half the night dealing with some broken piece of machinery."

She then looked at Graham with a very worried look on her face. "Sorry, but this has been a bad time at the mill. It is the worst year I can ever remember. There seem to be problems all the time and the mill is way behind its production schedule."

Carol stopped the music. "What do you want us to do?"

"Oh, show Graham around. Go for a walk or something. What time does you bus go, Graham?" Mrs Boothby replied.

"Four thirty, Mrs Battersby," Graham answered.

Mrs Battersby glanced at an ornamental wall clock and nodded. "So be back by about two thirty and we can give you afternoon tea before the girls walk you to the bus."

"Okay Mum," Carol said, standing up.

Kirsty and Billy both stood up as well and Carol said, "You kids can't come."

An argument began, quickly silenced by Mrs Battersby putting her finger to her lips and shushing them. "Yes, they can, young Miss. You are not to go wandering around on your own. There are some nasty looking types working at the mill, the roughest I have ever seen. So stay in a group, and stay away from the mill."

Carol met Graham's eyes and his heart leapt. *Surely, she didn't want to be alone with me this early in the relationship?*

There was then a delay while hats and shoes were found. Billy began to make a fuss but was silenced by being told he could not go if he was not wearing a hat, shirt, and something on his feet.

Billy grinned and piped up, "Don't I need pants?"

Carol turned and hissed at him. "Don't be a little smart arse, Billy. Go and get dressed or we will leave you behind." She then blushed and turned to Graham. "Sorry, he has always been a little rudey-nudey running around with nothing on."

Mrs Battersby shook her head. "He's only little. Don't make a fuss. Now get your hat too, Kirsty."

Once Billy was dressed the four made their way down the back steps. Graham had expected them to go out the front gate and perhaps to the old steam locomotive in the park but there were some of the local kids playing on that so Carol led the way out through the back gate.

This put them on a gravel road which ran along behind the row of houses and then along behind the mill. Looking both ways Graham saw that it was the same gravel road that ran along behind the buildings of the town. He also noted that just beyond it was a railway line, a proper 3 foot 6 inch gauge line.

That's the line that takes the sugar from the mill to the main line, he thought, remembering seeing the loading hoppers during the mill tour.

These were visible a hundred metres away and he noted that the railway split at a set of points to give a siding under the hoppers. By looking left he could see that there was a Y-junction, which obviously connected to the main line.

So that trains can go either north to Cairns or south to Townsville or somewhere, he reasoned.

On the other side of the spur line was a newly harvested field of sugar cane and on the other side of that a line of dark green foliage that indicated a creek. The creek angled towards the mill. Carol led the way to the right, towards the mill, and they strolled along in the shade of a line of Mango trees and Tamarind Trees while Billy explored and Kirsty asked questions or flirted.

The road skirted some sheds at the back of the mill and then around huge piles of mill mud and bagasse and then the sugar loader hoppers and siding. As they walked along Graham was able to study the layout of the mill and could see into it through the gaps where no lower walls existed or through large doorways. The whole interior looked to be a mysterious maze of pipes, girders, machines, billowing steam, and lights casting their reflections on shiny metal. From time to time he glimpsed men working there. One worker even seemed to stand and stare at them.

They strolled on along between some sheds and a molasses storage tank on their right and the open field on the left until they came to where the light railway looped back around from the unloader at the main mill building to rejoin the marshalling yards. This area really got Graham's interest and he was happy to study the Railway Workshops for maintenance and repair of the rolling stock and the rows of small engines. He was particularly impressed by the dozen sidings on which stood seemingly endless lines of empty cane bins, all waiting to be taken out again.

Another hundred metres on past the locomotive sheds and beside the marshalling yards, the smell of the sugar and molasses came wafting over them and Graham sniffed with delight. They were now downwind of the mill, and he thought it a wonderful aroma. The others did not even appear to notice the varied smells.

But then, if you live here and smell it all the time you wouldn't, he reasoned.

The gravel road turned to dirt and the field ended as the creek got closer. The dirt road was under another line of Mango trees and the sugar train lines were just the other side of the trees. Graham began to get glimpses down into the creek through gaps in the trees and head-high blady grass and guinea grass that lined it banks. It looked to be about 25 metres wide, and the water was crystal clear and flowing over a sandy bottom. It looked shallow and very nice.

Billy thought so too. "Can I have a swim please?"

Carol nodded. "I suppose so."

"What about me?" Kirsty asked.

"You didn't bring any bathers and Graham might be embarrassed," Carol answered.

Kirsty sniffed and gave him a cheeky grin. "Huh! I'll bet he wouldn't mind."

Carol turned to Graham. "Would you? The kids will have to swim in the nuddy."

Graham was surprised and embarrassed but also excited. He shook his head. He had been 'skinny dipping' with a number of girls over the last few years and had always found it most enjoyable. But he didn't want Carol to think he was a deviate or something.

"No, that's alright," he replied.

"Yipee!" Billy cried and he raced on ahead and then turned down a foot track in the long grass.

Carol hurried after him. "You wait for us you little monster!" she cried. Kirsty and Graham hurried to catch up.

The foot track went steeply down through the very long grass and weeds and Graham had a few anxious thoughts about possible snakes lurking in it. But the others just ran down the track which ended at a steep little beach at a bend in the creek.

There was a big tree there with several large branches overhanging the water and Graham noted a rope hanging from an upper branch, obviously a swing put up there by the locals. It was over a deep pool on the outside of the bend.

Then he looked at the creek more critically. He was conscious that only a couple of kilometres ahead was a mass of jungle-covered mountains. He was also conscious that all the creeks in that area flowed into rivers that emptied into the Coral Sea.

"What about crocodiles?" he asked.

Carol shook her head. "There's never been a croc seen in this area. We are too far inland. If there was any danger, the parents wouldn't let us swim here," she replied.

Graham nodded but wasn't entirely convinced. But then crocodiles were just swept out of his thoughts as Billy and Kirsty both proceeded to strip. Kirsty was undressed first, just peeling her skirt over her head and then pulling down her panties. She was too young to wear a bra.

Graham did not know where to look. Blushing with embarrassment, he decided to just act 'cool' as that was how Carol was acting. But Billy put this to the test when he took off his shirt and shorts and stood there laughing without a stitch on. Both Billy and Kirsty splashed into the water and began splashing each other and crying out in pleasure.

"They are having a good time," Graham said.

"They are. Would you like to have a swim too?" Carol asked.

Graham wasn't sure if he had heard her correctly. "I didn't bring any bathers, and I need to keep my duds dry to go on the bus," he replied.

Carol shook her head. "That's alright. You can go in the nuddy if you like. We won't mind."

Now that did put Graham on the spot and his mind raced with excited speculation. *Surely Carol isn't going to take her clothes off where I can see?* he wondered.

"I don't want you to get the wrong idea," he said.

"Oh piffle!" Carol cried. "You mean you don't want me to think that you just want to know me for sex?"

Graham nodded and croaked, "Yes. I'm not like that."

Carol smiled. "I know that! I can tell. But if you aren't interested in me as a girl then our friendship isn't going to go very far!"

That was a new viewpoint for Graham, but he was still scared. "I agree, but I don't want to get into trouble," he muttered, fear of her parents now coming to the fore.

Again, Carol shook her head. "You won't. Nobody will tell, and besides we swim that way all the time and mum and dad know."

"Your dad won't be pleased if he hears about me being with you," Graham suggested. His gaze roved anxiously along the bushes and tall grass that covered both banks of the creek.

Carol shrugged. "Huh! He won't make a fuss. And mum just says that if you haven't seen it before it will be educational, and if you have it doesn't matter."

"Only if you have a swim too," Graham said, his heart now hammering very fast with rising excitement.

"Sure. You won't mind?" Carol queried.

Now Graham did blush fiercely, amazed that a pretty girl should just say such a thing. He nodded and croaked, "What about Kirsty? She's too young to see things like that."

Again Carol shook her head. "She sees Billy's every day and I'll bet the boys at her school show her theirs. Come on, don't be shy."

With that she began to take off her sandals. Graham knelt to undo his joggers, his heart now hammering so hard he could hear it thudding in his ears. To add to Graham's emotional turmoil, Carol now stood and pulled her top over her head and then reached behind her to undo her bra. She looked over her shoulder.

"You look away until I am in the water, please," she said.

Blushing furiously, but wishing he could watch, Graham did as he was told. He heard splashing and Carol saying, "Stop it, Billy! Stop splashing me." Then she called, "Okay Graham, you can turn around now."

Graham did and his gaze immediately travelled to look at where Carol's head stuck out of the water. Her naked body was just visible as a blurry shimmering in the clear fresh water. By now Graham's blood was afire.

Then Kirsty added to his fierce emotions calling, "Come on Graham, come in! The water's lovely."

Carol smiled and said, "Come on, please Graham. We won't be offended."

Now Graham was awash with emotion: lust, desire to show off, fear. He hesitated and then took a deep breath, wondering if he was being subjected to some sort of test of manhood or courage.

Come on Mister Brave Guy! he chided himself. *You've done this before. Be a man!* "You girls don't look," he called.

With his heart pounding with emotion, he sat and pulled off shoes and socks and then stood and peeled off his shirt. Then he had to muster the courage to actually strip. Again he took a deep breath and then undid his trousers and slid them down. As he did, he was hotly aware that Billy was staring at him.

Heated memories of swimming naked with the girls in Kuranda the year before added to his arousal but that time Stephen had been there with him and the whole social scene had been different. Here it was much more intimate and that added to his anxiety. He wanted to but was scared and he knew it!

Casting the trousers aside, Graham hooked his thumbs in the waistband of his underpants and then hesitated. "Don't you look," he croaked, lust drying his throat.

Kirsty giggled and glanced back, and Carol shook her head. "Stop peeking, Kirsty. It'll be alright Graham. Hurry up," she answered.

With a gasp that was motivated by desire and fear, Graham pulled the undies down, hotly aware that he was now very aroused. Quickly he waded in, hot with embarrassment as Billy was staring. As soon as he joined them, the two girls turned around.

"Is that alright?" he croaked.

Kirsty answered first. She glanced down and her pupils widened. "Oooh yes! Oh, you'll like that, sis," she cried.

Carol snorted. "Don't be vulgar, Kirsty! Don't listen to her, Graham. I'm a virgin and I am going to stay that way until I meet Mr Right and he promises to marry me."

Once again, Graham was shocked by her directness and by the fact that Kirsty was standing close beside him watching and listening, and bursting into embarrassed giggles.

Graham tried not to stare while his pulses raced. His hands clenched and he had to master an almost uncontrollable urge to reach out and touch Carol. He had to summon all his willpower not to reach across. Carol sensed that and moved back a pace.

She said, "Let's swim."

Graham could only nod and turn to follow her as she swam out across the creek. As he did, he realised that the water was quite cold.

Coming off the mountains, he thought, glancing up the creek to where a jungle-covered ridge was just visible above the steep banks. As he swam, he experienced the wonderful free sensation of the cold water flowing over his skin. They both swam almost right across and then turned and swam back. Back near the beach they stopped and stood in chest deep water.

"Good?" Carol queried as she knelt with just her head above water.

"Wonderful!" Graham cried, staring hard at where her breasts could be seen moving in the water.

Kirsty and Billy joined them, and Billy climbed up onto Kirsty's back and then looked over her shoulder. They all bobbed around and swam gently. After a time, Billy slid off Kirsty and dog paddled over to Carol. She took his hands and then held his hands while he swam in a circle.

Then Kirsty splashed across and grabbed Graham from behind and climbed up so that she had her arms around his neck, her legs around his hips and her head looking over his left shoulder. He could feel her smoothness on his skin and that felt very nice as well, but he was hotly conscious she as only a little girl.

Carol frowned. "Get off, Kirsty! He's my boyfriend, not yours," she snapped.

Kirsty pouted but then slid off. She then swam ashore and waded out to stand naked on the beach. Graham blushed and looked away. He was embarrassed at looking as she was only a young girl.

Carol wasn't amused either. She frowned at Kirsty. "What are you going to do now?" she asked.

"I'm going to have a swing," Kirsty said.

With that she turned and walked the twenty paces to the big tree and then climbed out along the large bottom branch that overhung the water. Ashamed at his desire to look, Graham looked away until he heard her splash into the water.

"Your go now, Graham," Kirsty shrieked, her eyes alight with excitement and interest.

Graham blushed and shook his head. So did Carol. "That's enough! Stop showing off, Kirsty. You are embarrassing Graham."

Graham met Carol's eyes and nodded. She gave a smile in return and then Graham saw her eyes widen and her mouth open in obvious dismay.

Graham turned his head to see what she was staring at. His gaze focused on the end of the track through the long grass at the top of the beach. To his horror, he saw that there were three people there: Betty from the shop and two younger girls!

Chapter 10

TERRIBLE SHOCKS

Graham stared aghast.

Sprung! I will be in real trouble now, his racing thoughts told him.

He was thankful he was neck deep in the water and began to wonder how he could get out of the situation without serious trouble.

As his worried mind took in what he was looking at, Graham's studied the younger girls. One looked like a little sister, but the other was a red-head with a pony tail and obviously not related. To his relief, he saw that Betty was grinning and her sister smiling. The other girl was wide-eyed and gaping.

Betty grinned and called loudly, "Oooh! Sprung yez at it!"

Carol shocked Graham by swearing softly. "Oh bloody hell! Just what we don't need." Turning to Graham she said softly. "Her name's Betty and she a saucy little minx and her little sister Rosie there is a nosy little bitch."

Betty now waved and called, "Hi Graham! How's the water?"

"Fine," Graham croaked, still anxious to avoid trouble but also hotly aware that Carol was now staring hard at him.

"Do you know her?" Carol asked.

Graham managed a nod. "Met her at her shop as I walked past. She came out and said hello," he lamely explained.

"She would, the little flirt!" Carol hissed. She turned to Betty and called, "Go away! We are having a swim and we don't want you here."

"It's a free country and we will do what we like!" Betty called back. "We came to have a swim and you can't stop us."

"Go away!" Carol called.

"No! We are having a swim too," Betty snapped.

To Graham's amazement she began peeling off her tight white shorts.

"I'll tell your dad," Carol called,

"And I'll tell yours!" Betty retorted. Then she pointed at Billy who had walked up onto the beach near her. "And tell your little brother to stop being rude to my little sister!"

Graham now joined in. "I don't have any clothes on."

At that Betty laughed and gave a very mischievous grin. "I know, I can see that! That's alright, we don't mind." With that she slid off her T-shirt and her large boobs bobbled in her bra.

Feeling almost mesmerised, Graham watched as Betty and her little sister Rosie began to strip. The third girl just stood and looked worried.

"Tell that other girl to go away if she doesn't want to see anything," he said. Then, ashamed of looking, he turned away.

Betty shook her head. "Moira is just shy. She'll be okay, won't ya Moira?"

Graham glanced back and saw Moira give a nervous nod as her eyes kept flicking from the group in the water to Billy then to Betty and Rosie. Betty now reached back and unclipped her bra and took it off, giving both Carol and Graham a challenging stare as she did.

She won't surely? Graham thought. But she did, turning to cast it behind her.

Graham gaped in wonder and scared delight and felt his body react. His mouth went dry with lust. For a moment he stared and then looked away as heated desire went surging through him.

Betty then stood up defiantly nude on the beach. Graham glanced back and then stared in lustful wonder. He noted that her breasts were twice as large as Carol's. Next to her, Rosie also undressed but she was just a little girl and Graham felt guilty looking at her and again looked away from her.

Betty now waded in, her breasts swaying provocatively as she did. Graham stared in delight and then felt guilty as Carol obviously wasn't amused.

He turned to Carol, "Do you want to go?" he asked.

"Not yet," Carol answered, moving closer to him as Betty approached.

As she reached thigh deep, Betty cried out and crossed her arms over her front. "Oh! Brrr! Fuck, it's cold!" she cried.

The expletive shocked Graham and he glanced at Carol and saw she was pursing her lips.

Betty came to a stop a few paces away in water just deep enough to cover her boobs. The sight was so erotic Graham became even more aroused.

Betty said to Carol, "Is Graham in your class at school?"

She kept glancing at him and also looking down and Graham blushed and wondered what she could see through the water.

They were now diverted by Billy starting to splash Kirsty who had waded out to get him. This quickly developed into a free for all with Rosie getting splashed and retaliating and then Betty splashing Kirsty and Billy.

After a couple of minutes the water fight subsided and Kirsty and Rosie, who both went to the same school and obviously knew each other well, waded ashore and began using the swing, to the embarrassed interest of the girl on the bank.

Betty returned to standing in front of them or sometimes swimming while she chatted to Carol. Several times she swam a few strokes on her back so that her boobs stuck out of the water like small wobbly islands. This looked so erotic that Graham felt an intense surge of desire.

To Graham's great regret and relief, Carol turned to him. "We have to go," she said.

It sounded as though she said this with genuine regret which fired Graham's imagination even more. She then waded ashore.

Graham hesitated as the other girl, Moira, was still standing watching everything. She looked anxious but very excited. *I don't want to offend her,* he thought.

"Don't look!" he called to her.

Only when she was looking away did he wade ashore. He went up past Betty, covering himself with his hands as well as he could.

Blushing and with his heart hammering with fear and lust Graham hurried across to where his clothes lay on the sand. As fast as his excited and fumbling fingers would function, he pulled on his clothes. By then Carol had picked up her knickers and she now dusted her feet and called loudly to Kirsty and Billy to get dressed. She then turned her back and began to quickly dress.

Kirsty came running across, chatting to Rosie and then to Moira. She went to her clothes, which were in front of Graham. He blushed and tried to stop glancing at her and made sure he kept his back to the other girls.

He was hotly aware that Carol was dressing and that both Kirsty and Billy were also looking. He now felt so aroused he began to tremble. Suddenly he felt ashamed, and he scooped up his shirt and pulled it on. He then sat on the beach to put on his socks and joggers.

That got him glancing out at Betty who was still standing in the water, her lovely bosom on full display. Then he saw Rosie staring at him and that caused a wash of shame. Now anxious lest he be in trouble Graham quickly did up his shoelaces and stood up. But then he had to wait while Kirsty and Billy finished dressing.

Carol turned to Betty and said, "We won't tell if you don't tell."

"That's a deal," Betty said with a nod. "See ya, Graham!"

Graham nodded and gave a frozen smile while Carol frowned. She pushed at Billy and said, "Get going, Billy. Come on, Kirsty, hurry up!"

Now almost overwhelmed by a mixture of lust, anxiety and embarrassment, Graham followed Carol and the other two up the foot track through the long grass. Several times he glanced back and each time he saw that Betty was still standing half exposed, and each time she gave a cheeky grin and a wave.

Bloody hell! he thought. *I was getting into hot water there!*

He found it a relief to be up on the dirt road under the trees next to a row of empty cane bins. Carol slowed and took his hand.

"Sorry about that," she said.

Graham wasn't sure what she regretted but he nodded and said, "That's alright. Sorry if I offended you."

To his relief, Carol shook her head and smiled. "You didn't! It was very enjoyable and at least I know you are normal man."

That glowed in Graham's ego, and he mentally preened himself. He was still aroused but with every step towards the sugar mill he could feel his desire subsiding. In place of the rush of adrenalin came an emotional let-down, and then fear began to seep in.

If her dad learns about this, I will be in real trouble! he thought.

That brought notions like being interviewed by the police and that caused more unhappy thoughts. He and Stephen had been in serious trouble with the police a few months before and at the edge of his consciousness was the knowledge that he would have to appear in court over the fights with the gang at Stannary Hills. There was still the niggling anxiety over whether or not he might be charged with assault because he had injured the youth when he knocked him into the creek while he was trying to get away from him.

Carol glanced at him and frowned. "Are you worried?"

"Yes," Graham admitted. "If your dad finds out..."

Carol shook her head. "It will be alright. Don't worry."

By then the group had passed the railway yards and engine shed and was almost at the start of the mill. Billy and Kirsty were scampering about ahead playing some game. Graham turned to look up at the mill which now towered beside them.

He noted movement at the top of the tallest of the two huge steel chimneys. "There's a man up there," he said, pointing.

Carol turned her head to look and nodded. "They stop the mill sometimes on the weekend to do maintenance and they clean out the chimneys," she explained.

Graham's eyes focused on the man. He was hanging just outside the top on some sort of safety harness and was doing something, painting or cleaning.

Suddenly the man began to fall. For a second Graham's brain did not register what he was looking at but then he cried out and grabbed at Carol who gasped and stared. The falling man began to scream and that sent spurts of fear shuddering through Graham.

It's not true! he thought, appalled at what he was witnessing.

There was a sort of flicker or movement and then Graham's mind registered a tiny black object go shooting off sideways and the scream instantly stopped. He saw the body flip over and then plummet down in a floppy mass to land on the roof. Because of the angle he did not see that, but they all heard it, a terrible thumping crash. Smaller noises followed and then silence.

"He fell!" Carol sobbed. "Oh, he fell!" She now gripped Graham's arm and clung to him.

For another couple of seconds Graham just stood there, transfixed by the horror of what he had witnessed. It was not the first time he had seen a man fall to his death, but it now came to him with terrible, shocking force that he had just witnessed a man die.

Carol turned to him, her face pale and anxious. "Do you think he is alright?" she asked in a quavering voice.

Through Graham's mind flashed the ghastly crashing noises he had heard, and he shook his head. "No," he croaked, "He couldn't survive a fall like that." He didn't want to say it, but he had a suspicion that far worse had happened.

"Oh my God!" Carol cried.

She then turned away and bent over and began to spew. That was what Graham felt like too, but he managed to fight down the nausea while he gripped her arm. He found his heart hammering harder than when he had been aroused and his whole being seemed to be focused on that roof.

So quick! Just like that! Gone! he thought. Not for the first time his mind flooded with the images and fear of death.

Then he heard laughter and happy cries and glanced to see that Kirsty and Billy were still playing and appeared to be chasing a grasshopper or something.

They haven't noticed, he thought.

Grabbing Carol and pulling her upright, he hissed, "The kids haven't noticed. We must get them away from here. Quick!"

Carol wiped her mouth and nodded, her whole expression one of shock and despair. But she was able to move, and she hurried with Graham to where the two little children were giggling and running around. She grabbed both by an arm and began hurrying along the road.

They both objected but sensing her mood only made token protests. Graham followed and as he walked kept turning his head to stare towards the mill.

Should we be telling the people in the mill or calling the ambulance, he wondered, apprehension gripping his throat and chest. But even as he thought this, he saw two workmen run out of the mill and turn to stare up at the roof.

Walking quickly, the group passed behind the sugar loader, and as they did Graham got glimpses through the steel framework supporting the hoppers. He saw that more men had come running out of the mill into the yard. They were staring up and around.

Then he noted a man point to something lying in the dust near the railway lines and as the man hurried over to it Graham's suspicions solidified.

That is the man's head! he thought. Once again, he was almost paralysed by horror, and he found he was breathing so fast he was almost hyperventilating. *We must get the kids away. Oh, I don't want Carol to see that,* he thought.

With that he hurried to catch up, ignoring the little stabs of pain from his ankle, and moved to her left to block the scene. As they came out from behind the sugar loader, Graham glanced back and saw that the man who had found the head was staring at it, his face aghast with shock. Other men were moving to join him.

"Keep going," Graham gasped, feeling his stomach heave.

Then Billy looked around and saw the men. They were 50 metres away, but Graham was appalled. An idea came to him in a flash and he acted on it.

"I'll bet I can skip faster than you can," he said to Billy. With that he began to hop on his good leg and then skip.

Billy at once accepted the challenge and so did Kirsty. For a moment Carol stared dumbly and then joined in, hurrying the two smaller children on along the gravel road.

As they did, Graham kept glancing back, partly out of morbid fascination and partly to check when the men were out of sight. Because his right ankle still hurt, he changed to hopping on one leg and that got the little ones giggling and stumbling.

"Run then. I'll give you ten paces start," Graham called. "One... Two..."

The two little ones began running and within half a minute they were all around at the end of the mill near the railway crossing and bagasse heaps. A glance back showed Graham that the ghastly scene was almost out of sight, so he slowed to cross the 3'6" railway.

As he did, he saw Carol's father come running out of the back gate of his house. He was still buttoning on a shirt and had his hard hat on. Then he saw them, and a puzzled look changed to anxiety. To Graham's consternation he turned and ran towards them.

"Where have you kids been?" Mr Battersby cried as he approached.

Carol answered, "Just for a walk along the creek bank past the mill," she replied.

Carol's father looked very agitated. "There... There's been an accident at the mill. Take the little ones home, Carol, now!"

"We know," Carol replied. "We saw it."

A look of anguish crossed Mr Battersby's face. He glanced at Kirsty and Billy and shook his head.

"Did the little ones see it?" he asked.

Graham answered. "No Mr Battersby. They were busy playing a game. They don't know what happened."

"But you do? You saw it you say?"

"Yes sir," Graham replied.

Then he had to swallow as nausea welled up. To his shame tears began to form and he started to shake. Then he realised that Carol was clinging to him and trembling as well.

"Oh you poor kids! Quick, take the little ones home and wait there. I will talk to you later. Keep them busy please. I must rush," Mr Battersby said. He then turned and continued running towards the mill.

"Oh poor Dad!" Carol cried. "He doesn't need this."

Nor did the poor man who fell! Graham thought.

But he agreed and helped her hurry the little ones on along the gravel road behind the house.

A minute later they were at the back of Carol's house, and as they turned in through the gate Graham saw her mother come hurrying to the back door.

"Oh thank heavens! You are safe!" she cried. "Did you see anything?"

Carol let go of Graham and ran to meet her mother who came hurrying down the stairs. "Yes Mum, we saw the man fall," she cried. Then she flung herself into her mother's arms and began sobbing. "Oh Mum! It was awful!"

That was what Graham thought too and he really felt the need for comforting at that moment. For a minute or so he stood there and shuddered and battled with tears while Kirsty and Billy stared at him in surprise. He was saved from that shame by Carol's mother urging them all to go upstairs for afternoon tea.

That helped and by the time cordial, soft drink, jam tarts and scones with jam and cream had been offered, and by the little ones consumed, Graham felt better. Carol still looked unhappy and pasty-faced, but she then nobly stepped up to help entertain the little ones. This was particularly important as Kirsty had now worked out that something bad had happened, but not what.

A glance at the wall clock told Graham that it was time for him to head off to catch his bus. He had been assailed by a variety of anxieties and missing the bus had been one of them.

"I'd better go, Mrs Battersby, or I will miss my bus," he said.

To his dismay, Mrs Battersby shook her head. "If you actually saw what happened I think you must stay to be interviewed by the police."

Graham swallowed with anxiety. Images of policemen scowling as their questions revealed that he had been naked with the girls flooded his emotions and he found he was gasping. To his embarrassment and relief, Carol put her arm around him and hugged him. He looked up and his eyes met Mrs Battersby's, but she just nodded and smiled.

"Poor boy!" she said.

"But how will I get home?" Graham queried. "Mum said she couldn't pick me up."

"Don't worry. We will take you home if need be," Mrs Battersby said. Then she indicated Kirsty and Billy. "Now, Graham, you phone your parents and then I will talk to them. Carol, you get out a game to entertain the imps."

Graham did and found he could not stop the tears or the shaking as he spoke to his mother. He found it a relief to hand the phone to Mrs Battersby. Then he sat beside Carol and helped play a simple board game while his mind dwelt on morbid images of sudden death and on what it might be like and if there was a hereafter.

* * *

Just before 4pm, Mr Battersby arrived home and with him were two uniformed policemen, a sergeant and a senior constable. Mrs Battersby met them at the front door and Graham overheard her ask if it was terrible and then say with a strangled gasp, 'Decapitated!'

I was right. The man lost his head, Graham thought. At that he shuddered as images of the black thing flying off in a flicker of ... of?

Then he heard Mr Battersby say, "Probably hit a guy wire or something. The forensic people are up there now."

"Who was it?" Mrs Battersby asked.

A name was mentioned but meant nothing to Graham. He then stood as a grim-faced Mr Battersby and the two policemen came through to the kitchen. Mrs Battersby suggested they do their interviewing in the room at the front of the house so she could keep Kirsty and Billy at the kitchen table playing.

As he made his way along the hallway, Graham felt ill with fear, hoping that Mr Battersby hadn't noticed that they had all had wet hair at the time of the accident.

That might lead to questions about what we were doing down the river.

Graham and Carol were then interviewed. To Graham's relief, there was no follow up on the statement that they had just been walking along the gravel road at the back of the mill. To his surprise, they weren't even asked which direction they had been walking. So he volunteered that information with the explanation they were on their way back.

During the interviews Mr Battersby was very hard-faced and distracted but Graham sensed it was not because of him and Carol.

He is angry and upset because of the accident, he reasoned.

That this supposition was correct was confirmed after the policemen had gone and Mr Battersby went through to the kitchen. He met Mrs Battersby in the hallway and Graham overheard snatches of their conversation. He listened because it concerned him as Mrs Battersby was explaining that he had missed his bus and must be given a lift home.

Then Mr Battersby said, "Oh Laura, this is very bad! There is a suspicion that it wasn't an accident and that could cause more trouble with the workers. They are very upset already, and this might just drive them to strike."

"Oh dear! We can't afford for the mill to close for long, can we?" Mrs Battersby replied.

"No. If there are any more disruptions like this the mill could fail this season. It is already having trouble making ends meet financially and if it isn't a successful season, it could go bankrupt and be closed."

Graham didn't hear any more as they moved away but it certainly sounded bad, and he felt sorry for Carol and her parents. As his own father's shipping business was also struggling, he understood the sort of pressure families could come under.

While they waited, Graham reached across and took Carol's hand. "Sorry about all this. Would you like me to come again tomorrow?"

Carol shook her head. "I'd like you to, but we will be going to church in the morning and after that we had planned to go to the markets at Garradunga. We usually have lunch there and won't be home till later. We may not go now but it would be best if you stayed home." Carol then put her hand on his arm. "Cheer up!" she said. "I have something nice to offer instead. My birthday is next weekend, and I am having a party. Would you like to come?"

Graham's heart leapt. "Oh yes please!" he cried.

"I will give you an invitation at school on Monday," she said.

Soon after that, Graham was bundled into Mrs Battersby's car with Carol beside him and he was driven home. It was nearly dark by the time he got home and by then he felt wrung out and very battered emotionally. His mum was all concern and the two mothers stood on the footpath and discussed the event for nearly half an hour. While they did, Graham was conscious of Kylie giving Carol hostile looks from upstairs and of Alex occasionally wandering by to glance out.

It was a relief to say goodbye to Carol and to go upstairs. But then Alex immediately began bombarding him with ghoulish questions.

"They said on the TV News that the bloke's head got chopped off by a steel wire," Alex said. "Did ya see that?"

Graham could only nod and feel upset. His mother quickly stemmed that flow of questions and sent him to have a shower and change before bed.

That night he did not sleep very well, his dreams turning to nightmares of death and dying and of being chased by... by? He wasn't sure, just nameless dark shapes.

Chapter 11

EMOTIONAL STORMS

For Declin, that Saturday turned into one of the worst days of his whole life. For some weeks now he had taken to fishing in his spare time. He had discovered an overhanging branch over a deep pool at a bend in the creek that he used to sit on. The branch was at the bottom end of a narrow foot track that led down the steep bank and was obviously rarely used. The start of the track was near the locomotive sheds and was hidden by some bushes.

The place had become a refuge where he could sit on his own and relax; where he could think things out and just enjoy doing nothing much. Whether or not he caught a fish was immaterial. He just liked to unwind and often he did not even try to fish.

But with the start of the warmer weather he had his solitude disrupted by the local kids coming to swim in the creek. None had ever come down his track, not that he could detect, he presumed because there was no beach and it was a dark and sheltered little nook on a steep bank, but many kids went to the next pool up the creek where the next big tree overhung the water and had a swing on it.

Thus, for a couple of weeks Declin had seen kids coming to swim, and mostly they swam naked. At first he had been surprised and ashamed, as he did not approve of that sort of behaviour. Nor did he think of himself as a pervert or 'Peeping Tom', but he had to admit he had enjoyed seeing young Betty from the shop and her sister and friend. To his added shame, he had found that he became very aroused by seeing her, even if she was nearly a hundred metres away and most details were not clear. But with boobs her size there was plenty to see, and to his own dismay he found he had become instantly aroused.

In fact he had seen Betty naked a dozen times or more as her bedroom was almost opposite his room on the top floor of the Caster Hotel and she often pranced around her room naked or changed without closing the curtains. That she frequently glanced towards the hotel as she did this made him certain that she knew people could see her and was doing it deliberately. He assumed she got a thrill out of doing so. So he did not feel particularly guilty or dirty when he watched through his own curtains. The only real fly in that ointment was stabs of guilt that by having lustful thoughts about Betty he was being disloyal to Carol.

And then Carol and her sister and little brother had begun swimming in that pool and usually naked. The first time he was aghast and had been torn by shame and guilt and the notion that he should hurry away; and by the conflicting urgent desire to see her nude. Since then he had often gone to the creek in the hope of seeing her, all the while mentally tormented by knowing he was doing something wrong but rationalising it from his worry that she might need protecting or saving.

But this Saturday afternoon it had all got infinitely worse. As the mill was stopped for maintenance, he had the day off and had been happily relaxing on his hidden branch. He was mildly stimulated by the idea that Betty and her sister might come for a swim when instead Carol and her sister and brother had appeared, and with them was Graham!

Oh bloody hell! Surely Carol is not going to take her clothes off with him there? Declin had thought.

But then, to his horror and torment she had! A fierce emotional storm quickly engulfed Declin: jealousy dominating over lust.

Oh, how could she! he agonised as he watched Carol shrug off her clothes to expose what he thought was her almost perfect female shape to the leering eyes of that boy!

Then worse followed. To his disgust, fury, and envy he saw Graham also strip and then join the others in the water. Even from that far away Declin could clearly see Graham was aroused and he burned with mortification and jealous rage. He had to master the urge to storm up the track and along the bank to stop his perfect maiden from being defiled.

But he had stayed hidden, held mostly by the knowledge that his secret observation would become public knowledge and might lower Carol's opinion of him.

If she thinks I have been deliberately perving on her she will be disgusted, he decided.

So he remained in hiding and had to endure the teeth-grinding torment of watching Graham enjoy the close proximity of Carol, even if both were neck deep in the water. It was almost too much for Declin, and he groaned in an agony of jealousy.

Only to be further stunned by the sudden arrival of Betty and her sister and friend! He had never seen the two groups at the pool at the same time but was initially pleased, hoping it would end the disgusting naked romp and save Carol from being exposed to further obscenity. But Declin was disappointed and further appalled when Betty and her sister stripped off and joined in the swim!

Seeing Carol snuggling up to Graham in the water had added to Declin's anguish. By then he was so engulfed by emotional turmoil, simultaneously fearfully aroused, deeply envious, and nauseous.

My angel must be able to see him, he thought, the notion of her being violated adding to his growing misery. He was even more upset when he heard Betty swear.

It had all been almost too much and Declin sat there being battered by emotional storms during the whole incident. It had been an enormous relief when they had dressed, the relief added to when they all stood with their backs to each other. But even then he had been enraged by the way Graham had cast glances over his shoulder at Carol and Kirsty while they dressed.

After Carol, Graham and the two little ones had gone out of sight up the track, Declin struggled with what to do. He was tempted to rush up and confront them but again he held back, fearful of Carol's opinion if she thought he had been deliberately spying on her.

But I must save her! he thought.

Then the notion of getting Graham alone and warning him off came to him, along with the desire to pound the lecherous little bastard to pulp!

To add to his upset, Declin heard the group go past on the gravel road. He then rolled up his fishing line and stowed it in its hiding place and carefully crept up the track, his heart pounding fast with fear and arousal, for, to his shame, the whole scene had made him so horny he squirmed with unsatisfied desire.

At the top of the track, Declin carefully peeked through the bushes and long grass and was able to watch the four children walking away back towards Carol's house. As they went out of sight around the slight bend, he made his way out onto the gravel road. To his dismay, he found he was actually trembling with rage and suppressed emotion. He ground his teeth and wanted to rush after them and punch that Graham as hard as he could!

Thus it was that he got another terrible shock. He saw Graham point up and Carol look and then heard that terrible scream. Looking around the end of the engine shed, Declin had been appalled to see Martin Appleyard plummet to his doom.

For a few seconds Declin had been too stunned to move. He just stood in shock and gaped, hoping against hope that Martin was alright, although his ears told him that he had landed very hard on the steel roof.

Then Declin had noticed Graham hurrying Carol and the little ones away along the road and had the good grace to concede that Graham was doing the right thing.

We don't want Carol or the little ones seeing anything like that, he told himself.

Next, Declin saw several men rush out of the main building to stare up towards the roof and then it had occurred to him that he should check if Martin was alright. Leaving the cover of the engine shed, Declin ran across to where a group of the men were gathering.

But only as he got closer did Declin realise what it was that the men were standing around staring at. It was Martin's head!

Declin came to a gasping stop and stared in horror. He was morbidly fascinated to note that Martin's eyes and mouth were still open and that the bloody sinews and threads of veins and flesh were splayed out in ragged ends where his neck had been sheared through. Then his stomach heaved and he spewed in the dust between two rail tracks. Other men were having the same reaction and that made it worse.

As Declin straightened up, gasping and shivering, he heard Rossiter's voice. "What happened?" he asked.

That sent stabs of anxiety through Declin and he turned to look, wiping his mouth as he did. Rossiter was standing among the others and was staring down at the grisly thing in the dust, but without any of the looks of horror that showed on all the other faces.

"We think Martin fell while cleaning the chimney," replied another man.

"How? Didn't he have his safety harness on?" Rossiter queried.

There were shrugs and murmurs and much shaking of heads. Someone said, "They will find out when they... they retrieve his body," he said.

Rossiter scowled and then snarled. "This place is unsafe! It is the most dangerous place I have ever had the misfortune to work."

"There are certainly problems," agreed another man.

Bill Plowman stepped forward. "Should we... should we pick that up... or at least cover it?" he queried.

Jack, one of the foremen, now intervened. "No! Leave it for the police and the Workplace Safety investigators. Here, Charlie, you stay here and make sure no-one tries to shift it or interfere with anything. The rest of you, get back to work."

That obviously wasn't a popular decision and Declin wondered if it was wise. But at that moment the sound of running feet made him look around. It was Mr Battersby, hurrying from the direction of his house.

"Here comes one of the bloody bosses," muttered Dennis, a skinny man who was a frontend loader driver and a crony of Rossiters.

Mr Battersby came to a gasping halt and Declin saw his face go pale as he blanched at the ghastly sight of Martin's severed head.

"What happened?" he croaked, plainly appalled. Several comments were made but as none of them really knew he pointed to the front buildings. "You men go and make sure your work sites are safe and then go to the Rec Room so we are all in one place, please."

At that, Jack said, "I told Charlie here to stay and make sure no-one interferes with... with this area," he explained

"Good thinking Jack. You okay with that Charlie? Thanks. Okay men, let's move," Mr Battersby ordered.

Declin moved with them. Even though he was not rostered on he knew he had been a witness and must be interviewed. After one last sad glance at the severed head he turned and started walking. Morbid thoughts swirled in his head as he contemplated death and fate.

All over, just like that! All his hopes and dreams and problems, all finished.

Declin shuddered as he wondered what thoughts had been racing through Martin's mind during those last few seconds. But then his thoughts were shockingly interrupted by Rossiter.

The man had sidled over beside him as they walked, and he now nudged Declin. "You be very careful what you say, young Declin," he hissed.

Declin was instantly gripped by almost paralysing fear. *This wasn't an accident!* he thought. *Rossiter or one of his cronies has killed Martin.*

It was an appalling notion and one that got him so scared he quickly became nauseous. All he could do was look back at Rossiter through misery laden eyes and nod.

And he was careful what he said when he was interviewed by the police and the safety investigators. To begin with, he had not really seen much and he knew he could not imply that it might not have been an accident. There was nothing in the police questioning to indicate whether they thought it was a suspicious death or not, so Declin was extremely cautious.

He was also not entirely truthful about why he had been where he was at the time of the accident. As he was not rostered on for work, all he had said was that he was taking an afternoon walk. To his relief, nobody questioned this or followed it up. The last thing he wanted was to get Carol into any sort of trouble, or, heaven forbid, reveal that he had been watching the children when they swam in the nude!

But Rossiter's comment deeply troubled him, and he remembered the other threats and a deep sense of dread gripped his stomach and bowels. To add to his anxiety, he wondered if Rossiter had seen where he had come from and knew what he had been doing.

* * *

That night, Declin could hardly eat his evening meal at the hotel and later he sat in his room and began to tremble as reactions of shock, morbid thoughts and fear all took hold. It was a terrible night and he had difficulty sleeping, spending many hours lying awake while contemplating death and what it might be like and the religious notions of heaven and the hereafter.

It was all very distressing and he was still shaken and upset next morning. As he made his way to the mill, Declin found his eyes being continually drawn to the huge steel chimneys that towered above the gigantic buildings.

Was it an accident? he wondered. More sickening thoughts of violent death came to swamp him and set him shivering.

That was the main topic of conversation when he joined the other workers on his shift in the Rec Room. Until the investigation was complete, the mill was not operating so all they could do was sit and talk. They were briefed by the General Manager and then offered counselling and given information to help them, then left to wait until they were all interviewed again.

While sitting there feeling very despondent, Declin noted Rossiter, Big dumb Marvin, and Dennis all sitting together in a corner. They were muttering and looking annoyed but not upset.

They look like they are stirring up trouble, Declin thought.

Again the notion that Rossiter might have had something to do with the death came to Declin. As it did, as though by malignant magic, Rossiter turned and met his eyes. He saw Rossiter's eyes narrow and then the man scowled and looked away. Declin was left shaking and wondering if the superstitious nonsense of people being able to read thoughts was true!

Once again, Declin began seriously considering resigning and moving to another town.

Chapter 12

MIXED EMOTIONS

Sunday was a day of mixed emotions for Graham. When he woke from a fitful sleep, the memory of the man falling from the mill chimney came to him and his mood went sharply down. Depression and apprehension took over.

For hours Graham brooded on the concept and shocking reality of death. He felt a real need to go to church and did not even mind sitting next to Margaret while he pondered the hereafter and the concepts of heaven and hell.

With that came shame at his behaviour during the swim, then worry about the nature of sin and of possible hellfire and punishment to come. But deep down he simply could not believe that God could be so harsh and ruthless as to think anything they'd done was of any importance.

His mother noted his mood and tried to draw him out and he was thankful she cared but did not want to discuss it. He knew she was deeply concerned lest he drop back into the deep state of depression and despair that he had reached in Year 8 when he had contemplated suicide after failing the Navy medical test.

"I'm alright," he assured her. "I'm a just a bit shocked and upset."

What he did not add was that he now had several reasons for very positive focus in his life: being a sergeant in the Army Cadets with the possibility of being the Company Sergeant Major next year; and his hopes for his relationship with Carol.

Sister Kylie was sympathetic and so was Margaret, but it seemed Alex had already forgotten and was too busy with his own life. Roger was in church, and he knew nothing about the death.

"What's wrong? You seem a bit down," he said after the ceremony.

Graham related the outline of the incident to him, and Roger looked very concerned. "You okay then?" he queried.

"Yes, thanks mate. It was just a real shock at the time," Graham replied, the images of that ghastly tragedy again playing across the screen of his mind.

"What are you doing today?" Roger asked.

"Nothing much," Graham replied, aware that he had been neglecting his friend a bit.

"What about coming over and helping me work on the railway?" Roger said.

The railway was a joint project which included Peter and Stephen and was located under Roger's house. From the outside it looked like an ordinary old-style North Queensland house standing in its own allotment with lawn and garden. It was on high timber posts with the living area upstairs. The downstairs had a concrete floor and was enclosed to provide a carport, laundry, storeroom, and a large room the boys called the 'Train Room', which ran the whole length of the western side of the house. Most of this space was taken up by a large model railway. The remainder of the room was a workshop with a workbench, cupboards, and two old tables.

The four friends had been working together to build the railway for three years and had reached the stage of developing the next section. This was to be based on the mining areas in the dry hills west of the Atherton Tablelands. The plan was to construct a narrow-gauge branch line modelled on the old 2' gauge line that used to run from Boonmoo to Stannary Hills and Irvinebank. It had been to research for the model railway that the boys had done their expedition to Stannary Hills and had resulted in their most recent adventure (and the injury to Graham's right ankle, which was still giving him twinges when he wasn't careful).

It was a plan of the mining area which Roger showed Graham after they had enjoyed morning tea at his house. "I would like to include a model of my mine," Roger explained.

Graham studied the plan and nodded. "I like it. It's a great idea, Roger."

Then he studied it a bit more closely and wondered if they could fit it all in: Roger's mine, the crook's mine, and also the Ivanhoe Mine and battery location.

For a time they puzzled over this and decided that a few compromises might have to be made. In particular they both agreed that the 'Gorge' section of the line, which both wanted, could not be in its correct position downstream of the mines but needed to be upstream, before the Black Bridge and Town area. But even that did not fit very well, and it was only after half a dozen sketch maps to illustrate ideas that it was agreed the Town should be the last part.

"We just turn the plan around and make that side the connection to Timbertop," Graham suggested, naming the small model town at the end of the 'Tablelands' section.

"But I want to make my mine so you can see into it," Roger said. "Like one of those ant farms they have at school where you have a glass wall and can see inside the tunnels."

"That's a great idea Roger!" Graham agreed.

He really wanted to support his friend and was uncomfortably aware that, in his pursuit of girls, he had been neglecting the friendship. He was also vaguely conscious that he was losing interest, that at the back of his mind he now thought himself grown up and that the model railway was little kid stuff he had outgrown.

The other problem Graham had when he got home was permission from his mother to attend Carol's birthday party the following weekend.

"Do you have an invitation?" she queried.

"Only from Carol," Graham answered. "She said she would give me one tomorrow at school."

"And where is this party?"

"At her house I think."

"And who is supervising?"

"Her mum and dad I suppose."

"And who is going?"

Graham could only shrug. "I don't know. Her little sister and little brother for sure," he replied.

"And how do you plan to get there? The party may finish too late for you to catch the bus," Graham's mother queried.

That stumped Graham. He had not thought of that. "I... er... I don't know," he admitted.

"Then we will have to wait for the invitation and then I will decide," his mother replied.

That really cast Graham down and he went to his bed and pretended to read, but in reality he brooded on life, and on death. He was also aware that Kylie was very annoyed with him and that Margaret was looking anxious and hurt.

His dreams that night were half nightmares of erotic swims and half of falling. That was easy to conjure up as he had nearly fallen to his death only a few weeks before when he had saved Peter and Cadet Carnes from plummeting to their death from the huge steel railway bridge across the Bunyip River. There were even more traumatising memories of hanging from the cliff over the Barron Gorge in Year 9 when the fake 'Tarzan' had tried to throw him to his death.

* * *

When he woke on Monday morning, Graham found he was washed out and trembling with reaction. For a few minutes he contemplated asking his mother if he could stay home as he felt sick. But then he remembered that Carol had said she would give him the party invitation at school, so he got up and pretended he was fine.

When he arrived at school, the first friend he met was Stephen. Once again, the awful incident of the chimney death had to be described and Stephen was obviously fascinated in a ghoulish way. To steer the conversation off such a depressing topic, Graham described Roger's plans for the model railway. When Roger and Peter arrived, they joined in and the new plans were agreed to.

Then Carol appeared. Graham got no chance to talk to her before the all-school assembly but on the way to class he walked with her.

"How are you, Carol? Are you okay?" he asked.

"Yes, thank you. A bit down. I've never seen anything so... so... so awful," she replied.

"I know. It was terrible," Graham agreed.

They reached her classroom, and she placed her school bag on the port racks and began to rummage and dig out books. As she did, Carol took out a bundle of envelopes. She leafed through these and then smiled and handed one to Graham.

"Here's your invitation to the party. Mum insists I go ahead with it," she said.

"Oh thank you!" Graham replied, feeling really pleased. He opened the envelope and began reading, his mind seeking times and places and the other answers to his mother's questions.

Then one of the answers was provided immediately when Carol turned to Stephen, who was passing, and handed him an invitation.

"This is for my birthday party, Steve," she explained.

Stephen looked pleased and began to chat about the party while

Graham stood and experienced a niggle of jealousy. *I didn't know she knew Steve that well,* he thought anxiously.

Carol then moved on to hand invitations to several of the girls from 10B: Ailsa, Rowena, Rosemary and Annette. Seeing that sparked Graham's desire to attend even more. He again thanked Carol and then followed the girls to his own classroom.

Later, during morning break, Graham broached the subject of the party with Stephen. "Do you think you will be allowed to come?" he asked.

Stephen nodded. "Yeah, I'm in good favour with my oldies at the moment. They weren't even put out that we had all that drama at Stannary Hills, so I'm not grounded."

"This party could go on into the evening. How do you plan to get there?" Graham asked.

Stephen shrugged. "My oldies might drive me. I'll ask tonight."

They had to leave it at that, and Graham was left fretting that he might not be allowed to go if the transport problem could not be easily solved. Stubbornly he did not want to ask Stephen to ask his parents.

If they offer, I will accept, he told himself.

For a few foolish moments he again contemplated riding his bike and even camping overnight and coming back the next day.

At lunch time, Graham sat with Carol and she asked if he was able to go to her party. Graham had to admit that there was a transport problem. Carol frowned and looked put out.

"Could you come for the whole weekend and stay overnight?"

At that Graham's hopes soared. "I could ask," he replied. "But where? Do you mean at your place?"

To his disappointment Carol shook her head. "No, sorry. I have four girls staying with me and there isn't room. Perhaps you could stay at the hotel?"

"You mean the one in the main street of Caster?" Graham asked, quite surprised by the suggestion.

"Yes, the Caster Hotel," Carol replied. "The horrible yellow place."

It was a thought and one he put to Stephen as he was now very anxious to go to the party and was clutching at straws.

To his relief, Stephen nodded. "That might be alright. Depends how much it costs. I'll ask my oldies," he replied.

That was the idea Graham put to his mother when he handed her the invitation at home that evening. She read the invitation and noted the address and times and then asked who else was going. After he named Stephen, she looked a bit more at ease.

"I will check on this hotel," she said.

While this discussion was going on, Kylie came into the kitchen and before Graham could stop her, she picked up the invitation and scanned it, then scowled at Graham and curled her lip.

Graham's mother then made a telephone call. Twenty minutes later she came out to where Graham was working on his homework.

"This hotel is cheap enough. Apparently, it provides long term accommodation for mill workers so has reasonable rates. It will depend on whether Stephen can stay there as well. You are not staying at some strange hotel in another town on your own."

"Yes Mum," Graham answered, his hopes soaring.

He at once ran to the phone and called Stephen. Stephen replied that he was allowed to go if suitable accommodation could be provided as his parents had planned to be at the Juvenile Eisteddfod in Innisfail, where Stephen's mother and father were to be judges and could drop them off on the Saturday and pick them up on the Sunday afternoon.

"They were planning for us all to stay overnight in Innisfail anyway," he explained. Then he sighed and added, "Thank God for this party! But for it I would have had to go with them to the Eisteddfod. Have you ever sat through twenty renditions of *Fur Elise* by little girls one after the other, and dozens of identical poems and songs? It can be pretty wearing if you aren't into that sort of thing."

"So ask about the hotel and get back to me," Graham replied. He then provided the details and hung up.

Stephen was back on the phone in ten minutes. "Yep, it will be okay. We can stay at the hotel," he said.

That sent Graham's hopes shooting up again and he went to bed a very happy boy. It was only later when he had a bad dream about being on a truck… or was it a train?… racing out of control towards a steep cliff, and then dead bodies appeared, that his mood changed. Once again, he had a bad night with gloomy introspection about dying and death.

* * *

Tuesday had its own little incidents that sent emotions up and down. There was annoyance when Kylie and Margaret scowled and poked tongues at him. There were niggles of jealousy when he saw Andrew sitting with Tina, heads together in the sort of relationship he hungered for; and even lustful envy when he saw Willy pashing with Marjorie (in blatant defiance of the school rules) in the library in class time.

And then, quite unexpectedly, it was his turn. When he went to be with Carol after eating his lunch, she said she had to do some research in the library. As they walked there side by side, he noted that she looked very down and pensive. When they were inside at some carrels in the far corner, he said, "Are you feeling okay?"

To his dismay tears sprang to her eyes and she shook her head. "No, not really," she answered. Then she began to sob.

Without conscious thought, Graham reached out and put his arms around her and pulled her tight. That got her really crying and he held her tight and began to soothe her.

For several minutes they clung together and then Mrs Standish, their English teacher and also a lieutenant in the Army Cadets, came along.

"What's going on here?" she asked.

Graham knew that physical fraternising was against the school rules, but he did not take his arms away. "Carol's a bit upset, Miss," he replied.

"Why is that? What has happened?" Mrs Standish asked

At that Carol lifted her head from his tear-soaked shoulder. "I... we... we both saw a man get killed in an accident at the mill on Saturday," she answered. Then she sobbed some more before adding, "And the funeral is today, and the poor man had a wife and four little kids and now they've got no dad."

Mrs Standish bit her lip and nodded. "I heard about that on the news. Sorry, I didn't know you were there."

Graham met her eyes and then images of the severed head in the dust swamped him and he felt tears spring to his own eyes. He trembled and bit his lip and managed to croak, "It was really awful, Miss. Sorry Miss, but Carol just needed a hug."

"From the look of it so do you," Mrs Standish replied. "So just look after each other, and nothing more."

But as soon as the teacher had moved away, Graham looked down at Carol's tear-streaked face and saw the misery in her eyes and he just found himself kissing her. For a moment he wondered if he had done the wrong thing, but then she responded, kissing with fierce intensity and gripping him even tighter.

So engrossed were they in what Graham found had become a somewhat frightening storm of emotion that it took several calls from Angus MacDougal before what he was saying penetrated.

"Ye'd best leave off," Angus said in his lovely Scottish accent. "Yon's Miss Hackenmeyer and I 'ave the notion she'll no be as understanding as Mrs Standish."

Graham eased back and looked and saw the much-feared Miss Hackenmeyer on the other side of the library. At that moment she had not seen them. But many others had, and he became aware that at least half his class were all gaping and watching. To his surprise, he found he was crying and also panting for breath.

"Thanks Angus," he said, then asked Carol if she was alright.

She lifted her tear-streaked face and nodded. "Yes thanks. I just really needed a hug."

* * *

That night he had a deep, dream free sleep and he woke on Wednesday feeling refreshed and happier. Wednesday also meant Cadets, so Graham prepared his uniform and packed it carefully.

During school that day, Graham hardly saw Carol and that got him a bit grumpy. And at Cadets he got a bit of a jolt. Sgt Crane had returned and had asked if he was still in the Flag Party. When told 'no' he gave Graham a sour look. Instead, he was sent to be 3 Platoon sergeant for the parade. His mood wasn't improved when, during the rehearsal of the prize giving, he was required to march over and take Graham's place so he could fall out to get his prize, thus ensuring that the flag was guarded the whole time.

As they were talked through this procedure, Sgt Crane was halted a pace to Graham's left and on command Graham took two paces forward. Crane took two short paces to his right to take his place. As he did, Crane hissed out of the side of his mouth, "Bloody sniveller! You'll get yours!"

That upset Graham as he did not consider he had done anything but earn his promotion, so he just ignored the comment and marched across to join the others who were receiving 'Best Attendance'. After the practice at receiving an award, the changeover drill was repeated, Graham marching back to halt beside Crane. Crane curled his lip and stepped forward.

After the rehearsal the company were seated in section lines and Capt Conkey reminded them that the Passing-Out Parade was on the Saturday afternoon in two weeks' time.

"You will be needed for the whole day so we can issue rifles and do some more practice and get our uniforms up to scratch."

As he said this, it occurred to Graham that he would not be able to go to Caster to see Carol on that Saturday. For the first time in years he had the fleeting notion that maybe she was more important than Cadets?

This idea was reinforced when Capt Conkey also called for volunteers to attend the Navy Cadets Passing-Out Parade on the Saturday after that. Graham and his friends had attended the ANC parade for the last two years and his hand shot up straight away as he really enjoyed seeing how the other services did their ceremonial. But then it crossed his mind that it was another Saturday.

I won't be able to see Carol then either! he thought. For a few moments he considered pulling his hand back down but then he shook his head and kept it up. *If I am to be CSM next year I need to lead by example,* he told himself. He also understood that for him Cadets was the most important thing in his life, probably even more important than Carol.

He saw Capt Conkey note his hand up and then write his name on the list he was compiling and that settled it. Graham knew that Capt Conkey had to do paperwork to the Cadet HQ to get approval for cadets to take part in every activity outside the school grounds and he did not want to cause him extra work. Seeing his friend's hands up strengthened his resolve.

Joining Instructions with Consent Forms for the Passing-Out Parade were then handed out and the company formed up for dismissal parade. It was then that the idea came to Graham.

I wonder if Carol would come to watch the Passing-Out Parade?

Deep down he sensed that if the relationship with Carol was to prosper, he had to know whether she would support him being in Cadets.

He knew he must put it to the test.

Chapter 13

PUTTING IT TO THE TEST

Graham went to school almost a bundle of nerves. The more he thought about putting it to the test, the more nervous he became. But he did not see Carol in the morning and as a result his anxiety built to nail-biting proportions.

Then, to his mixed relief and concern, he saw her at morning break. She looked very down and that added to his worries. After taking several deep breaths, he marched determinedly towards her. To his relief, she gave a brief smile when she saw him approaching. She pushed along the bench seat to make room for him.

"How are you?" he asked. "You look a bit down."

Carol nodded. "I'm still upset over Martin's death," she said.

Graham nodded and agreed. He felt an urge to reach out and pat her or hug her but didn't.

Then his courage temporarily deserted him, and after asking her how her sister and brother were and chatting about nothing much, he assured her that he was coming to the party.

"Steve and I are booked in at the Caster Hotel," he said. Then he took a deep breath and took his courage in both hands and said to her, "Er... er. Carol, in two weeks' time, on Saturday afternoon, is the Army Cadet Annual Passing-Out Parade. I think you saw it last year."

Carol nodded and looked him right in the eyes. Her face crinkled with mirth. "That was the parade when Willy Williams flew his model plane in to break up your parade," she said.

A mix of emotions swirled in Graham along with images of Willy's red DR1 Fokker Triplane model zooming between the ranks before crashing into him. Anger, annoyance, and a desire for justice made him gruffly reply, "It wasn't Willy who did it. Someone else flew it to get him into trouble," he said.

At the time he had been ready to punch Willy but since then he had come to have a high regard for him.

"Why did he do that?" Carol asked.

"Because Willy was winning with a chick named Petra and the other guy was smitten by her and was jealous," Graham explained.

Carol looked thoughtful for a few moments and then pursed her lips. Graham felt his anxiety shot up, thinking she was going to say no. Instead she nodded and said, "Okay, but only if you agree to come to the Civic Theatre that evening for a Chamber Music performance."

Chamber Music! Graham thought but did not say. Instead he nodded and said, "Sure, if my mum agrees."

They had to leave it at that as the bell for classes went. As he made his way to his next class, Graham met up with Stephen on the steps. "Steve, what is Chamber Music?" he queried.

Stephen looked at him as though to check he wasn't having him on. Then he shook his head. "Very high-brow old-fashioned stuff, the sort of music they played at court before the French Revolution. Strings and stuff like that," he explained.

"Do you think I'll like it?" Graham asked.

Stephen looked doubtful. "Don't know," he said. "Seriously, music is something you either like or you don't, and you don't know until you try it."

Graham nodded but still didn't know what to think. Stephen said, "My oldies reckon you should never just reject different types of music until you have heard a good sample. And they also keep advising me not to reject particular types just because of peer pressure from mates who put down what you actually like."

That was all food for thought and Graham went to class deep in thought. It was also at the top of his mind when he mentioned it to his mother that evening.

"The Civic Theatre? Straight after the Passing-Out Parade? Oh, I don't know. You might be too tired," she said.

"Oh Mum! Fair go! I can go for days without sleep," Graham cried, his mind crowding with incidents from Cadet camps and other adventures.

"And who will be at the theatre?" his mother queried.

"Carol's mum and dad and probably her little sister and little brother," Graham answered. He wasn't sure if the little ones would be there but threw them in to try to make his case sound better.

His mother looked thoughtful. "Hmm, a bit of culture might do you some good," she said. "I will phone Mrs Battersby and discuss it."

Which she did and the upshot was that Graham was allowed to go. "But you need to hurry home from Cadets and have a shower and change very quickly," she added.

Graham saw no problem with that, but his mother's next comment brought him up sharp. "This birthday party on the weekend, have you bought a present yet?"

Present! Graham thought. Something close to panic immediately replaced his happiness. "No Mum, not yet," he mumbled.

"Well you had better get a wriggle on! You've only got tomorrow afternoon to buy one," she said.

That shocked Graham even more. *How could I be such a noddy as to forget I needed to get a present.* Suddenly it loomed as the biggest problem in his life. "What do you suggest I buy mum? What do you buy a teenage girl?"

"Depends what her interests are," his mother replied. "What does she like doing?"

That added to Graham's mounting sense of panic. With a mental jolt he realised he actually knew almost nothing about Carol. *I don't know what hobbies she has, or what movies she likes or what sports she plays,* he thought.

"I don't really know," he admitted.

His mother gave him a look and pursed her lips. "Then you had better do some discreet questioning tomorrow," she suggested. "Now go and finish your homework."

* * *

It took a while to bring up the topic of presents when he saw Carol the following morning. Partly this was because he did not want to admit he had not thought about presents, and partly because she looked very unhappy.

"What's the matter? You look like you've lost your last brass razoo," he said, using an expression his father often used

"The mill workers have gone on strike and are demanding danger money and other things," Carol replied.

That mystified Graham a little and he shrugged and shook his head. "It will blow over, won't it?" he suggested hopefully.

Carol shook her head. "It might, but the mill is having a very bad crushing season and if it makes too much of a loss it could close. Then my dad would have to look for another job."

"Would that be easy do you think?" Graham asked.

In the back of his mind was the notion that highly qualified mechanical engineers should not have too much trouble finding employment.

To his surprise, he saw that Carol was on the edge of tears. She shook her head again and then let out a little sob. "Yes, but it might be in another town. I don't want to leave Cairns. I love this part of the world and I like this school," she cried.

That gave Graham another mental jolt. The notion that their relationship could be fractured by her having to move away shocked him. "Oh, I hope not!" he cried.

His sincerity obviously moved her, and she gave a sad smile and reached across to gently stoke his cheek. "Oh, you are sweet! Now, are you still coming to my party tomorrow?"

"Yes, Stephen's parents are giving me a lift and will pick us up afterwards," he said. Then, before he realised it might be a blunder he added, "What would you like as a present?"

She gave him an odd look and then looked thoughtful. "A diamond necklace and matching earrings, please," she said. Then she grinned and trilled with laughter at the look that came onto Graham's face. "Oh Graham! You should see your face. Sorry, I'm only teasing. Just buy me some music please," she said. "Classical stuff, you know Beethoven, Bach and the like."

Graham didn't know. He had heard the names but really did not know what she was talking about. He nodded and pretended he was more knowledgeable.

They chatted for a bit longer until the bell went. Graham went off to class deeply bothered by the notion of losing Carol because her dad might lose his job; and by fretting about what to buy her.

The present problem he managed to solve by making a special effort after school. He walked home and jumped on his bike and rode to the nearest shopping centre. Luckily it had a music shop, and he took the bull by the horns and took his problem straight to the nice ladies behind the counter. After describing his problem, not without some embarrassment at his obvious ignorance, they made some very helpful suggestions.

With their help he purchased several music cards Carol could download with a wide range of work by classical composers on them. It made a very small bundle, so he also purchased a music video, one of Andre Rieu's concerts in Maastricht. That eased his worst anxieties, so he went looking for wrapping paper.

As he walked through the shopping centre, Graham passed a jeweller's shop. Remembering what Carol had said he detoured over and looked in the display windows. There was a diamond necklace there, and it had matching diamond earrings and he thought they were things of exquisite beauty. But the price!

Holy mackerel! he thought. *Maybe when I am older and have met the girl of my dreams.*

Which made him realise that not only did he not know much about Carol, but he wasn't even sure if he was in love with her. He knew he admired her and admitted to having a crush, but he dimly understood that real love wasn't like that.

Next, he went to a newsagents and bought gift wrap and a card. It took him longer to find a card he thought was suitable than it had to buy the present. Satisfied he had done sufficient he made his way home and set to work writing and wrapping.

While doing this, Kylie walked past several times and scowled. Alex took the opportunity to tease him as well. When his mother got home from work, he showed her the presents and described them and she nodded with approval. He went away to pack for the weekend, humming happily. Even some snide comments from Kylie did not dint his good mood.

It was only when the bad dreams came in the middle of the night that fear and nameless apprehension replaced it.

* * *

Graham woke to a mixture of pleasurable anticipation tinged with anxiety. Kylie knew what was happening and would not even speak to him, so he chose to ignore her disapproval and told himself that he wasn't married to Margaret and that she didn't own him. It was what he had said to Kylie several times before and had only served to enrage her.

Packing was more of a challenge as it wasn't a camping trip. He owned a small suitcase and he took this and his hiking pack with his pillow and sleeping bag stuffed into it. Four changes of clothes were carefully stowed in the suitcase along with the usual collection of toiletries, socks and underwear. He even packed his bathers. *Just in case.*

The last things he packed were the present and card. Satisfied he had everything he might need he sat and waited, trying to read but hotly aware of Kylie's frequent glares.

It was a relief when the Bells arrived in their car at 8:30. But then there was a frustrating and irritating fifteen minutes while the adults talked and Kylie scowled. Then Graham's mother kissed him goodbye and offered her last warnings and advice.

"Promise me you won't do anything wrong in that hotel," she said.

"Mum! I don't sneak and drink alcohol. And I don't take drugs or smoke," Graham cried.

"Good! Then just behave this time, and don't get into any dramas like you usually do," she added.

"No Mum. We will be good," Graham promised.

Thankfully he took his seat beside Stephen in the back of the Bell's car and sat back to enjoy the trip. Now that he was away from Kylie and her constant reminders of Margaret, and with hopeful thoughts of what lay ahead, he started to smile.

Then heated memories of the swim swept into his mind and he became strongly aroused and also confused. One of the things that bothered him was that it was images of Betty's bouncing boobs that filled his mind, both in the T-shirt and quivering for all to see, that came to him more often than images of Carol. He had told himself that his love for Carol was pure, that she was a good girl, but ever since then he had begun to revise his estimation. Several times she had so shocked him that he realised he not only knew very little about her but that she was a much more down-to-earth person than he had at first thought.

She can also be very direct, he mused, remembering some of her statements or questions. But then images of her nude form swept away such worries in a torrent of hopeful fantasies.

As they got closer to Caster, Graham found his excitement increasing, along with a frisson of anxiety. In the distance he glimpsed the chimneys of the mill above a field of standing cane and his heart gave a few little rapid beats.

Not long now! he told himself.

Graham now acted as guide and was able to direct Mr Bell where to turn off. But his assistance in finding the hotel was not needed. Its yellow paint stood out boldly and was visible as soon as they turned off the highway.

"Oh yuk!" Stephen cried. "They should be paying us to stay in that horrible looking place. What an awful yellow, like custard the cat has sicked up."

"Stephen!" cried his mother.

Stephen grinned at Graham and muttered, "Sorry Mum." But he obviously wasn't.

Mr Bell stopped the car at the front of the hotel and they all climbed out. Mrs Bell then went inside. "I will just check the bookings," she said.

Stephen shrugged and turned to help Graham unload their gear. Graham put the luggage on the footpath and smiled. He was just happy to be there and did not care what colour the hotel was. He wasn't planning to spend much time there. Then he looked around and had to grin.

Looking out of the door of the shop was Betty. This time she wore a tiny and very tight yellow T-shirt and very short white shorts. Betty stared and then her face lit up with recognition.

"Oh hi, Graham!" she called, waving as she did.

Graham waved back, hotly conscious that Mr Bell was looking from one to the other. Stephen pushed his glasses up his nose with one finger and raised his eyebrows at the same time.

"Who's that?" he asked.

"Betty the Babe," Graham replied, then realised he should not have added her nickname as Mr Bell frowned and Mrs Bell obviously heard him as she came back out of the front door.

"Who is she?" Mrs Bell queried, also frowning as she cast negative glances towards Betty.

To Graham's relief, Betty retreated into the shop. "Just one of the locals," he answered, not really wanting to explain. Scorching memories assailed him and he blushed. Guilt and anxiety began to build.

"Hmmpf! Yes, well!" snorted Mrs Bell, her disapproval plain. She turned to Mr Bell. "It's a cheap and nasty dump. It smells and the bar is just there and full of rough looking types. Maybe we should look for alternative accommodation?"

That got Graham all worried. He looked both ways along the street. There wasn't another vehicle or person in sight. The only movement were cars on the highway. He could just see the other hotel, but he was not keen on going there.

That will add half an hour to our walking time, he thought.

He was saved by Mr Bell who said, "Doesn't matter dear. We aren't staying here and if it is a low-class dump then it might be a good lesson in life for Stephen." He turned to Stephen and continued, "You can take it as a lesson. If you work hard and study and get a good job you have more options in life, including where you live."

"Yes Dad," Stephen replied.

His mother then took over, making Stephen again promise not to go anywhere near the bar or to get up to any mischief. As he did this, Graham noted Betty peek out of the shop door and grin, and he saw that Stephen was trying to look sincere. Luckily his parents had their back to the shop, and by the time they moved to the car Betty had vanished back inside.

The Bells did a U-turn and drove back to the highway. Graham and Stephen picked up their gear and went into the gloomy little vestibule where a small office window was marked as 'Reception'. As they did, Graham looked around. Directly in front of him was as set of stairs leading up to the second story and beside that was a hallway through to the back of the hotel. On his left, a door led into a pleasant enough looking lounge room, and on his right another led into the public bar.

A quick glance at the drinkers showed a dozen or so working-class looking types, some quite young but mostly middle aged. A couple of old codgers sat at a small table near the door and on the other side sat four men that definitely fitted Mrs Bell's description of rough looking types.

Graham then noted a thin young man sitting at the far end of the bar. He was reading a newspaper and had a half-finished beer in front of him.

That's that Declin bloke who works in the control room, he thought.

Then he saw the barmaid and his mouth dropped open. She was a lovely looking brunette of about twenty and she was topless. All she wore was a tiny pair of briefs. She was pouring beers and when she looked up and met his astonished gaze she smiled and then gave a wink before leaning forward to hand the beers to a man.

Graham had heard about topless barmaids but had never seen one, and the sight got him instantly excited and aroused.

At that moment a middle-aged, blousy-looking woman arrived from the back. She saw where Graham was looking and a sardonic smile formed on her face.

"Yes, well. You young boys just stay away from the bar. You are too young to see things like that."

Graham could tell she was not really concerned, and when he noted the astonished look on Stephen's face he nudged him and said, "You hear that? You stop looking. You already need glasses."

The woman laughed at the old joke and got them to fill out the register and handed them keys. "Room One, top of the stairs, turn left," she said. "And no hanky panky or funny business, or you'll be out on yer ear."

"Yes ma'am," Stephen replied.

He cast a lingering look at the barmaid and then picked up his bags. Graham also cast a last look at the barmaid again she grinned and winked, and he knew that he was blushing, and very excited.

The boys made their way up the stairs and as they reached the landing at the top Stephen turned and chortled. "Geez! Just as well mum didn't see her or we would have been hustled straight back into the car."

"Or your dad," Graham added.

Stephen shrugged. "Dad's alright, but mum wouldn't have let him look. But Mum was right, this place stinks."

The whole place smelt of stale beer and stale urine. And it was old and dirty, the paint peeling from the timber walls and the lino was worn through in places to expose floorboards. And the floor creaked when they walked on it.

Graham led the way along to where two doors stood open at the back corner of the hotel, a toilet and a bathroom. There was a corridor there leading right towards the front of the hotel. There were three rooms on both sides of the corridor and the hallway was dark and stank. Room No. 1 was the first on the left, next to the bathroom. He opened the door and was even less impressed.

There were two beds, one either side of a tiny room, with two old brown wardrobes beside them. A double, frosted glass bay window opened out and through it he could see into the windows of another building.

And even as he looked out, Graham realised it was the shop as into the room directly opposite came Betty. She was looking their way and she immediately waved. She waved so hard her boobs quivered and Graham experienced a surge of fierce lust.

Stephen's gaze followed and his face split into a grin. "I don't care if this dump is a hundred years old and is falling down and smells. The place has definite potential. What did you say her name was?"

"Betty. She works in the shop next door."

"What does the shop sell?" Stephen asked.

"I don't know," Graham replied.

Stephen tossed his bag onto the bed on the right, glanced at his watch and then said, "Then let's find out, and we can check out that barmaid on the way past."

Chapter 14

DEEP DISTRESS

After breakfast on Saturday morning Declin did his washing and then walked to the newsagents to buy the paper before settling at the far end of the bar to enjoy a quiet beer.

For a time he sat there reading and brooding over the fact that Carol was having a birthday party and he could not go, nor even give her a present. He knew about the party from Little Billy who had been playing on the old steam loco Friday afternoon. Declin often saw him and Kirsty there, along with other local kids, as he crossed the park on his way home after work and he frequently stopped to push them on swings, or to be an engine driver. Yesterday he had been roped in by Billy to help drive the train and Billy had told him about the party.

Then the atmosphere in the bar was further spoiled when Rossiter and his cronies arrived and sat at the table in the corner behind him, muttering and laughing. With Rossiter were Marvin, the skinny little weed named Dennis, and another ugly looking thug. Rossiter then annoyed and frightened Declin by pretending to be very friendly and by saying a cheery hello. To Declin it had come across as a direct threat and that was how he interpreted the group behind him now.

Rossiter is reminding me that he is not the only one in this gang, Declin thought, with the vague notion that soon pressure would be put on him to do something to stop the mill. It was all very stressful and quite spoiled his enjoyment of what should have been a relaxing Saturday morning.

I wonder if it was one of them that let those cane bins run loose on the other side of the creek? he thought. It was really only a minor incident but on top of everything had caused more trouble at the mill.

And then Sheila, the Irish barmaid, came into the bar topless. Declin realised he should have expected something like that as the hotel often hired topless girls to be barmaids or raffle ticket sellers on Friday evenings and Saturday mornings. While Declin appreciated her attractiveness, and his body reacted to her sheer physical alure, he was not in the mood.

And then it got worse. Those damned boys arrived. Declin looked up from his paper when he saw people walk in the front door of the hotel. Immediately he recognised Graham and his emotions went up a notch as jealous concern was added to the turmoil of depression and fear. Surmising that Graham was there for Carol's birthday party just added to his distress.

Declin almost ached to protect Carol, to keep her safe from lechers and crudity. He wished he was going to the party and had several times contemplated buying her a present. But how to explain his reasons? That difficulty had stopped him, but it still hurt.

And now here was Mr Smoothy Graham and a mate, a freckle-faced kid with glasses. They then went upstairs with their gear, which surprised Declin even more.

They must be staying overnight? he decided.

He heard the boys moving about upstairs on the creaky old floorboards and envy slowly simmered in his distressed mind. Memories of Graham being naked with the girls in the creek deepened the distress. *Oh, I hope they aren't going to do that again this weekend!* he thought.

And then his annoyance had gone up another notch when the boys came down the stairs, peeked into the bar to look at the barmaid and then went out onto the footpath. They turned left and walked past the open front door of the bar, leering in again (and earning a wave and another wink from the Irish barmaid).

He then turned to watch them through the window, to be instantly annoyed even more when he saw Betty exit the shop and greet them like long lost friends. The boys and Betty then vanished into the shop.

Declin sat there torn by even more complex jealousy as, in some odd way, he considered Betty to be someone he could secretly lust over. So to see the two boys openly flirt and ogle her caused him to boil with unreasonable anger. He was also angry with Betty.

She's only 14. She shouldn't behave like that! he thought.

Declin expected the boys to purchase something and to reappear within a minute or so, but five minutes went by and then ten and they were still in the shop and Declin's mood worsened. Then he heard Betty's brute of a father shouting from somewhere in the building for Betty to get her sister to take over the shop so she could come and help him clean out the storeroom.

Only then did the boys come out onto the footpath again, both with ice creams and a Coke. The boys walked back past the hotel, once again ogling the barmaid who smiled back. Then they walked on along the sidewalk towards the highway. Declin sat there and seethed and wondered if there was some way he could let Carol know what they were like.

How can I keep her safe? he fretted.

Still very conscious of Rossiter and his cronies behind him, Declin finished his beer and reluctantly took himself off upstairs.

For the next hour he had sorted washing and then used the hotel laundry. The wet clothes were hung on lines at the back of the hotel and Declin went back up to his room.

He pushed his window slightly open to let some air in and then lay down to finish reading his newspaper. Thus he heard the boys arrive in the room next to him.

Oh drat! Why did they have to be put in that room? he thought peevishly.

He tried to concentrate on reading as the boys began talking. Mostly he could not understand what they were saying but then he quite distinctly heard Graham say, "There she is again, the little bloody tease!"

Declin went stiff with anxiety. He knew instantly what Graham was talking about. *Betty is flaunting herself at her window,* he thought. Driven by emotions he could not even name, he cautiously lifted his head to peek through the curtains.

Sure enough, Betty was just visible to him, and obviously fully visible to the boys. (Declin had often wished he was in Room No1 because it looked more directly into her room, but he had been afraid to ask to change rooms and had rationalised it by telling himself it was next to the bathroom and the noises would annoy). And, in truth, he was sure that Betty knew he watched her and deliberately stood or sat where he could see her. But now she was obviously standing where the boys in the next room had a better view and the knowledge really hurt.

A sharp stab of jealous rage smote Declin. He had come to think that Betty somehow liked him and only put on a show for him. But here she was changing her top, and for God's sake her bra!, where the boys could see her. Before his aroused and angry gaze, he saw her take off her T-shirt and fling it aside before gripping her breasts and studying them in the mirror. Declin's mouth went dry with lust. Somehow it felt like betrayal by a spouse, and he knew it hurt. It also hurt to know that the boys were looking.

That Graham is just a... a... a... Declin fumed. *He isn't fit to clean the gutters near Carol.*

The notion that he was just leading (misleading?) her to try to get sex from her made him even more distressed, as did his inability to come up with a plan to thwart this.

What can I do to save her? he fretted.

Betty abruptly turned and even as she quickly pulled her curtains closed, she gave a mischievous grin in the direction of the boys. That annoyed Declin as well. He understood that someone had knocked on her bedroom door and she was moving to conceal her lewd behaviour.

Stephen's snickering comment that, "She's got a good set of bouncers on her that one!" added to Declin's fury.

Graham's reply of, "Never mind her, let's go and see Carol," only sent Declin deeper into distress.

The boys went away and Declin lay down again, his emotions in turmoil. He was deeply upset, and also tormented by the fact that he was also now fiercely aroused with his excited body in conflict with what he believed his morals to be. On top of the fear of Rossiter and his gang, it all added up to deep distress. And he feared there might be worse to come.

He tried to calm himself, but without much success. He felt too upset to have lunch, and when he lay on his bed and tried to calm himself he found he was just brooding and getting upset and aroused again. So he went for a long walk out to the highway and across it for several kilometres and back.

For a while he lay on his bed, but then a check of the time told him he must get ready for work. The strike was over, and the mill was working again and now needed to run 24 hours a day to make up for lost time, including on Saturdays and Sundays as well. Reluctantly, Declin got up and had a shower and changed into work clothes. He did not feel like eating but knew he needed the energy, so he brushed his hair and went out, locking his room as he did.

Only to walk into another situation. As he started down the stairs, Declin met the two boys coming back up. A spurt of jealous emotion he did not like to name as hate surged in him and he felt like hitting Graham and knocking him down the stairs. But instead he just gave a nod and noted the recognition in the boy's eyes.

Declin felt so upset he could barely make himself think. Still seething with jealous upset, he made his way to the dining room and forced himself to pretend he was relaxed and normal. He managed to eat a reasonable amount but felt tired even before the shift began.

As he was finishing his meal, creaking on the stairs made him look that way and he saw Graham and Stephen go past the doorway. They were now dressed in long trousers and neat casual shirts and had obviously just showered and groomed themselves. In their hands were parcels in pretty gift wrap.

Going to Carol's party, Declin thought, grinding his teeth.

After quickly finishing his meal, Declin made his way upstairs to clean his teeth. Then he looked at himself in the mirror and experienced a spurt of self-pity, very aware that he was not very handsome. Images of Graham's good looks added to his feelings of envy.

Noting that he would be late if he didn't hurry, he went back downstairs. As he went out onto the sidewalk to walk to work, Declin was relieved to note that Rossiter and his gang had gone and that the Irish girl was no longer flaunting herself in the bar. Nor was Betty visible in the shop as he walked past it. But in the distance a few hundred metres ahead were Graham and Stephen, going in the same direction and obviously heading for Carol's house.

Still brooding and feeling emotionally torn, Declin followed them along the street to the Mill Estate. He was just in time to see the boys go in the front gate at Carol's as he crossed into the park. There was a large gathering of people on the front and side lawns and streamers and party balloons festooned the fence and garden.

Another spurt of envy stabbed Declin. He came to a stop and stared enviously. *I wish I was invited,* he thought.

And there was Carol! From amongst a cluster of very pretty teenage girls, she had emerged to greet the two boys. And now Declin experienced another even sharper stab of jealousy as he watched Graham bow and hand her a present, then Carol lean forward to give him a kiss.

Declin could only stand there in the park near the old steam locomotive and stare in jealous distress. He ground his teeth in frustrated rage and clenched and unclenched his fists.

Suddenly a voice next to him jerked him back to reality. "Hello there, Declin me boy! Wishin' yer was at the party with all the pretty girls are yer?"

It was Rossiter. Declin spun to stare at him, both frightened and aghast lest Rossiter had guessed his secret. "No. Just wondering what the party was for," he answered, trying to sound as casual as he could.

"Is that so?" Rossiter said. "Do yer like little girls, do yer?"

Declin blushed, knew he was blushing and blushed even more. "No!" he blurted out.

As he did, he saw that Rossiter had been with three other men, sitting at a picnic table on the other side of the steam locomotive. The men were all watching and looking unfriendly. They had beers on the table and food.

Rossiter snorted in obvious disbelief. "Well it looks that way. You need to be careful, young Declin. That could get you into trouble," he replied in a voice laden with scepticism.

"It's not like that!" Declin cried. He started walking again.

But Rossiter reached out and grabbed his arm. "Not so fast, boyo! You remember what we said. When we want you to do something, you do it. Or else!"

Declin experienced such a spasm of fear he was quite unable to move for a few seconds. His eyes met those of a killer, and he broke into a sweat. Then Rossiter let him go and he hurried on in a state of deep distress towards the mill.

Chapter 15

DOUBTS AND MORAL DILEMMAS

For Graham, the afternoon and evening were testing times. To be sure they were very pleasant and also very stimulating, but they also provided numerous opportunities for him to feel doubt and temptation.

So many beautiful, desirable girls! he thought as he and Stephen arrived at Carol's.

For a few seconds his senses were swamped by gorgeous scents and wonderful sights. Everywhere he looked there were lovely females. His nostrils were filled by pleasing aromas of scent and his vision with smooth, attractive female skin and arousing, curvy shapes. These were accentuated by the fact that some of the girls were delectably bosomy and the sight of all those bouncing, quivering breasts made him think he was in heaven.

Except they were not the girl he was there to meet! *And there she is!*

Carol appeared from amid the throng of pretty, very pretty and downright beautiful teenage girls. She saw Graham and her face lit up and she hurried over, making him feel guilty for admiring those around her.

Mustering his social graces, he made a bow and presented her with the gift. Carol accepted with a smile and then stepped forward to reward him with a nice kiss on the cheek.

"Thank you, Graham," she murmured.

She then turned to Stephen and accepted his present but did not offer him even a peck on the cheek. She then ushered them over to join in. Graham again found his vision and senses swamped by lovely females. Everywhere he looked there were pretty dresses, bright ribbons, tiny sparkles of jewellery, shining, brushed hair of many colours, smiling lips, sparkling eyes, and happy faces.

He knew most of them although there were a few children from the estate. Their fellow corporal, Gwen from 10A, hurried over and greeted him and Stephen. She was followed by Rosemary with the big boobs from his own class. Then he saw the heart-stoppingly beautiful Rowena that he had admired ever since Year 4. With her were Louise and Ailsa. Seeing them caused a little niggle of doubt and a reminder that he must be very careful to choose when he finally did. At the back of his mind was the notion of getting attached to a woman he might later regret having committed himself to. There were just so many pretty ones to choose from!

Graham instinctively understood that this was one of life's absolute realities, and one which caused a deep, elemental fear: that a person could chose a partner and then later meet another person who seemed even better.

God, I must get it right when the time comes! he thought.

There were other pretty girls including Lynne, Annette, and Judy from Carol's class, her little sister and a couple more he did not know and never got to meet. Fat Donna was there looking anxious and trying hard to have a good time, and also a tall, slender girl Graham had seen around the school.

But there are always snails in life's garden, and he noted Vince Brooks scowling at him and Joseph Chandler looking down his nose. There were other boys from 10A, but he noted that only he and Stephen were there from 10B.

I wonder if that tease Betty is here? Graham thought, looking around while smiling and moving to meet Carol's mum who was laying plates of cupcakes on a table. She greeted him warmly and that vote of approval helped keep his emotions on a high.

And there was Betty, and she immediately caused him embarrassment and worry. She was obviously under dressed compared to the other girls; wearing only her tight white short shorts and a sort of halter neck top which left her back and much of her sides bare.

"Hi Graham!" she shrieked, rushing over to give him a hug.

Graham saw Carol frown and other girls look around and creases appear in their brows.

But luckily Stephen saved him. "What about me?" he called loudly, holding his arms out.

"Oh hi, Steve!" Betty cried, letting go of Graham and flinging herself into Stephen's embrace.

"Good luck!" Graham called, for once thankful Stephen was cutting him out.

Carol shook her head and Graham smiled and nodded. But then he had to say hello to two shy but hopeful younger sisters: Betty's and Carol's. Graham could not remember either name, but he did note the looks in their eyes and he mentally set up his guard. He was nice and polite to them but did not give either any encouragement.

But when he met Carol's eyes, he noted that she was smiling but had a quizzical look in hers.

"They like you," she said.

Graham could only shrug and shake his head. "I came here to be with you," he answered, but also dimly conscious that he was sorely tempted by some of the girls around him.

Graham enjoyed the party. It went on until 10pm with a BBQ meal and later supper. There were games and music and even a bit of dancing. Graham felt too inhibited to take part in that, but the girls liked it and he liked watching them. Later he would remember it as one of those magical evenings of bright lights, sparkling eyes, happy faces, and the waft of hope.

And there was a bit of romance. Carol devoted a fair amount of time to him. Despite his fears and doubts, Graham told himself that he really liked Carol and that he must make the effort to get to know her properly, just in case she really was 'The One'. He dimly understood that this was fate type stuff.

Like buying a lottery ticket that wins; or buying a ticket on a plane that then crashes. And the only way to find out was to take the risk!

There were a few little incidents to irritate or annoy, such as Vince Brookes sneering at him when he was at a table getting some cheesecake, and Annette looking disapproving at him and Stephen.

There was a brief meeting with Carol's dad who was doing the cooking on the BBQ. He nodded and said, "Oh hi! You're Carol's boyfriend. Good you could make it." Then he went on cooking.

To Graham he looked distracted and a tired and worried man. *If the mill is in trouble and he might lose his job I suppose he would be,* he thought.

And there were little twinges of jealousy and regret, like seeing Chamberlain obviously impressing Lynne and noting Stephen and a smirking and dishevelled Betty walking back into the lights from the back lawn.

Steve has taken Betty for a bit of a pash, or worse! he thought.

Then he shook his head. He was aware that Stephen was much more successful with girls than he was and that rankled. Graham considered himself to be better looking and nicer but somehow Stephen, in spite of his freckles and glasses, clearly had something the girls liked.

In some ways it was an odd party, half little kids and half teenage. There were some simple party games like Spin the Bottle (which Graham enjoyed as he got to kiss Rosemary, and that bothered him as he had kissed her several times over the years and thought she was very nice); Hide & Seek (but not 'Sardines' so, to his regret, he did not end up squashed in among some girls), and some skipping and hop scotch. But it was too 'tropical' and sweaty for too many physical games.

There was a moment of embarrassment when Carol blew out the candles on the cake and they all sang 'Happy Birthday'. As they finished Judy said to her, "Well, you are sixteen now, Carol. That makes you legal."

As she said this, Carol blushed but glanced at Graham and then half the others looked at him as well.

Bloody hell! he thought. *What does she mean by that?*

The real tension came at the end. Parents began to arrive to collect children. Because many came from Cairns this was at about 10pm. Then Betty's father appeared.

"Where are Bet & Rosie?" he called loudly.

Graham heard this and looked around. There was no sign of them, nor of Stephen. *Bloody hell! I hope Steve hasn't wheeled her off again!* Graham thought. To check, he quickly walked around to the side of the house while Betty's dad walked over to talk to Carol's parents.

And there was young Rosie peeking around the corner. Graham hurried over and, as he did, she looked around and then looked anxious.

"Your dad's here," Graham said. "Where's Betty?"

Rosie giggled and pointed, "Round the back with Steve," she said.

"What are they? Oh, never mind! Get going before your dad gets angry. He sounds like he's in a bad mood," Graham said.

"He always is! He's probably drunk," Rosie replied, but she was clearly afraid of him and did as she was told.

Graham walked around into the shadows in the back garden and quickly spotted two people standing behind a tree. It was Stephen and

Betty and as far as Graham could tell Stephen had his right hand right up inside her top.

At least they are both dressed and aren't doing anything too serious, Graham told himself.

"Sorry to interrupt, but Betty's dad's here."

"Oh bugger!" Betty cried, taking her arms from around Stephen's neck. "I'd better go. See ya later, Steve!"

"You bet Bet. See ya," Stephen replied, giving her another quick kiss and then a final fondle before sliding his hand out.

Betty squirmed and muttered something and then hurried off.

Stephen sighed. "Oooh! She's a hot one that!" he muttered.

Graham wondered what plan he and Betty might have made but knew Stephen would resent any interrogation, so he held his tongue. In fact he was aroused and jealous and that helped keep them both silent as they rejoined the party at the front.

Soon there were only the three girls who were staying plus Carol's little sister and little brother and parents. Graham thought it was good policy to help clean up, so he moved to help Carol's dad while Stephen stood and chatted to the girls.

Then there were regretful goodnights. Graham did not want to leave. He wanted it all to flow on to some magical romantic interlude, but the little ones were ordered upstairs and the big girls all followed.

At the bottom of the stairs, Carol stopped and turned and Graham's hopes went up. Rowena, who was halfway up, also looked back.

"Give the poor bugger a kiss Carol," she cried. "He's earned one."

"That's right," Rosemary called. "If you won't, I will."

That earned her a sharp look from Carol and caused Graham a few heated flashbacks and he could only blush and grin. The girls all cheered and offered words of advice and encouragement when Carol came over and put her arms around him and kissed him.

"See you tomorrow," she said as she ended the kiss.

Graham was all hot and his frustration made him squirm. "What time and where?" he asked.

"Nine O'clock over on the old steam loco there," Carol replied. "See ya, sweet dreams."

"They will be. They'll be of you," Graham answered.

"Oh good boy! You deserve another kiss for that," Carol replied. So she gave him another hug and a kiss while the others teased and called out and laughed.

Graham then realised that it was Carol's dad beside him. "Come on poppet, upstairs and to bed! You've had all evening for that sort of thing."

"Dad!"

So it was a much happier Graham who released her and waved goodnight as she and the others made their way up the front stairs. Graham then turned and walked out the front gate with Stephen.

As they walked along the bitumen ring road in the cool night air Stephen said, "You look like you are winning mate."

"We are getting to know each other," Graham agreed.

Stephen chuckled and Graham badly wanted to say it wasn't like that, but then he pictured Carol naked and wasn't so sure. Instead he said, "Sorry to interrupt you and Betty."

"Huh! That's alright," Stephen replied.

By then the boys were crossing the main railway line. They made their way along the quiet and deserted street past the silent houses. The only sounds seemed to be distant clanking and hissing from the mill and the equally distant hum of traffic on the highway.

They walked past the front of the shop and Stephen glanced up and then chuckled again. Graham noted this and wondered.

I hope Steve's not thinking of doing something foolish, he thought.

But he was. The boys used their key to get through the front door of the hotel and then carefully crept up the dimly lit stairs, or tried to as the old treads all seemed to creak and groan under their weight. So did the floorboards upstairs.

Having reached their room, Graham whispered, "I will just go to the toilet and clean my teeth."

"Good idea," Stephen agreed.

They both crept into their bedroom and then turned on the light. Graham made sure the curtain was closed, remembering that Betty had been able to partially see into the room from her bedroom.

He dug out his towel, toothbrush, and toothpaste. Stephen did the same, but then sat on his bed and began taking off his shoes. Graham hurried to the toilet and did a pee, then he went to the bathroom next door and turned on the light. Quickly, he washed his face and then began scrubbing his teeth. As he did, he glanced sideways out the window.

Across above the shop all the windows were in darkness, but Graham thought he glimpsed movement. *Is that Betty?* he wondered, unsure if he had seen a pale blob appear at the dark rectangle of her window or not.

Not wanting to be thought a Peeping Tom, he hastily looked away and finished cleaning his teeth. After rinsing his mouth and having a drink he made his way back to the bedroom.

Stephen met him at the door and Graham saw that he was only wearing PJ shorts by then. Stephen also had his towel over his shoulder. "Don't wait for me. Turn the bedroom light out. I'll be a while. I need to go to the dunny," he said.

Graham nodded and then went to his bed. Stephen left the room and closed the door behind him. As Graham turned back his bedclothes, he glanced up and then frowned.

I thought that curtain was fully closed, he told himself.

Unsure, he decided to leave it to let some breeze in. Acting on Stephen's advice, he switched off the light and changed into his PJ shorts and then climbed into bed. Then he began to wonder what Stephen was doing. Minutes crept by and the sound of the toilet flushing suggested that his more serious business was accomplished. But then Graham's ears detected what he thought were stealthy sounds: floorboards creaking and noises on the stairs.

Is Steve going downstairs? Graham wondered.

Notions like raiding the kitchen crossed his mind but when he heard more stealthy steps on the steps and then across the floor into the bathroom he began to relax, until he heard whispers and a distinctly female giggle.

"Shhh!" hissed Stephen from the bathroom.

Christ! Has he got that Betty in there? Graham wondered.

He sat up, making the bed creak loudly, then realised he needed to be much more silent. Carefully he twisted his head round to look out the window, just in time to hear the bathroom door close and get locked and to see the bathroom light go off.

Oh God almighty Steve! What are you doing? Graham thought, anxiety, even fear for his friend flooding in.

For a few minutes he sat there straining his ears and thinking deeply. What he was trying to decide on was whether to interrupt what he thought might be going to happen.

I am his mate, but is it really my business? he agonised.

Left sitting in the darkness while being torn by a turmoil of moral options, Graham found he was also very jealous and, stimulated by suggestive little noises from the next room, highly aroused.

The moral dilemma was complicated by the fact that Graham knew for a fact that Stephen had 'done it' with several girls and that Betty had obviously come to him willingly, and by secret agreement. Then he flamed with shame knowing he was an absolute hypocrite, that he fervently wished it was him in there, and with Betty, not Carol.

For a while he considered saying something to remind Stephen not to do the wrong thing. But he could not bring himself to do that, so he decided not to intervene. Instead he eased back onto his bed and lay listening, his fevered imagination forming images of fantasy while his conscience smote him with guilt. He then wondered if he was a coward but rationalised not acting by thinking Stephen would just say he was jealous. And he was!

After some time, Graham heard the bathroom door squeak slowly open and then more whispered speech. No light showed under the bedroom door, so he deduced that Stephen and Betty were sneaking out.

The sounds died away down the stairs. Graham had to suppress an urge to peek through the window to see if he could see Betty going home. He resisted this and lay back, his heart hammering and body squirming with arousal and emotional turmoil.

Then there was the dilemma of what to do when Stephen came back. *Do I mention it and try to find out what happened?* he wondered.

Thus, when he heard more stealthy footsteps approaching the bedroom door a few minutes later, Graham lay in the darkness in a lather of perspiration and anxiety.

Chapter 16

CLOSE TO HEAVEN

As he heard Stephen's stealthy footsteps approach the bedroom door, Graham bit his lip while his mind raced.

What will I do if he speaks to me? Lie? Pretend I heard and saw nothing? Offer advice or express censure? And what if he starts to boast? Do I express my disapproval or join in with stories?

Unable to decide, Graham closed his eyes and pretended to be asleep while despising himself as a coward and a hypocrite.

The door slowly squeaked open, and he heard Stephen creep in and then close and lock the door. Stephen then made his way to his bed on the other side of the room and eased himself onto it. Graham lay there trying to keep his breathing slow and regular and found he was trembling with tension and jealous lust.

Stephen's shoes were placed quietly on the floor and his bed emitted several loud squeaks as he rolled on his side. It was then obvious that Stephen was not going to speak to him and only then was Graham able to relax slightly. He lay back and continued to pretend he was asleep, sure he wouldn't!

Only to slip into a deep but broken sleep filled with erotic images and an awareness of unpleasant odours. Several times Graham came to a state of muzzy consciousness. Through blurred eyes he looked across the darkened room to check if Stephen was still in bed. Each time he saw he was and that he was apparently sleeping peacefully.

When he woke to find it was daylight, Graham lay for a while wondering how the conversations might go and still worrying about what policy to pursue. Finally it was the urgent need to pee that drove him from his bed and he tiptoed out to the toilet.

On his return, he found a bleary-eyed Stephen sitting on his bed. For a few seconds Graham felt quite tongue-tied. Then he gabbled, "How did you sleep?"

"Better than you I think," Stephen replied with a grin. "You moaned and groaned and tossed and turned and farted. You even cried out once.

Who were you were trying to save this time?"

Graham remembered fleeting glimpses of an erotic dream and blushed then gave a wry grin. Careful to not let slip any hint that he was aware that Stephen had left the room the night before, he chatted and picked up his toilet bag.

"Shower and shave for me," he said.

Only to immediately walk into another unpleasant situation. When he reached the bathroom door it was closed, so he had to wait; and when the door opened ten minutes later, he found himself face to face with the mill worker Declin.

Graham tried to ease the situation, not liking the unfriendly look on Declin's face. "Good morning," he said.

Declin gave him a sour look and grunted a reply, then pushed past him, wiping his face with a towel as he did.

Unfriendly bugger! Graham thought.

Then he went into the bathroom and closed the door, and immediately had all his thoughts directed across to Betty's bedroom. Her curtains were open, and she was standing naked in front of a mirror while brushing her hair! Graham could only gape while admiring her quivering, out-thrust bosom. He began to experience an instant rush of lust.

Then Betty turned and the lust was tempered by shame at being found staring at her, even if the bathroom window was mostly closed and he could only see through a small gap. To his astonishment, Betty suddenly grinned and waved.

Is she waving at me? Graham wondered.

Unsure and embarrassed he half raised a hand to return the greeting and his face formed a lopsided grin. But then he focused his eyes and decided that Betty was actually looking at the bedroom next door.

She is waving to Steve, he thought. *Oh, what a brazen little witch!*

Quickly he moved aside so as not to be visible, then put his eye to the tiny gap between the window and its frame. *She's a horny little chick alright,* he thought, now fully aroused and wanting to see more.

But he didn't. Betty suddenly reached across and pulled her curtains closed and the show was over.

Regretfully, Graham took himself to the shower. Soon after, Stephen hammered on the door. "Come on, Graham, don't use all the bloody hot water!" he called.

As quickly as he could, Graham finished and dried himself and opened the door. "Your go," was all he could manage to say.

Stephen smiled and took his place. Graham returned to the bedroom and completed dressing, short-sleeve shirt, shorts, and joggers, then carefully combed his hair. While he did, he thought he heard the bathroom windows being pushed open more and that puzzled him. Then a glance showed that the bedroom curtains also had a small gap.

Was Steve watching Betty too? he wondered.

Then the embarrassing thought crossed his mind that Stephen might be returning the favour by standing in the bathroom with nothing on where Betty could see him. That thought got Graham peeking through the gap and he stared hard at Betty's bedroom, trying to decide if she was looking through what looked like a tiny gap between her own curtain and window frame. Ashamed of his own wicked thoughts, Graham moved away and resumed dressing. Then he lay on his bed and waited until Stephen returned and began pulling on shoes and socks.

"Breakfast?" was all Stephen said.

As it had been paid for along with the cheap board, Graham agreed. Self-consciously he led the way downstairs to the Dining Room. There was then more embarrassment. There were six mill workers sitting at various tables and one of them was Declin, who again gave him a sour look.

What's his problem? What have I done to annoy him? Graham wondered.

Then his mind was diverted by discovering that the waitress was the Irish girl who'd been the topless barmaid the day before. Now she wore a respectable white shirt and black skirt and acted friendly but demure.

"Good morning boys. Did you sleep well?" she asked.

Graham tried to think of a witty comment while trying not to stare at the soft swelling of her shirt just in front of his eyes. But Stephen beat him to it.

"No," he said. "I kept having hot dreams about you."

"Oh, don't get fresh, you cheeky boy!" the Irish girl cried-and then she laughed.

To Graham's embarrassment, the nearby workers had heard the exchange and one of them turned and frowned.

"Cheeky ratbag!" he growled.

Graham glanced at him and blushed and then noted Declin positively scowling at him. Ashamed of his thoughts and Stephen's comments, he looked away.

Stephen just grinned and said, "What can you offer us?"

"There's the menu. If you can read that is," the Irish girl replied.

That drew a laugh from the workers and caused Graham more embarrassment. He reached for the printed menu and studied it while Stephen continued to flirt. She then took their order and went back to the kitchen before returning with trays of food for the workers.

A full breakfast of cereal and toast, bacon, eggs and sausages, and fruit juice did much to restore Graham's morale and good humour, as did the knowledge that he would be seeing Carol soon.

* * *

After breakfast, the boys went and cleaned their teeth (Yes, the bathroom window was wider open!) and packed their belongings. The boys then booked out and set off along the street towards the mill.

As they approached the shop, Graham half expected Stephen to say something or to make an excuse to stop and talk to Betty but the shop was closed and there was no sign of life at any of the upper floor windows, so the boys just continued on.

It was hot by then and there was very little breeze. There wasn't a cloud in the sky or a car on the street. The only signs of life were a dog that strolled across the road and a loaded cane train that went purring and clanking past on its way to the mill. Graham got a whiff of the new cut cane and breathed deeply.

"Aaaah! That's better than that smelly old hotel," he commented.

"It certainly stank," Stephen agreed.

A discussion of the shortcomings of the hotel began, making Graham worry that there might be some mention of the creaky floorboards and stair treads. But there wasn't.

Stephen diverted the conversation by saying, "But none of that matters when you get a barmaid like that Irish chick. Holy mackerel, weren't they nice tits!"

Graham could only agree, and then his gaze noted Carol and the girls at the old locomotive a hundred metres ahead.

Everywhere he looked, it seemed there was desirable female showing. All the girls wore fairly revealing and skimpy clothing, and all looked beautiful and amazingly attractive. Carol wore a short 'shift' type dress with five bands of colour: white, blue, white, red, and white. It was so short it revealed almost all of her legs and the way her bosom moved in the cloth got him wondering if she was wearing a bra.

Rosemary wore a white T-shirt and lavender slacks and sandals, and her large breasts strained at the thin material of her top. Rowena was a picture of sheer beauty, her glossy black hair framing her heart-shaped face and held in place by a well-chosen hairclip. She wore a blue shirt and white shorts and her long legs looked most delectable. And when Graham tore his gaze from them to look at Ailsa his eyes nearly popped out. She looked the horniest of all. While she was wearing jeans and sandals her top was a thin, almost see-through shirt made of red cloth with a pattern of yellow flowers on it. But what got his attention was the fact that most of the front was undone and only held by a knot which revealed a lot of cleavage.

And there was young Kirsty trying to compete with the older girls by wearing a short wrap around skirt and halter top.

Young Billy was there acting as the pretend engine driver with Rowena holding him up so he could reach the controls and look through the small driver's window. He just wore a short-sleeved loose cotton shirt and shorts.

Graham's senses reeled as pleasant aromas of scent and girl wafted across. For a few moments the sheer eroticism and beauty of the scene held him speechless. *Oh my God! This must be what Heaven is like,* he thought.

But Stephen wasn't rendered speechless, and in response to cheery greetings and queries as to how well he had slept he replied with witty banter that just made Graham jealous.

He was helped in the social situation by Billy. He called to Graham to come up and play and Graham was glad to do so. He quickly put down his bag and heaved himself up the steps onto the footplate. Rowena gave him a friendly smile and stepped back, still holding Billy so Graham could take over.

But Rowena didn't help by calling all the others to come up and help drive the train. When they were all up on the footplate it was so crowded that Graham and Stephen had girls pressing on them from both front and back. It was heaven, even if it was embarrassing!

Stephen revelled in the situation and Graham was sure he took advantage of it to surreptitiously feel a couple of the girls. Graham was sorely tempted to try that as well but fear of getting into trouble kept his hands away and he just enjoyed it when one or other of the girls pressed against him. There were giggles and laughter and much puffing and chuffing as they imitated steam engine noises. All in all it was one of the happiest hours of Graham's entire life.

As the game became boring, the girls climbed up onto the boiler or back onto the coal tender. Billy lost interest and asked Graham to push him on the nearby swings. He reluctantly assented. Kirsty then insisted that Stephen push her on the swing although it was patently obvious a girl her age was quite capable of doing it for herself.

After half an hour of talking, swinging, telling silly jokes and generally having a good time, Carol commented that they should all go to her house for morning tea. That led to another pleasing situation for Graham. When he picked up his bag, Carol came and took his other hand and walked beside him, the other girls all flicking glances and smiling.

When they reached the house, Graham and Stephen dumped their gear on the front veranda and the whole group seated themselves on chairs and lounges while Carol's mum fussed with cold drinks and cake and other sweets left over from the party.

"These all have to be eaten," she said.

After morning tea a walk was suggested. Carol's mum reminded them all to back by 1230 for lunch and then almost shooed them out of the house so she could do some cleaning. They all made their way down the front stairs and out through the front gate. To begin with, they strolled across the ring road and lawn towards the steam loco, Carol again holding Graham's hand.

Along the way, Graham saw that Declin, the mill worker, was walking across the park towards them. He looked a bit hot and anxious, but Graham did not care. He was too happy. But he was surprised when Carol waved to him.

"Hi Declin! Are you off to work?" she called cheerfully.

Declin gave a half smile in return and shook his head. "No, just going for a walk to keep fit. I do too much sitting in this job," he replied.

He passed on behind them, heading for the mill and the group strolled on across the park. "Who's he?" Rowena asked.

"Just a young bloke who works at the mill. He operates the computers," Carol answered.

Billy piped up, "He helps me drive the train and we play horsies and tiggy," he said.

Graham did not care. He thought he was in heaven and just happily strolled along, savouring the sights and sounds and aromas. The sugar mill smells melded with the girl's scents and the aroma of mangos to provide a mix he would remember forever. He was just so happy to be there.

There was no real interest in either the play equipment or the old loco, so when Rosemary pointed on along the road and asked where it went they agreed to explore it. Laughing, joking, and teasing, the group strolled across the park and followed the road that ran northwest between the mill and the workers houses.

To add to Graham's pleasure, this led them along beside the cane train marshalling yards and he was able to study the layout and watch two loaded trains come rattling in and an empty one go out. It was hot but the sweat did not bother him. The others all seemed happy enough, so they walked on.

After ten minutes, they came to the northern end of the rail yards. Here the road split. A gravel road went left across the last few rail tracks, and another went right into the cane fields. A rail track went each way.

Carol pointed left. "The creek's just over there and there's a good bridge. Sometimes you can see fish," she said.

By common consent they walked that way. They passed a line of trees and came to another gravel road that ran both ways along the creek bank. Graham noted it as the road he had walked along during the previous visit. For just a moment he was assailed by a series of flashbacks, naked girls in the creek, and brutal sudden death as the worker fell from the chimney. He was half inclined to suggest they turn back but didn't.

The group strolled across to where the railway and gravel road led onto a long, narrow timber bridge. This was a dual road and rail bridge. Stephen led the way out onto the narrow bridge.

"Be no joke if you were driving across this and a train came along," he said.

"It's like the bridge across the Mulgrave on the way to Kearneys Flats," Graham commented.

His eyes followed the light railway and he noted that it had a very sharp bend to the right at the other end before running up over what looked to be a long rise covered with fields of cane. Beyond it was the jungle-covered slopes of the mountains.

"The trains must puff a bit getting up over that," he suggested.

Carol nodded. "They do, but they are empty going that way and full coming back down."

That made sense to Graham, so he shifted his attention to the creek below. To his surprise, it was quite deep but the bottom, being clean white sand, was still visible. Just beside the bridge on the downstream side he saw that there was a jumble of loaded sugar cane bins lying in the water.

Four, no five, he thought. Pointing to them he said, "Was there a bit of an accident?"

Carol nodded and pointed up the distant rise. "That happened on Friday. They were parked up on the top of the hill waiting for a train and something must have gone wrong as they just rolled down and derailed. Dad's organising a crane to lift them out."

Graham studied the tumbled and twisted cane bins and spill of cane billets in the water, then he shifted his attention to the creek. Luckily, a few small fish were flitting around among the timber piles and the long guinea grass which lined both banks so Billy and Kirsty were happy.

Then Rowena said, "Gee, that water looks nice. Pity we didn't bring our bathers. We could have had a swim."

That got Graham instantly alert and both anxious and hopeful. And Billy had heard the word 'swim'. He looked up from kneeling on the bridge deck and said, "Can mine have a swim please, Carol?"

Graham saw Carol blush and then glance at the others. "We didn't bring any bathers."

"We didn't wear them last time," Billy retorted.

Graham saw the other girls all glance at Carol, and she blushed. "That was just us. There are big girls here now," she replied.

"That's alright. I won't mind," Billy replied.

At that Carol laughed. "I was thinking of them, not you little brother! They may not want to see you being a rude little water baby."

Rowena laughed and said, "We won't mind. He can have a swim."

At that Kirsty also stood up. "Can I have a swim too please?"

"Yes, but not here," Carol said, gesturing downstream to where Graham could see the big tree with the swing at the next bend to the left.

At that Billy and Kirsty set off at a run, ignoring calls to wait. The others all began to follow. By then Graham's mind was in a ferment. He did not want the other girls to know he had been swimming nude with Carol and her little sister and brother, but he was also swamped by erotic memories and became very hopeful.

They reached the end of the track down to the beach and Graham stopped. To make it appear that he was a nice boy, he said, "Steve and I will just go away so as not to embarrass anyone."

"It'll be okay," Carol replied.

Carol met his eyes and a mischievous smile flitted on her face. "What if the other girls want a swim too?" she teased.

Graham's mouth went dry with lust, but Stephen answered at once. "As little Billy said, we won't mind."

At that both Rosemary and Rowena laughed. Rowena turned and called back, "We won't mind either. Come on you two boys."

Hot memories of Rowena's nude form when she and he had swum in the fountain in Munro Martin Park when they were in Year 5 rose to heat Graham's mind even more. The idea of seeing Rowena naked now she was a 'big girl' had enormous appeal and he did not know what to say.

As the group made their way down the path through the long grass, Ailsa surprised him by saying, "I'd like to have a swim, if nobody minds me having nothing on."

Ailsa! Graham thought.

His mind exploded with hope. He had admired her female form for years and could not believe his ears.

By then they had reached the little beach, to be confronted by Billy pulling down his shorts. His shirt already lay on the sand. To Graham's embarrassment, the girls all looked and he saw blushes mottle the necks and cheeks of Carol and Rosemary.

Billy dashed into the water and Kirsty peeled off her clothes and stood there jumping up and down, quite nude and looking very cute.

"Come on!" she cried, wading in after Billy.

"Don't get your hair wet!" Carol called. "We don't want mum to know we have been swimming."

Graham now said, "Steve and I will go away."

But Carol shook her head. "You girls don't mind if the boys join us, do you?" she asked.

To Graham's surprise, they all shook their heads and said no. Rosemary blushed but grinned and said, "Won't be the first time, from what I hear."

Graham did blush at that, but he was now also scared. "We don't want to get into trouble."

"You won't!" Carol assured him. "Now you boys turn your backs until we are in the water."

Graham and Stephen turned away until the girls were all undressed and in the water. This was accomplished with a lot of embarrassed giggling and gasping at how cold the water was. Carol then called, "Okay boys, you can come in now."

Graham glanced around and saw that they were all neck deep in the water. "Don't you look," he called.

"Why not?" Rosemary replied.

"Because I... we... I don't want to embarrass you." He was actually afraid of possible legal consequences but did not want to say so.

"You won't," Rosemary called back, and all the girls giggled.

"What about Kirsty? I don't want to do the wrong thing," Graham croaked as he toyed with the waistband of his shorts.

Carol snorted and shook her head. "She sees Billy's every day and she didn't mind last time," she commented.

"Last time?" Rosemary queried.

Carol obviously realised she had said the wrong thing and cast a bushing glance at Graham. "Er... er we had a bit of swim a few weeks ago," she admitted.

The other girls shrieked and giggled, and Graham glanced over his shoulder to check that the girls weren't looking. As he did, he got a glimpse of Ailsa's magnificent bosom and thought he was in paradise. Nerving himself he glanced at a leering, smirking Stephen and began undoing his pants.

By then his heart was hammering fit to burst and his vision had gone blurry. With trembling, sweaty hands he slid down his shorts and then straightened up to undo his shirt.

Carol suddenly called, "Kirsty! Stop looking."

Graham blushed and glanced back to see Kirsty hastily turn her head away. A flush of embarrassment and desire surged through him. With his heart hammering with desire, he turned and waded quickly into the creek. Stephen followed. The water was refreshingly cool and, to Graham's added delight, crystal clear so he could still see almost everything. As he stood in waist deep water, he noted that while the girls were all now neck deep he was getting tantalising glimpses of their naked bodies. He thought it was wonderful!

They stood or knelt in a circle and then Billy started to splash but Carol at once stopped him.

"Don't wet our hair I said!" she snapped.

This is heaven! Graham thought.

But as always there were worms in life's apple. What began to bother Graham was that he was so lustfully attracted to the other girls, and he had the notion that if it was true love with Carol he would have eyes only for her. The fact that she was so open and that she did not seem to be jealous of Rosemary also bothered him.

And does she know that Rowena and I used to swim in the nuddy?

Luckily, Stephen provided most of the conversation with jokes and banter so Graham could just enjoy the situation. And then it occurred to him that he wasn't bothered by Stephen seeing Carol naked.

Do I really love her? Or is it just a crush? he wondered.

At that moment, he heard voices and fear stabbed through him. Anxiously, he looked around and to his dismay saw heads moving through the long grass of the track.

"Uh oh! Someone coming," he cautioned.

But the others had heard them too and were looking and all the girls lowered themselves so that only their heads were out of the water.

Then Betty and her sister Rosie walked into view. Betty grinned and called loudly, "Yeah, thought yez might be here."

Betty now waved and called, "Hi Steve! Hi Graham! How's the water?"

"Fine," Stephen replied. "Come and join us."

Carol turned to stare hard at him, then turned to Betty and called, "Go away! We are having a swim and we don't want you here."

"No! It's not your creek. You don't own it. We can swim here if we like!" Betty called back.

"Go away! We've got boys here," Carol replied.

"Lucky you! We don't mind," Betty snapped.

To Graham's delighted amazement she began peeling off her tight white shorts. But he was also worried about any complaints so he called, "We don't have any clothes on."

At that Betty laughed and gave a very mischievous grin. "You didn't have last time either," she replied, earning him surprised and interested looks from the other big girls. Betty now slid off her T-shirt and her large boobs bobbled loose.

Graham found the sight incredibly arousing. Feeling almost overwhelmed by lust, he watched Betty and her little sister Rosie strip. Because Rosie was just a little girl, Graham felt guilty looking at her.

Betty did not call on the boys not to look and now waded in. Graham stared in delight and then felt guilty as Carol obviously wasn't amused.

He turned to Carol, "Do you want to go?" he asked.

"Not yet," Carol answered, moving closer to him as Betty approached.

Betty came to a stop a few paces away in water just deep enough to cover her boobs. The other girls obviously didn't quite know what to make of her, but they did introduce themselves.

Betty then swam over and put her arms around Stephen's neck and kissed him, very obviously pressing her bosom against him as she did. She then ended up in his arms with one of her arms around his neck. All the big girls watched this performance with almost open amazement. Stephen had the good grace to blush but made no move to push her away.

And then Graham saw Betty's father appear at the end of the track and his pleasure became a flux of passion and fear!

At that moment, Stephen had his back to the beach. But Betty was facing the shore and she saw her father at once. With a gasp she let go and pushed herself away. Stephen tried to hold her on until a roar of rage from close behind him sent a look of alarm across his face. Stephen was obviously having trouble seeing without his glasses and he blinked and stared until he realised who he was seeing. Then the look of alarm immediately changed to fear.

Betty's father was a big brute of a man with a beer belly and fat, ugly face. His arms looked massive, and he wore only dark blue shorts and a blue singlet. And he was angry. His piggy eyes flicked around, taking in the scene with astonishment and obviously growing rage.

"Betty, you little slut! Get out of there and get home!" he shouted. He waved his fist and glared around. Then he spotted Rosie and pointed at her. "And you, you little minx! Get out and get home!"

Stephen turned to face Betty's father while all the other girls sank lower so that only their heads were showing. Betty and Rosie both splashed quickly ashore, both sobbing and obviously frightened.

Oh my God! We are in trouble now! Graham thought.

When Betty's father saw that both girls were naked, his face suffused to bright red and he glared and then shouted and smacked Betty hard on her wobbling, white bum.

"You shameless little slut!" he screamed. "Get dressed and get home!"

Betty bent to pick up her undies but, in her haste and panic, had trouble getting her wet feet into them. Next to her, Rosie also struggled to dress but her father made no attempt to hit her or speak to her.

Betty's father now turned and shook his fist at Stephen. "If you've done anything to my little girl you bastard, I'll get the police! You'll regret it," he shouted.

To Graham's surprise and admiration, Stephen answered him quite calmly. "We are just having a swim," he said.

"Swim you call it! Fornication I call it! I will get the police onto you! She's under-age!" yelled Betty's father, again shaking his fist at Stephen.

By then a weeping Betty had her undies on and was pulling up her shorts. "No you won't!" she screamed. "If you get my friends into trouble, I'll tell them about you and mum!"

To Graham it looked that Betty's father went even redder in the face, verging on purple. "You do and you'll regret it," he snarled.

"Then don't call the police," Betty snapped back. She was obviously recovering from her surprise and was getting angry.

And then suddenly another person appeared down the track: Declin. He was running and skidded to a stop on the beach and Graham saw his thin, anxious face turn from side to side as he took in the scene.

Bloody hell. It gets worse and worse! he thought.

Chapter 17

JEALOUS MISERY

For Declin, they had been among the worst 24 hours of his young life. All of Saturday night he had been at work, but he was tormented by knowing that Carol's birthday party was taking place only a hundred metres away across the park. In his jealous mind he formed images of Graham kissing Carol (and maybe even trying to do other things to her).

She wouldn't let him surely? he had tried to tell himself, but then searing images of Carol stripping down at the creek and swimming with naked Graham had risen to add to his doubts and torment.

There were more problems on Sunday morning. When he returned to his room at 6:30am, Declin could hear the boys talking in the next room. Just knowing they had been to the party aroused his envy. Feeling quite peeved, he took his toilet bag and went to the bathroom to shower.

Only to encounter another unpleasant situation when he opened the door ten minutes later and found himself face to face with Graham. Graham gave him a friendly greeting, but Declin was in no mood to be friendly to someone he considered his main rival. In reply he gave him a sour look and grunted a reply then pushed past him, wiping his face with his towel as he did.

Bloody kid! Declin thought.

He went into his bedroom and closed the door, and immediately had his thoughts directed across to Betty's bedroom. Through his own half-closed curtains he saw that her curtains were open and she was standing naked in front of her mirror while brushing her hair! Declin could only gape at her.

Then Betty turned and the lust was tempered by shame at looking at a young girl, and of being a 'Peeping Tom'. Even though he did not think she could see him, he felt guilty. But then his shame turned to astonishment and anger when he saw Betty turn and face the hotel and then grin and wave.

Is she waving at Graham? Declin wondered. Unsure, he focused his eyes and decided that Betty was actually looking at the bedroom next door. *No, she is waving to that kid with the freckles and glasses,* he thought. *Oh, what a brazen little bitch!*

His emotions boiling with anger, envy and lust Declin put his eye to the gap between the window and its frame. *She's a horny little creature alright,* he thought, now fully aroused and wanting to see more. But he didn't get that pleasure. Betty suddenly glanced towards the bathroom and then reached across and pulled her curtains closed.

Regretfully, he dressed and took himself downstairs to the dining room. As he made his way past the next bedroom and the bathroom, he eyed the doors malevolently.

How come that Betty is so forward with that kid with the glasses?

Which got him fretting about what might have happened at the party during the night. Once again, the green monster stirred his emotions.

In the dining room there was more embarrassment. There were six other mill workers sitting at various tables and he nodded and forced a smile to them but then sat on his own. Then his mind was diverted by discovering that the waitress was Sheila, the Irish girl who'd been the topless barmaid the day before.

"Good morning. Did you sleep well?" she asked.

Declin again forced a smile and shook his head. "I've been on nightshift," he explained, then ordered a full breakfast.

This was served and he was eating it when the two boys appeared and sat at the remaining table. Declin cast them a sour look and was pleased to note a puzzled frown on Graham's face. That caused him to rethink.

I had better be more careful. I don't want anyone to suspect I am interested in Carol. Shame at the possibility of being labelled a paedophile made him blush.

But the boys again attracted his attention when Sheila the waitress spoke to them in a friendly tone. He scowled his disapproval and tried to calm down, to think straight while he ate. That did something to restore his battered emotions. But he found it a relief to finish and to take himself back upstairs.

Feeling quite frustrated and cast down, Declin threw himself on his bed. He then endured hearing the boys return upstairs and go through the process of cleaning teeth and packing. It was obvious they were leaving, and when he heard them go down the stairs he peeked through his window. His deductions were correct.

Going to Carol's? Declin thought, which was the source of more jealous regret as it was what he dearly wanted to do.

Then his imagination became his worst enemy and he lay there conjuring up images of Graham kissing Carol (and worse) so that he almost became physically ill.

Tiredness from the nightshift then eased his mind as he drifted into a restless sleep. When he woke, he saw it was only 10am and all his tormented worries rushed back to bother him.

"I have to know!" he muttered.

So Declin dressed and set off walking towards the mill. He had no plan, and knew he really could not just barge into the social situation without exciting comment and suspicion. But he was so upset and irritated that he felt he had to be up and moving. And as it was, he was lucky enough to encounter them at the park. As he crossed the main railway, he saw a group of children come down the front steps of Carol's house and walk through the front gate towards the playground and the old loco.

Declin kept walking but his mind was in a ferment. *Do I keep walking or just go somewhere else?*

Then he decided it would look odd if he suddenly detoured so he stubbornly continued walking, angling to pass close to them. As he did, he studied the group and was astonished to note that there were only three boys: Little Billy, Graham and the one with glasses. All the others were girls, and apart from young Kirsty, extraordinarily attractive teenage girls.

As he got closer to them, Declin's senses were almost swamped by visions from the five girls of erotic loveliness. His whole focus was filled by images of real and very desirable females. All wore revealing and skimpy clothing, and all looked beautiful and amazingly attractive.

To Declin's consternation, the scene caused him an instant involuntary erection. This had never happened to him before and he was appalled and broke into a sweat of anxiety, hoping that none of them would notice.

Young Billy was with them, and he saw Declin first and smiled. Declin was unsure what to do, but then Carol turned and her face lit up with a smile.

She waved and called in a cheerful voice, "Hi Declin! Are you off to work?"

Declin gave a half smile in return and shook his head. "No, just going for a walk to keep fit. I do too much sitting in this job," he replied, burning with jealous resentment as he did.

He passed on behind them, heading for the mill and the group strolled on across the park. As Declin walked on, he heard the girl with the back hair say, "Who's he?"

"Just a young bloke who works at the mill. He operates the computers," Carol answered. That hurt to hear but Declin rationalised that she could not say more.

She doesn't even know I adore her, he told himself.

He continued on towards the mill, his body and mind in a ferment. From time to time he glanced back to see where the group was going. Thus he watched them go past the play equipment and the old loco and saw the busty blonde point on along the road. He did not hear what was said but it was obvious they had decided to follow it. Just watching the happy group laughing, joking, and teasing as they strolled along the road that ran northwest between the mill and the workers houses set Declin ablaze with envy. And seeing Carol still holding hands with Graham was the worst part of it.

By then Declin was near the mill offices and he realised he had to decide where to go next. As he wasn't rostered on for work until the next day, and he knew it would look odd to go in there, he detoured to the left to go around between the manager's houses and the mill. He decided to go to his secret spot to reflect.

They are going the other way so I should be alone, he told himself.

So, nursing his jealous misery and his aroused and out of control body, he made his way to the creek bank and down to his secret fishing spot. But he was in no mood to fish. Instead, he just sat and brooded. A few tears of self-pity crept out and he again wondered if he shouldn't leave and go to another town and get a new job.

And then his emotions received an even worse battering as he heard laughter and girls giggling and saw the whole group emerge from the long grass onto the little beach.

They must have walked right up to the bridge and come back along the other road. But surely they aren't going for a swim?

But, to his stunned amazement, the girls and Billy all began stripping off. Even those fabulously beautiful and desirable girls began to undress, albeit with a lot of embarrassed giggling.

At least they made those two horrible lecherous boys turn their backs! he thought, grinding his teeth in fury.

And it got worse. Little Billy pulled down his shorts and dashed into the water. Declin saw the girls all look and he saw blushes mottle the necks and cheeks of Carol and the blonde.

Then Kirsty peeled off her clothes and stood there jumping up and down, quite nude and looking very cute. "Come on!" she cried, wading in after Billy.

"Don't get your hair wet!" Carol called. "We don't want mum to know we have been swimming."

Declin did not hear the next exchanges but he gathered that Graham had suggested that he and his friend go away. To Declin's chagrin and surprise the girls all shook their heads. There was some banter and giggling but then they all began undressing. Declin really did not want Carol exposing her loveliness to anyone but he could think of no way to stop her. He could only stare in shameful misery as she reached down and pulled off her shift, revealing that she wore nothing under it. Declin was shocked and gaped and then blushed furiously and thought of going away so he could not see.

But emotional forces had him in their grip and he stayed to watch, his own body aroused by the sheer erotic quality of what he was seeing. Now lust really surged and Declin stared in heated arousal, his breath coming in urgent gasps.

Then his feelings got another horrible jolt when Graham and the boy with glasses called on the girls not to look and then both undressed.

Jealous hurt engulfed Declin and he wept with rage and had to master the urge to rush over there and assault Graham. The one with the glasses, Stephen he now learned, then took off his clothes and that angered Declin as well. And seeing young Kirsty peeking and the other girls giggling really upset him

Seeing the pair of naked boys wade in to join the girls, who were now neck deep in the water, was almost too much for Declin. Noting that the water was so clear he was sure they could all see more than they should, also upset Declin. He was sure that if they had not then moved down into the water he would have lost control, probably with violent consequences.

Then Declin heard voices up in the long grass and Betty and her sister

Rosie walked into view. Betty grinned and called loudly and waved. Soon, as Declin thought she might, she began peeling off her tight white shorts.

After some banter with the boys, Betty then slid off her T-shirt. Declin found the sight of those large boobs incredibly arousing and, feeling almost overwhelmed by lust, he watched as Betty and her little sister Rosie stripped. His heart thumped and his mouth went dry.

So aroused was Declin that he remained very tense, balanced on his branch among the leaves. But suddenly he was assailed by a cramp in his calf muscles. Quickly he changed position with his feet but then slipped. As he fell, he managed to grab another branch. Through his mind flashed the awful prospect of his secret being shamefully revealed and he clung on desperately, swinging down in full view of them from the bottom branch.

Driven by fear, Declin used all his strength to haul himself back up onto the branch and then back among the sheltering leaves. To his relief, he saw that his presence had not been detected. It seemed everyone was focused on Betty, who barely covered herself as she waded in, a saucy grin on her face. Declin he kept looking in lustful wonder, now tinged by shame.

Carol then moved across and appeared to cuddle up to Graham. Once again, jealousy surged in Declin and for the first time he understood the concept of a 'killing rage' and realised that he might not be the quiet, gentle person he had always thought himself to be.

Betty introduced herself and then swam over and put her arms around Stephen's neck and kissed him, very obviously pressing her bosom against him as she did. She then ended up in his arms with one of her arms around his neck. That got Declin speculating about what might have gone on at the party the previous night. It was nearly all too much for Declin, and he sobbed in emotional distress.

And then Declin saw Betty's father appear at the end of the track and anxiety immediately over-rode his arousal.

Oh no! This is bad! he thought.

Betty's father was a big brute of a man with a beer belly and fat, ugly face. And he was angry.

"Betty, you little slut! Get out of there and get home!" he shouted. Then pointing at Rosie, "And you, you little minx! Get out and get home!"

Heart in mouth out of fear that there might be real violence and anxious that Carol be safe Declin stared and held his breath. Stephen turned to face Betty's father while all the other girls sank lower so that only their heads were showing. Betty and Rosie both splashed quickly ashore, both sobbing and obviously frightened.

Oh my God! This is bad. They are in trouble now! Declin thought. *I must help!*

He wasn't sure how, but he was now so overwrought that he just scrambled back onto the bank and went running up the track, casting fearful glances back as he did.

He saw Betty's father's glaring face suffuse bright red as he shouted and smacked Betty hard on her wobbling, white bum as she ran past.

"You shameless little slut!" he screamed. "Get dressed and get home!"

Declin then lost sight of them as he ran up the track through the long grass. Sobbing with emotion he turned left at the top and raced along the gravel road to the top of the other track and went down it. As he ran, he could hear the shouting and just hoped he would get there in time.

He heard Betty's father shout, obviously at Stephen. "If you've done anything to my little girl you bastard I'll get the police! You'll regret it."

To Declin's surprise and admiration, Stephen answered him quite calmly. "We are just having a swim," he said.

"Swim you call it! Fornication I call it! I will get the police onto you!"

By then Declin was getting glimpses over the top of the long grass and he saw Betty's father shaking his fist at Stephen. By then a weeping Betty had her undies on and was pulling up her shorts.

"No you won't!" she screamed. "If you get my friends into trouble I'll tell them about you and mum!"

To Declin, it looked that Betty's father went even redder in the face, verging on purple.

"You do and you'll regret it," he snarled.

"Then don't call the police," Betty snapped back. She was obviously recovering from her surprise and was getting angry.

Then Declin arrived on the beach and skidded to a stop, to be confronted by astonished and anxious looks from everyone. For a few seconds there was a sort of frozen tableau and then Betty's father turned and glowered at him.

"Who are you? What the fuck do you want?"

For a few moments Declin did not know what to do or say. Then he shook his head. "Leave them alone! They're just having a swim," he lied, determined to save Carol.

At that he noted Carol give him a surprised and shocked look. But it was Betty's father who spoke first.

"Who are you and what are you doing here?" he snarled.

Declin realised he could not admit he had been watching. *Carol will despise me as a pervert if I do,* he thought.

So he lied again, pointing back up the creek bank. "We can hear you at the mill! I heard the shouting and thought someone was in trouble, so I came to help."

"Well nobody needs your help, so piss off!" shouted Betty's father, waving his huge fist in Declin's face.

Declin was scared and knew he would get bashed if it came to a fight, but he was determined. So he stood his ground and looked around.

"Is everyone alright?" he managed to say.

As he did, he noted that all the teenagers had lowered themselves so that only their heads were out of the water. Little Billy was standing waist deep looking scared. Rosie was struggling into her shorts and Betty had hers on and had straightened up when he had come running down. Now she turned and bent to pick up her top.

"Piss off!" Betty's father shouted at Declin.

At that Betty turned and said, "He was just trying to help!"

Before Declin realised what he intended, Betty's father stepped forward and punched Betty in the head, sending her sprawling hard on her bum, her boobs bouncing wildly as she fell. Anger surged in Declin and he reached out and grabbed at Betty's father, who had moved to kick at her.

Betty's father's response was to whirl around and punch him. The blow struck Declin full in the chest and half winded him. He went to defend himself, but Betty's father was faster. His boot came up between Declin's legs and hit his testicles. Searing agony lanced through Declin and he clutched at himself and doubled up. Betty's father began to kick at him, and Declin curled into a ball and tried to protect himself.

"Leave him alone, you bully!" shrieked Carol.

By then Declin was down on the sand and shuddering as waves of terrible pain stabbed through him but he saw, to his astonishment, Carol came splashing up out of the water, shouting and waving her fists.

Carol stood between Declin and Betty's astonished father. Declin looked up and saw that his eyes were goggling at Carol's nakedness. So was he but then nausea engulfed him, and he rolled over and vomited.

He heard Betty's father shout, "You keep out of this, missy! It's none of your business!"

"It is! He's a friend of mine, and you have no right to bash him. If you hit him again, I'll have the police charge you with assault," Carol screamed back.

There was more splashing and, as he rolled onto his front, Declin saw that Graham, also still naked, had come wading up to stand beside Carol, his fists raised. That caused Declin to grudgingly admit that maybe Graham wasn't all bad.

At least he's got some guts!

Betty's father wasn't amused, and his mottled face looked even uglier. He shook his fist at Graham, "You get dressed you disgusting little bastard! I don't want my little girls polluted by seeing crude things like that." He gestured to Graham's genitals.

At which Betty, who had been crouching holding her face, sneered and retorted, "So why do you keep waving your ugly great slug at us at home? Why do make me undress for those dirty old men?"

At that Declin thought Betty's father would completely lose control. He gabbled and spluttered and then shouted, "You keep quiet you little moll, or it will be the worse for you!"

"So stop calling me names," Betty screamed back.

By then the waves of agony had begun to subside but Declin still couldn't get up. All he could do was watch as Stephen, also naked, strode up to stand near Graham.

Betty's father scowled at him but shook his fist at Betty, "Shut up. Shut your mouth if you know what's good for you!"

Carol now spoke again. "Leave her alone. You hit her and I will have the police charge you with child abuse!"

Betty's father turned and glared at her, his gaze running up and down her naked body which she defiantly made no attempt cover.

"You're just a little trollop too! I'll tell your dad."

That threat chilled Declin but it was Betty who spoke next. "You do and I'll tell the police about you and mum and the gambling you and those people do out the back after the pub is shut."

"Shut up!" Betty's father shrieked. But he then shook his head. "You just get dressed and get home. Rosie, get home, now, this minute!"

Both Betty and Rosie pulled on their tops and then their thongs. A sobbing Rosie went running up the track and Betty went to follow.

As she did, Carol called to her. "Betty, you tell me if he hits either of you. If he does, I will report this all to the police." She then turned to Betty's angry father. "You hear me mister? You hurt them and I will report you. And don't you tell my father any stories either."

Betty's father scowled and did not reply to her. Instead he swore and shook his fist at Graham and Stephen.

"You little bastards keep away from my daughters! If I see you with them again I'll cut your cocks off!"

With that he turned and went lumbering up the track behind his daughters. A sort of collective shudder ran through the group as he went out of sight. By then Declin was able to straighten up but still could not stand. He simply could not believe how much the kick had hurt and how much it had disabled him. Now he could only stare up at the naked teenagers who stood around him and feel ashamed of his failing and weakness.

To add to this, Carol crouched down and bent over him. "Are you alright, Declin?" she queried.

Declin nodded and wiped his lips. "Yes, it just hurts," he croaked.

To add to his misery he could not help seeing her nude form in all its intimate detail. And, to add insult to injury, those of his rivals!

Carol patted him and stroked his face. "Thanks for coming to help. That was very brave of you," she said.

That helped. Declin tore his gaze from her body and looked into her eyes. "I hope you don't get into trouble," he said.

Carol shrugged and then stood up, apparently oblivious to the fact that she was still naked. "I don't think he will. What a nasty piece of work!" she said.

"It certainly sounds like he is doing some disgusting things with his daughters," Rosemary called.

Carol now took charge. "You boys look away while us girls get dressed," she commanded.

Declin rolled away to allow them to dress without him looking (although heaven knows he wanted to!). Instead he found himself watching the boys as they stood with their backs to the girls and pulled on their shorts. The girls all waded ashore and quickly dressed.

For the next few minutes Declin lay there, trembling and occasionally shuddering as misery and emotion flowed through him. Then he painfully struggled to his feet. He had trouble straightening up and was concerned to feel stabs of pain still emanating from his testicles.

I hope there isn't any permanent damage, he thought.

By then all the group were dressed. They stood there looking anxious while waiting for Billy to finish dressing. Declin found himself exchanging wary looks with a hostile Graham.

When everyone was dressed, Carol came over and studied Declin's face. "You sure you're alright?" she asked.

"Yes. Still hurts a bit but I'll be alright," he replied, blushing at the nature of his injury. To end it he muttered, "Anyway, you are safe. I had better get back up to the mill."

He turned and started walking up the track, but Carol hurried after him and called, "Declin!"

"Yes?"

"Thank you! It was very brave." With that she leaned forward and gave him a little kiss on the cheek. "Don't tell on us, please," she asked, her eyes pleading.

Declin was nearly overcome with emotion. "That's alright. I'd fight anyone to keep you safe. I won't tell anyone," he croaked in reply.

"Oh that's sweet!" Carol whispered.

"I think you are the most wonderful girl. I adore you!" Declin whispered back.

Then he blushed and turned to hurry up the track.

Chapter 18

ANXIETY

Graham did not hear what Carol and Declin said before he limped away up the track, but it bothered him.

He's sweet on her, he decided, noting the expression on Declin's face.

And the fact that she had intervened to stop him being assaulted was also food for thought, as was the peck on the cheek she gave him.

When Carol had run up out of the water to stop Betty's father kicking Declin, Graham had been astonished. Concerned that she might also be hit he had moved up beside her, anxiously aware that he was still naked. And the fact that she had dared to just confront such a big, angry man while herself stark naked was also a revelation.

And she didn't seem to care that Declin could see everything too, he thought, a niggle of anxiety and jealousy worming in his brain. *She has certainly got guts!*

By the time they were all dressed and Declin had gone, they all begun to talk rapidly as the tension eased.

"What will that man do, do you think?" Rowena asked.

Carol shook her head. "Nothing, I reckon. I think Betty has got something over him," she replied.

Rosemary glanced up the track. "It sounds like that Betty is being abused or something," she suggested.

From the look on Carol's face Graham deduced that she did not care much about what might be happening to Betty. But he was appalled at what had been implied. But more importantly for him was anxiety about word of the incident reaching Carol's father.

That could get me into trouble and end the relationship, he thought.

Stephen picked up his glasses and put them on. "Who is that young guy?" he asked Carol.

"Declin. He's a worker at the mill," she replied.

"You were pretty matey with him just then," Stephen observed, echoing Graham's thoughts.

Carol shrugged. "I've met him a few times. He plays with Billy and

Kirsty sometimes. I think he's just a young man who's lonely and away from home for the first time," she said.

"He likes you," Ailsa observed.

Carol made a wry face and shrugged again and did not answer. She glanced at Graham, and he got another niggle of envy.

She does like him, he thought. He wanted to say that Declin was too old for her but decided that might be poor tactics and expose his anxiety to her and everyone else.

At Carol's urging the group made their way up to the gravel road and she led the way back along it towards her house. The incident had changed the whole mood of the group and several times Graham shivered as the tension eased out of him. But it had been such an intense experience that his mind kept reliving it, particularly the images of the girls. He realised he did not know much about Carol at all and now wondered if they were at all suited. But there was no doubt he really admired her.

As reaction set in, Graham felt sick as the anxiety built up. His main concern was of Mr Battersby learning they had been swimming nude. Therefore he was very relieved when they reached the back gate to Carol's house and she stopped and said very forcefully to Kirsty and Billy.

"Don't you tell mum and dad we've been swimming, or anyone else. Promise please." Both did, and Carol added, "And don't tell anyone about Betty and her dad either. Now, let's just pretend nothing has happened and go in and have lunch."

And that is what they tried to do. Graham suspected that Mrs Battersby could tell that something was wrong, but she did not ask and lunch developed into a pleasant affair. Stephen kept exchanging glances and Graham badly wanted to discuss the whole weekend with him but did not get a chance. Just as they were finishing lunch, Mr and Mrs Bell arrived to pick them up.

After introductions, Stephen's mother asked, "Did you have a good weekend?"

Stephen smiled and nodded, then glanced at the girls. "Yes, really great," he replied.

Mrs Bell turned to Carol's mother. "I hope he wasn't any trouble."

"None at all. He was very well behaved," Mrs Battersby replied.

At which Stephen grinned and had the good grace to blush, as did Graham and the girls.

Then Ailsa's parents arrived to collect the three girls and there was more social chit chat by the adults and more embarrassed squirming by the teenagers. All in all it was nearly 2:30pm before Graham and Stephen loaded their gear into the Bell's car.

As they did, Carol's mother said, "Are you still coming to the Chamber Music next Saturday after your cadet parade, Graham?"

"Ye,s Mrs Battersby. I would like to," he replied, glancing at Carol and getting an encouraging smile in return.

His spirits got another boost when Carol said, "See you tomorrow then."

"Yeah, see you," Graham agreed.

Now he felt more hopeful, quite what of he wasn't sure, but at least the incidents had not caused them any problems.

* * *

At home, Graham went to the kitchen to say hello to his mother.

"Well, how was the party? Who was there?" Kylie intervened.

Graham managed to list most of the people, ending lamely with, "And some local kids I don't know." At which he had searing images of naked Betty form in his brain, causing him to blush.

Kylie noticed this immediately and said, "Oooh look at him go red! Well, did you sneak out with Carol and do a bit of smooching?" she demanded to know.

Again Graham suffered heated memories, in this case of him and Carol being naked down at the creek and he went even redder, try as he might to stop it.

Kylie watched closely and then shook her head. "Oh he did, Mum. Look how red he's gone! He's been sneaking out to kiss that Carol."

At that Mrs Kirk shook her head. "That's enough, Kylie! It's what boys and their girlfriends do. Now stop picking on your brother and go and finish your homework. You too, Graham."

Kylie stamped her foot. "Oh Mum, it's Margaret he should be kissing. I'd approve then," she cried. But she did as she was told and left the room.

Graham hurried away too, annoyed with his sister and also bothered by niggling guilt over Margaret.

I like her, he told himself, *but she doesn't own me.*

He then went to tell himself that he couldn't imagine swimming in the nude with Margaret when he experienced more arousing memories of the half dozen times when he had done just that, with her enthusiastic participation.

"Oh bugger girls!" he grumbled as he made his way to his worktable on the enclosed front veranda that was also his bedroom.

* * *

Graham woke with his whole being in a tingling, semi-frustrated state of arousal and anticipation. This was tinged by anxiety over whether Carol might now regret what she had done or whether her parents had been told. The ugly threats by Betty's dad kept swirling to the surface of his worries.

He went to school hopeful and scared. His main aim was to meet with Carol and to find out how their relationship now stood. But he also wanted to talk to Stephen. Initially he got no chance to do either as Carol was with other girls, and while she gave a friendly wave she made no move to join him. Also, when Graham found Stephen there were other friends there, including Peter and Roger. The best Graham could do was return Stephen's grin.

The topic of conversation was a dramatic rescue some of the Air Cadets had been involved in during the weekend. Chief of these was Willy Williams who even had his photo on the front page of the newspaper, standing in front of an aircraft Graham recognised as a vintage Catalina flying boat.

When Willy came walking by, Stephen waved and called him over. "Hey Willy, tell us all about it," he said.

Willy joined them and proceeded to tell his tale. While he talked three navy cadets joined them: Andrew Collins, Arthur Blake, and Luke Karaku, a Torres Strait Islander.

By the time Willy had finished his story, more students had joined the group. Among them was red-haired Barbara Brassington from Year 9. Graham smiled a welcome and thought she was everything he dreamed off: intelligent, strong-willed, beautiful, long-legged, slim-waisted, and with very prominent boobs.

Graham noted Willy's girlfriend, Marjorie, walking towards him. On reaching the group, Marjorie pushed through and slid in to sit beside Willy, squashing hard against him as she did. No one seemed to notice, their relationship was so well known they were treated like an old married couple.

Willy finished his tale and pointed to a magazine that Stephen had been reading. "What's that?"

"A magazine about vintage aircraft," Stephen answered. "It's got some really interesting articles about old, restored planes and replicas, and there is a really good one about plane wrecks in North Queensland from World War Two."

The title of the magazine was *Classic Wings* and it held no interest for Graham. He looked around, wondering where Carol was.

Willy called to him, "What's the matter Graham, are you still wondering how we caught all you army cadets on that field exercise a few weeks ago?"

Graham scowled. That was still a sore point and at that moment he resented being teased. Suddenly, Graham spotted Carol walking on her own. He immediately stood up and pushed his way past Andrew and walked off.

He caught up with Carol over near the tuckshop. To his relief, she turned and waited for him and then gave him a big smile.

"Did you enjoy the weekend?" she queried.

"Loved it," Graham answered. "It was fantastic. Thank you."

Carol's face dimpled into a mischievous grin. "You just liked swimming in the nuddy with the girls," she suggested.

"I did!" Graham replied enthusiastically, noting Ailsa in the group beyond. "But I really liked being with you."

"That's sweet of you," Carol commented.

Heartened by this Graham grinned. "I hope you weren't offended?"

"Not at all. I liked seeing you and Steve on the weekend."

That was also a bit of a revelation to Graham, and he shrugged. He blushed and wondered what to say next. Luckily, he was saved from having to answer by the bell for classes.

Carol grinned and said, "See you at lunch time then."

"Yes please," Graham replied. He turned and went back to his class, his hopes soaring.

After the next bell went and the two friends walked to another class,

Stephen nudged him. "That was a fantastic weekend. I reckon it was the best in my whole life. I wish we were going to Caster again this weekend."

"Me too!" Graham replied.

Stephen grinned and winked. "You are randy as a dog with two dicks at the moment," he said, then laughed. Graham could only grunt as Stephen shook his head and said, "That swim with those naked chicks was the horniest thing I have ever done and Betty was the icing on the cake. I hope we can get there again. She's hot stuff that Betty!"

Graham felt a mixture of jealousy and concern. "You better be careful, Steve."

Stephen shrugged. "I won't. She is on the pill."

"At her age!" Graham cried.

He was astonished. Then images of naked Betty and of Stephen caused him to blush in jealous embarrassment.

Stephen shrugged again. "So she told me. Anyway, I've agreed to go to Beck's Air Museum to look at vintage aircraft. Sorry, you'll have to go on your own."

That set the pattern for the whole week. Driven by an almost frantic urge to be with Carol, Graham carefully raised the subject when neither Alex nor Kylie were present that evening.

"Mum, could I go to Caster again this Sunday?" he asked.

To his intense disappointment, she shook her head. "No you may not! We have arranged to go to Mareeba to see Grandma Cynthia and Grandad Bert. You will have to put your romance on hold for a few days. Besides, don't you see this Carol at school every day?"

"Yes Mum," Graham agreed, his disappointment so sharp he had to battle to hold back tears. And then he remembered what Stephen had said, and added, "Then while we are in Mareeba can we go to see Beck's Air Museum?"

"If we have time maybe. Why? What's the reason?"

Graham explained that Willy and Stephen were going there for a visit and his mother looked doubtful and then said, "We will see. Maybe for a half hour or so."

Graham had to be satisfied with this and took himself off to study and complete his homework. Then he went to bed to again almost be overwhelmed by erotic images of naked girls.

* * *

The only time he was quite free of erotic urges was during the Cadet Home Training Parade on the Wednesday afternoon. Here Graham was so focused he had no thought for anything else. He was determined to do the very best he could to make the parade a success.

This time Graham was able to march properly and take part in all the activities without any problems. But there was a problem that Capt Conkey had to solve: Sgt Crane had again asked to be put back in the Flag Party. To Graham's anxious satisfaction, Capt Conkey shook his head at this request and Sgt Crane was told he must act as 3 PL sergeant. He accepted this with bad grace. The rehearsal went ahead but to Graham's eyes the company needed a lot more practice before trying to perform in public.

During the Admin Parade at the start of the activity Graham was able to do all the drill with only a few twinges in his ankle. That pleased him and he ignored the grumbles from cadets who still resented him being appointed as their platoon sergeant. The sergeants gave their reports one by one to the CSM. He then handed the parade over to the OC, Captain Conkey.

Captain Conkey fell the Cadet Under-Officers in and then stood the company at ease. After talking administration for a few minutes, he reminded the cadets that the selection list for the December Promotion Courses would go up after the Passing-Out Parade that weekend.

"This is a test of loyalty. To make the parade look good we need numbers. If you don't turn up, I will move your name to the bottom of the list or off it," Capt Conkey said.

Graham heartily agreed with that sentiment. *If they can't be bothered to turn up for an important event like the Passing-Out Parade they aren't worth promoting,* he thought. Then he chewed his lip with anxiety. *I hope I still get selected to attend the Warrant Officers Course.*

The parade rehearsal then went ahead, and Graham was pleased with the Flag Party drill and his part in it. *We should be alright on Saturday,* he told himself.

Thursday turned out to be a frustrating day. Graham did not get a chance to sit and talk to Carol as she spent both breaks in the Home Economics room baking and icing a cake. That put him in a grumpy mood and he discovered an equally moody Andrew walking around on his own because Tina was also in the Home Economics room.

"Let's go and see what the gang are doing," Andrew suggested.

So the two boys walked to where their friends usually sat, to arrive just as Stephen said, "I don't make the rules. Anyway, who is coming to Beck's Air Museum next Sunday? I need to telephone to let them know we are coming."

Willy was there and immediately said yes and explained that he would take Marjorie and Stick with him.

"What time are we all meeting up then?" Stephen asked.

It was agreed that 2:00pm would be a suitable time. Andrew raised his eyebrows and asked, "What is this all about?"

"Steve's got as bee in his bonnet about old aircraft wrecks," Willy replied.

They discussed World War 2 B24 crashes and Willy provided some details. Stick then mentioned the 'Airacobras' which crash-landed all over Cape York in 1942.

At that Graham sat up and was interested. He said, "My Grandfather was involved in that. He was the captain of a small ship taking supplies to the airbases up in the Cape and he told me he took several air force work parties to the wrecks to take out the guns, radios and instruments, and engines and so on. There are even some old photos he took somewhere at home."

Willy immediately looked very interested. "Do you think you could find them?"

"I suppose so. Grandad has been dead for five years, but Gran might still have them," Graham answered.

Noddy Parker now said, "I heard there was the wreck of a B25 or something like that in the jungle near Babinda."

"See if you can find out more details, please," Stephen asked.

"I heard that a plane crashed up on Black Mountain back during World War Two," Stick added.

They discussed all the plane crashes they had heard about, and Graham realised there were a lot. Stephen then nudged him and said, "So you aren't going to Caster then?"

Graham shook his head. "No, damn it! Mum has made plans to go to Mareeba to see Grandad and Grandma."

Stephen made a wry face and then grinned. "Too bad! You'll just have to bottle it up till you get another chance."

"Soon I hope," Graham cried. "Anyway, I will check again if we can join you on Sunday."

"You bet! It should be interesting," Graham agreed.

"Not as interesting as seeing Rowena swimming in the nuddy!" Stephen replied, again sending Graham into arousal at the images conjured up.

At school on Friday, Graham sought out Carol to check that she was still coming to the Passing-Out Parade the following afternoon. This now became a significant source or anxiety for him.

I hope we don't muck up and I hope I do well when Carol is watching, he thought.

Chapter 19

PROGRESS?

When Graham woke on Saturday morning, he was in a state of nervous tension that got him concerned.

This is a big day. I mustn't stuff up! he told himself.

Which got him wondering what else might go wrong or who else might ruin their parade, either by mistake or intentionally. Memories of Willy's red painted model aircraft zooming down to disrupt the parade the previous year added to his anxieties.

Graham shook his head and muttered, "No, Willy wasn't responsible for that last year, so he won't do anything."

But Graham was uncomfortably aware that there were people and groups who did not approve of Cadets or anything military.

Because Cadets had a whole day activity, morning for preparation and rehearsals and parade in the afternoon, Graham had to get organised quickly. He hurried to the shower to shave. Then it was breakfast and polishing and getting ready. Next, he had to make sure his good clothes were laid out ready for the evening, and that caused more worry and more scowls from Kylie. For this Cadet activity his mother drove him, as he had his best uniformed ironed and on a coat hanger and that would have been awkward to walk with.

The whole unit was at school for the day. After the admin parade to mark the roll, they were briefed and then issued with innocuous F88 Steyr rifles and slings. These were provided by the army and were brought to the school in an army truck with two soldiers who stayed the entire day to supervise. They were both 'Queys', one middle-aged and the other in his thirties and not very fit, but they were soldiers all the same and Graham studied them with interest, having now resolved on a career in the army after he left school.

The fitting of rifle slings and some static revision of rifle drill took up the next hour, followed by a 20-minute break with cordial and biscuits. The entire unit then marched down to the oval and did a complete rehearsal. This took them through to lunch time and despite the summer heat, none of the cadets fell out. The rehearsal seemed to go well, with no obvious problems other than some of the individual drill not being very good.

Lunch followed, up under the shade of the main school buildings. There was then a uniform check, particularly to ensure all the Hats KFF were being worn at the correct angle (tilted to the right front, one finger width above the right eye). Embellishments were then issued: woven unit lanyards (in school colours of blue and white) were placed on right shoulders and checked.

Then scarlet sashes were issued to the CSM and sergeants. For Graham, that was a moment of particular pride and he glowed with a sense of achievement, ignoring the jealous and resentful looks and murmured comments from his rivals and enemies. The members of the Flag Party were also issued with white gloves and as he tugged them on Graham felt very proud. By then he was in a state of heightened awareness and was fretting about whether Carol would actually come to watch the parade.

She did, but she was not the first girl he noticed when the unit made its way down to the oval at 1600hrs. First, he saw Margaret and she gave him a smile and a hopeful look, and he could not resist smiling back. Kylie was next to her and gave him an admiring look and a smile as well. The girls were with their mothers and Graham was glad of that. He would have liked his dad to be there to witness his moment of glory in the Flag Party, but as a ship captain he was at sea somewhere in the Gulf of Carpentaria.

In fact, Graham did not see Carol until the activity was underway. By then he was standing at the side while the section demonstrations went on and he had just marvelled at the size of the crowd that had gathered. He estimated that between three hundred and four hundred parents, friends and family had come to watch the event.

As he stood there scanning the crowd, Graham also noted a couple of clusters of white uniforms and blue uniforms: the Navy Cadets and Air Cadets who had come to watch the parade. Knowing that rivals would be critically evaluating their every move caused another little spurt of worry to Graham.

We'd better not stuff up! They will never let us live it down if we do! he thought.

While he waited, Graham noted Lieutenant Hamilton, who had been walking along greeting people stop and speak to an Air Cadet. It was Willy and Graham saw him stand up and self-consciously salute.

Lt Hamilton returned the salute then spoke to Willy, who appeared to shake his head and blush before replying.

Lt Hamilton must be warning Willy not to spoil our parade, Graham deduced.

He watched Willy sit down and then noticed that he was with his parents and his girlfriend Marjorie. Graham was also pleased to note that Andrew, his sister Carmen, Tina, and a couple of other Navy Cadets were there in uniform. Seeing Tina caused a few moments of regret.

The actual passing-out parade began a few minutes later. The VIPs: Captain Conkey, the Principal, Mr Croswell, an army Lieutenant Colonel who was the Reviewing Officer, two Air Cadet Officers, two officers from the Navy Cadets, and a few other civilian dignitaries moved to the front row of seats and the displays began. Captain Conkey then took over, speaking over the PA system to the parents. As he did, Graham remembered that, in his youth, Captain Conkey had been a regular soldier and had fought in the jungles of Southeast Asia. The row of bright medals hanging from their coloured ribbons pinned to the left side of his shirt showed that. Seeing his teacher wearing the army ceremonial uniform gave Graham a feeling of pride and hero worship.

He then watched the section competition, noting that Roger, a lance corporal in Number 4 Section, was doing a very effective job of leadership. Stephen commanded 6 Section and was obviously capable and Peter, in charge of the HQ Signals Section, had his group functioning very well. Graham also admired Barbara as she stood in her section behind Gwen. For a few moments he focused on Barbara.

Should I ever ask her for a date?

He could not decide and then felt guilty at being disloyal to Carol. Once again, he looked to where Carol and her mother sat and hoped he was making progress.

The section displays began, two races between the sections. The first race was to carry out First Aid on a 'snakebite' victim and get them on an improvised stretcher quickly (1 minute and 15 seconds for the winners!). The second race was much more entertaining and involved the sections erecting a shelter using only two broom handles, some thin rope, six pegs and two Shelters Individual.

To Graham's annoyance,e both races were won by 2 Section. The company then moved off for a drink, being very hot and humid, even at 4:45pm, and then to prepare for the formal ceremonial parade. The Flag Party remained in position, ready, Lt McEwen bringing them cups of cold mango cordial.

Graham really enjoyed the parade. With considerable satisfaction he watched his friends trying their very best to do their drill. When it was the turn of the Flag Party to march on, Graham tried his very hardest, sweating with anxiety and effort. He was so focused he did not dare glance sideways to see if Carol was watching him. To his relief, no-one in the flag party made any mistakes as they marched into position. Graham felt very proud as he marched beside the CUO carrying the Australian flag. Part of his mind settled with a vow to defend his country's flag, to the death if necessary.

Then there was the 'Present Arms' for the National Anthem and then another for the Reviewing Officer. This was followed by the inspection. Graham was able to relax a little, even though the Flag Party remained at attention throughout. Thus he was able to look at Carol. He saw she was smiling at him, and they gained eye contact. Seeing her there sent his spirits up even more and he felt puffed up with pride. And he was very conscious that with almost every movement he made, out of the corner of his eye, he could see that scarlet sash across his chest and that made him even prouder.

I have really achieved something this year, he thought.

The unit then did a march past and an 'Advance in Review Order', followed by a speech by the Reviewing Officer. After the speech was the presentation of prizes. To Graham's complete surprise, his name was called out to get the award for Best Junior NCO, it being explained that he won the award while still a corporal. Sgt Crane had to march over and take his place in the flag escort. As he did, there was muttering and Graham heard the word 'sniveller' but he was so pleased he just shrugged the jealousy off. He marched over and halted in front of the colonel and snapped his very best butt salute, then pushed the rifle back on its sling to shake hands and take the shield that was the prize.

He had to pose for a photo, then stepped back and braced up to salute before doing a left turn and marching over to where Lt Standish was standing beside a table to receive the prize. As he marched across,

Graham found his eyes locked with Margaret's and she looked so happy and proud that he had to smile back. That made her clap even more and only then did Graham remember that Carol was watching.

Now worrying about how he looked marching, he made his way back around to the rear of the parade and re-joined the Flag Party. "I was sure Peter would win that," he muttered as he stepped sideways to replace Sgt Crane. In reply, Crane just gave a surly grunt.

Graham had to fall out again for a 'Best Attendance' award, but he was expecting that so had less trouble. And this time he made sure he looked towards Carol as he returned to his place.

Just as the sun was dipping behind the mountains to the west, the unit farewelled the Reviewing Officer and then marched off to where the army truck was parked. After falling out the Flag with due ceremony, rifles were handed back. Graham regretted that as he really felt good carrying a real rifle. The whole experience confirmed him in his decision to join the army as a career.

When all the rifles and swords had been returned and accounted for, the red sashes, gloves, and lanyards were handed back. It was with real regret that Graham peeled off that scarlet sash. To him it had become a symbol of hope and achievement.

I can do this and I'm good at it! he thought with deep satisfaction.

While this was being done Graham saw cadets clustering to peer at a nearby noticeboard. *That will be the list of who is going on the Promotion Course,* he thought, hurrying over to have a look.

Even though he had been told he was selected for the Warrant Officers Course, there was still that niggling doubt. But there was no mistake. A quick glance showed his as the only name listed for the WOs Course.

And Pete and Steve have been selected for the Sergeants Course and Roger for the Corporals Course.

That was good news, and he quickly went to congratulate them.

There were then work parties to return chairs to the hall and to clean up the area. This all took twenty minutes. Captain Conkey then thanked the unit for a splendid parade, and they were dismissed. Along with most of the other cadets, Graham made his way back to where tables had been set up with refreshments for the families and friends. And he immediately walked into an embarrassing situation. As he walked with Stephen and

Roger, Margaret appeared. She ran up to Graham and for a moment he thought she was going to throw her arms around him and kiss him. He was sure that was what she wanted to do, and he broke into a sweat of anxiety about what Carol might think if she saw that.

Margaret's eyes sparkled and she bubbled with enthusiasm and pride as she congratulated him. He had to grin back and even took her hands for a moment. Luckily Kylie arrived next, and she did hug him and it was at that moment Carol and her mother arrived.

Carol raised an eyebrow and then smiled and offered her hand to shake congratulations. Perversely, Graham was glad she didn't hug him as he knew that would really hurt Margaret's feelings. But Carol did give him a quick peck on the cheek and then place her hand on his arm in a possessive way.

Then the Air Cadets arrived. Willy, Marjorie and her brother Stick came and offered their congratulations. Graham felt extremely pleased.

They were joined by several Navy Cadets, resplendent in their dress whites. These included Andrew Collins, his big sister Carmen, and Tina Babcock, Andrew's girlfriend. For a few minutes they discussed the differences between the drill done by each service.

Stephen joined them. "What are we doing tonight?"

To Willy's embarrassment, Marjorie giggled. That made the others all look from him to her, then grin. Willy blushed and Marjorie went red when she realised what she had done.

He said, "We are playing board games at Marjorie's."

"Board games, eh?" Stephen said in a suggestive voice.

"Yes," Marjorie said, trying to look indignant.

Stephen turned to Graham. "What about you, Graham?"

Graham gestured to Carol and said, "We are going to the theatre."

He did not want to admit it was to a Chamber Music concert. That reminded Graham that time was an issue so he hastily made excuses and led Carol away.

But there were more challenges to meet. To start with he had to face Kylie and Margaret, both of whom had heard what he said. Graham glanced at Margaret and was sure that there were tears forming in her eyes as she struggled to hold a smile. But Kylie had pursed lips and was just hostile.

Struggling to keep his composure, Graham introduced them. "This is Kylie, my sister. She's in Year 8. And this is Margaret, her best friend. She's another Year 8."

Carol smiled at the two and nodded. "I know. I've seen you guys around the school. Nice to meet you." She then looked around and said, "There's my mum. I'd better fly if we are going to be at the theatre before seven. See you!"

With that she hurried off and Graham found himself looking into Kylie's angry eyes. Kylie pursed her lips again and watched the departing Carol.

"She needs her broom and pointy hat if she's going to fly," she muttered.

"Be fair, Kylie!" Graham retorted. "She's alright."

Kylie gave him a disbelieving look. "She's not suited to you, you'll see," she said.

At which Margaret did start to cry and hurried away. Kylie cast Graham an accusing look and hurried after her friend while Graham stood feeling all mixed up and unsure. The arrival of his mother helped solve the situation.

"Come on, Kylie, say goodnight. We have to get Graham home so he can change," Mrs Kirk called.

For a few moments Kylie hugged Margaret and talked to her, and Graham wondered if Kylie was going to indulge in some delaying tactics to sabotage his date. But then she said goodbye to Margaret and joined them, casting another scowl at Graham as she did.

The sibling friction continued in the car on the way home and again at home. Kylie kept up her attacks and Graham became quite annoyed. The real blow up came after he had hurried through the bath and changed into good clothes.

"So where are you going all dressed up?" Kylie asked.

"Out," Graham replied.

"Out where?" Kylie persisted. "Are you going to the movies?"

Feeling quite pressured Graham retorted, "No, to the theatre." The moment he said this he regretted it.

Kylie instantly seized on the information. "The theatre! You! Are you going to a play or a musical then?"

Graham blushed and wished he had not spoken. He knew Kylie often went to the theatre as she did ballet and dancing and musicals.

He blushed and muttered, "For Chamber music."

"Chamber music!" Kylie shrieked. "Give me a break! The only sort of music you like is thumping big drums and marching stuff."

At that their mother called, "That will do, Kylie, thank you."

"Oh but Mum! Chamber music! He's a real Philistine and wouldn't know a banjo from a bassoon."

Then she burst out laughing. To Graham's embarrassment, Alex had overheard this. He also laughed and then sneered.

"A bit of culture is what the little toad needs. Do him good!"

Their mother again intervened and told them to stop it. Then she looked Graham up and down.

"Yes, that should do," she said with a nod.

Alex again butted in and called, "Shouldn't he be wearing a tuxedo and bow tie?" Again he cackled with laughter and Graham burned.

"Alex!" their mother warned. "Okay, Graham, get in the car."

Graham fled, glad to escape the teasing and tormenting from his brother and sister. But the comments gave him food for thought.

Am I really like they say? he wondered.

The event suddenly loomed as more of a challenge than he had anticipated.

Chapter 20

WORRIES

Declin endured a week of fear and jealous torment. Whenever he thought of the incident down at the creek, his emotions quickly boiled and he felt consumed by a mixture of intense arousal and jealous rage. The thought of Graham and Stephen seeing Carol when she was naked hurt so much he experienced several intense pulses of rage. The desire to smash his fist into Graham's face was almost overwhelming.

There was also the problem of what to do when he encountered Carol. He wanted to see her, to be with her, but he did not want to embarrass or shame her. He could not decide on a policy, other than trying to avoid her.

Thus it was that he accidentally met her while walking to work on the following Saturday morning. She was playing with Billy on the playground in the park near the old locomotive.

Billy saw him first and came running across. "Declin! Declin! Come and steam the twain for me," he cried.

Declin smiled and then his eyes locked with Carol's. She blushed but then smiled back and he felt better.

"Only for a few minutes," he said. "I'm on my way to work."

He and Billy climbed into the cab of the small locomotive and were busy pretending to shovel coal into the firebox when Carol climbed in to join them. That surprised Declin, as he thought she would be so ashamed she would try to avoid him and wish him gone.

For a few moments the two looked into each other's eyes and then Carol said, "Sorry Declin. I didn't mean to embarrass you last weekend. Thank you for coming to save us from that horrible man."

Declin was astonished. He blushed and mumbled before getting control of his racing emotions and tongue. "That's alright. I just wish I hadn't offended you by rushing in and shaming you like that."

"You didn't shame or offend me," Carol replied. "I've been worried that I embarrassed you."

Declin could only shrug as he was embarrassed and, as the naked images of her and the other girls flooded his mind, he went bright red.

"I couldn't help looking, sorry," he muttered.

Carol shook her head and grinned. "You wouldn't be a normal male if you hadn't looked. It was my fault for being a rudey-nudey."

Now Declin was so much in emotional turmoil he could hardly think straight. Flustered, he stammered and then shook his head.

"You shouldn't take your clothes off like that," he muttered.

"Why not? I like it and the others didn't mind. The boys enjoyed it," Carol replied.

Which almost sparked an intense outburst as hot flushes of envy boiled in his mind. Once again, Declin struggled to control his jealous rage. He found he was trembling and gritting his teeth and clenching his fists.

"I'd rather you didn't," he cried. "Those boys…"

"Why Declin, you are jealous!" Carol cried. "Anyway, those boys are alright. And if you don't like me the way I am then too bad. I am not going to change."

"But I love you, Carol. I want you to be safe!" Declin cried, his emotions now spilling over into tears.

"Oh Declin! That is so sweet! I'm sorry. I didn't realise how much you cared," Carol said, reaching across to touch his cheek.

At that Declin trembled, being distracted by Billy demanding he check the steam gauges.

"I do," he muttered, knowing that with such an open declaration their relationship must now change: she must now tell him to leave or admit she liked him.

Their eyes met and she looked worried, and she also shook her head. "I do like you Declin, but…"

"But I'm too old and you already have a boyfriend," Declin finished.

"Oh, I don't know about that," Carol replied, sparking a glimmer of hope in his heart. Then she swore, upsetting his feelings some more. "Oh bugger! Here comes Kirsty. What does she want?"

"I'd better get to work," Declin said, seizing on the opportunity to ease the tension. "You keep driving the train, Billy. Look out the front and then ease the brake off and the regulator open." With that he turned and climbed down.

Carol moved to look down at him. "It'll be alright," she said. "I won't tell anyone."

"Thanks," Declin replied. Tears began to mist his eyes, so he turned and gave Kirsty a smile.

Kirsty grinned back but then called to Carol. "Come on, Carol! Mum said you have to get home and have a shower and get changed if you are going to this army cadet parade."

Declin saw Carol blush and she glanced at him. "What cadet parade?" he queried, again feeling the niggle of envy.

Carol shrugged and looked embarrassed. "Oh, Graham and his friend Stephen are army cadets and they are having their end of year ceremonial parade at the school this afternoon. Graham's getting some sort of a prize and he asked me to come."

That news further dismayed Declin and his gut twisted with jealous emotion. All he could do was nod and mutter, "Well, have a good time."

"You too. Okay Kirsty, you look after Billy. See ya Declin!" Carol called as she climbed down and hurried away.

Kirsty grumbled but climbed up into the cab to join Billy. Declin turned hastily to hide the tears that had suddenly sprung out and he then hurried off across the lawn towards the mill.

I've done it now, he thought miserably, sure that he had frightened Carol with his declaration of love.

Only to walk into another upsetting situation. As he approached the mill office, he saw Rossiter and Marvin standing just outside. It was obvious that they had been watching and Rossiter gave him a false smile and stepped across to block his path.

"Hello there, young Declin! Having a good chat were ya?" he said.

Declin nodded and tried to step around, but Marvin blocked him. Rossiter frowned, "Now that's not very friendly! We were just concerned about yer social life, boyo. Do yer like the young girls, do yer?"

The implication chilled Declin and he felt his stomach churn with a mixture of fear and nausea. "No. I was just being friendly, helping Billy drive the train," he muttered.

"So yer do like the boss's daughter, do yer eh?" Rossiter responded, giving a leering grin as he did.

"She's a nice kid," Declin replied.

"Yeah, that's right. She's a kid. So you be careful, young Declin, or people might get the wrong idea. Her dad might not take to kindly to a paedophile sniffin' around his daughters."

"It's not like that!" Declin retorted, but even as he did, he felt his stomach gripped by a sour swirl of real fear. He realised that both his reputation and his job were in peril from these horrible men.

Rossiter nodded. "Yeah well, we don't mind how yer get yer thrills, but we do mind that you do what we say, when we say. So when we say stop the mill, we mean stop the mill, get it?"

Declin 'got it', the ugly implied threat chilling him and making him feel physically sick. Trembling with emotion, he stepped past the men and hurried into the mill office to sign on. Then he exited through the back door, casting an anxious glance over his shoulder as he did, and made his way to the Control Room.

By the time he got there he was so upset he was sweating and shaking. Swallowing to keep down the bile that rose to sour his throat, he made his way up the steep steps and into the Control Room. Mr Parsons was there, and as Declin came in he turned to greet him. Then his cheerful expression changed.

"You okay?" Mr Parsons queried.

Declin could only shake his head as nausea swirled in his insides. Tears misted his eyes so that he could hardly see. With an effort he swallowed and spoke.

"Not really Mr Parsons. I... I've got an upset stomach."

Mr Parsons looked concerned and studied him. "You look a bit pasty-faced. Is it something you've eaten do you think?"

Steve Mullany, the Rail System Operator snorted and called, "More likely something he's drunk!"

That upset Declin even more as he was very scrupulous about not drinking any alcohol on days when he was rostered to work. He opened his mouth to make a defensive rebuttal but as he did the room seemed to move and he had to grab at the back of his chair. To his horror, he felt vomit rising and he gagged and turned towards the door.

He only just made it to the door before he realised he had no chance of reaching a toilet or washroom. Gripping the door post he leaned outside and spewed, the vomit cascading onto the steel grating of the deck and then dribbling and trickling down. Through tear misted eyes, Declin glimpsed upturned faces down near the tipper controls. Shame coursed through him, making him feel worse.

The upshot was that a thoroughly ashamed and embarrassed Declin was helped back to the office to the Sick Room. It was decided by the Manager, Mr Conners, that he should be taken home. That resulted in one of the office staff driving him back to the hotel. After thanking them, Declin made his way inside, noting as he did that the bar was packed and that the Irish girl was again serving as a topless barmaid. That didn't help, merely increasing his mental and emotional turmoil.

Feeling utterly miserable and drained, he groped his way up the stairs to his room and flung himself on his bed.

* * *

For a time Declin just lay there quietly sobbing and torn by a mixture of emotions: hope, jealousy and fear. But it was thoughts of Carol that got him up and moving. Knowing that she was going to Cairns to watch the army cadet parade brought back memories of her kissing Graham. Jealous images caused Declin to grind his teeth and waves of rage and despair got him clenching and unclenching his fists.

"The bastard!" Declin muttered as images of Graham flitted across his mind. "He is not fit to clean her shoes. I'd like to... to..."

Mentally he noted he had not called Graham a 'little bastard' and he realised that Graham was nearly as big as him, and looked broader in the shoulders and a good deal fitter.

And he's better looking, Declin conceded.

Another wave of self-pity engulfed him, and he lay and brooded, wondering how to retrieve the situation. So upset was he that he could not drive the jealous thoughts from his mind. He kept picturing Carol with Graham and knew it was like picking at the scab on a sore and knowing he shouldn't but not being able to stop.

And then another more chilling thought came to Declin. *Rossiter threatened that he might do something to Carol if I don't do what he said.* But what? *And how can I stop that, other than just giving in?*

From that grew the notion that he must make every effort to keep Carol safe. The 'how' niggled at him and the urge grew to watch over her, even though he knew it would only increase the pain of his jealousy if he saw that she and Graham were happy together. Knowing in his heart that it was self-torment he decided to go to Cairns to watch.

The problem then was how? He did not own a car or motorbike

and did not know anyone he might ask for a loan. But having made the decision, Declin found he could not lie there any longer. A check of his watch told him it was already nearly 2pm and he did not know what time the parade was scheduled for.

Quickly, Declin showered and changed into good casual clothes. Then he made his way downstairs, thinking to look into the bar to see if there was anyone there he knew who might be going to Cairns. In this he was luckier than he expected. As he went down the stairs, Frank and Jonny, two young mill workers who worked at the Milling Train, came out of the side door of the bar and headed for the front door. As they did, they looked up and saw him and called hello.

"You wouldn't be going to Cairns would you?" Declin asked.

"We are," Frank replied.

"Can I get a lift? I want to see the doctor," Declin lied

"Sure. Come with us," Frank answered.

So Declin climbed into the back of Frank's car and by 3:30pm was at the Cairns Hospital. He got out on the pretext of seeing a doctor, but as soon as the workers had driven away he turned and went hurrying along the footpath in the direction of the high school. It was only a few blocks but walking in the afternoon sun soon had him hot and sweaty.

As he got closer to the school, several problems raised their heads. First was a desire not to be seen by Carol as he did not want to bother her. The second was the location of the parade.

If it isn't already over!

In this Declin was lucky. As he came along a side street, he saw the school oval ahead and noted that cars were pulling in to park along the wide grassy verge outside the fence and that people who looked like parents and family were all climbing out and making their way through a gate to seats arranged at the south end of the oval. That told him that he was in time and answered the 'where?' question.

Declin paused at the corner to see if Carol and her family were in sight. In this he was again lucky as he noted their car parked amid the others and then saw her and her mother walking along the footpath towards a gate. He drew back and waited, peeking through the crotons in the garden of the house on the corner until they were inside and seated.

As soon as they were, Declin hurried across to the line of parked cars and then lingered at the side fence to the oval, keeping back so that he was behind the seated crowd. He was surprised at just how many people were present. He estimated it was several hundred and that was good as it gave him cover. He was also pleased to note that there were a few other people, young boys mostly, lounging along the fence to watch.

Good! I won't be as conspicuous, he thought.

It took him some time to locate Carol among the throng and he only managed it by recognising the hats she and her mother wore. *It looks like her dad and little Billy and Kirsty aren't coming,* he decided.

He was glad of that as he was sure Billy would have wanted to run around so Carol would have been more likely to turn around and look.

His sense of the importance of the event was further increased when he saw the group of invited guests and he recognised the mayor and the local state and federal members of parliament. There were also, as he had expected, a number of army or army cadet officers in ceremonial uniforms but Declin knew so little about the military he could not judge their rank or status. They just looked important. Seeing the brilliant white uniforms of Navy officers and Navy Cadets and the blue of Air Force uniforms added to his dismay.

This looks like a really important event, he thought, fretting that this gave his rival advantages he did not enjoy.

Declin then watched the parade with a mixture of amazement and resentment. There had been no cadets at the school he had attended and no-one in his family had ever served in any of the armed forces, so he'd had very little exposure to such events. Despite his dislike and resentment, he grudgingly admitted that the cadets did well and that it all looked good.

He was also surprised to see that many of the cadets were girls. He had not known they could join, just assuming that the army cadets would be an all-male organisation.

And some very attractive ones too! he noted as he eyed a long-legged, red-head in the front rank.

Declin's first real emotional test was when the Flag Party had marched on and he recognised Graham as one of the cadets with a red sash escorting the flag.

How can I compete with someone as good looking and confident as him? he fretted.

When Graham was called forward to receive the prize for being the

Best Junior NCO, that feeling of hopelessness deepened. Seeing him again rewarded for Best Attendance just deepened that dejection.

As the company marched off at the end of the parade, they came marching back past Declin and he stared angrily at Graham. An emotion that Declin did not like to name as hate seethed in him. Again he ground his teeth in jealous frustration.

And then Declin realised he should have moved because most of the crowd had turned to watch the cadets march away and for a few seconds he clearly saw Carol. She was looking in his direction as the rear of the marching column went past.

I'd better move, or she might see me, Declin thought.

Quickly he turned and moved out of sight behind a tree. Declin stayed near the tree, glad that some people were now making their way out their cars so he could mingle with them. He kept note of where Carol and her mother were and when they moved up into the school area to where the parents and friends and the invited dignitaries and officers were crowding around tables with cakes and sandwiches.

Despite the risk of being seen, Declin moved to where he could still observe. There he remained watching as the cadets came back from handing back their rifles and returning chairs. Then he found it difficult to recognise Graham when he joined the crowd. There were so many male cadets, all looking similar that Declin was irritated. Then he saw a dark-haired girl rush up and throw her arms around a male cadet and then others lean forward to shake his hand. It was only when he saw Carol arrive and then lean forward and give the male cadet a kiss on the cheek that Declin realised the boy was Graham.

Declin watched enviously as Carol stood with her hand on Graham's arm while other cadets, including some from the Navy Cadets and Air Cadets, came to offer congratulations or to talk.

And then Carol and her mother turned and began walking quickly towards Declin. He had to hastily retreat. Walking quickly away from them, he hurried off along the footpath and managed to get out of sight behind an SUV before they came out the gate. Feeling quite demoralised, he watched them get into their car and drive off.

The whole event thoroughly depressed Declin as he felt sure he could not compete with a younger, fitter, better looking male who appeared to be so confident and capable.

And then he realised he had the problem of getting back to Caster! It was getting on for 6:30pm by then and he knew the last bus left at 7pm. To catch it he had to walk as fast as he could in the humid tropical evening to get to the bus depot at the City Wharves in time.

Luckily, he made it with a couple of minutes to spare so he could manage a quick visit to the toilet before hurriedly boarding the coach. By then he was tired, hungry, thirsty, and thoroughly depressed.

* * *

All the way back to Caster, Declin brooded and considered his options. He felt sure he had dished his chances with Carol but felt a deep sense of obligation to keep her safe. That got him thinking about his fears and the threats from Rossiter and his gang. Declin was sure they were a gang and that made it hard to consider running away when the gang had said they knew who his family were and where they lived. It was sickening stuff. And what to do if Rossiter asked him to cause a stoppage at the mill?

Still undecided and feeling utterly wretched, Declin stepped off the coach at Caster and watched it drive on south into the darkness. Then he sighed and shivered and looked around. It was the grumbling of his empty stomach that claimed his attention.

I'd better eat something, he told himself.

There, just a hundred paces away on his left, was the other, classier hotel, the Imperial. Light streamed from the doors and windows and there was obviously a crowd in the public bar. Declin had been there several times for a meal over the last few months, so he now made his weary and unhappy way across to the front entrance.

A quick glance into the crowded public bar told him that he knew no-one there, so he went in along the hall to the door on the left and into the dining room. There were only two couples in the room, a young man carrying on an animated conversation with a pretty, young woman and an older couple he thought might be enjoying a Saturday night out. That left six spare tables, so after selecting and paying for his meal Declin moved to a vacant table and sat.

Not wanting to go back to his lonely hotel room, Declin sat and ate slowly, brooding over the events of the day and trying to decide what to do.

When he was halfway through his main course, a middle-aged businessman, by his tailored grey trousers, white shirt and tie, stepped through the doorway. The man stopped and looked around and for a moment his gaze met Declin's. Then the businessman moved to a vacant table and sat with his back to the room.

Ordinarily, Declin would have paid the man no more notice but a few minutes later two men appeared at the door and then made their way directly over to the businessman: Rossiter and Marvin. The sight of Rossiter and his bully boy sent an instant stab of anxiety through Declin, but their behaviour also aroused his curiosity.

What do those two thugs want to meet with that businessman for?

Rossiter gestured with his head and Marvin nodded and turned to go back into the bar across the hallway. Rossiter walked over sat opposite the businessman without any greetings or introduction and began talking, making it obvious they knew each other. It was a short conversation and Declin saw both the businessman and Rossiter nod several times.

Then Rossiter stood up and started walking out of the room. As he did, his eyes noted Declin. Declin saw his eyes widen and then a frown cross his face. Rossiter detoured across and stopped beside the table.

"Hello, Declin me boyo! What are you doin' here?"

To his annoyance and shame, Declin had to swallow to master his fear. "Just having some variety in my meals," he replied, trying to appear calm and disinterested.

"Bit up market for you isn't it, coming over to this side of the tracks?" said Rossiter with a sneer.

To Declin's relief, the bully turned and made his way out into the public bar. But the meeting quite spoiled Declin's appetite. Resentfully, he finished his main and started on his desert. From time to time he glanced at the businessman or across through the door into the public bar. To his relief, there was no sign of Rossiter or Marvin. But Declin's mind was now working fast.

There's something fishy going on here. What do Rossiter and this businessman have in common? he wondered.

He resolved to find out. Having finished his meal Declin began to put his plan into action. *I need to watch these people,* he thought. The obvious and inconspicuous place to do it from was from in the public bar. *It will look perfectly natural if I have a beer after my meal,* he reasoned.

There was some anxiety that Rossiter or Marvin might still be in the bar, but a quick glance around as he stepped across the hallway and through the door quickly revealed that they were not. Declin almost sighed with relief and went to the bar to order his drink.

To his further relief, there was no topless barmaid or topless ticket seller there, just a nice, cheerful middle-aged lady and the male publican. The lady took his order and was just taking his money when movement out of the corner of his left eye caught Declin's attention. It was the businessman, and he was walking out of the dining room towards the front door.

Damn! I have just paid for this drink, Declin thought. Quickly picking up the frothing glass he moved away from the bar and went to follow the businessman. But then he paused. *No, too obvious,* he reasoned.

A quick glance gave him a plan. Like most hotels built on a corner, the public bar had an entrance leading out on to both streets so Declin quickly turned and walked out of the other door.

Outside were four tables, three with people seated at them. Declin quickly placed his beer on the vacant table and moved to the corner, trying to saunter casually but actually almost squirming with the desire to hurry. He was not sure why, but he just felt he was on to something.

On that side of the hotel were alternating trees growing in garden beds and bitumen parking spaces leading onto the side road. Beyond the road was semi-darkness, lit only by a streetlight at the nearby junction of the side street and the Bruce Highway. On the other side of the road was the narrow-gauge railway that led across to the mill. There were pools of shadow under the mango trees and as they seemed to offer good cover Declin stepped through between two parked cars and strolled over to them.

A glance showed him that none of the people at the tables were taking any notice of him, so Declin moved into the shadows of the trees and made his way towards the front to the hotel, the Bruce Highway side. There was a bitumen car park between the front of the hotel and the highway and as the rows of parked vehicles came into view Declin hissed with satisfaction.

Yes! There they are, he observed.

The businessman and the two thugs were standing on the other side of the cars but there was enough light from the hotel and the streetlights for them to be clearly visible. Declin made sure he was in the deep shadow and behind some bushes as he moved closer. But to his annoyance he could not get close enough to overhear the conversation.

Now why is Rossiter meeting that businessman? And what are they discussing? Declin wondered. It all just looked so odd that Declin felt sure something illegal was being discussed. *Oh, I wish I could hear what they are saying!*

But he could not do that. All he could do was note that the businessman then got into a grey BMW with a white top. As the car began moving off, it came to Declin that he should memorise its registration, but all he managed was a part index.

"871 Y... or is that V? Or..., oh bugger!" he muttered as the car swung away through the car park.

It pulled out onto the Bruce Highway and headed towards Cairns. Rossiter and Marvin then got into a ute and drove off towards Innisfail.

"Now what was that all about?" Declin wondered.

For several minutes he stood there in the semi-darkness. Then he shrugged and decided he would go home. He was in no mood to go back to the hotel, and he just shrugged about leaving his beer. Mainly it was because he did not want to be near happy couples enjoying romantic relationships or even just good company.

Brooding on his failures and weaknesses, Declin made his way across the highway and along the quiet street to the Caster Hotel.

Chapter 21

CHALLENGING

Graham's mother dropped him off near the Civic Theatre at 7:10pm. As she drove away, he looked nervously around. Almost at once he felt out of his depth and wished he had not agreed. To his embarrassment, most of the people going in were much better dressed than he was and, to his dismay, a few were in evening dress.

For a few seconds he considered not going in but then he scorned himself as a coward. "Come on weakling! Move!" he told himself.

He began walking towards the entrance, his eyes scanning the hundreds of people milling around. And then he saw Carol. She was standing on the outskirts of the crowd looking up and down the street. To his relief, she was dressed in quite an ordinary frock and had no special accessories.

He was even more relieved when she saw him, and a big smile lit up her face. "There you are! We'd better hurry," she cried, running over to take his hand.

As they started to make their way through the throng, Graham saw a couple of ladies in what looked to him like ball gowns and they also appeared to be dripping with jewellery. In his flustered state he said the first thing that came to his mind.

"Sorry I'm a bit late. I couldn't find my bow tie."

Carol glanced back and gave a quizzical smile but kept on walking. "I left my tiara at home too," she replied. Then she broke into giggles.

Graham laughed too and relaxed. But there were more challenges. He had been to the theatre a dozen times, either to watch Kylie perform or with the school, but never with such a different audience. Most appeared to be elderly, and most were much better dressed than he was. They seemed friendly enough but had a serious sort of air about them.

The next challenge was saying hello to Carol's mum. She was already seated inside in the seventh row back. For something to say he said, "Kirsty didn't come then?" He had guessed that Billy wouldn't be there.

It was Carol who answered. She giggled and made a face and then said, "Huh! She's more into 'Country and Western' or 'Rock'."

Carol's mum shook her head. "Don't say horrible things about your sister please."

"Yes Mum, but it's true. Anyway, she will probably become one of those punk rockers and start listening to headbanging music at home."

"Carol!"

"Yes Mum," Carol answered, letting go of Andrew's hand and gesturing to the seat between her and her mother.

That was not where Graham wanted to be, and he broke into a cold sweat of nervousness. He had hoped to be on the other side of Carol, and he was left feeling quite stressed. He knew he could not try any advances such as he and other girls had indulged in at places like the movies.

No kissing and cuddling tonight! he told himself.

And then Carol pressed against him and images of her and the other girls naked swamped his mind. Having her mother close beside him got him all anxious, adding to his emotional and physical discomfiture.

And the music wasn't really to his taste. It was very melodious and soothing enough but he found that lots of the tones seemed to be inaudible to him.

And it certainly doesn't set the blood on fire! he decided.

But there was no doubt the audience appreciated it and they sat in utter silence, apparently listening to every note. Graham found sitting still and concentrating a bit of an ordeal, but Carol seemed to listen with rapt attention.

All in all he was glad when it ended. When asked for an opinion on the music he avoided offering a real opinion and muttered nice things, but he didn't think Carol believed him. As they made their way out and to the Battersby's car, she chattered away, discussing various performers and tunes with her mother. Graham just strolled along holding her hand and relieved that his arousal had subsided. He did want to get Carol away on her own but understood there would be no chance of that.

He was driven home by Mrs Battersby. On the way she said, "Well, Graham, did you enjoy that?"

Graham did not want to lie. "It was interesting," he replied.

"Well, that was tactful! No in other words. Never mind. We all have different tastes. Are you coming to visit us at Caster tomorrow?"

"I'd like to, Mrs Battersby, but my family are going to Mareeba to visit my gran and grandad," Graham replied.

Mrs Boothby quizzed him about them for a few minutes and then said, "What about the following weekend? We like to have young people around for Carol and Kirsty to play with. Some of the local children are a bit low class."

Instant images of naked Betty and of her and Stephen sprang to mind. He felt quite anxious for a moment but then decided that it meant that Mrs Battersby had no idea what he and Carol and the others had been doing. Then he remembered he had already promised to go to the Navy Cadet Parade. For a few moments he was tempted to say yes and find an excuse but then shrugged and said, "Sorry. I'd really like to, but I have to go to watch the Navy Cadets do their Annual Parade."

At that he thought he caught a glimpse of a curled lip in Carol's expression, and he blushed. To his relief, Mrs Battersby nodded and said, "We'll that's fair! They came to yours. It was very well done by the way, and congratulations of your awards. You have done very well I hear."

"Thank you, Mrs Battersby."

Emboldened, Graham turned to Carol. "Would you like to come to the Navy Cadets parade?"

Carol made a face and shook her head. "Thanks, but no. I am not that interested in military stuff," she replied.

Graham nodded and sensed there was more to her opinion, but he did not want to push it into a debate or argument at that moment.

"That's okay. I will get to see you when I can."

Then they were at his home and he was presented by the dilemma of whether to give Carol a little kiss or not. To his relief, her mother said, "Come on Carol, give the poor boy a kiss so he can go, and we can get on our way home."

"Yes Mum!" Carol answered. So she drew his head to hers and kissed him. "Good night. Sweet dreams. See ya Monday!"

Graham climbed out and smiled, still hopeful the relationship was progressing. Happily, he waved as the car drove off and then he turned and made his way in the front gate and up the steps.

To his relief, Kylie was already in bed and Alex was in his room reading and just glanced up as he went past. His mother was waiting in the kitchen.

"How did it go dear?"

"Okay Mum," Graham replied, sliding onto a stool.

"So how was the music? Did you like it?"

"Not really. Not my thing," Graham replied. "Thanks," that for the cup of Milo she slid across to him.

His mother smiled. "I didn't think it would be, but you never know until you try," she commented. "So, let that be a lesson to you. If you can try things without harming yourself, and I don't mean being afraid in case your friends tease you or dare you, then you should try as many things as possible to find out what you actually like and are good at."

"Yes Mum."

Graham did not really want to discuss either the Chamber Music or his relationship with Carol, so he took a sip of Milo. The question of Carol was now bothering him. He wasn't at all sure how he felt about her.

Is it admiration? Or is it just that I really want a girlfriend and to be normal? he wondered.

He knew it wasn't love, but also understood that real love only developed over time and with mutual friendship and attraction. The fact that she could do things like go 'skinny dipping' where other people could see her bothered him and got him wondering what she actually thought of him.

It was a somewhat confused boy who took himself off to bed. But there the thinking went on with alternating doubts and searing erotic images. He spent hours fantasising about scenes in which he was the hero and in which nudity was always involved and then passionate actions.

* * *

On Sunday morning the family set off just after 8am and drove via Smithfield and Kuranda to Mareeba. They arrived mid-morning to warm greetings from Grandam and Grandad. A full morning tea with fresh, hot buttered scones with jam or cream followed and then a lot of family chatter. The whole family then set to work for a couple of hours doing household chores. Graham picked up mangos off the back lawn and then pruned fruit trees while Alex mowed the yard and Kylie and their mum did some washing and ironing.

They were rewarded with a big lunch of roast duck and baked vegies.

Graham really enjoyed that and was just finishing when Stephen arrived. He knocked on the door and Graham thanked his Gran and then arranged for his mother to pick him up. He then went out and got into Stephen's dad's car. The Bells were very friendly and they chatted all the way on the drive south along the Kennedy Highway.

At 1:10pm the two boys were dropped off at the entrance to Beck's Museum. The parents arranged a pick-up time and drove on. They were going on to an Orchid Show in Atherton.

Beck's Museum was 5km south of Mareeba, set back from the highway and separated by a 100m wide belt of open savannah woodland. Parked outside the front gate was a yellow painted World War 2 'Matilda' tank.

Graham and Stephen chatted for a bit and then climbed up onto the tank. Stephen began discussing World War 2 tanks, of which he had several plastic kit models. Graham was not very knowledgeable but tried to discuss them intelligently.

Luckily for him, a car pulled in and he saw that it was Willy and his parents and his girlfriend Marjorie and her brother. The two boys waved and then slid down and hurried in along the entrance road behind the car to the car park

As Willy and the others climbed out, Graham and Stephen walked over to join them. The group made their way to the ticket office inside the front gate and were met by the museum owner, Mr Syd Beck, and his son Norman. Mr Beck, a red-faced elderly man, was expecting them and was very pleased to show them around.

"Is there anything in particular you want to see?" he asked, after being reminded they had all been there before.

"The Airacobra," Willy answered.

Mr Beck led them out into the large semi-circular hangar and past other aircraft including a Neptune, a Sea Venom, and a Canberra. They made their way past several armoured vehicles and lots of aircraft engines and propellers to the Airacobra.

For nearly ten minutes Willy carefully studied the plane and asked Mr Beck questions. Graham listened and looked at the aircraft but was not really interested. He did not think the Airacobra was a particularly good-looking plane.

After studying the aircraft from all angles, Willy said, "Mr Beck, do you have any information on the others that crash landed on Cape York Peninsula?"

"I certainly do," Mr Beck answered helpfully. He led them back to the front office, which also housed a very large collection of extremely well put together models and a small library. The models were mostly plastic kits on 1:72 or 1:35 scale but they were so well done they really aroused Graham's interest and even jealousy.

They are much better done than mine, he thought, noting the care in assembling and the fine details in the painting and decals.

Willy then asked, "There are some of these still where they crashed aren't there?"

"Yes, there are," Mr Beck answered. He then named four places where he knew of wrecks.

Stephen looked up from a book he was leafing through. "There are a few other wrecks up there aren't there, like P40 Kittyhawks and some Beauforts or Beaufighters?"

"Yes. I know where there is a Kittyhawk in quite good condition and also most of a Beaufighter," Mr Beck answered.

Stephen frowned. "If you know where they are why don't you go and get them?" he asked.

Mr Beck laughed. "It's called money. And you need permission, permits and so on. They are in very inaccessible places, and you can't get a truck in to them. It means either hiring a big helicopter, or a barge of some sort."

At that Graham spoke up. "My dad owns a landing barge," he said.

"Does he now? And who is your dad?" Mr Beck asked, interested.

"Bert Kirk, of NQ Marine Contractors," Graham answered. "He owns three ships and a big dumb lighter."

"Is that like a cigarette lighter?" Stephen quipped.

Graham wasn't amused and gave him a look suggesting he was dumb. "No, a dumb lighter is a barge that has no engines. It has to be towed. Dad uses it to move oil drums and things like that," he explained.

Mr Beck nodded but then shook his head. "I can't afford to hire ships. And anyway, I would also need men to help with the work."

"We could do that," Stephen offered. "The school holidays are only a few weeks away. We could go on a trip to help you find these things and then provide you with some volunteer labour."

Mr Beck looked interested but made a wry face. "You and who else?" he asked. "It would take half a dozen at least."

Stephen looked around at the group. "Us?" he suggested.

Graham found himself liking the idea. Up till now they had loomed as nothing much, except for the 9-day cadet promotion course at an army base near Charters Towers in the last week of school.

Willy was obviously very keen on the idea. He turned to his father. "Could I do that dad?" he asked.

Willy's father rubbed his chin, then nodded. "I suppose so. It would depend on who else was going and how the expedition was organised."

Now that there was a glimmer of hope Willy turned to Graham. "Can you come, Graham?"

Graham gave a wry smile. "I will be at sea on dad's ships anyway, at least after Christmas. It would depend on when and where."

"Would your dad help with the shipping?" Stephen asked. He was obviously keen on the idea.

"I don't know. I would have to ask," Graham answered.

Mr Beck now spoke. "I can cover some cost, but not a great deal. I might be able to pay freight and the cost of the day or so lost from a voyage while we load a plane."

"Whereabouts are these planes, Mr Beck?" Graham asked.

Mr Beck shook his head. "Ah, that is secret."

"Why?" Stick asked.

Mr Beck laughed. "Because there are a dozen other collectors and museums in Australia, all thirsting to get their hands on some original aircraft, even on parts. And there are lots of overseas collectors. We are talking big money here."

That was a revelation to Graham. It obviously was to Willy as well, as he said, "We won't tell."

Mr Beck looked thoughtful. "Well, I suppose if you are going to volunteer to help." He reluctantly reached down and pulled an air chart of Cape York Peninsula from under the counter. This was spread on the desk and he pointed to two locations. "There is a P40 Kittyhawk here," he said, "and a Beaufighter further north, up here near Cape Sidmouth."

The friends bent to study the chart. Graham studied the chart and then nodded. "That is right beside the main shipping route. I might be able to persuade Dad to pull up for a few hours."

Mr Beck nodded. "Please try. I have the permits to remove the wrecks, and the permits to go onto Aboriginal land. The longer I leave this the more likely some rival collector will learn about them and snap them up."

Willy looked around at them for agreement. "So we will organise an expedition during the holidays then," he stated. He pointed on the chart, and said, "Which wreck is the best one to try for first?"

Mr Beck pointed to the shore of Bathurst Bay, just west of Cape Melville. "This one, the Kittyhawk. The only real snag is that it is almost two kilometres inland, with a lot of scrub between it and the sea. The Beaufighter is right on the beach."

Stephen studied the map and then said, "If it is right on the beach, how come someone else hasn't found it?"

"Because it is in among some low sand dunes, and a few bushes have grown up to hide it. It was only luck that I found part of the tail poking out of the sand," Mr Beck replied.

"How did you know where to look?" Willy asked.

"I read the pilot's report. He wasn't sure where he had landed, and he walked along the coast for days before some Aborigines found him and took him to Coen. I worked out the general area and then hired a plane and flew over. That didn't show me anything, so Norman and I went walking with metal detectors. Took about two weeks," Mr Beck explained.

Stephen chuckled and wiped his glasses. "What if we shift tons of sand and find it is all rusted away? We would look silly then!"

Mr Beck smiled and shook his head. "It is all there, a complete Beaufighter. We dug it out to check, then buried it again. Took us three whole days. But this time we covered it with canvas tarpaulins to help protect it from the sand and salt."

"So we need some fit people and three days of time," Willy suggested.

"And a ship or barge," Stephen added.

Graham considered this. Even though he was only a teenager he had done dozens of sea voyages of one- or two-weeks duration and had acquired quite a store of nautical knowledge.

He said, "Even then it might not be possible. What is the shore like, Mr Beck? How deep is the water offshore and are there any rocks or reefs?"

"I don't know. It looked like an ordinary beach to me," Mr Beck answered.

Graham frowned and added, "It would depend on the weather too. Any sort of surf and it might not be possible to get a landing craft onto the beach safely."

"Oh Graham! Stop being such a Gloomy Jimmy!" Stephen cried.

"Just trying to help by being realistic," Graham replied, adding, "And there is the tide too, don't forget. That would determine the best time to make the attempt."

Mr Beck looked very thoughtful. He said, "We will look up the tide tables and you can work out a suitable time. Then we will go as soon as we can arrange a ship."

Willy agreed. "We will work it all out and then come up again next weekend for a planning conference to get things organised," he said.

"Now steady on young Willy," his father said. "There are adults to consult yet. Your mother might not approve."

"Aw Dad! If she doesn't then I will try to make another airship," Willy replied.

Dr Williams laughed, then said, "No emotional blackmail, thank you, and no underhand deviousness either. We will see."

Graham shook his head. "I might be busy next weekend," he said.

"Oh Graham, give it a break!" Stephen snorted. "She can live without seeing you for one weekend."

Graham sniffed and blushed. He wanted to say it wasn't like that, but he knew it was. He was now so involved that he wanted to be with Carol every day.

I will find ways to be with her, he told himself.

Chapter 22

ANGER

After an almost sleepless night, Declin woke feeling utterly exhausted and depressed. He was tormented by jealousy and fear and could not decide what to do. His mood wasn't helped when he went to the bathroom to shave and freshen up and saw young Betty flaunting herself over in her bedroom.

Angrily, he slammed the window. "I don't need that sort of pressure either, the teasing little trollop!" he muttered.

And he knew he had to make some decisions. *Do I tell the bosses what I know?* he wondered.

But then fearful thoughts of the possible consequences when the gang found out flooded in to unnerve him. And what about Carol? His gloomy assessment was that he had lost her and that just sparked more self-pity and envy, and he again felt the urge to hurt Graham somehow.

"I suppose I'd better go to work and report in," he decided.

Not doing so could result in him being sacked and he did not want a work record like that. So he dressed in his work clothes and made his way down to the dining room and forced himself to eat breakfast, served by the delectable Sheila.

After breakfast, Declin set off for the mill. It took him an effort to make himself keep walking as he did not want Carol to see him, yet he ached emotionally to meet her! Knowing it was Sunday morning made the tension worse as he expected to meet Carol and her siblings at the locomotive or in the playground.

All the way along the street his eyes kept focusing on the distant park and he could see people at the playground. Several times he stopped and considered turning back.

I'm not rostered on until tomorrow, he told himself.

But then the moral dilemma of reporting Rossiter's threats seemed to rise up and choke him. With a sigh that was more of a sob Declin forced himself to keep walking. Only to discover that the people at the park were not Carol and her brother and sister.

Those are Frank Hamilton's kids I think, he noted, nodding to a teenage girl he had seen before who was obviously minding four younger children.

On reaching the mill office, Declin was again torn by fear as he went in, but again it was all wasted emotion. None of the managers were there and only one of the admin staff. She was bright and cheerful and noted Declin's information about time off and told him he could work the evening shift to make up if he wished as another worker had just phoned in sick.

Declin accepted this and then wondered how he could fill in the day. Feeling washed out and thoroughly down he took himself back to the hotel, once again walking past Carol's in a state of emotional turmoil, and again seeing no sign of her.

Back at the hotel, Declin went to his room and threw of his work clothes and lay down. For an hour or so he lay there brooding and nursing his self-pity before he dropped off to sleep. He woke a few hours later feeling groggy and ill but made himself dress and go down for lunch. He then returned to his room and lay down and dozed.

But sleep wouldn't come and instead he was tormented by images of Carol and the other girls swimming nude, making him very aroused and also very angry. Adding to his anger were jealous images of a naked Graham standing beside Carol and the other girls. What particularly upset Declin was the fact that Carol very obviously was not offended or concerned.

She shouldn't do that! he thought, a tear creeping out and sliding down his cheek.

But now the anxious fear of her getting into trouble gave him the excuse to rationalise his desire to go to see if she or her sister were at the creek. Knowing that he was being driven by lustful desire added a sense of guilt, but that did not stop him. Declin changed into old clothes and set off along the gravel road at the back to go to his secret fishing spot.

That meant walking past the back of Carol's house and again he was on emotional tenterhooks as he approached and passed by. But again he saw no sign of anyone, although her mother's car was parked under the house and the family was obviously home.

The angst then grew with anticipation as Declin walked past the back of the mill. There was anxiety at being seen by Rossiter or his cronies, but the only person he saw was a man named Williams who was working a front-end loader at the bagasse pile and who gave him a friendly wave. Then worry and shame about possibly being caught peeking at Carol became his next emotional hurdle.

But he felt as though an invisible force was dragging him along and he kept going to his secret fishing spot, only to find the creek deserted. The relief and disappointment were so sharp that Declin just slumped down and brooded. For the next hour he pretended to fish but his heart wasn't in it, and he kept glancing up the creek to the little beach where the kids usually went swimming, his mind full of remembered images and his body torn by arousal and guilt.

Finally it was too much for him. Seeing that it was nearly four o'clock and knowing he had to be at work by six, Declin rolled up his fishing line and placed it in his small backpack then made his way back up through the long grass to the gravel road.

Only to have what he dreaded but hoped for happen: he met Carol. She was walking towards him along the gravel road from the direction of her house. It was clear she had not seen him until he stepped out of the long grass onto the gravel road and to add to his anxiety she seemed to hesitate. She wore only Lycra bike pants and a cotton top and joggers. To Declin, she looked to be a vision of loveliness that made his heart hammer and caused him to catch his breath. As they got closer, Carol gave a puzzled smile and Declin forced one in reply.

"Hello Carol," he managed to croak.

Carol stopped a few paces away. "Hello Declin," she said. She appeared to frown and think and then she said, "I saw you at the cadet parade. I didn't know you were interested in army stuff."

"I'm not," Declin replied, his mind racing to come up with a good explanation. He could see that she was puzzled, and he began to fluster. "I was just worrying about you," he muttered.

"Worrying about me!" Carol cried in astonishment. "Were you following me?"

The surprise and concern on her face got Declin even more flustered. Again, he groped for a sensible explanation but all he could do was shake his head and say, "Carol, you need to be very careful."

That really got her frowning, and he knew he wasn't handling things well. She looked him in the eyes and said, "What do you mean?"

Now starting to perspire from anxiety as well as the heat, Declin replied, "Don't go anywhere on your own, and don't go down the creek on your own."

"Why? What is the problem?"

Declin did not know what to say and just spread his arms and shook his head. He knew he looked miserable.

Carol pursed her lips and he saw her eyes narrow. "Have you seen us swimming down the creek?"

All Declin could do was nod, the anxiety and misery almost paralysing him.

Anger flared on Carol's face. "Have you been watching me?"

Declin was appalled. "No!" he cried.

"It looks like it! Every time I go somewhere I seem to bump into you. And please don't come and perv on me down at the creek!" she snapped.

"But you mustn't go there. It is dangerous," Declin cried.

"Dangerous? How?"

"From strange men," Declin replied, now battling to keep his misery form turning to the public shame of tears.

Carol snorted and put her hands on her hips. "Huh! You are the only strange man I need to worry about! Leave me alone and stay away from me!"

With that Carol stepped past him and started jogging towards the bridge.

Declin was stunned. *Oh no! What have I done!* he thought.

Despair flooded his emotions and now the tears came. Feeling utterly defeated, he watched Carol as she ran away. But when she cast a glance back over her shoulder he quickly turned and began hurrying back towards the hotel.

Feeling more wretched than he could ever remember, Declin walked quickly back past the mill, only to encounter yet another problem. As he went back past the bagasse pile, a dirty ute came driving over from beside the main buildings, and driving it was Rossiter.

"Hello Declin, me boyo," Rossiter called through a wound-down window. "I see you are working tonight."

Declin could only nod, appalled that Rossiter had such inside knowledge and now anxious about what he wanted.

Rossiter changed facial expression and gave him a hard look. "Good, so tonight make this mill stop, and make sure you do it, or else!"

Declin was appalled. He was so scared he could hardly bring himself to speak. "But... but there's always more than one of us in the Control Room. And the system will tell who did it. I will be in trouble then," he replied.

Rossiter curled his lip. "Just do it! The bosses are the least of your worries. You need to be more afraid of us. So make the mill stop," he snarled. With that he accelerated away.

Declin stood there and watched it go. He felt stunned and fear slithered in his stomach like an evil serpent uncoiling. He broke into a real sweat and had trouble making himself keep moving. Once again, he considered going to the management and telling them but as before fear of the repercussions stopped him. Knowing he was scared just made it worse and he despised himself for being a coward.

In a fog of indecision and gnawing anxiety,y Declin walked back to the hotel, his mind swirling with options and arguments. To his horror, he found himself considering ways he could bring the mill to a halt. He was so upset he was quite unable to eat any dinner, so he just showered, changed into work clothes and made his way back to the mill, all the while feeling like he was somehow enmeshed in a nightmare and hoping he would wake up soon.

* * *

Declin went through the next few hours in a sort of daze. He was so unfocused that the Control Room manager, Mr Ferris, twice asked him if he was alright.

"You were sick yesterday. Are you still not feeling well?" he asked.

"A feel a bit off," admitted Declin. "I'll be alright."

"Then focus on the job please. Safety is the main priority. There are men's lives involved," Mr Ferris retorted.

Declin was very aware of that and the notion that his actions might harm or kill a person caused him to break into a cold sweat. With an effort of will he concentrated on his work and managed to calm himself. But all the while his mind and emotions were racing and in turmoil.

Stop the mill! Do it tonight! kept pounding in his brain. But how to do it? And how to do it without harming anyone and without getting blamed for it?

After several hours of wracking his brains, during which he considered all the options on how the computer system operated, he came to the same conclusion: He couldn't do it without the system pointing an electronic finger at him.

So how else can I do something? he wondered, hoping that if he did some small thing it might get Rossiter to leave him alone. What he did not want to do was anything that might possibly harm a workmate.

Then a stoppage occurred anyway and that gave him an idea. Something jammed part of the milling train and the process had to be halted. The panel lights warned the Control Room and again it was Declin who quickly shut the equipment down. But then he scanned the CCTV monitors to see where the problem was.

Not covered by a camera, he noted.

"I'll just nip out and see what the problem is," he said to Mr Ferris.

"You do that, lad," Mr Ferris agreed, his eyes also scanning the bank of CCTV monitors.

Declin went to stand up but even as he did a worker opened the door and called loudly, "Shut it down! Shut it down!"

"We have," Declin answered. The worker had obviously run as he was puffing.

Mr Parsons also stood up. "What's happened?"

The worker pointed up along the milling train. "A drive chain has come uncoupled and some part is jammed in the gears." With that he turned and went hurrying back along the steel walkway into the mill.

With nothing else to do until the damage was repaired, Declin followed him, with Mr Ferris and Steve Mullaney following. By the time they reached the area of the breakdown, a team of workers was already there, laying out tools and inspecting the damage.

Portable lights were organised to be rigged and to make room Declin and Steve Mullaney were ordered back out of the way.

"Go back to the Control Room and be ready to restart. You are just in the way here," Mr Ferris ordered.

Declin followed Steve Mullaney back along the steel walkways and on the way detoured to visit one of the toilets organised on that floor so that workers did not have to go too far from their workstation. Steve

Mullaney continued on, and when Declin came out and glanced back along the floor to where clanging noises and bright lights indicated repairs had begun, an idea came to him.

Could I just do something like that?

With that in mind he slowly made his way back to the Control Room, counting paces and measuring distances with his eye.

Back in the Control Room, he discussed the breakdown with Steve Mullaney while looking at the monitors and studying the map of the mill layout. He noted that there were large areas of the mill not covered by CCTV.

If I do something I must not be seen, and I need a good alibi, he reasoned.

It took over an hour for the repairs to be completed. During that time, Steve Mullaney grumbled about conditions at the mill and how he might try to get a job at the South Johnston Mill during the next crushing season.

"This place sucks," he said. "I have never been in such an unhappy workplace in my life. And besides, I live in Innisfail and South Johnston is closer."

Declin could only agree. The whole social work environment felt toxic to him. *And that is because of Rossiter and his scaly cronies,* he mused. Once again, he considered telling management what he knew. *Why can't they see what is going on?* he wondered. But he also wondered what Rossiter's motives were. *What is he aiming to achieve? How does shutting down the mill and losing pay help anyone?*

But fear stopped Declin from saying anything to Mr Ferris when he returned to the Control Room a few minutes later.

"They reckon another quarter of an hour," he said.

On the pretext of curiosity, Declin said he would go and look and come back as soon as the workers were finished the repairs. Mr Ferris nodded and agreed so Declin went out and slowly made his way along to the worksite. As he did, he carefully looked around, searching for something he could break and not be found out.

If I do something that might get Rossiter off my back for a while.

From that came the idea of dropping something down into one of the drive chain sprockets to jam it. But what? And how to get away undiscovered?

And back at the site of the repairs he found just what he needed. The repair team were packing up by then and lying on a steel girder off to the side was a huge steel wrench they had been using. The workers gathered up their tools but none of them appeared to notice the wrench.

That might do, Declin decided, hoping they would not notice and would leave it there.

Declin was surprised to see that Mr Battersby was down with the foreman inspecting the repairs. He looked tired and had obviously been roused from sleep and hastily dressed. As he climbed back up, he saw Declin and frowned.

"What are you here for Declin?" he queried.

"Mr Ferris sent me so I could report back to the Control Room as soon as we are ready to restart," Declin replied.

Seeing the strain on Mr Battersby's face caused him a pang of sympathy. *I am planning to add to his problems,* he thought, quite smitten by guilt.

Mr Battersby nodded and said, "We are ready to go. Go back and tell Mr Ferris and let's get this bloody mill milling. We are days behind schedule as it is."

"Yes sir," Declin replied.

Turning, he made his way back along the walkway, noting as he did that the repair team were dismantling the portable lights and still had not noticed the wrench which now lay in the shadows.

But will they see it and take it? he fretted.

As he made his way back to the Control Room, Declin again studied the layout and refined his plan. *If I get caught that will be me out of a job,* he thought.

He broke into a sweat despite the cool of the night air and then shivered when it occurred to him that he might even face criminal charges and end up in jail.

That could ruin my whole life!

From that it came to him that his life was a bit of wreck already. Carol had rejected him and told him to stay away; he was in fear of Rossiter, and he could not even keep his family safe from their threats of vengeance. It all looked very black and depressing and he sobbed a few times as he made his way back in the semi-darkness of the walkway.

Back at the Control Room, he reported in and they got the mill started again. Declin sat and did his job and then brooded while studying the system diagrams, flow analyses and safety lights, his mind and emotions churning with fear and depression.

For the next hour Declin sat at his workstation, his mind and body in a ferment of fear and distress. All the while he struggled to pretend he was calm and efficient, but once again his stomach threatened to let him down and several times he had to swallow vomit as it rose to the back of his throat. He broke into a cold sweat and was tempted to again claim he was sick.

At 0400hrs Declin knew he could not put it off much longer. But anxiety held him in his chair, and he sweated through another 15 minutes of mental anguish before he finally nerved himself to act.

"I need to go to the toilet," he said to Mr Ferris, rising from his chair as he did.

Mr Ferris just glanced at him and nodded. "Something you ate?" he casually queried.

"Might be," Declin agreed.

It was obvious the other two suspected noting and he felt a real Judas as he opened the door and stepped out onto the walkway.

Outside he looked around but the whole vast cavern of the main mill building was just its usual mix of bright lights and pools of shadow. The familiar noises of grinding machinery and mechanical sounds filled his ears, and the aroma of the sugar and molasses filled his nostrils. No-one was in sight and that was part of Declin's plan. He knew that very few workers were out among the machinery, that the whole process was now automated and mostly controlled by the computers in the two control rooms. But he was also conscious that he would appear briefly on two CCTV monitors and that got him anxious about the timings of his move.

But there was still a chance of being seen by a foreman or maintenance man and that idea caused Declin to break into a fit of trembling and to sweat even more, or was that just because he was now out of the air conditioning in the Control Room?

With a sob of near despair, Declin forced his legs to move and he hurried along that level, eyes still flitting from side to side to check no-one was around. As he approached the toilet, he let out another sob of self-pity. Once he was passed that his actions became suspicious and questionable.

It took an effort of willpower, even courage, for him to walk on past the toilet. Anxiety then drove him to hurry, the squelching thud of his rubber-soled boots sounding very loud to him as he strode along the steel walkways.

As he approached the selected location, his eyes began questing for the wrench. To his dismay, he could not see it. When he got to the spot where he had seen it, he stopped and stared down into the shadows.

It was here. Where is it? he thought, his anxiety shooting up another level.

But it wasn't there. And he was sure he was in the right spot. Below him he could see quite clearly where the repair team had been at work. There was no mistake. After all that angst his plan had come unstuck because somebody had removed the wrench!

What can I do now? Declin fretted, fear rising to gag his throat.

Chapter 23

CRUEL DILEMMAS

For several minutes Declin just stood there in the semi-darkness amid the grinding machinery of the milling train, his heart hammering as something close to panic seized him.

My plan has failed! Now Rossiter will have it in for me, he thought. So emotionally overwrought was he that he suddenly felt dizzy and had to cling to the steel safety railings.

Now awash with adrenalin and anxiety he gripped the rail and wondered what he could now do. But no idea came to him, or at least none that made any sense. *If I do something I haven't thought through I will be blamed and sacked,* he reasoned.

Shivers of apprehension kept him gripping the rail. For a few more seconds he stood there until it came to him that he must make himself do something.

Forcing himself to slow his breathing he took several deep breaths, trembling as he did. *I'd better get back to the Control Room and try to come up with another plan,* he told himself.

Now anxious lest his absence be too long, he turned and quickly made his way back along the walkway. And it was just as well he did because just as he was passing the toilet he saw the Control Room door open. Quickly he stepped into the toilet and hurried into a cubicle.

Must make it look like this is where I've been, he reasoned.

Hastily he pressed the button to make the WC flush and then he 'casually' stepped over to the washbasin and began washing his hands. As he did, Steve Mullaney came in. To Declin's guilty relief, he did not speak but just nodded and went into the cubicle and shut the door.

Declin felt an extraordinary wash of sickening guilt in his stomach, even though he had actually done nothing wrong.

I meant to. I tried to! he thought as he washed his face and studied the pale reflection in the mirror. Feeling even more wretched and anxious he made his way back to the Control Room.

As Declin resumed his seat, Mr Ferris just glanced at him but was focused on one of the lights on the flow diagram panel. Declin saw it was flashing amber. Muttering he made a few adjustments with the keyboard and the light changed back to green. Mr Ferris nodded and settled back.

"Good. We don't need any more breakdowns. This mill's in enough financial trouble as it is," he muttered.

Which made Declin both glad he had not sabotaged the works, and afraid of what Rossiter might do. But having watched Mr Ferris make an adjustment got him again considering if he could somehow stop the crush without damaging anything. But how to do it without the system recording that he was the operator that did it?

Declin could not think of a way to do that, so he sat there for the remainder of the shift in a state of growing apprehension.

And he needed to because when he went back to the hotel for breakfast Rossiter was there and he came over and sat opposite him. His cronies Marvin and Dennis were seated at the next table.

Leaning forward, Rossiter hissed, "I thought I told you to stop that bloody mill when you were on shift?"

"It did stop. Something broke a drive chain pinion," Declin retorted. He had to swallow to keep the rising bile of fear from his throat.

Rossiter snorted. "Huh! That was just Mar... er... someone dropping a steel rod into the chain sprockets. But that only stopped it for an hour or so. We want it stopped for a whole day."

"I can't do that," Declin replied, ashamed that his reply came out as a frightened squeak.

Rossiter leaned closer and glared at him. His ugly red face filled Declin's vision and he smelt his bad breath and gagged. Rossiter stared hate at him.

"Yes, you can. It's all controlled by those computers you work with. Make them do something."

Declin was now so afraid and flustered he had to pause to get control of his vocal cords. Perspiration trickled on his face.

"But that can be tracked and they would know I did it. I could lose my job!"

"Better than losing your life! Next time make it happen big time or else! Now get it organised," Rossiter snarled. "Stop the mill when we say so or you will meet the same fate as O'Malley." He then pushed back his chair and stood up, returning to his own table.

Declin sat there as though stunned as he realised what Rossiter was saying. *O'Malley did not just walk off and leave town for another job. He has been murdered!*

The implication chilled Declin and he found he was shaking. But even with such a statement he found it hard to believe. *Surely Rossiter isn't going to admit to murder,* he thought.

It just didn't seem credible. But it certainly sounded like it and with that notion came the flashback to that ghastly image of that arm pushing Jack Henley into the start of the milling train.

Declin swallowed to keep down the bile as a wash of fear swamped him. Unable to face the prospect of food he stood up. At that moment, Sheila appeared and came over but Declin felt so bilious that he could only stand and shake his head. Hounded by fear and the knowledge he was possibly going to throw up again, he fled upstairs to his room.

Shaking with emotion he threw himself on his bed and lay there, his depression deepening to despair. For hours he lay there, tossing and shifting uncomfortably, his mind and emotions churning with doubts and despair. Declin felt completely torn and he again considered all the options: tell management; go to the police; run away; or give in and help damage the mill.

And thinking that he had lost with Carol deepened his sense of failure. From that another option crept insidiously in: end it all. As thoughts of suicide clouded his mind and emotions, Declin felt even more distressed. Those thoughts led his mind down more dark corridors as he wrestled with the morality and consequences of killing himself. Feeling that he was trapped and that he lacked the courage to face the situation did not help.

At last he fell into an exhausted sleep from which he woke feeling utterly exhausted. He was so weak from lack of food that he lay there shivering and then crying as self-pity again gripped him. But his bedside alarm clock also nagged at him, telling him he was due at the mill for his normal roster.

Despising himself for even being too weak to run away, Declin rose and showered and changed back into clean work clothes. Feeling exhausted and ashamed, he made his way downstairs. He was too late for the normal lunch session, so he went into the bar and ordered a counter lunch.

Sheila handed him the menu and then looked at him with concern. "You look a bit of a wreck dearie. Are you alright?"

Declin shook his head and felt his eyes prickle with tears. With an effort he held them back, not wanting to shame himself that much. "Just not happy at work," he muttered.

"You being bullied by that prick Rossiter?" she said.

That stabbed right into the heart of the matter and Declin stared at her aghast, wondering how much she knew. All he could do was nod and make his watering eyes concentrate on the menu.

Sheila also nodded and pursed his lips. "He's a mean mongrel. He and those thugs of cronies pick on lots of the guys," she commented.

"Does he give you trouble?" Declin asked, lifting his gaze to meet her eyes and suddenly concerned for her welfare.

Sheila shook her head. "Nah! He leers at me and makes the usual smutty jokes and suggestions, but I don't think he's up to it, and that Dennis I think is gay."

That made Declin feel a bit better but also got him worrying about whether Carol might be in any sort of danger.

"Thanks," was all he could say. He then ordered his meal.

As he finished and went to leave the bar, Sheila came along to take the plate and cutlery and gave him a smile. "You just hang in there, luv. Don't let 'em get you down."

Declin managed a smile in return but inside he was feeling ill with apprehension. His mind still a maggot's nest of doubts and possible solutions to the problems that seemed to be crowding in on all sides he walked slowly back to the mill.

And her comment about 'hanging in there' did not help. It kept recurring in his mind, along with other notions of how he might commit suicide. But deep down he was repelled by the concept. Not only was he terrified of dying, it just struck him as all wrong.

It hurts too many innocent people, he reasoned.

But he was still in a funk of fear and black despair all that day and on into the week. Every day he was anticipating some action by Rossiter, and he began to dread even going down for meals, let alone going to work.

Somehow, he made himself keep up with his normal roster but he felt ill and exhausted and had trouble eating and with keeping food down.

Bouts of black despair got him arguing all the options repeatedly and life became just one huge black pit of despair.

There were several more smallish breakdowns or incidents, but none that could be attributed to any particular individual or act of negligence. But Declin was sure it was the work of Rossiter and his gang, and his gloom deepened.

Thursday came around and Declin had to wrestle with his courage to even get up and get dressed. Somehow, he forced down some lunch but the effort left him shaking and nauseous.

Chapter 24

PLANS & PARADES

The moment Graham arrived home that Sunday evening after the visit to Mareeba he put the idea of the expedition to his mother.

She listened and then raised an eyebrow. "I will have to speak to your father. Haven't you got some cadet camp coming up?"

Graham nodded. "Yes Mum. The Promotion Course. It is during the last week of school and the first few days of the holidays. After that I presume I will be shanghaied into being crew anyway."

"Oh, don't speak like that!" his mother said. "You know we need to economise to help the business to stay afloat during the holidays."

"Pressganged then," Graham replied.

Alex had overheard this and laughed. "As long as it's only the business that we are trying to keep afloat and not the bloody ship!" he cried.

Their mother frowned. "Alex. Don't joke about things like that please. And don't swear."

Alex muttered an apology and Graham went away, surprised at just how much nautical superstition had rubbed off on his mother, who came from a farm.

What was also taking up his thoughts, apart from girls, was his future career. Now that he had decided that he would make the army his career the notion of being an officer had lodged in his brain. He knew he wanted to be a Cadet Under-Officer and it just seemed a logical step to go from being an officer in Cadets to a real officer in the Regular Army. But that meant the Royal Military College and the Australian Defence Force Academy.

And you need good school marks to get selected, Graham thought ruefully. *I'd better study if we have exams in the next few weeks.*

He knew that the Year 10 exams would not be counted but now determined to improve. He also resolved to do some research to find out exactly what subjects he should be enrolling to study the following year. So he settled to doing homework and studying.

His mother then called him to the radio telephone that the family used to communicate with the ships when they were at sea. Graham spoke to his father. After describing what Mr Beck wanted, his father gave him agreement, depending on the dates.

Satisfied he had done what he could, Graham returned to studying.

* * *

Monday morning found Graham at school full of hopes concerning Carol. But she was nowhere to be seen so he joined his friends in their usual spot. He had only been there a few minutes, discussing the Passing-Out Parade and again congratulating his friends for being selected for promotion when Willy came along.

After the usual causal greetings, Willy asked if there was any chance that Graham's father could help. To his relief, Graham nodded and said, "Yeah. I spoke to dad last night on the radio. He said it would depend on the ship's schedules, but he might be able to see his way clear to help. What really helps is that it won't take any ship far out of its normal route."

On hearing that Willy looked very anxious. "You didn't say where the wrecks are, not over the radio?" he asked.

"No. I'm not that silly. We not only learn radio security in the Army Cadets, we actually practice it," Graham replied.

Willy laughed with relief, then grinned and retorted, "So how come we were able to monitor all your radio traffic and track all your patrols on that last field exercise, the one that WE won?"

This brought a chorus of cries and denials from the army cadets. Willy chuckled and Graham fumed with hurt pride. It was not often that the Air Cadets were able to get one up on the Army Cadets in a field exercise and Willy was obviously relishing the victory.

He asked, "So, who would like to come on this expedition? Can you come, Graham?"

Graham gave a rueful smile. "If it is dad's ship, I will probably be pressganged into being aboard anyway," he answered.

"Does your mum agree?" Willy asked.

Graham laughed. "'Only the good die young,' she said. Anyway, it's normal for us kids to help out on the ships during school holidays."

"Pete?"

Peter shook his head. "I'd love to, but I have to go and spend this Christmas with my dad in South Australia."

There was a short, embarrassed silence. Graham knew that Peter's parents were separated and felt very sorry for him. Having his own two loving parents in the same house felt very comforting to him.

Willy turned to Stephen. "What about you, Steve?"

Stephen looked worried. "Mum says yes, but Dad is a bit undecided. But I reckon I can win him around. But it can't be until after 'Promo'."

"When is that?" Willy asked.

Peter answered that. "In six week's time, starting on Saturday the fifth of December. That includes the last week of school. It ends on the fourteenth and we will be home the next day."

Willy pulled out a pocket notebook and a pencil and made some notes. As he did, they were joined by Andrew Collins and his three Navy Cadet friends. Andrew again congratulated the army cadets on their Passing-Out parade.

"Pity it won't be as good as ours," added Arthur Blake.

"Oh pull the other one!" cried Stephen. "You lot can't march for nuts." He stood up and called to an imaginary parade, "Ship's motley crew, Ho! Crew, swab the decks. Aye, aye sir!" Then he swept his hand across to his waist and added, "That's a navel salute. Get it? A navel salute."

Graham saw Andrew go red and for a moment he feared Stephen had gone too far in his teasing. But Andrew just gave a wry grin. Then he grinned again as Roger made a comment about the 'Belly button cadets in their belly bottom trousers'.

"Better than being 'Space Cadets," Blake retorted.

"Yeah, space between their ears!" Luke Karaku cried, his black face splitting into a huge grin.

Andrew turned to Willy and said, "Anyway, what are you doing here plotting with these troublemakers?"

Willy looked at Andrew and his face lit up. He then outlined the idea, explaining he had to keep the location secret. Then he asked, "Would any of you be interested in joining us as voluntary unpaid labour?"

They were interested. Andrew nodded and said, "I wouldn't mind a trip up the east coast of Cape York Peninsula. I've never been up past Cape Tribulation. But you might have to allow my sister Carmen to come along."

"That's alright," Willy replied. "Marjorie will probably be with us, so she won't be the only girl."

The bell for classes ended further discussion and Graham made his way to class, getting a distant glimpse of Carol as he did. During the morning break he again sought her out, but while she smiled she shook her head.

"Sorry Graham, but I have to study for exams this week and next. My marks aren't very good, and Dad says I need to pull them up if I want to get into university."

That surprised Graham, so he said, "What do you want to study to become?"

"An Industrial Chemist. What about you?"

"I was thinking of being an officer in the army," Graham replied, feeling a bit embarrassed as he did.

"Hmm, I sort of guessed that," Carol commented.

She did not sound very enthusiastic, and he was left feeling a bit flat. However, they agreed to sit together to have lunch and he had to be content with that.

* * *

By Wednesday, the friends reported whether they were allowed to join the expedition to Cape York Peninsula or not. Stephen was. So were Andrew and Carmen. Blake wasn't and Luke said 'maybe'. Roger confirmed he was not allowed. Because Carmen could go Marjorie was also allowed, but only for the first expedition as she was going south to visit family after Christmas.

That afternoon was a Cadet Home Training Parade to prepare people for the Promotion Course. Everyone present was required to step up to be mentored for their new roles and ranks. As Graham was to be CSM, he stood out front to conduct the Admin Parade at the start of the activity. CDTWO2 Cleland stood beside him to advise him on what to do or say next. That peeved Graham a bit as he was sure he already knew all of this, having watched closely for a couple of years. Still, it felt really good to be out there in that role and he was confident he would be able to do it the following year.

During the training session, Graham checked who else was allowed to attend the Navy Cadet parade. He then took that information to Captain Conkey. To do this he went to the cadet office and knocked on the door, not without some trepidation as he was new to not being in a squad all the time. Captain Conkey was doing some paperwork, but he looked up. Graham saluted and Captain Conkey raised his eyebrows.

"Yes CSM?"

Being addressed by that honourable title almost flustered Graham and he stood up even straighter at attention. "List of names of cadets who wish to attend the Navy Cadet's parade on Saturday, sir."

"Oh good. Here are some consent forms. Hand them out please and then you and any sergeants can get issued a red sash for the parade."

"Sir!"

Graham took the offered forms and then stepped back and saluted. Now he felt very good. *CSM!* he thought, relishing the status and looking forward to the promotion it implied. He then went to the Q Store as ordered, feeling even more pleased to have the scarlet sash in his hands again.

The prospect of wearing it and showing it off to the navy cadets made attending their parade even more attractive.

* * *

Thursday brought a change. When he met Carol, she did not look happy but she would not tell him what the problem was and just shook her head and muttered it was 'just something at the mill.' Not being able to help made Graham feel even more frustrated. But there was nothing he could do so he went off to study.

Friday came around and during the lunch break Graham sat with his friends because Carol had gone to the library and asked not to be disturbed while she studied.

Willy joined the group and said, "We might even be able to find our own local plane wreck."

"Oh yeah?" Stephen commented. "Where?"

"In the Graham Range behind Caster," Willy replied.

Graham at once sat up. "Behind Caster? What type of plane? What happened?"

From the grins on his friends' faces Graham guessed that they knew exactly why he was suddenly interested. He blushed but kept a smile on his face.

Willy explained, "I read about it last night in a local history story. It happened back in 1942. Apparently an American B25, a Mitchell bomber, got lost during bad weather at night while returning from a raid on the Pacific Islands. Some local farmers said they saw a big explosion right up near the top of the mountain just before ten o'clock that night. But they never found any wreck. The Americans admitted they lost three planes out of a flight of five, so it could have been a plane crash."

Stick looked puzzled. "But if it was seen to crash, why didn't the Americans send a search party?" he asked.

Willy shrugged. It was Peter who answered, "Probably short of men and with too many more pressing concerns with a war going on."

"We could look," Graham suggested.

Willy looked pleased at that. "When?" he asked.

"Next weekend?" Graham answered.

Willy shook his head. "Sorry, no chance. We are going back up to see Mr Beck on Sunday and we have exams starting on Monday."

Graham nodded and looked disappointed. Andrew added, "And we have our Annual Parade on Saturday afternoon. I was hoping you blokes might come and watch."

"We will," Willy replied. "It will cheer us up to see that we are much better."

"Better! Oh, piffle!" Andrew snorted. He then muttered about 'blue orchids' and 'show ponies'.

Stephen frowned. "So when can we go looking for this B25?" he asked.

They discussed the calendar of events for the next few weeks. With the Navy Cadet's parade on the Saturday and the Air Force Cadet's parade on the Friday night a week later, and with two weeks of exams at school, they agreed that the earliest they could plan on was the weekend after the exams finished.

"Ask your parents so we can do some planning," Willy requested.

This was agreed to, and Graham went home that afternoon feeling very hopeful.

* * *

Graham considered asking his mother if he could go to Caster on the Sunday for a day trip, but when he plucked up the courage to ask, she just shook her head.

"No. We are going to Mareeba again. We are going to help Grandma repair her hen coop. A branch has fallen from the mango tree and broken part of the roof and the fence, and I don't want her or Grandad climbing up on ladders and getting hurt. And if you aren't willing to do that you can stay home and study."

Graham then remembered that Willy and his friends were planning to go to see the Becks again that day. "Could I do some work at Grandma's in the morning and then go to Beck's Air Museum in the afternoon please? They are going to discuss the expeditions up the Cape during the holidays."

"Yes, alright, as long as you make up for it," she replied.

"Can I take Stephen with us?"

His mother looked annoyed but agreed. Graham immediately went to the phone and called Stephen and put the idea to him. He liked the plan and went off to ask his parents. They gave approval so times were agreed on and Graham felt better.

He then settled to study but could not seem to think straight. What niggled was a tiny doubt that his relationship with Carol, which had seemed to start so well, wasn't going quite as well and he had hoped.

* * *

The Navy Cadet parade the following afternoon did not have the numbers or the marching spectacle of the Army Cadet parade, but Graham still found it impressive. Partly it was the setting and partly the uniforms. The navy cadets stood facing the setting sun. This shone on their white uniforms so that the cloth appeared to glow. The sunlight also shimmered on the blades of the swords and cutlasses held by the Cadet Midshipmen and petty officers.

Nine army cadets in their best ceremonial uniforms stood in a group behind the chairs occupied by the parents and guests. Graham stood tall and erect and feeling very proud as he wore his sergeant's scarlet sash. With him stood Peter, Stephen, and Roger. Beside them stood Barbara and her section commander, Gwen. Nearby stood a group of air cadets, including Willy, Noddy, Stick, and Marjorie. Among the guests was Captain Conkey in his ceremonial uniform and medals. Feeling very self-conscious, Graham called the others to 'Stand Fast!' and saluted when Captain Conkey arrived. Captain Conkey smiled and returned the salute and gave them a few words of welcome before he sat down. The AAFC CO was there too but he merely returned Willy's salute and gave the group of air cadets a brief nod.

The Reviewing Officer was a navy captain, resplendent in dress whites and with a bright splash of colour made by his medals. Seeing him caused Graham some very unhappy memories. From his earliest days he had set his heart on being a naval officer, to go to sea. But in Year 8 he had his hopes shattered when he discovered his eyes were not good enough to ever be a 'General Service' officer in the RAN.

Feeling hurt and dejected he had left the Navy Cadets which he had joined so proudly only a few months before. For some months he had been so depressed he had several times contemplated suicide and his behaviour had deteriorated so badly that he was threatened with expulsion from school and worse. It had been joining the Army Cadets that had saved him and he was very conscious of that. So while he admired the naval officer's cap with its gleaming black brim glinting with gold leaves and startling white top reflecting the afternoon sunlight, he was able to watch without too much emotional angst.

This parade looks really good, Graham thought.

Obviously, some of his friends were not as impressed, or at least pretending not to be.

Stick sneered and muttered, "Their drill isn't nearly as good as ours."

Nor ours, Graham thought. But despite that he enjoyed watching, and he liked seeing the little differences in the way things were done. His gaze roved along the ranks of navy cadets while they were being inspected. *There is Andrew,* he noted. *He looks very proud of himself. And there is his sister Carmen.*

For a good few seconds, he studied Carmen. She was in Year 11 and was the petty officer standing at the rear of the group on Willy's left. *She looks very attractive, very much the lady,* he thought. Then he briefly admired Tina Babcock and the memory of his failed courting caused him to give a little sigh, before he felt guilty at even thinking of another girl.

After the parade there was a barbeque. During it Graham sought out

Andrew and his friends and congratulated him. He ended up talking to Andrew, Blake, Carmen, and Andrew's girlfriend, Tina. Willy and his friends joined them.

Andrew drained a cup of orange cordia,l then said, "Willy, are you still planning this expedition to the Cape in a few weeks' time?"

"Yeah, why?"

"Because Carmen and I still want to come. But we might have to work to pay our way," Andrew answered.

"Work? What sort of work?" Willy asked.

"Graham's dad is going to put us on the payroll. We have to join the Seaman's Union. That costs a bit, so we need the money," Andrew explained.

That did not surprise Graham as he had a working knowledge of such 'waterfront' stuff. What did surprise him was that Andrew and his parents had obviously been in contact with his father.

Willy then said, "Mr Beck, the man who owns the Air Museum in Mareeba, is going to pay for most of it."

"I've heard of him. Is the museum very good?" Andrew asked.

Willy nodded. "Yes. He has lots of interesting things. He even has three tanks and a couple of armoured cars, plus a lot of planes and things. They are all in a big old hangar. We are going up there tomorrow afternoon to talk to him."

"Can we come too?" Carmen asked.

"If you like," Willy replied, adding, "You might have to pay the museum entry fee though."

"That's alright," Andrew replied. "That is fair."

The conversation was interrupted by Willy's mother, insisting they go home. After that it was just co-ordinating with Stephen for the next day and then home with his mother.

Chapter 25

EXAMS AND ANXIETIES

Next afternoon, Graham and Stephen were taken to Beck's Museum by Graham's mother. There they met up with Willy, his parents, Marjorie, and Stick. Graham was in a bad mood because he had not slept well and because he was so frustrated.

I wish I was in Caster with Carol, he thought.

Andrew and Carmen arrived with their parents. They were introduced and taken on a tour of the museum. The others strolled along behind. Graham spent most of his time looking at the tanks. The one that really impressed him was the Centurion.

Am I brave enough to serve in a tank? he wondered.

He had seen a number of images on the TV news of tanks being hit by anti-armour weapons and then erupting in flames and the idea of being inside one at that moment appalled him.

Mr Beck pointed to the 50 ton, green-painted monster and said, "This one and the Saracen APC and the Ferret scout car all still work."

"Oh! Can we see one drive around?" Stick asked.

Mr Beck shook his head. "No. Sorry. There are all sorts of legal reasons why not, insurance and that sort of thing," he explained.

That was a disappointment, but Graham could only accept it as one of those things he knew he would have to face up to one day. He strolled over to join Willy at the Airacobra. Stick and Marjorie joined him, then Mr Beck and the others.

Mr Beck explained the aircraft to the adults, then said, "We are hoping to add to the collection by adding a Kittyhawk fighter and a Beaufighter."

"These are the ones crashed up on Cape York that the kids want to help you find?" Mr Collins asked.

"Yes, that's right," Mr Beck answered.

Marjorie piped up to add, "We are not the only ones trying to get them either."

Mr Beck looked at her. "Aren't we? Who else is trying to get them?"

Marjorie screwed her face up in concentration and said, "I can't remember his name. A man who collects old aeroplanes. He has an aircraft collection too."

Willy broke in. "Mr Jemmerling."

To Willy's surprise and dismay, Mr Beck looked suddenly very anxious. "Mr Jemmerling!" he cried. "How do you know?"

"He visited the Air Cadets on Friday night," Willy explained. "He showed us slides of his collection and we looked through his restored Catalina."

"I hope you didn't mention our plans," Mr Beck asked, his anxiety plain to see.

Graham saw Willy glance at Stick, who blushed. Willy then said, "I'm afraid we did."

"I hope you didn't give away any details," Mr Beck replied.

Willy again glanced at Stick who shifted uncomfortably from one foot to the other before admitting, "I told him. I'm sorry. I didn't think. We, that is Noddy and I, were talking about Kittyhawks and that man must have overheard us. He then got us talking about Kittyhawk wrecks and we told him we were going to look for one. He then asked where it was. I... I... er... I just didn't think. I pointed to Bathurst Bay on the air chart on the wall."

Mr Beck frowned and pressed his lips together.

Stephen cried, "Oh Stick, you bloody nong! I hope you didn't show him where the Beaufighter is as well?"

Stick shook his head. "No, I didn't."

"Did you tell him we were looking for it too?" Stephen asked.

Stick swallowed and went red, then nodded. "Yeah, sorry. It just sort of slipped out."

Mr Beck shook his head. "Did you show him exactly where the Kittyhawk is?"

Willy answered before Stick had time to. "Not exactly. He only pointed to the general area before I dragged him away."

Graham was now worried. He asked Mr Beck, "Who is this Jemmerlane anyway?"

Mr Beck sighed. "Mr Francis Mortimer Jemmerling, millionaire. He is my greatest rival. We have been trying to beat each other to wrecks for twenty years. Unfortunately he has a lot more money and is doing much better than I am. Now it looks like he may beat me yet again."

Willy looked very guilty. He said, "We will do our best to help you find the planes first, Mr Beck."

Mr Beck smiled. "That's fine, young William. Let's hope we can, but he has a couple of planes he can use for aerial searches."

"He said a Cessna 180 and a PBY Catalina," Willy replied.

"That's right. The Catalina is painted black and he calls it the *Pterodactyl*. I didn't know he was in North Queensland. I wonder what brought him up here?" Mr Beck replied.

"Maybe he was here for the same air show as Mr Southall?" Willy suggested.

Mr Beck shook his head. "No. I would have heard of that. No, I'm afraid Mr Mortimer Jemmerling has picked up some clue and is now sniffing around for more information."

"Then we must make sure he doesn't find any," Marjorie cried.

Mr Beck gave a short laugh, then said, "Easier said than done, my dear. But I must ask you again not to speak to anyone, not even your friends."

"We won't," Willy promised.

Graham now mentioned the B25 that was rumoured to have crashed in the jungle up behind the sugar mill at Castor. Mr Beck nodded. "Yes, I've heard of that one but never had time to go and look. It is up in very thick jungle, and no-one has ever been able to find anything. Why do you ask?"

"We thought we might have a go," Graham answered.

"Good luck!" Mr Beck replied. "When are you doing that?"

"Two weeks' time, after exams are finished," Graham replied.

They settled to discussing expeditions and timings and Mr Beck made arrangements to meet with Graham's father when his ship docked in Cairns the following week. By then they had run out of time and began dispersing.

Graham and Stephen were picked up by Graham's mother and they went back to Mareeba for another couple of hours of home handyman work at Grandma's. Then it was home back to Cairns

An evening spent completing an English assignment that was due the next day followed.

That night Graham had some very mixed dreams. Two of them started with him trying to impress Carol but Margaret kept appearing and he ended up with her, being caught kissing by Rosemary! The other was more of a nightmare. In that he was being chased by shadowy figures at the sugar mill and to escape he had to climb steel ladders and run along slippery catwalks between hissing machinery. Somehow, he ended up at the top of the chimney and there was a clutching hand reaching out for him. He woke in a lather of sweat and had to go and have a drink to calm down.

Monday was all study and revision for exams. Graham handed in his English assignment and worked hard. Being now focused on becoming an officer in the Regular Army helped him work hard as he had now set his heart on that. The only other things that enlivened the day were sitting with Carol during the breaks between classes and having a quick kiss when he met her in the library during a class when 10A were there at the same time.

During the day Graham also thought frequently about their planned expedition and he wondered how he could do that and get away to be with Carol. It seemed possible.

If I can run back down the mountain early, or join the others later, he speculated.

That night he did not sleep well. He was aware that the relationship seemed to have cooled a bit and a sense of anxiety was creeping in.

Carol seems to have gone all distant, he thought.

Tuesday was two exams: English in the morning, and Maths A in the afternoon. After school Graham went straight home and studied. That evening he did another assignment, History this time. He also went on the internet and looked up Army Careers. The part that most interested him was the Royal Military College at Duntroon and he was surprised to learn that he had two choices. He could try for a direct entry and do 18 months there, or he could do three years at the Australian Defence Force Academy and then another year at Duntroon. The direct entry looked to be an easier option and he noted it was even open to serving soldiers. For a few minutes he considered the option of joining the army as a recruit and then later applying for RMC. But he also suspected that it might not be the best option.

It was certainly food for thought, and that night he slept well.

* * *

Wednesday was just a day of revision and study. During the school day the only incident that later stuck in Graham's mind was sitting with Carol during the lunch break.

I was right, he told himself. *She seems to have gone all remote. I hope she isn't regretting having known me and is trying to find a polite way to dump me.* To him she certainly looked a bit tense. *If she wants to tell me it is over, I will make it easier for her,* he resolved.

After a couple of hesitant false-starts, he finally plucked up the courage to say, "Is everything okay? You look very distracted."

Carol shrugged and looked at him and he noted that her eyes had a far-away look in them and that she was on the edge of tears.

"No, just problems at home and at the mill. The workers are very unhappy, and something seems to go wrong almost every day so there are lots of stoppages and the mill is way behind in the crushing schedule. Dad is really worried, and he has even hinted the trouble is being stirred up deliberately."

Graham was amazed. "Surely people wouldn't deliberately stop the mill? It would cost them money, wouldn't it?"

Carol nodded. "It would, but Dad has even used the word 'sabotage' to mum. He tries to hide the situation from us kids, but I know they are both very worried."

Sabotage! Graham thought.

That did not sound likely to him, although he then admitted he had heard stories from his dad about waterside trouble in the old days where the wharf labourers would deliberately damage cranes or winches or cargo as an excuse to strike when their bosses told them.

But they were run by the Communist Party back then and their aim was to ruin the free countries' economies. There are no Commos anymore so why would anyone slow down the mill?

For something to say he blurted out what was on the top of his worries. "I was worried you were regretting being my girlfriend," he said.

At that Carol first looked alarmed, then she gave a wry smile and shook her head. "No. I just wish I could see more of you," she said.

Graham smiled, "Me too. I just wish I could get to see you more often. We might be coming to Caster in a few weeks to go searching the mountains looking for some aircraft wreck that Willy Williams wants to find."

"Why not next weekend?" Carol asked.

Graham sighed. "I have promised to go to the Air Cadet parade on Friday night and we are all going to up to Mareeba on Sunday. My dad's parents live there, and he hasn't been to see them for a couple of months."

"What about Saturday?" Carol asked.

Graham scowled, but not at her. "Because we will be helping with the ship," he said. "Dad gets home tomorrow, and we always get roped in to help with cleaning and maintenance so the crew can have some leave." He didn't really want to burden Carol with the family business worries but he decided that more of an explanation was needed. "Ships are very expensive to run, and business isn't doing so well at the moment so the family pitch in to help keep down costs."

"That's really good," Carol cried, placing a sympathetic hand on his arm as she did. Then said, "Well, the weekend after is the Mill Christmas Party. Would you be able to come to that?"

"I'd love to!" Graham cried. "When is it?"

"Two weeks' time. The twenty-first of November, a Saturday night."

When he realised that was the same weekend as the proposed expedition into the mountains, Graham was dismayed. "Oh, that's when we promised to go and look for the crashed plane," he replied.

"Ask anyway, please," Carol said, obviously disappointed.

On seeing her expression, Graham at once resolved to go to the party instead. "No, I will come to the party. I'd rather be with you," he said firmly.

"That's sweet, but if you have promised your friends you should go with them," Carol said.

Graham felt torn. He shrugged. "I didn't really promise. I just said I'd like to go. Anyway, I can probably be with them some of the time. When does the party start?"

"Middle of the afternoon and it goes on into the night. There will be a barbeque tea."

"I will ask," Graham promised.

He took himself off to class puzzling how to do both activities. Making 'time and space' calculations kept his mind busy for the afternoon. During the last lesson, Graham sat next to Stephen and after a few minutes he led the conversation to the Mill Christmas Party.

"Would you like to come?" he asked.

Stephen's eyes lit up. "I'd love to. If it's going to be anything like the last trip, it will be fantastic fun."

"We will probably have to stay in that ghastly hotel again."

"That's okay. Betty might put on a show for us like she did last time," Stephen replied.

That made Graham blush, but he also itched to ask if Stephen had done anything to Betty at the hotel that night. To lead up to it, he said, "You looked like you were doing alright on Sunday down at the creek."

Stephen grinned, a self-satisfied smirk, Graham thought. "We were! Pity her dad came along when he did."

"You are bloody lucky he didn't see what you were doing," Graham commented.

Stephen laughed and grinned again, more ruefully. "My word, yes! He would have had my nuts on toast if he had."

"You want to be careful," Graham said.

He struggled to find the right words to be tactful but also had to admit he was very jealous.

Stephen shrugged. "It's okay. Betty's on the pill. She told me that she has sex lots of times, and not always because she wants to or with blokes she likes."

"Is... is," Graham tried to ask, wondering if Betty was being made to do things by her parents. He struggled for the right wording, but at that moment the final bell went and the question stayed unasked.

Instead, he and Stephen made their way out to their school bags. Being Wednesday meant Army Cadets and they both hurried off to the toilets to change into their uniforms. They then made their way to the Cadet Q Store area.

As they did, they met Willy. He reminded them that the Air Cadets had their Passing-Out Parade that Friday night. "Are you blokes coming to watch?" he asked.

Graham nodded. "I am. I will ask on parade who else wants to come and I will get them consent forms."

He knew Captain Conkey had been invited and that he had done the required paperwork to get HQ approval for any cadets to attend.

As the trainee CSM, Graham had lots to do so he hurried down to the Cadet Office to get Platoon Roll Books and to check with the officers if there was anything else that needed to be done. Then he went out onto the grass quadrangle and marked out the parade ground with coloured plastic cones under the supervision of WO2 Cleland. Once again, WO2 Cleland stood with him during the parade and then helped him mark the Company Roll, once the others had gone to a lesson.

During the break between lessons, Graham found himself standing near Captain Conkey who called him over. "Graham, you are doing very well as CSM, and I note that your schoolwork has picked up too. Well done!"

"Thank you, sir. I've decided to try for the Royal Military College when I finish school," he explained.

"Good for you!" Captain Conkey replied.

For a few minutes they discussed the various options for entry to Duntroon. Captain Conkey then gave Graham some real food for thought by saying, "Of course, if you really want to do well in the army, to get to be a colonel and a general, you need to be in at the start, to do the three years at ADFA first and then the one year. They are the Corps of Staff Cadets, the people who are the inner circle who actually run the army. The others might get to the top, but it is much harder."

Graham was a bit shocked by that but could understand what Captain Conkey was talking about.

As dad says: Not what you know but who you know!

After Cadets it was home to study and then to once again look at pictures of the 'Staff Cadets' at Duntroon. Graham studied these carefully and imagined himself there.

I had better aim at ADFA, he decided.

He also plucked up the courage to ask his mother if he could attend the Sugar Mill Christmas Party.

She frowned and looked doubtful. "I thought you were going bushwalking with your friends, to look for some crashed plane from the war," she said.

"Yes Mum. We are doing that, but Steve and I have also been invited to the Christmas Party."

"So how will you do that if you are up in the jungle?" she asked.

Graham could only shrug. "We will leave the others when they are setting up camp and go to the party and then join them again the next day," Graham said, uncomfortably aware that his plan had lots of holes in it.

"But what about your friends?" she queried.

Graham shook his head. "There will be a whole bunch of them, at least six or eight. They won't miss us for a few hours."

To his relief, his mother just looked thoughtful and nodded, "Only if you promise it can be done safely."

"Yes Mum," Graham replied, thankful that she hadn't asked where he and Stephen planned to spend the night. He felt a bit guilty about that and tried to rationalise that he hadn't actually lied, just not given all the facts.

Thursday was a Science exam (Physics) which Graham felt he had done all right. *Better than 1ˢᵗ Semester anyway.*

He then studied hard for the next exams and also completed a Geography assignment. For interest sake he did this on the way the early development of Cairns was dictated by the pattern of swamps and sand dunes in Trinity Inlet. To illustrate this, he used the military topographic map and also a selection of photos, some from tourist brochures and some he had taken himself.

During the day there was also a bit or rising tension caused by the knowledge that his father was due home later that day. Graham did not exactly fear his dad, but he certainly respected him and there had been enough problems caused by his own behaviour over the last few years to generate some anxiety.

But the worry was for nothing. When he got home, he discovered his father was already there and was asleep in bed. To Graham's huge relief when his father woke just before dinner, he was very friendly and congratulated him on his Cadet prizes and on the fact that he had been selected to be the CSM and was to be promoted.

"Well done son!" was his gruff comment.

There was no shaking of hands or anything like hugging as the family wasn't like that. Because he was always coming and going the family had long adopted the custom of not making arrivals or departures too emotional.

Friday brought more anxiety and another exam. This was in the afternoon and was Maths B. Once again, Graham was sure he had done better than before and that gave him hope for the future. Immediately school was over he made his way home and, to his mother's astonishment, did his homework immediately and then prepared his uniform for the Air Cadet Parade.

Chapter 26

AIR CADETS AND PROGRESS

After a shower and dinner, Graham dressed in his Army Cadet uniform with particular care, pulling the sides of his tucked-in shirt around into small folds to smooth out the wrinkles. The scarlet sash was carefully positioned, under the black belt at the front and over at the back. That done, he stood in front of the mirror and admired himself, adjusting the angle of his Hat KFF to set it at the regulation angle. He then did a few practice salutes.

If I am going to be CSM I will be doing lots of saluting, he told himself.

As he made his way out to the lounge room, he wished his father was there to see him but knew he would be down at the wharf at Portsmith supervising the unloading of the *Wewak,* the ex-Landing Craft Tank that he was currently commanding. But he did note a gleam of approval in Kylie's eye and a look of pretended indifference on Alex's face, which he took to indicate jealousy.

His mother then drove him to the Air Cadet Depot at the General Aviation section of the Cairns Airport. As he marched across the bitumen car park among parents and other guests, he felt very self-conscious, mainly because he thought his red sash was very conspicuous.

The parade was to be on the small bitumen parade ground in front of the old wooden hut that was the Air Cadet Depot. The guests were seated on chairs placed along the front of the hut. Graham moved to the edge of the crowd and stood looking around, trying to pretend he wasn't nervous. He found it a relief when first Peter and then Stephen joined him, both in uniform. The friends chatted and watched the Air Cadets forming up to the side of the bitumen car park that was the Parade Ground.

Stephen shook his head. "Their ceremonial uniform is better than ours," he commented.

Graham could only agree. The Army Cadets wore the same DPCU shirt and trousers for all training and ceremonial, just adding a black belt and some embellishments and turning the side of their KFF up. The

AAFC on the other hand had a nice blue polyester uniform for parades and it looked very good: neat and ironed and more comfortable.

The only thing Graham thought was better was that the Army Cadet sergeants and WO2s had the scarlet sash, whereas the Air Cadet Warrant Officer and the sergeants who were the Banner Party escorts wore a blue sash that was not nearly as dramatic in appearance.

White uniforms appeared in the lamplight and Graham saw Andrew and Carmen, plus several other navy cadets. One of their officers took his place among the seated VIPs in the front row, his white dress uniform a splash of brightness

And there is Captain Conkey talking to the Mayor, Graham noted, seeing Captain Conkey in his ceremonial uniform.

At 1930 hours the parade began. It was a hot, sultry night but a breeze coming in from the sea and across the airport kept it reasonably cool. As far as Graham could tell, the parade went without a single hitch. The three friends made quiet asides to each other as they compared the drill and procedures with their own.

"More like bloody ballet than drill!" Stephen commented.

Graham could only agree. The Air Cadets moved their feet so slowly and so high and far out to the front when coming to attention or standing at ease that he thought it looked more like something choreographed.

But he still thought it all looked good. He searched the ranks and saw Willy. He stood tall and erect, chest out with obvious pride. When a Banner Party was marched on, Graham watched with jealous interest. His conclusion was that the army did it better. His only annoyance was the doubt over whether to salute or not as the AAFC OOC who was doing the commentary on the PA System made no mention of what people should do when the Banner was marched on. It was obvious to Graham that Captain Conkey wasn't sure either.

They should have told us what to do, he thought. He was vaguely aware that there were flags that should be saluted and unit flags that should not be. *And there are Regimental Colours and banners that have been consecrated and they definitely get saluted,* he remembered. But the details eluded him, and he hoped that he would learn such knowledge on his Warrant Officers Course.

But was the banner being paraded in front of him consecrated? He didn't know and so felt embarrassed when some people stood and saluted and others did not. He was astonished when the CUO carrying the Banner did a slow march across the front of the parade without an escort. But watching the drill also reminded him of how proud he had been to be part of the Flag Party.

I am really glad I got to do that, he thought.

Graham did admire the excellent co-ordination of the AAFC CUOs and sergeants. Just watching the squadron command group all move in flawless unison as they turned and stood at ease impressed him. And when he saw the CUO commanding the parade saluting with his sword, Graham was filled with a burning desire to reach that rank.

That will be me when I am in Year 12, he told himself.

The regional Wing Commander was the Inspecting Officer, and he was received with the appropriate salutes and then conducted the inspection. Graham gave a wry smile when the Wing Commander just went past Willy but then stopped to talk to a busty female cadet he now recognised as Marjorie

Stephen noted it too and muttered, "I see the boss man has chosen the most outstanding cadet to speak to!"

Graham chuckled. For a few seconds he wished he was somewhere else with a busty girl who liked him and who might offer him some delightful pleasures. That got him worrying because the first face that had flitted across the screen of his mind had been Rosemary's, not Carol's.

The inspection over the squadron turned to the right to march past. After the march past and advance in review order came the awards. It was no surprise to Graham when he heard Willy's name called out as the winner of the Service Knowledge prize.

"He's a bright bugger!" he commented.

"Mad as a cut snake," Stephen offered.

"Bugger beat us with his gadgets on that field exercise," Peter reminded him.

At which they all scowled and muttered. There were at least a few moments of malicious satisfaction when Willy just stood there as though stunned before he stamped to attention and stepped smartly out of the ranks. To Graham it was really obvious that Willy was having difficulty preventing his emotions flustering his drill.

But his drill is good, he conceded as he watched him trying to make his marching as perfect as he could.

Having been under the same pressure not to muck up such an apparently simple skill, Graham understood how very self-conscious he must feel and how his arms and legs probably felt very stiff and gawky.

Willy stamped to a halt and saluted. The wing commander returned the salute, then shook his hand and handed him a small trophy, a shiny gold coloured aeroplane mounted on a small wooden base with an inscription on it. Camera flashes flickered, among them one held by Willy's mother who had moved to the front. Then Willy stepped back, saluted, turned left with his best turn at the halt, then marched over to hand the trophy to an OOC. He then marched proudly back to his place in the ranks while the crowd clapped.

He did that well, Graham conceded.

When the parade was over, Graham and his friends moved to congratulate Willy. But Marjorie was the first person to do that. She rushed up to him and flung her arms around his neck.

"Oh Willy! I am so proud of you!" she cried before kissing him.

That obviously worried and embarrassed Willy but nobody seemed to think it odd or even notice. Then his mother stepped forward to hug him and he disentangled himself from Marjorie's arms. Willy's father shook his hand and then Graham and his friends could step forward. Graham smiled with genuine pleasure while holding out his hand.

Graham's own satisfaction increased when he got home and found his father there. His father eyed his uniform and then nodded and smiled.

"That looks good, son. Just stand there so I can admire you, please."

Feeling both very pleased and self-conscious, Graham did so. His father again nodded, and then said, "Hat on son." Graham complied and again his father nodded. "You certainly look the part, a real 'Aussie Digger'. Well done, son! And I hear good reports about your schoolwork as well. That is good. Keep it up."

"Yes dad. Thanks Dad," was all Graham could reply, having received more praise in those couple of minutes than in the preceding couple of years.

It sent him to bed with a deep glow of satisfaction and a feeling of making real progress in life.

* * *

Saturday was as he predicted. After being woken at 6am and given an early breakfast, the family drove to the port and set to work. The barge was unloaded by then, so Graham and Kylie got the job of removing some hydraulic fluid and oil spilt by the fork lift that had done the unloading ("And make sure none of the bloody stuff gets into the harbour!"). That and sweeping and picking up the loose bits of dunnage (the baulks of timber used to wedge and secure cargo) and other odds and ends and then sweeping kept them busy for several hours. Down in the 'Tank Deck' in the blazing tropical sunshine was sweltering work, but they were used to it and kept steadily at it.

Morning tea was allowed and then they began cleaning the wheelhouse, inside and out. Dust, diesel grime and dried salt were washed and wiped off and then Graham was sent to clean the windows. This entailed lying on his stomach up on the 'Monkey Island' above the wheelhouse while he used a mop and then a window cleaner squeegee to get the salt and grime off. It wasn't particularly hard work, but the deck was so hot that Graham had to get a blanket to lie on and then he forgot he was only wearing shorts and got sunburnt on the backs of his knees.

After a good lunch, Graham's father handed him some cleaning cloths and a can of metal polish. "Seeing that you are now so well trained at polishing brass by the bloody army, you can put a bit of a shine on the binnacle and anything else on the bridge made of brass," his father said.

Alex laughed loudly until he had his grin wiped off by being ordered to go and chip rust off the anchor chain and the chains that raised and lowered the bow ramp.

"And grease those pulleys well too!"

It was a long and hot day and Graham got very sunburnt, but he actually felt good about most of the work. It was helping the family and he did think the old barge looked better for a good clean up.

Saturday evening was relaxing in front of the TV and they were allowed a sleep in before a late breakfast, morning routine and then a drive to Mareeba.

Sunday afternoon found the family at Beck's Air Museum. As introductions were made to Willy's family, Graham's studied his father. He saw a solid, weather-beaten man with a serious face. He suspected from seeing old family photos of uncles and grandparents that he might look just like him when he was older. Even when his father was dressed in casual civilian clothes, Graham found it easy to recognise him as the tough ship captain he was. He knew he respected him enormously, even if he wished he might stay at sea a bit more.

Especially when exam results come out!

Graham's father shook hands with Mr Beck and then said, "So you'd like to charter one of my ships to move some wrecked aircraft?"

Mr Beck nodded. "That's right, two World War Two wrecks."

"Are they easy to get to? Can a vehicle collect them and drive them on?" Capt Kirk asked.

"One is. It is right on the beach. But the other is in a fairly inaccessible place. We might need to take our own vehicle with us, and then think about winching or using a crane. There are no roads leading to either area," Mr Beck answered.

"Beaches, eh? Hmm. So we need to worry about the depth of water, the tides, and any underwater obstructions. Can you show me which beaches please?" Capt Kirk said.

As a chart of the East coast of Cape York Peninsula was spread on the bench top Graham noted Willy looking anxious.

He is worried the secret might leak out. But Dad has to know where the wrecks are to plan the voyages, he thought.

Capt Kirk was shown the approximate locations and bent to study the chart. After a few minutes, he straightened up and said, "No obvious problems. It depends on the weather and the tide. When are you planning to do this?"

"Four weeks' time, after the Year Tens have finished school," Dr Williams answered.

A calendar was consulted and then Capt Kirk opened his phone and brought up the tide tables and studied them. "Should be alright," he commented. "Depending on the weather of course. You can get a lot of northerlies at that time of the year, and they could build up a dangerous surf in Bathurst Bay. It is also the cyclone season," Capt Kirk said.

"Are they likely?" Mr Beck asked.

"December to March is the cyclone season, but they are very rare up in that part of the coast. They usually come in much further south; Bowen and the Whitsunday Islands for example. But the weather people will give us plenty of warning, so it shouldn't be a problem. I still have to sail anyway."

"So you think our scheme is feasible?" Mr Beck asked.

"Certainly. We can use the *Wewak*. She is our old Landing Craft Tank. We could drop you off with some vehicles and supplies on our way north to Thursday Island. We always do a run with Christmas supplies at that time and could pick you and your wreck up on the return trip a week later," Capt Kirk said.

Mr Beck looked anxious. "Wouldn't that be a bit unsafe, not having any transport if we had an accident?"

"Not really," Capt Kirk replied. "If you had a good radio or a satellite phone you could just call the Emergency Services helicopter from Cairns. It would be there in an hour or so."

"I will be there as well," Dr Williams added, "So you will have a doctor on the spot."

"So, what date are we looking at?" Capt Kirk asked.

"Friday the eleventh or Saturday the twelfth of December," Mr Beck answered.

At that Graham groaned. "Aww! That means Steve and I will miss out."

"Why is that?" Capt Kirk asked.

"Because our army cadet promotion course doesn't end till Tuesday the fifteenth," Graham explained.

Capt Kirk shrugged. "Stiff! Life is going to be full of those sorts of choices. You must choose. Which do you want the most; promotion in the army cadets or a trip on the landing craft?"

Graham grimaced and shrugged. He said, "Couldn't the trip be put off a few days?"

"It probably could be, but the ships are trying to run to a schedule. Other people are involved. They are depending on vessels being available. I have another contract with a mineral exploration party in that area about then. If you like you can pay to hire the ship for five days and we will wait."

"No thanks," Graham hurriedly answered.

He knew it cost thousands of dollars a day to run a ship and he did not even have hundreds!

The discussion moved on to what vehicles and cranes might be needed, and how the various parts they might salvage would be moved, protected and stowed.

Mr Beck pointed out the far end of the big hangar. "I am building a new shed to restore the wrecks in and then to display them in."

Graham looked and saw a concrete slab and a steel framework with a few sheets of corrugated sheet metal fastened to it.

"It isn't finished," he commented.

"No," Mr Beck replied. "Norman and his friend Jeff are working on the roof and hope to have that done by next weekend. Then they will start on the walls."

Norman now said, "It'd go a lot faster if we had a few more workers."

"What about a working bee?" Willy's father suggested.

"That would be a great help," Norman answered. "Even if they just held things or passed tools and so on. It would speed it up a lot."

"We could do that," Willy offered.

"When?" Norman asked.

"Can't be next weekend," Willy answered. "We are searching the jungle near Caster then. It would have to be the weekend after."

"That will do," Norman replied.

Timings were then agreed on. Marjorie also volunteered and so, reluctantly, did Stick. Graham did not want to but felt pressured to agree. There was then a discussion about who was going. Capt Kirk was concerned as he explained that none of his vessels were registered to carry paying passengers.

"I understand there are a few who might come as non-paying passengers," he commented.

"That's right," Mr Beck answered. He looked at Willy who said, "There are myself and Dad, and Andrew Collins and his big sister, Carmen. They are navy cadets so should be useful. Then there might be Stick and his sister, Marjorie."

"Girls, eh? And who is going to chaperone them?" Capt Kirk asked.

Willy said, "Oh, they are all big girls. They don't need anyone to look after them."

Capt Kirk smiled and said, "Maybe not, but I don't want the responsibility of looking after two or three teenage girls. We need an adult female."

"Mum might come," Kylie suggested.

Capt Kirk looked at her in surprise. "I doubt it! Are you planning on joining this expedition 'Hickety Boo'?"

Having her family nickname used in public caused Kylie to blush deep red. She vigorously shook her head. "No. I am going to Port Douglas with Sally. Besides, we all have to do the trip just before Christmas, don't we?"

"Yes, you do," Capt Kirk agreed.

Dr Williams now said, "I will ask Helen if she will go."

Capt Kirk nodded, then turned back to Mr Beck. "Which of these two jobs do you wish to do first Mr Beck?" he asked.

Mr Beck hesitated. Willy had no doubts. "We must go to Bathurst Bay first," he said.

Mr Beck nodded. "Yes, you are right. If we are to beat the opposition that is. Bathurst Bay Captain."

Capt Kirk nodded. "That suits me fine. I have to take the mineral exploration people to Bathurst Bay at about that time. Maybe we can fit the two trips together to keep down the costs."

* * *

Back in Cairns that evening, Graham settled to studying for his exams with a much easier mind. He went to bed full of hopeful thoughts about Carol.

The week that followed had both good and bad experiences. To Graham's disappointment, he hardly saw Carol as her exam program was different and during the breaks she wanted to study. But she did cheer him up by checking that he and Steve were allowed to come to the Mill Christmas Party.

The exams were mostly hopeful. They were on Geography, Chemistry and History. For Geography and History Graham felt very confident he had done well. '*Bs' if not 'As'*, he told himself. But the Chemistry? He was not confident of even passing that. *All those bloody SO2 s and Hs and so on!* he lamented.

Cadets on Wednesday was better. He particularly liked the fact that he was allowed to run both the First Parade and the Dismissal Parade on his own. CDTWO2 Cleland just stood behind the company and nodded or made gestures if it looked like he was going to forget what to do next.

By Thursday Graham was all a-tingle with anticipation about the weekend trip to Caster. He discussed it with Stephen and they agreed on details, but he did not pass on the fact that he and Stephen were not going to be with the others all the time. He felt a bit bad about that but rationalised it by thinking there were enough of them.

But then it just came out when the group of friends were discussing the weekend expedition during the lunch break. It was very obvious to Graham that Willy was very excited and full of hope for finding the wreck of the crashed B25 in the jungle in the mountains behind the Caster Mill.

The truth came out when Willy asked Graham directly if he was still joining them.

Graham made a face and shrugged, not wanting to disappoint the group. "I might join you for a little while," he conceded.

"Why? Where will you go then?" Stick asked.

Graham felt quite uncomfortable and then shrugged. "Down to Caster. The sugar mill is putting on its annual Christmas Party," Graham explained.

"Oh, I see," Stick commented, obviously not seeing at all.

Willy understood though. Graham saw him give a wry smile and nod. That made him blush.

Willy then said, "So who is going? Are you going, Steve?"

To Willy's evident surprise Stephen shook his head. "No. I'm going to the party with Graham."

"Why?" Willy asked in astonishment. Then he shook his head. "No, don't tell me. I can guess. So what about you, Pete?"

Peter nodded. "Yes, and young Roger here. And Andrew and his team say they are still interested."

"That's good," Willy replied. "How are we getting there and back?"

Details of transport were discussed and then timings. While they discussed these details the sound of radial aero engines came to them and Willy looked up. Graham followed his glance and had just enough aircraft general knowledge to identify the aircraft.

A Catalina flying boat, he thought, remembering Willy and the Air Cadets had been for a flight in one.

But Graham did feel a few gnawing doubts about how he would balance his desire to be with Carol at the Christmas Party against his wish to go searching the jungle. He did not want to admit that his lustful urges were probably stronger.

Chapter 27

DESPAIR

That Friday afternoon, despite feeling ill and depressed, Declin made his way to the mill. Only to find that he wasn't starting shift as planned at 2pm. Instead, all the workers had been called to the Recreation Hall for a union meeting. Some very unhappy looking managers and foremen, including Mr Battersby, stood around outside the mill offices watching as the workers made their way into the hall. Declin went with them, his mind again in turmoil and his anxiety at a higher level, dreading what the outcome might be. In an effort to make himself inconspicuous, he sat near the back and in the middle of a row of chairs and then hunched down.

He then looked around to check where Rossiter and his cronies were. To his surprise, they were on the other side of the hall and also near the back. Declin had expected them to be near the front or even up with the union rep and organisers. To Declin, the feeling in the room was one of wary tension and he noted quite a few workers casting worried glances around the room.

This is not a happy workplace, he thought.

He then learned that there had been another safety problem during the last shift. A steam pipe had come loose and squirted superheated steam across a walkway. As soon as he heard that Declin glanced across at Rossiter and noted that Dennis had a tiny smirk around his mouth.

Did Dennis make that happen? he wondered.

Once again, the idea of telling management what he knew and suspected crossed his mind. But that was followed by a bout of almost paralysing fear. So Declin just sat and listened while several workers complained about how unsafe the mill was and how they should stop work until the problems were fixed.

Other workers then objected, saying that they couldn't afford to go on strike as they had families to feed and rent to pay. This led to some furious arguments. Declin would have loved to speak but he found he lacked the courage.

What was obvious to even him was that the workforce was deeply divided. He noted quite a few casting anxious glances back towards Rossiter and Marvin, and that gave Declin the notion that he was not the only one being pressured to cause a stoppage.

In the end it was a close vote and that was on a compromise. It was voted to have a two-hour stoppage while the union people went around with a couple of the more vocal workers to do a safety check. The meeting broke up with a lot of muttering and grumbling. Nobody was really happy, and they filed outside and stood around in groups talking. Many of the groups casting worried glances at other groups.

Declin took himself aside and sat in the shade near the mill office. Something close to panic gripped him as he tried to summon the courage to go in and talk to the bosses. But images of his mother and his little sister kept bringing Rossiter's threats to mind and the fear held him there.

But as he sat, he saw Carol appear on the gravel road over behind the houses. She was still in her school uniform and had obviously just arrived home. His heart leapt and he let out a sob of anguish. With eyes that hungered with a need to love, he watched her walk along the gravel road until she vanished out of sight behind the buildings of the mill.

Declin was tempted to go after her, to try to win back her affection but could not think of what he should say. So he shook his head and stayed where he was and felt even more miserable. But even as he decided to stay there, he noticed a man he thought worked in the loco repair shed go walking quickly past towards the back of the mill, his gaze fixed on where Carol had just gone out of sight.

Where is he off to in such a hurry? Declin wondered, looking around to see if anyone else was also going that way.

But the only workers he could see were a small group at the front of the main mill building and they were busy arguing amongst themselves.

Puzzled, Declin watched the man hurry to the far corner of the mill. When the man abruptly stopped before the corner and then appeared to peek around it, his suspicions went up.

Is he watching Carol? he wondered.

The man then vanished around the corner, walking quickly in the same direction Carol had gone. Declin's suspicions immediately moved to concern. It certainly looked like the man was watching her.

Is he stalking her? he wondered.

Driven by concern for Carol's safety, Declin stood up and began walking towards the far corner of the mill. As he strode across the lawn, a glance back showed that nobody was paying him any attention, or not that he could detect.

On reaching the far corner of the mill, Declin did the same as the man, stopping then looking carefully around. He did not want to appear to be doing anything strange himself and blunder into an innocent situation. But that quick look settled things in his mind. The man was now just visible, peeking around the corner of a shed over near the bagasse heaps.

He is watching Carol! Declin decided.

His concern for her shot up another notch. He knew she often did walks and even went jogging along that gravel road after school and he was also aware that while it was a fairly open road on the mill side it was out of the sight of most people.

Is this guy a pervert? Is she in danger? he thought anxiously.

As soon as the man slipped out of sight Declin followed, hurrying across the railway spur line and the dusty open yard past the bagasse heaps and to the shed. Here he also stopped to peek around the corner, and his suspicions hardened when he saw the man again appearing to hide behind another structure near the loading hoppers while still looking in the direction Carol had gone.

The man again moved on and Declin followed, trying to appear he was just sauntering but actually walking fast. Now his heart was starting to hammer with anxiety and perspiration was beading on his face and arms. So far he had been unable to see Carol, but as he reached the base of the loading hoppers he got a glimpse of her in the distance. She was passing the loco workshops. The man moved to the molasses tank and then on to the loco workshops.

Maybe that is where he is going? Declin considered.

As the man worked there it was a reasonable assumption, but when the man moved on past the workshops on the creek side of the building Declin's worry grew again.

Now feeling quite stressed, Declin followed the man past the locomotive workshop. As he went past the building, he looked in the windows but saw nobody else in there.

Then another horrible thought came to Declin, sending his emotions shooting up even higher: Carol sometimes walked to the creek after school to have a swim, and she swam naked. Now really concerned for Carol's modesty as well as he safety, Declin continued following as Carol walked on past the parked locomotives and the lines of parked cane bins. He moved now from mango tree to mango tree as the only cover. The man was doing the same thing, and by this time Declin was absolutely certain the man was stalking Carol.

But why? Declin fretted. Was he just sneaking up to watcher her naked, or were there darker motives like rape in his mind?

And then Declin saw Carol turn and go down into the long grass along the track to the swimming beach. That instantly raised a dilemma: how to keep her safe without also being a Peeping Tom? To his dismay, he saw the man move to the end of the track and also vanish from sight.

The idea that the man might actually attack Carol got Declin moving. He hurried forward along the gravel road, going past his own secret fishing track and now quite determined to confront the man if need be.

But at the top of the track he dithered. *Do I just go down her track and warn her before she goes in, or do I just watch and wait?* Declin wondered.

The memory of her berating him last time gave him pause and he stood there, almost hopping from one foot to another in his indecision and anxiety. But would he hear her if the man attacked her?

And what would he do? Anxiety about what he would then do caused him more upset, as he presumed he might have to fight the man. As he had never been taught how to fight, the prospect filled him with dread, but he vowed that for Carol he would fight anyone.

Unable to decide but still driven by anxiety, Declin decided to go for the compromise of going down to his fishing spot to see if he could keep an eye on her from there. Feeling really stressed and ashamed, knowing he might also see Carol naked (and being torn by wanting to but not wanting to), he walked back to his secret track and pushed into the long grass.

Heart hammering with anxiety and arousal, Declin made his way down to his fishing spot and carefully peered through the leaves and long grass. And there was Carol! She had stripped off and was wading into the water.

Oh! She is so beautiful! Declin thought, blushing with shame at seeing her but unable to make himself look away. *But where is that man?*

Carefully he crouched to watch, his eyes scanning the bushes and long grass of the creek bank. To his relief, Carol was now submerged up to her neck, so she was not on embarrassing display. But the sight and the memories of seeing her nude on previous occasions caused him to become very aroused and that made him ashamed and anxious as well.

I love her! It's not just lustful desire, he told himself.

But it was still stressful to be acting like a Peeping Tom and Declin remained torn by his shame and by the urge to watch over her to keep her safe. He watched her wade back onto the little beach and then stand in the afternoon sun while she allowed the wind to dry her skin.

Oh, I hope that creepy man can't see her now, he thought. *But oh, she is so lovely and desirable!*

To Declin, Carol's nude form appeared to be the very vision of female perfection and he became so aroused he shivered and kept blushing with shame. Even watching her dress held his gaze. With fascinated interest he watched and then sighed with relief when she vanished from view back up the track.

Now another dilemma presented itself, when to go back up to the road himself? For the next few minutes he crouched there, listening intently in case the man grabbed her or did something.

It was cramp that got him moving and he crept back up the track, sick with shame at what his actions might look like if he was caught.

At the top of the track, Declin paused to listen and then carefully peeked out. To his relief, Carol was now a hundred metres away, walking quickly back in the direction of her home. But where was the man? Declin looked in all directions but could see no sign of him.

Where has he gone? Is he still down the creek? Declin worried.

He looked in all directions again but there was no sign of him. By then Carol had gone out of sight, so he straightened up and walked out onto the gravel road, again scanning the surrounding area for any sign of the man. Nothing! It was a mystery and Declin could only shrug.

I'd better move away from here in case he sees me, he decided. So he began quickly walking back along the gravel road towards the mill.

As he got closer to the loco workshops, Declin considered cutting across the many rail tracks to the Control Room, which he could see above the unloader. But there were several lines of parked empty cane bins standing on the tracks waiting to be taken away and he did not feel like climbing through them. He also knew that such an action would be recorded on the CCTV and people might wonder why he was doing that.

They might associate me with the sabotage of the rail tracks, he thought.

But then another idea came to him: had the CCTV recorded the man following Carol along the gravel road? He had never looked at the images closely to see what the cameras actually covered in the distance but now he decided to have a look. He felt a need to know where the man had gone, and when.

By then he was passing the loco workshop and he looked in to see if the man was there. There were a couple of workmen in there, but the man wasn't so Declin continued on. But as Declin approached the far end of the building, Carol suddenly stepped out, a very angry looking Carol with fists on hips.

"What are you up to? Are you following me?" she snapped.

Declin came to an embarrassed standstill and gaped at her, his mind groping for what to say. "I was... I was..."

Carol frowned and glared at him. "I told you to stay away from me! Why are you following me?"

Declin was tempted to say he wasn't but that did not sit right so he shook his head and blurted out, "To keep you safe."

"Safe! From who?" Carol snapped.

"There was a man following you," Declin replied.

Carol's lip curled in disbelief. "Oh there was not! Who?"

"I don't know his name. A tall thin guy who works here, in the loco worskhops."

Carol turned to look into the workshop and then looked back at Declin. "I don't believe you! When was this?" she cried.

"Just this afternoon, when you walked along the road from your house. I was at the mill office and saw him follow you. He was watching you from behind trees and buildings. I was worried about you, that he might... might, you know?"

Carol looked doubtful. "You sure? You aren't just making it up?"

"No. Honest I'm not!" Declin cried, wishing her to believe him.

"But you were following me then?" she asked.

Declin nodded. "Yes, I was, but Carol, I'm not stalking you! I just wanted to be sure you were safe."

"Did you watch me have a swim?" Carol asked, anger glinting in her eyes. Then, before Declin could reply she pursed her lips. "You did! I can see by the way you are blushing. I asked you not to. Stop sneaking around watching me, okay?"

Declin blushed furiously with shame and embarrassment. "Carol, I only did it because I care about you. I am not some obsessive weirdo. I did it because I was worried you might be in danger."

Carol snorted. "Huh! What sort of danger?"

Declin blushed some more and was tongue-tied. He did not want to use sexual words like rape to her and could only shake his head and mutter, "I… I thought he might... might attack you or something. You shouldn't go down the creek on your own. It's not safe."

"Not safe from you!" Carol snapped.

"No, from the men!" Declin cried in near despair.

"What men?"

Declin shrugged, desperate now to be believed. "From the men who are trying to close the mill."

"Oh, what men are trying to close the mill?" Carol cried in disbelief.

Declin went to tell her and then realised he might be saying too much. Fear of Rossiter made him reword what he had been going to say. "Some of the workers. They want the mill closed," he replied, casting an anxious glance towards the mill as he did.

"Oh I don't believe that! Prove it," Carol demanded.

At that moment, Declin's anxious gaze noted a man looking at them from the main mill building and it felt like ice suddenly clutching his heart. "I... I can't say," he replied.

Carol looked so doubting that all Declin could do was say, "There is danger, Carol. Please be careful. Oh I love you!" he cried.

At that Carol shook her head but her expression softened. "I like you too, Declin, but I am too young," she said.

And then the whole situation suddenly changed. Out of the workshop stepped Mr Battersby and the workshop foreman. They were obviously discussing some technical issue, but the moment Mr Battersby saw them he frowned and changed direction. "What's going on here? What are you doing here, Riley? Is he bothering you, Carol?"

To Declin's immense relief, Carol shook her head. "No Dad. He was just worrying about my safety," she said.

That got Mr Battersby to give Declin a very sharp look. "Why should you be worried about her safety?" he snapped.

Declin couldn't make his mouth work to answer as he could see Dennis watching from near the loading hopper. His throat just dried up from fear and he could only shake his head.

"Well?" demanded Mr Battersby. "What's going on?"

"We were just talking, Mr Battersby," Declin replied, while cursing himself for being a coward.

Here is your opportunity to tell management you weakling, he castigated himself. But he couldn't bring himself to do it.

Mr Battersby gave him a hard stare. "Well don't. You stay away from my daughter, Riley. She's only a child. I've warned you before and I won't warn you again. If I hear of you causing her any trouble you will be given notice and you will be out of here on your ear. Do you hear?"

"Yes sir," Declin croaked.

He could feel tears forming in the corners of his eyes and he had to swallow as the upset caused a nauseous reaction in his stomach.

Mr Battersby pointed, "Now get to work!" He then turned to Carol, "And you, young lady, you get home. Riley is right, it isn't safe for a girl to be walking around places like this alone. So don't! Now get going!"

Declin noted Carol cast him an anxious and worried glance and then she fled. With misery welling up to bring the tears he quickly turned and began stumbling his way across the railway tracks towards the unloader and Control Room.

I have really mucked things up now! he thought, misery deepening to despair.

Only for things to get much worse. As Declin approached the mill, he saw Rossiter and Marvin waiting near the unloader. Dennis was slinking away into the dark interior. The sight of the men instantly sent a chill of fear through Declin and he hoped they weren't waiting for him.

But they were. As Declin reached them, they stepped across to block his path. Rossiter did the talking, Marvin just standing and looking belligerent. Rossiter jerked a thumb towards the loco workshop.

"What were you talking about with the boss man?" he queried.

"Mr Battersby just told me to get back to work," Declin replied.

"Don't be a smart-arse, Declin me boy. He said much more than that. What were ya doin' over there?"

"I just went for a walk after the meeting," Declin answered, a film of sweat breaking out from the nervous tension.

"Horseshit! You were down the creek pervin' on the boss's pretty little daughter while she was swimmin' in the nuddy," Rossiter said with a leering grin.

That stunned Declin speechless, and he could only stare back, his heart hammering with fear. *Does he know that? Or is he just guessing?* Declin thought.

The horrifying thought that they were watching him caused him to almost throw up, until the thought occurred that they might also be watching Carol. Terrible ideas of what they might do to her caused him to reel with emotional turmoil.

I must keep her safe! he vowed.

Rossiter obviously felt he had the advantage as he gave Declin's upper arm a punch and said, "So you keep your trap shut and co-operate if you know what's good for you, and her."

At that Marvin spoke for the first time. "Yeah! You wouldn't want something horrible to happen to your little girlfriend!" He then turned to Rossiter, a lascivious grin on his face. "Yeah, we could have a lot of fun there!"

Declin was so horrified he could only shake his head and swallow the bile that rose to his throat.

Rossiter also grinned and leaned closer. "So, boyo, when we say stop the mill, we mean stop the mill. If yer don't we might tell the boss that you are a paedophile and that you've been stalkin' his lovely little daughter."

Marvin chuckled an evil chuckle deep in his throat. "He probably is storkin' her! I know I'd like to," he said. With that he gave Declin another punch on the upper arm and walked away.

Rossiter glared at Declin for a few more seconds and then muttered, "So stop the mill, or else." He also turned and walked away.

Declin stared at his retreating back with revulsion through eyes blurry with anxiety. He found he was breathing so hard he was dizzy from hyperventilating. He had to grab at a steel upright to keep his balance.

Oh my God! What will I do? he thought as despair flooded his whole being.

Chapter 28

GRAHAM DISTRACTED

At home that Friday night, Graham found he could hardly sleep for excitement. Exams were over, he was selected to do the Warrant Officers Course, and he would be in Caster with Carol the next day, and tomorrow night he might just get to be alone with Carol.

Saturday morning dawned clear but hot and humid. Graham was woken by his mother at 6am and he at once set about his morning routine and packing. By 0730 he had eaten breakfast, dressed and packed. For the expedition he wore a pair of old DPCU trousers, an old, long-sleeved, jungle green shirt, and a cloth hat. On his feet he wore his black leather ex-army hiking boots. A bag containing clothes for the party, a towel and toiletries was prepared. While he packed his gear the excitement and anxiety both increased.

When he was ready, his mother bundled him and his gear into the car and they set off to pick up Stephen. An hour later, the car turned into the main street of Caster. Graham felt his arousal and anxiety both increase as he glimpsed the trees in the park and the mill beyond them.

His mother drove on past the hotel to the end of town and across the main railway. Graham saw two parked cars at the side of the park and a group of teenagers clustered on and around the old steam locomotive. His interest increased and he leaned forward to peer at them. To his relief, he recognised them as his friends and noted the jumble of assorted hiking gear on the lawn nearby. He also noted three more girls walking across the road towards the group and recognised Betty and her sister and friend.

Mrs Kirk parked near the other cars and Graham and Stephen climbed out. As Graham did, he saw Carol and his heart leapt. He had not expected that and was pleased. He smiled and waved and, to his relief, she smiled and waved back. He and Stephen then lifted their packs and webbing and bags out of the boot.

"See ya, Mum," Graham said, offering a cheek for her to kiss.

Mrs Kirk kissed and said, "Remember, be safe. There has been more than enough trouble with you kids on weekend expeditions."

"Yes Mum. We will be careful. We will keep out of trouble. See you Sunday afternoon," Graham assured her.

Wanting to get out of the emotional situation he hurried across the lawn, dropping his pack and webbing near the other gear before heading for the group. On joining them there were greetings all round. Graham saw that Tina was there and he gave her an embarrassed smile, memories of that kiss during the field exercise in June lying between them even now. Andrew and Carmen were very friendly and so were Willy, Marjorie, and Stick. Little sister Kirsty was also very welcoming, to Carol's obvious annoyance. Even Betty gave him a friendly greeting before turning her attention to Stephen.

Graham had been half hoping that Carol might hint that he give her a welcome kiss or even give him one. But she just stood and smiled and that worried him as he sensed that her greeting wasn't as fulsome as he thought it should be. Brushing his worries aside with hope, he gave her a cheerful hello.

Graham and Stephen then handed the two bags containing their civilian clothes for the party to Carol and her sister.

"Can you leave this at the front of your house please?" Graham asked.

Carol held the bag up and looked at it. "What is it?"

"Our civvies, clothes for the party," Graham explained.

"Aren't you staying at the hotel?" Carol queried.

Graham glanced to check that his mother was not within earshot and then shook his head. "Nope. We thought we might just camp on the edge of the jungle or something, so we can re-join the search easier tomorrow."

"You sure?" Carol asked, plainly astonished.

Graham could see that the notion of just sleeping anywhere was quite foreign to her. He smiled. "We do it all the time in Cadets. We will be fine. We've got all the camping gear. Besides, if we went up the mountain with these guys that is how we would be sleeping."

Carol still looked doubtful but took the proffered bag. Graham then looked around and studied the hiking apparel of the others. As he had expected, both Peter and Roger wore their old army boots and army camouflage trousers and cloth hats and long-sleeved work shirts, their normal hiking clothes. For the hike, the four boys had all brought their army basic webbing and packs.

And the Navy Cadets look fine, Graham thought, noting that all three wore dark blue long trousers and long-sleeved shirts. These had the appearance of being navy cadet issue, as did the black boots and dark blue baseball caps they wore.

His gaze met Tina's again and she gave an embarrassed smile. Graham experienced a moment's regret but then told himself they were not really suited.

Good luck to Andrew, he thought.

Next, Graham studied the Air Cadets and had to control his face. Willy looked okay in long blue trousers and black boots and a long-sleeved shirt, but both Stick and Marjorie wore jeans and short sleeved shirts. In Marjorie's case this was only a yellow T-shirt which was too tight, so that her boobs strained at the thin material. Graham almost gaped at the spectacle and wondered if he should hint at more appropriate clothing in the jungle, but in the end he only shook his head.

There was more chatter and some flirting as Betty and her little sister competed for Stephen's attention. Betty even made a few flirty comments to Graham and they obviously annoyed Carol. Graham was half conscious of this and when he saw Carmen purse her lips and shake her head at a cheeky comment by Betty he blushed with guilt at his secret lustful thoughts.

Graham did think that Betty's top was a bit revealing but he had been enjoying the sight. Then Graham saw his mother cast a frowning glance at Betty while chatting to the other mothers.

Oops! I'd better make sure Mum doesn't think I am interested in Betty in any way, he cautioned himself. He found it a relief to see his mother wave goodbye before driving off.

Peter looked at his watch and said, "Let's get moving. It is after half past nine and we have a long way to go."

"Where are you going?" Carol asked.

Peter had an army 1:50 000 scale topographic map which he unfolded and orientated. He then pointed to the jungle covered mountain two kilometres to the west.

"The book says that the local farmers saw a big flash up near the top of Mt Graham there, and then a glow from a big fire. They said it was just on the other side of the peak," he explained.

Graham had seen that mountain several times before but had not actually studied it. Even now he only glanced at it because the view of most of the mountain was obscured by the trees in the park and by the mill buildings. Then he turned back to listen to a smart comment by Betty.

Willy pointed to the map. "We could go up this ridge that runs up directly behind the mill," he suggested.

"That's what I thought," agreed Peter. Turning he said, "What do you think, Graham?"

Graham merely shrugged and said, "Whichever way you think best."

Dimly he understood that he was not really interested in the expedition. His whole mental and physical focus seemed to be consumed by the girls. He realised that he just did not want to go up the mountain.

I want to stay here, he thought.

Peter pursed his lips and shook his head before saying, "Fine, I will lead. Packs on and let's go!"

As Peter moved to hoist on his pack, Graham was vaguely aware of the undercurrent of tension. He was also conscious that Carol and Betty were giving each other hostile glares.

I had better make peace here, he thought.

But then Betty said something witty, and he could not help grinning. Carol looked quite peeved, and Graham wondered how to extract himself from the problem.

Betty is supposed to be interested in Steve, not me, he thought.

* * *

The expedition got under way, Peter leading. Roger gave Graham another odd look and followed. After Willy helped Marjorie to pull on her pack, they also started walking. Stick, Andrew, Tina, and Carmen all set off after them. Peter detoured across to say goodbye to his mother and the mothers then waved and called the usual 'Take care' and 'Don't do anything silly,' and 'Watch out for snakes'. Peter's mother asked him to check that the mobile phone he was carrying was working and Peter did so, then resumed walking.

Still Graham stood and talked. Stephen stayed with him. Graham knew he must start walking but was now torn by conflicting desires. Dimly he understood that he was not handling the social situation very well, but he was concerned about the state of his relationship with Carol. He sensed that his feelings for Carol, and probably hers for him, were now different in some worrying way. The relationship no longer had that wonderful feeling of falling in love and he could not decide if it was his feelings that had changed, or hers.

Or both?

What he did know was that he was worried, and that there was a fine edge of desperation in his emotions. There was an intense desire to know exactly where he stood in her mind and for that reason he just wanted to be with her. But when he saw Peter, now about 50 paces away along the ring road, look back and then shake his head he knew he must move.

My mates will bag me out if I don't start walking, he told himself.

Reluctantly, he said goodbye to Carol and then found he had to say something in response to Betty's trill 'cheerio!'. Stephen also said goodbye with obvious reluctance.

Steve isn't very keen on this expedition either, Graham thought. *But then he's not thinking with his brain! And nor am I,* he added.

By the time he and Stephen began pulling on their gear, the group were near the last of the worker's houses. After a last smile at Carol, Graham started walking. Stephen gave Betty a final muttered comment that set her nodding and giggling, then hurried to join him. For the first few hundred metres the two boys walked along the bitumen ring road to the right.

Graham was familiar with the layout, having walked that way before. But then he had been very distracted by the presence of all those pretty girls. Now he had a chance to look around. First, he studied the mill, noting the steam and smoke billowing from the chimneys.

That's because they are now working every day to try to catch up after all the breakdowns and problems, he thought.

Then he remembered Carol's comment about possible sabotage, and he frowned. But it all looked very ordinary so all he could do was shrug.

Carol was his real focus and he glanced back, hoping she was watching. To his consternation he saw that she and her sister appeared to be arguing with Betty and her sister, and as he watched he saw Carol turn and walk towards her house. Her sister followed, carrying both his and Stephen's bags.

Oh, I hope our relationship is alright! he worried.

After passing the last house, Graham noted a side road off to the right that he hadn't noticed before. He became conscious that the palm trees and brilliant clumps of Bougainvillea gave the place a very tropical appearance. The hot sun and humid air added to the tropical feel. He began to perspire freely but didn't care.

The group had turned left to go along the side road, so Graham and Stephen followed. This meant that they had a cane field on their right and the cane railway marshalling yard on their left. Several loaded cane trains stood on sidings waiting to be unloaded and another came rattling in behind a small, yellow painted, diesel locomotive. The driver gave them a cheerful wave as he passed.

The side road curved slowly to the left, crossed two narrow gauge railways that came in at different angles from across the cane fields and then curved left across to the line of mango trees that grew along the bank of the creek. The gravel road that ran along behind Carol's house and the mill joined them from the left. At that point another branch of the light rail network went off under the trees and across the creek on the high timber trestle bridge. The bridge was a dual purpose one with a timber deck for road transport and with rails laid down the middle for the cane trains.

By the time he and Stephen arrived there, the others had crossed the bridge and were a hundred metres up the long slope beyond. Graham checked there were no trains coming and walked out onto the bridge. As he did, he looked down at the creek and was assailed by fierce surges of erotic memories of swimming nude with the girls. He also noted that the cane bins that had been tumbled in the water during his past visit were now all gone and that the creek was deep and the water very clear.

"We'd better catch up," Graham suggested to Stephen, feeling a bit guilty at letting Peter and Roger down.

They were still a fair way ahead, walking along a dirt vehicle track between the light railway and two cane fields. Both cane fields had been harvested so there was a clear view across it to the mountains. The road went up a long, gentle slope.

"They look pretty big," Stephen commented, his gaze roaming over the steep, jungle-covered slopes that now loomed high above them.

"About seven hundred metres the one we are going up," Graham answered, studying the mountain more carefully with the eye of experience.

Bloody hell! That looks pretty thick jungle, he thought.

Memories of other 'scrub-bashing' expeditions and the resulting scratches and stings came to make him regret he was not back with Carol.

Stephen indicated the nearest spur of the jungle-covered mountain. "I suppose that is the ridge we are going up."

Graham nodded. "Yes. That should be the easiest way up."

He saw that Peter had led the others to the left along a vehicle track between two more cane fields. He was heading straight of the bottom of the prominent spur line.

At 10:30 the leaders reached the edge of the rainforest and stopped for a moment. Graham saw Peter take out a pair of garden secateurs and begin to trample and cut a track through the green tangle of vegetation.

Here we go! Graham thought, mentally bracing himself for the pain of climbing in thick jungle.

Chapter 29

JUNGLE

Graham watched Roger follow Peter into the thick wall of scrub. The hesitation of the others was obvious, even from a hundred metres away and Graham gave a derisive smile and mentally prepared himself. Now he felt even more torn. His body wanted to be with Carol and the girls, but his emotions were half with the challenge of the jungle and the mountain. He knew that he normally relished such expeditions and was half aware that he was not his normal self.

By the time he and Stephen arrived at the edge of the jungle, the others had vanished from sight. But their trail was clear and easy to follow. Graham swung off his pack.

"We will leave our packs here," he said. "No point in lugging them up the bloody mountain when we don't have to."

Stephen nodded and took off his pack as well. The two packs were placed just out of sight then Graham took out his own secateurs but had little need to use them. Now their fitness and the experience from previous jungle expeditions paid off. The two boys quickly caught up with the main group.

As they did, Graham saw that Peter and Roger were explaining 'wait-a-while' to the others. Thinking he had nothing more to learn about the vicious vine, Graham just gave a sardonic grin and trampled his way up to join them.

"What's up?" he asked as he reached the rear of the group.

Peter answered, "Just explaining wait-a-while to the 'Blue Orchids' and 'Matelots'."

Stephen snorted and said, "If that's all they are worried about they will be lucky."

Roger then said, "Steve doesn't like the jungle, not since he got lost at Kanaka Creek a couple of years ago."

"I wasn't lost!" Stephen snapped back, giving Roger a glare. "I was being chased by those crooks."

"Yeah, whatever," Roger answered.

Graham noted the animosity between the two and understood that Roger had just taken the chance to get a bit of his own back. He knew that Steve could be a bit harsh with his tongue and that Roger had been the victim of it on more than a few occasions.

Graham now said, "I suppose we should have warned them it wouldn't be a stroll in the park."

"That's right," Roger agreed, adding, "There are lots of little nasties to watch out for."

"Like what?" Andrew asked.

"Stinging tree, ticks, snakes, spiky bushes, leeches," replied Roger with a wide grin.

"Leeches!" Marjorie shrieked, looking around her.

"Yes, leeches," Roger agreed. "Big, fat ones that suck your blood. They wriggle in where the skin is softest and juiciest and start sucking."

Marjorie went pale and glanced around. "Do they hurt?"

Roger chuckled but Peter cut in to say, "Not a bit. They spit some sort of anaesthetic on your skin so you don't feel them bite. It contains an anti-coagulant too, so the blood flows more freely."

"Are they poisonous?" Marjorie asked.

Peter shook his head. "No. They just fill up with blood and drop off. In the old days, doctors used to put them on patients to draw blood out of them."

"Yerk!" Marjorie cried in disgust.

"The ticks and mites are the real danger," Peter went on. "Some ticks are really poisonous and can even kill you; and there are mites that bite you and can give you scrub typhus and that can be fatal."

Willy looked quite uneasy, and said, "How do we stop getting bitten?"

"You should have put mite/tick repellent on," Peter answered. "My fault, I should have checked you had some. We had better do it now."

He swung off his webbing and dug in his pack to extract a small grey plastic bottle. After unscrewing the lid he squirted a small amount of liquid into the palm of his hand. Rubbing both hands together he smeared the liquid on the tops of his boots and around the bottom of his trouser, which were tucked into the tops of the boots.

"You only need a thin smear," he explained. "If you can see splotches on the cloth then you have put on too much. You must not get it on the more sensitive parts of your skin. It burns if you do."

"That's right," Stephen added. "Don't use the repellent and then go and have a pee."

Willy looked both concerned and embarrassed. Carmen was not amused. "Don't talk like that please, Stephen," she reproved.

"Sorry, just giving fair warning," Stephen replied.

Graham added, "The army repellent melts plastic too, so make sure there is none left on your hands before you touch a compass, or the face of your watch."

"Or the lenses of your glasses," Stephen said.

"Or in your mouth," Roger said. "It burns your lips and tongue, and it tastes horrible. And keep it away from your eyes."

Andrew let out a short laugh and said, "Are you trying to put us off?"

"Just making sure you know what you are letting yourself in for," Peter replied.

Ten minutes were spent applying mite/tick repellent before the journey was resumed. When it did Roger led the way, secateurs in hand, while Peter followed. He had secateurs as well but also held a compass. Graham did not mind.

Pete knows what he is doing, and is a very good navigator, he told himself. This time he was happy to be at the back.

The course Peter chose led them away from the creek line. As they angled slowly up the slope, dodging around clumps of wait-a-while, they got further and further from the creek until Graham could no longer hear the water gushing down over the stones.

And the going was as hard as his experience had led him to expect. At almost every step he got caught up by something: a vine which hooked their equipment; or a tree root which tripped them; or a rock or tree they had to detour around. There was wait-a-while everywhere and it was so thick in places that Peter and Roger did not try to detour but slowly snipped a path through it, with much muttering and under-the-breath swearing as they did.

Even when a path was cut, there were always tendrils they missed and these snagged those behind, causing cries of dismay and pain. It was slow going and also very hot and humid. Perspiration trickled and soaked clothing so that shirts clung to them. It was quickly apparent to Graham that Marjorie was not enjoying herself and was sure she wished she had not come. For himself there was no way he was going to admit it was hard, not with the air cadets and navy cadets there to note any weakness on the part of the army cadets!

I'm not going to give them any ammunition for later put-downs, Graham resolved.

For the next hour they struggled up the ridge. At 11:45 they came to a panting, sweating halt on a small ledge. Marjorie wiped her face and groaned, then said, "Are we nearly there yet?"

For an answer Peter laughed. "Not even a third of the way up, I reckon," he said.

Hearing that obviously dismayed some of the others, but Graham kept a smile on his face. In an attempt to check whether Peter was correct he looked around, hoping to get a view out through the thick vegetation. But everywhere he looked was a tangle of growing things: leaves, vines, ferns, and trees. There wasn't a single gap large enough to allow him a glimpse of any of the farmland he knew was out there.

Willy also looked around. Then he shook his head. "The vegetation is too dense," he commented.

"We are the ones who are dense," Andrew replied, wiping his face with his sleeve.

Willy looked at Marjorie to check how she was coping. Graham saw that she looked tired and unhappy. Her hair was a rat's nest and her clothes torn and dirty and she had scratches on her arms. Then Willy pointed at her bare arm.

"Marjorie, what's that?"

Marjorie looked, then used her other hand to touch the black object the size of her finger that was on her upper arm. Suddenly her eyes went wide and she began to shriek in fright and jump up and down.

"Eeek! Eeek! Oh, take it off! Take it off! Get it off me!"

Graham saw that it was a leech and just shrugged. He had had dozens on him over the years. Now he watched with sardonic amusement as Marjorie scraped the thing off. That left a smear of blood and a very clear wound from which more blood trickled.

Marjorie continued to cry out while Stephen sneered and said, "Bloody hell! It's only a bloody leech, not the end of the world!"

Willy stepped across and put his arms around her. After a minute or so she calmed down and snuggled into his embrace.

"It's alright," he said soothingly.

Suddenly Marjorie jerked back and began to shriek again, her eyes wide with alarm. "Oh! Oooh, lookout! Oh, there's one on you too!"

She pointed to Willy's neck, her face a mask of horror. Willy put his hand up and felt a slimy thing. Amid a mild attack of panic he scraped at it, ignoring Peter and Graham who cried not to pull it off. The leech came loose and he flicked it away, shuddering with disgust as he did. Then he saw the blood all over his fingers and looked amazed.

Worse was to come. Marjorie pulled out her handkerchief and pressed it to the bite and then wiped at it. Graham was not impressed and, he could see, nor were his friends.

"It's only a little bite," he said. "You won't die."

They all now checked themselves for leeches, and all found at least one or two. Most were thin and small, only a millimetre or two in thickness and a centimetre or so long but a couple had gorged themselves and were slick, fat slugs which Willy found repulsive. There were more shrieks and cries of horror and disgust. Trouser legs were pulled up and a dozen at least were plucked from around the tops of socks and one even from the inside of Andrew's thigh.

Stephen laughed. "You don't want them any higher up," he joked.

Carmen wasn't amused. "Don't be disgusting!" she snapped.

"Just trying to warn you," Stephen replied.

To Willy's obvious annoyance, the army cadets had hardly any on them and only one or two in the top of their boots. They all took the opportunity to apply more repellent and Graham even smeared it around his collar and seams and around the brim of his hat.

That done, they found rocks or tree roots to sit on and settled to eat their lunch. While they ate, they all kept glancing down to try to spot more leeches before they could get on him. Willy spotted one moving with its head-tail-head-tail movement onto Marjorie's shoe.

"Look out!" he said, pointing.

Marjorie again almost had hysterics. She hit at it and tried to flick it off. Laughing, Graham reached down and plucked it off with his fingers, then rolled it in a ball and flicked it away.

"You can't squash them," he explained. "You can try to mash them but only repellent, fire or salt kills them."

"And that is supposed to be an agonising death for the poor little things," Peter added.

"Poor little things! What about poor little me," Carmen retorted. That caused a burst of laughter and morale began to pick up.

Then it began to rain.

As the heavy drops dripped from the leaves, Willy complained at how cold it felt. He took out his raincoat and pulled it on, as did Marjorie, Stick and the three navy cadets. Not so the four army cadets. They laughed the idea to scorn.

"It's summer, in the tropics," Peter said.

Roger nodded. "In the steaming tropical jungle," he grinned.

Graham laughed. "The raincoat will make you twice as wet. You will sweat like pigs in it. Better to just let the rain cool you," he commented.

Willy obviously did not believe this and did his raincoat up. For a few moments he looked thoughtful, and Graham wondered if he had changed his mind. But then stood up and said, "Well, come on. Let's go and find this plane wreck."

As before Roger led, followed by Peter. The route was still up the ridge and as they struggled slowly up this it became an ever-narrower spur with steep slopes on either side. There were stretches with no wait-a-while, but they were few and the narrowness of the spur meant they had to cut a path.

After ten minutes of sweating and panting and hauling themselves up from tree to tree, they stopped again. By then the rain had stopped. Graham then had the sardonic amusement of seeing Willy casually unbutton his raincoat and peeled it off. It was stuffed back in his pack. The others did likewise, and Graham had to resist the temptation to make a teasing comment of the 'I-told-you-so!' type.

Instead, he took out his map and studied it. He was sure they were making good progress. Looking around he got glimpses back through the canopy of open fields and even of a distant farmhouse. That allowed him to judge their height. Putting his map back in its waterproof case and then into the map pocket on his trousers, he again looked around. A view upwards that showed a ridge top almost at the same level cheered him even more.

Well over halfway up, two thirds probably, he estimated.

He just wanted to find the aircraft wreck and then get back down to Carol. Niggling in his consciousness was how fast time was slipping by.

Another heavy shower of rain swept across, the rain drops hammering on the leaves so loudly they had to almost shout to make themselves heard. This time Willy left his raincoat off. Again Graham had to resist the temptation to tease, but when Tina put hers on he held his tongue. He liked her too much to want to hurt her feelings in any way.

The upward slog was resumed, 1:00 pm came and went, then 2:00 pm. By then Peter announced them to be more than two thirds of the way to the top.

Graham looked up the slope. "I was hoping we would have been at the top by now," he grumbled.

At the front of his mind were the Christmas Party timings. *The party starts at 5pm. It will take us at least an hour and a half, no, probably two hours to get back down. And we need to have a bath and change. Hmmm!* Having worked that out he started to get quite agitated as the maths said he needed to start back now.

Stephen took off his glasses and wiped them with a handkerchief he had kept dry in a plastic bag.

"We would have been if it was just us," he said.

The implication that it was the air cadets and navy cadets that had slowed them down annoyed Willy, but before he could reply Carmen snapped angrily, "I hope you aren't suggesting it was because we are girls that we took so long?"

Stephen did not reply but gave a lopsided grin. This annoyed Carmen even more. "I don't know why you even came," she said. She looked hot and annoyed.

"Neither do I," Graham replied. He made a show of looking at his watch and said, "Time we started back anyway, Steve."

"Well, goodbye then!" Carmen cried.

"I hope you regret it when we find the plane wreck," Stick added.

Graham felt quite embarrassed, but Stephen scowled. "All right then. We will see you tomorrow," he said.

By then Graham was feeling quite ashamed of himself and was annoyed that his mother had been right.

"See you then," he said.

Stephen also muttered goodbye and the pair turned to make their way back down the mountain. As they did, Marjorie made Graham feel worse by calling after them, "And you'd better work out which girl it is you like Graham, or you will both end up with none!"

Stephen's response was to shake his head, but Graham just hunched his shoulders and hurried on down the slope. Within seconds they were both out of sight of the main group. Graham now felt so upset that he forced himself to hurry down the steep slope regardless of the snagging vines and snatching wait-a-while.

"Ow! Slow down, Graham!" Stephen called from behind him.

Graham stopped and looked back and saw that Stephen was caught up on some wait-awhile and his glasses were half off.

Stephen got himself free with his secateurs and then adjusted his glass. "Bloody hell! If we have an accident, we won't make it to the party at all," he growled.

"Sorry," Graham croaked.

He realised he was gasping for breath and that sweat was running down into his eyes. He wiped them and then paused to have a drink.

I must stink of sweat. I really need a bath, he thought.

Stephen also had a drink and then, as he screwed the cap back on his canteen said, "You need to be careful. That teasing little bitch, Betty, looks like she has her eye on you today. Carol was looking a bit pissed off."

"I know," Graham agreed.

He wanted to discuss his worries about Carol but decided it was too personal and potentially embarrassing. Seeing Stephen was ready he resumed the downward slog.

As he went down, often from slimy tree trunk to slippery tree trunk, Graham kept glancing at his watch. He was appalled at how fast the time seemed to be flying by.

After four o'clock already! Bloody hell.

He mentioned this and wasn't amused when Stephen came back with the silly joke, "Time flies like the wind but fruit flies like bananas!"

Despite grumbles from Stephen Graham continued to force the pace. Luckily both boys were dressed and equipped for the activity and were quite fit, so they were able to keep it up. But thirst became a problem when their water bottles were emptied. Graham shook his head and noted that his shirt was actually dripping with his sweat.

No problem yet, he told himself, well aware of the effect of tropical heat and humidity in causing heat casualties. *It is when I stop sweating I really need to start worrying.*

After what seemed like forever, but was actually only about fifteen minutes, the boys reached the lower slopes and a few minutes later burst out of the jungle onto the edge of the cane field. Graham heaved a sigh of relief and checked the time.

"Now we need a bath," he said.

Stephen joined him, his glasses fogged by condensation and plastered with dead leaves. "Can we do that at Carol's?" he queried.

"I hope so, otherwise we will have to wash in the creek," Graham replied.

He was annoyed with himself for not thinking through the details of the weekend and realised he had been far too ambitious in his planning.

I have certainly overestimated my own ability, he thought ruefully.

He and Stephen recovered their packs from the edge of the jungle and swung them on. Another check of his watch told Graham it was 4:30pm.

Damn! We will be late if we don't hurry, he fretted.

He would have liked to jog but knew Stephen would object. So, rather than annoy his friend, he set off at a fast walk. Five minutes of striding along had them at the light railway and they turned right and hurried up the long slope.

A few minutes later, the pair crested the rise beside the light railway. In the distance, Graham saw the chimneys of the sugar mill begin to appear above the skyline and his emotions began to change, from deep anxiety to a sort of worried anticipation.

Won't be long now, he told himself..

Chapter 30

CHRISTMAS PARTY

As the two friends strode down the long slope towards the creek, Graham looked towards the mill. The two huge steel chimneys stood up above the trees along the creek bank like beckoning beacons. Graham observed with satisfaction the billowing white steam and smears of brown smoke and a waft of the burnt sugar smell caused him to breathe deeply with pleasure. It seemed to him that every step he got closer to Carol his anticipation increased.

The boys walked quickly down around the curve and onto the bridge. Gesturing downstream, Stephen said, "I hope we get to have another swim this weekend."

Graham grinned and nodded in reply, eager to hurry. On reaching the other bank, he led the way to the right, striding along the gravel road under the mango trees and sweating heavily in the afternoon sun. A glance at his watch informed him that it was almost 5pm. Knowing that the Christmas Party was about to officially commence, he became anxious about being late and began to walk even faster.

Stephen objected. "Take it easy, Graham! She'll still be there. Slow down! I'm sweating like a pig," he cried.

He glanced at Stephen and noted he was perspiring heavily and that his glasses were starting to fog up. Then a person began speaking on a loudspeaker system somewhere over at the mill and he felt bad about being late. Music began and it was obvious that the party had begun.

But it took another five minutes of rapid marching for them to pass behind the mill. It was 5:07pm before they came out from behind the large mounds of mill mud and bagasse and were able to see the park. As it came into view, Graham was astonished. The whole park had been transformed into a fair ground!

What had been an empty park a few hours before was now covered with tents, trailers, vehicles and people, lots of people. He now began angling across the lawn towards the front of Carol's house. He did not feel it was right to walk in the back way, or not yet anyway!

Stephen walked with him, blinking in an attempt to see through his fogged glasses. The pair angled across the lawn between the mill and the front left corner of Carol's yard. At the corner they stopped, by mutual consent, and studied the layout.

"Bloody hell! Like Pig Day at Goombungee!" Stephen cried, using an expression Graham had heard Stephen's father use. He had once been a teacher at a school near Toowoomba and was full of quaint sayings.

Right around the outside of the ring road, including in front of Carol's house and the other houses, were parked hundreds of cars. They were side by side on the grass, and more were arriving and cruising slowly around looking for suitable places to park.

Inside the ring road were a large circle of tents, shade structures and various food trailers and amusement rides. Right at the entrance to the park a large jumping castle was just visible, the upper parts shaking and vibrating as children jumped on it. Inside the ring was an open area where organised games and activities were taking place and there looked to be hundreds of people.

Stephen blinked through his glasses and then took them off to wipe them. "Holy Moses! This is a much bigger deal than I imagined," he said.

Graham agreed, amazed at the number of people and scale of the event. He led the way along the front fence to the gate and then shrugged off his pack there.

"We will leave our gear while I find Carol," he said, unbuckling his webbing and placing it inside the fence on the front lawn beside the path.

Stephen did likewise and the two boys then made their way across between the parked cars and across the ring road. As they picked their way between vehicles and vans, Graham realised that many of the vehicles were food trailers. Next to him on his left was one providing hamburgers and chips, and the one on the right was serving hotdogs and the like. A line of little kids was getting pink fairy floss.

In the middle was a roped off area and a group of adults was taking part in a sack race, to the hilarity of families and friends. A loudspeaker began blaring and the Master of Ceremonies declared that the next event would be an Egg and Spoon race and calling for competitors from the mothers and daughters.

Stephen blinked and looked around. "All the fun of the fair!" he cried. "Oh, there's Betty!"

Graham followed his pointing finger and saw Betty and her sister. They were talking to a group of youths, and he noted wryly that Betty was wearing her usual provocative short shorts and cut-off T-shirt.

"Good luck then Steve!" he called sarcastically. "You'll have to compete with the local yokels from the look of it."

Stephen swore softly but headed for Betty. Graham watched for a moment and then looked around, his eyes seeking for Carol. And there she was. She was wearing jeans and a floral shirt and looked happy. Then his anger surged.

She is talking to that Declin git!

Which meant he had to summon up his own courage! Swallowing to get his nervousness under control, he walked over to her. He was not at all pleased to see how happily she was talking to Declin. Once again, he wished he wasn't wearing smelly, sweaty bush clothes.

"Hi Carol!" Graham called as he approached. To his relief, Carol turned and her face lit up when she saw him.

"Oh hi! You made it then?" she replied.

Graham nodded, very conscious that Declin was positively glowering at him. Carol seemed not to notice.

"You two know each other I think?" she said.

Graham glanced at Declin and nodded. "Hello," he managed to mumble, not wanting to be rude in front of Carol.

Declin was less forthcoming and just nodded and glared. Carol sensed that and grabbed both by the arm. "Oh don't be like that you two. It's a lovely party. Don't spoil it please."

"We won't," Declin replied, flashing another hostile glance at Graham.

Graham forced a smile and nodded. He was aware that he was jealous and stressed but he did not want to put Carol off by being overtly aggressive.

"I need a shower and to change," he explained.

Carol looked him up and down and nodded. "Yes, you look a bit grubby. Did you find that old plane crash?" she asked.

"No. They weren't even at the top when Steve and I had to start back," Graham answered.

Carol now took his sleeve. "Come with me and we will get you cleaned up. Excuse us please, Declin. We won't be long," she said.

Declin looked unhappy but nodded and went back to trying to sell raffle tickets. Graham didn't care what he did as long as he stayed away from her. His spirits rising, he followed Carol towards her house.

Then he remembered Stephen and saw him and Betty in the middle of a crowd who were all talking and laughing. Walking that in that direction, Graham caught Stephen's eye and pointed towards Carols house.

"Shower!" he called.

Stephen nodded and turned to join him. They made their way out of the ring past a barbeque at which Carol's father was working, apron on and egg slice and tongs at the ready. Carol led them over to her house and up the front stairs. They stopped on the veranda.

Carol pointed. "There are your bags. I'll just show you the bathroom."

She led the way through the house to the rear. Graham expected to meet her mum or sister but there was nobody else at home. It crossed his mind that it would have been a good opportunity for a kiss, if Stephen hadn't been there.

Carol must have been thinking something similar as she gave Stephen a sideways glance and whispered, "Pity!"

Graham could only grin and nod. "You go first Steve," he said, hoping that once Stephen was showered and changed, he and Carol might get a chance to be alone together.

But it was not to be. By the time he had showered and changed into clean clothes Kirsty had appeared and she at once began to flirt, to Carol's obvious annoyance.

The interruption to his plans put Graham into a grumpy mood, which he had trouble hiding.

* * *

As they all strolled back across to the Christmas Party, Graham was aware that he was feeling frustrated and irritable. Seeing Declin giving him sour looks from his Chocolate Wheel did nothing to ease his jealous anxiety.

For a time the group strolled around, seeing the sights and watching the games, a Three-legged Race now, and, for Graham and Stephen, admiring the other pretty girls.

Twenty minutes was taken up with having something to eat. Graham opted for a hamburger from Carol's dad and Stephen for hot dogs and tomato sauce. Carol had hot chips and the group sat on some plastic chairs. The food was good, and Graham's mood improved when Carol's mother walked past and gave him a cheerful hello and a smile.

There were more races and games and both boys had a drink of Coke. Kirsty and Billy kept coming over and then going to play. For Billy the old locomotive was still the main attraction and Graham watched Declin get called over to help drive the train. That caused a sour spurt of jealousy.

The bugger lives here. That gives him an advantage, Graham mused.

He now saw Declin as a definite rival and the fact that Carol was so friendly to him caused Graham considerable anxiety. He felt his position wasn't quite as secure as he would like it to be!

The sun went down while they sat there talking and eating and rows of coloured fairy lights strung overhead were turned on, adding to the carnival feel. Carol suggested they try some of the games and Graham immediately got up, intent on pleasing her. Stephen did so but he was obviously busy looking around for Betty.

A happy half hour of fun followed. They played a game of tossing coins onto floating polystyrene frogs to win little prizes, then small quoits at hooks on a board and then darts. Graham won a fluffy panda bear, which he promptly gave to Carol. In return he got a smile and she took his hand while they strolled on to the next thing. Graham began to really enjoy himself and feel good.

It was while they were watching Kirsty and Billy enjoying themselves on a merry-go-round that was positioned between the jumping castle and the playground swings, that the next little annoying incident occurred. Betty and her sister and friend appeared and at once came over and began flirting.

Carol frowned at Betty and Graham felt her displeasure and tried not to respond to Betty. After a few minutes, Betty made a face and walked away. The tension eased a bit.

Only to return a few minutes later when the group had moved on. They were at one of the games with Carol trying her hand at mini golf when Betty came from behind and pushed in between Graham and Stephen.

"Hi boys!" she trilled, putting her arms around both boy's waists as she did.

Graham reacted instinctively to the cheery greeting. "Hi Babe! How's tricks?"

"Good!" Betty responded, giving Graham a squeeze.

As she did, he glanced anxiously towards Carol, hoping she wasn't watching. To his relief, she was focused on her putt. He was about to make what he thought was another witty remark when Declin's angry face appeared in front of him.

"Stop hurting Carol, kid!" Declin snapped.

"I'm not hurting her!" Graham retorted, his guilty conscience sparking his anger.

"You are! Stop flirting with... with Betty and... and with other girls. That's hurting her," Declin cried.

Graham's temper flared. "Mind you own business!" he cried, stepping away from Betty and Stephen. In his anger he clenched his fists and placed them on his hips.

Declin responded and the two males eyed each other. Declin then wagged his finger angrily in Graham's face. "You are just playing with her. Every time you run around making eyes at other girls, she gets hurt!"

"I'm not making eyes at other girls!" Graham shouted, guilt fuelling his emotions. He was vaguely aware that other people were looking and that added to his reaction.

"You are! I've seen you! Now back off and leave her alone!" Declin shouted, his face red with anger. He then stepped forward and pushed at Graham.

The shove stung Graham's ego. "Leave me alone, you cradle snatcher!" he cried.

"Don't you call me names you two-timing lout!" Declin retorted.

"I am not!" Graham shouted, his mind racing with guilt and hurt feelings.

Declin curled his lip and then called, "Yes you are! You've got another girlfriend named Margaret. I asked about you and you aren't fit to lick Carol's boots!"

That really inflamed Graham's feelings. "Mind your own business. You are too old for Carol," he yelled.

"She can choose. You just stay away from her and don't hurt her," Declin retorted, shoving at him again.

"I'll do what I like!" Graham answered, his pride now taking up the challenge. He brought up his fists ready to fight.

Declin did likewise and Graham braced for blows, determining that he wanted Declin to swing the first punch so he could be in the right.

Instead, Carol pushed angrily between them, shoving them both apart. "Stop it you boys! Stop it! No fighting!"

Graham found his emotions all in a jangle of anxiety, anger, and hurt pride. He stepped back and found Stephen pulling at his upraised arm. To his own surprise he found he was shaking with rage and realised he was taking great gulps of air.

Declin glared at Graham but stepped back and lowered his fists. It took Graham a few seconds to focus his thoughts as a fierce desire to lash out gripped him. Feeling a bit like a rhinoceros tangled in a thorn bush, he took several deep gulps and looked around. Through eyes that were misted with jealous rage he noted Carol urging Declin further back, Stephen's worried face near his as he gripped his arm, Kirsty looking all concerned but excited, and Betty also looking worried. Then his gaze focused on three workmen sitting at a nearby picnic table. They wore bright yellow Hi-Vis shirts with the usual silver reflective stripes. One of the men Graham dimly recognised, a big, burly brute, beer in hand.

He was the man who gave Carol the fright during the mill tour, up on that high platform, he thought.

The man had a sardonic smile on his face and for a moment his eyes met Graham's and there was no friendliness in them. Graham looked away, noting an even bigger brute of a worker next to him. A third, skinny man was with them, and their table had a dozen beer bottles on it, some full, most empty.

But Carol was his focus, and he shifted his attention back to her. She turned from Declin and again gave Graham a gentle shove.

"Come on Graham, no fighting please. It will upset the little kids and just get you into trouble. Dad's frowning at us and I can see the manager looking as well."

Reluctantly Graham lowered his fists and nodded, giving Declin another challenging stare as he did. Then he took some deep breaths and looked around at Carol. She was looking concerned but also a bit puzzled. The expression on her face worried Graham more than anything.

Maybe I have offended her? he thought.

That left him somewhat baffled as he was sure that Betty would have been thrilled to have him fight over her. That was what the excited look on her face seemed to indicate. Feeling suddenly deflated, Graham nodded and seemed to slump.

"Okay," he croaked.

"Let's move away," Carol suggested, taking hold of his free hand and leading him across towards the food stalls.

Graham went with her, his emotions in a flux as he sensed things weren't working and that he needed to change tactics. With an effort of will power he forced himself to calm down. Glancing over his shoulder he noted Stephen and Betty following. He was pleased that his friend was supporting him but equally did not want him to witness any rejection or humiliation.

For a few paces Graham thought that Carol was leading him across to where her father was, but then she swerved and went to the right, heading along past the front of the food stalls. He was about to say that he did not want anything else to eat when Carol said, "You shouldn't have called Declin horrible names. Please don't do it again."

That touched him on the raw and his temper immediately flared. "Why not? He's big enough to take it. Anyway, he's years older than you. He shouldn't be trying to win on to young girls."

"Oh! I'm a young girl am I!" Carol snapped back, letting go of his hand.

"You know what I mean," Graham cried, aware that he had blundered. "You are the same age as me and he's an adult."

"He's only four years older," Carol retorted angrily. "There are five years between mum and dad."

Graham was hotly aware that he had made a mistake but was now too upset and flustered to think of a suitable reply. "It still isn't right," he muttered, having trouble meeting eyes.

"You are just jealous," Carol cried. "You need to lighten up and stop being so bloody stodgy and... and military."

Graham was conscious that they were the centre of an interested ring of faces and that did not help. His mind seemed to have gone foggy with anxiety and embarrassment.

What can I say to retrieve the situation? he wondered.

Chapter 31

DARKNESS

For a few moments Graham stood there in an embarrassed fluster. Knowing that Stephen and Betty were beside him and that others were watching and listening added to his emotional turmoil. His hurt feelings tried to grapple with the comments from Carol and he knew he had to be very careful or he would definitely lose her affection.

Carol gave him what looked like a grim smile and then said, "I think you should go for a walk and calm down. Then we can talk."

That hurt too, but Graham could only nod as tears began to mist in his eyes. Not wanting her to see him cry (or anyone else in the audience, especially Stephen) he nodded and turned away. Mustering what dignity he could he walked away, pretending he wasn't hurting.

But it was a real sense of relief to pass between two stalls and out into the ring road area as there were no people there and he could let his feelings flow. Tears began to pour down his cheeks and he started to sob and take deep gulps of air. Hardly able to see, he now hurried across into the relative darkness beyond the parked cars.

He moved towards a tree in the large area of lawn between Carol's house and the mill. What he wanted was just a quiet place to regain control and the tree seemed to offer some sort of sanctuary. But as he got closer, Graham realised that there were two people there. They were standing in the darker shadows beyond the tree.

Local lovers? Graham thought, noting that they were standing entwined in each other's arms and leaning against the trunk. Then he wondered if it was Stephen and Betty. But then he shook his head. *No, they can't be. They were back there with me. Steve's a fast operator, but not that fast.*

Which caused more upset as he conceded that he was jealous of Stephen's 'cool' social skills and apparent success with the girls. So as not to blunder into another unpleasant scene, Graham deviated towards the mill and walked quickly on, pretending not to notice the kissing couple.

But that direction was towards the bright lights of the mill and rather than angle back to the ring road and the Christmas Party, he turned left and walked across the lawn between the tree and the mill.

This took him out across the railway spur line to the gravel road that ran behind the manager's houses and the mill. Here Graham stopped and blinked back his remaining tears before looking both ways. All was quiet, any night sounds drowned out by the loud music and noises from the party. To his left Graham could just see the twinkle of streetlights in the distance behind the houses and hotel. A brief flicker of lights indicated a car passing south along the Bruce Highway.

For a few seconds he just stood and steadied his breathing. By now his tears had dried up and he was feeling more ashamed of his outburst than angry. But he knew he was jealous and anxious.

That bloody Declin! He's too old for Carol! I should have punched his ugly face in. Feeling more down than he cared to admit he now berated himself for losing control. *I didn't impress Carol. She obviously did not like me calling him names or of wanting to fight,* he thought.

But as his mind went back over the incident it still seemed to him that his reaction had been justified. He certainly understood that he was not going to back down if challenged to a fight. He felt his honour was at stake and that he would fight rather than stand accused of being a coward.

Dad is right, better to get a bashing than have to live with the knowledge that you despise yourself for being a weakling, he thought, remembering an incident a few years before.

On that occasion, his father had been home and had overheard an altercation with a friend. When Graham had tried to run away, his father had blocked him and pushed him back outside to face the situation. There had been a brief bout of fisticuffs but then the two boys had settled their differences and resumed their friendship. It had been a good lesson.

But Declin is not a friend. He's a rival, Graham reasoned. But was a fight the way to win Carol's affection and respect? *Obviously not,* he thought. But how to win her interest and love? *And do I really want to?* he wondered.

It came to him that he was not really in love with Carol and that they actually had very little in common. It took some effort to admit that as he knew his pride was also involved. Being dumped in public was a humiliating thing to experience and he did not want his friends to think less of him.

But what to do? Graham stood there for a few more minutes and then felt the urge to walk. Once again, he glanced to his left towards the town and the highway but then shook his head and turned right to walk along the gravel road behind the mill.

This turned out to be something of a mistake as he had wanted to be alone in darkness but found the road was actually a mixture of brightly lit areas and pools of deep shadow. The whole mill interior was lit up and the rail yards were flood lit. There were even lights on in the locomotive workshops. But having started, Graham stubbornly kept on.

He passed the bagasse heaps, the loading hoppers, the molasses tanks and then the workshops, and only stopped when he reached the start of the rail yards. A loco was reversing to pick up a line of empty cane bins and that operation held his interest for a few minutes. Only when the train was hooked up and went rattling off into the distance did he resume walking.

Graham was glad of the shadows cast by the line of mango trees as it gave him cover and the darkness also matched his mood. As he walked slowly along, he began to wonder if his relationship with Carol was over. Had she dumped him? Did he care? Well, yes, he did, massively! But was that because he yearned for her love, or because his male ego was dented?

And having realised that he really did not love Carol, did not even like her much, he began to fret over how to end it.

How do I let her down and say it is over without hurting her feelings? he wondered.

Already in his young life he had experienced several break-ups with girls, but he realised, with something of a dismaying shock, that in every case he could think of it had been the girl telling him it was over.

Is that because I am no good? Is there something wrong with me? Graham thought.

As he walked on along the dusty road from one pool of shadow to the next, his spirits sank as he began to have gloomy thoughts. Self-pity welled up and Graham moved from dejection to depression as he listed all of his alleged faults and failings. That hurt because he considered himself to be a good and honourable man, well boy really.

But I am loyal, and I can be loving, he told himself.

But as he thought about loyalty, he remembered all the pretty girls he had been tempted by and squirmed internally with guilt. Then an image of Margaret formed in his mind, and he blushed in the darkness. *She is loyal and loving,* he admitted. *But she's just a little kid. She's too young to... to...* Intensely erotic mages of Rosemary and Rowena naked in the creek rose to swamp his emotions with a mingled mixture of lust and despair.

And there was the creek! He realised he was passing the track to the swimming hole even as he thought about the delights the older girls seemed to offer. Another bout of heated memories got him aroused and that added to his confusion and guilt.

Is it just my body taking control? Is it just because I am at that age and seemed to have no control over myself?

Shaking his head with unhappiness he trudged on, more tears starting to form as he mentally flailed himself for being selfish, too macho, too blind to what girls liked, not sensitive enough. One girl had called him arrogant and said he was too aggressive, too...

Now tears did come, and Graham had to stop and lean on a mango tree. And it was as well that he did as first a train came rolling noisily past only metres away and then a vehicle. He hid from both behind the thick bole of the tree. The vehicle was a battered 4wd with dog or pig cages on the back and it went on past the mill and on towards the town.

Still in the grip of what he knew Peter would call a 'Fit of the dejections' Graham walked on, his mood growing darker as he got further from the lights of the marshalling yards. After a few more minutes of walking, he found himself at the end of the road-rail bridge over the creek and he turned onto it and stood there in the darkness, staring down into the dark water and thinking darker thoughts.

At the end of Year 8 he had been so depressed over the failure of his Navy Medical that he had several times seriously considered suicide. Now he stood there, his mind groping in a mist of self-pity while he again thought about ending it all.

Then his conscience began to bother him. *If I killed myself, Mum will be devastated,* he thought. *And Kylie will be really hurt and spend the rest of her life wondering how she could have prevented it. And poor Margaret, she will be broken-hearted.*

Those thoughts led to others and he finally gave a wry smile. *It's not the end of the world. It is just a girl saying we aren't suited,* he reasoned.

Then one of his mother's little sayings came to him and he smiled. 'Girls are like trams,' she had said. 'There'll be another one along in a few minutes.' Which he had always thought was funny as there were no trams in Cairns! But the essential truth of it struck him.

Carol is not the only girl in the world. There are others, he told himself. And this notion was reinforced by delightful images of Rosemary, Ailsa, and naughty Cindy. So he now stood and wondered what course of action to follow. *What do I do now?*

Still feeling very down, Graham looked around. In the distance he could see the lights of the mill and the billows of smoke and steam coming up from the chimneys. Except for the occasional chirp of some night bird it was very quiet. Only a dull rumble of the mill operating and the occasional clang of metal on metal disturbed the silence. He sighed and began to relax. Then he turned and looked up at the dark mass of jungle-covered mountain.

I wonder if they have found the crashed plane? he thought.

For a few moments he imagined his friends camped up in the jungle. Having spent a few uncomfortable nights in jungle on mountain sides he could easily picture it. And then he shook his head.

And they are my friends. They are true friends, he realised.

In his mind's eye he pictured Peter, Roger, and Stephen, and even Andrew and Tina. The image of Tina and her magnificent bosom gave him a few more regretful thoughts.

After a few minutes of this, Graham found he was shivering. A cool breeze had sprung up, blowing down the valley from the mountains. That caused him to remember Captain Conkey's Geography lesson on Katabatic Winds and then the image of Captain Conkey made him think of Cadets.

My life isn't a complete failure. I am doing very well at Cadets. Captain Conkey wants me to be the CSM, he told himself. Positive memories of cadet camps and challenges he had faced and beaten came to lift his morale even more. *Captain Conkey won't think much of me if I just give up,* he reasoned.

It was that thought that got him going. He shrugged. *I just have to go back and make the best of things,* he decided.

So he turned and started walking back off the bridge. Now the lights of the mill seemed to beckon, and a whiff of the raw sugar and molasses made him smile. Turning right on to the gravel road he walked back the way he had come.

He had only gone a hundred metres or so when he noted the headlight of a locomotive coming towards him. Not wanting to cause the driver any concern, Graham stepped over behind the nearest mango tree and stayed there using the trunk for cover until the locomotive had rumbled past.

He was about to step out onto the road when he heard a vehicle coming from behind him. Thinking that the driver might question what he was doing there at that time of night, Graham stayed at the tree and hid behind the trunk again, moving around to keep it between him and the vehicle as it went past. It looked to be a work utility and just drove on by. It went past the rail workshops and stopped at the back of the molasses tanks.

Graham watched it moodily for a minute or so, noting two men doing something and hearing a steel lid being dropped before the vehicle drove on towards the town. As it drove away, he resumed walking.

Now the bright lights of the mill tended to irritate but he still enjoyed looking at all the activity and the twinkle of interior lights and shiny steel inside. The cloud of steam billowing from the main chimney caught his attention and he was thinking how impressive and beautiful it looked when memories of the man falling to his death changed his mood back to darker thoughts.

That got him hurrying past the workshops and the molasses tanks and on past the loading hoppers. Now he began to hurry, worrying that something might have happened back at the Christmas Party. It occurred to him that Carol might be wondering where he was.

Or Steve.

And there was Stephen! Lying on the grass at the last mango tree past the mill were two people, and the one on top was Stephen. Graham nearly tripped over them in the darkness of the shadows.

"Oh, sorry! Oh bloody hell, is that you, Steve?" he cried.

It was. And he was lying on Betty. To Graham's relief they were both dressed but there was no doubt they had been in a passionate embrace, and he was sure Stephen had intentions.

Stephen half rolled over and sat up. "Oh bugger you, Graham!" he muttered, obviously annoyed at being interrupted.

Graham felt embarrassed and then irritated and then laughed. "Serves you right! My turn this time," he said, alluding to the incident the year before when Stephen had interrupted him and Millie in Munro Martin Park.

Stephen blinked up at him and Betty swore and told him to go away. But Graham had glanced towards the Christmas Party, that area now just visible across the area of lawn.

"How's the party going?" he asked, noting that the loudspeakers and music had stopped and that most of the cars and people had gone.

Stephen looked that way and so did Betty. Then she swore again and sat up. "Shit! What's the time?" she cried.

Graham glanced at his watch and was surprised to note that it was 8:40pm. He told her and she swore again and quickly got up. "Oh bugger! Rosie and I have to be home by 9 o'clock or my dad will belt us," she said. "Quick, Steve, brush me down."

Stephen began brushing her back to remove dead leaves and grass while she used her hands to brush at her hair. Graham stood there waiting and worrying.

I've been gone more than an hour, he thought, worry about what Carol might have been thinking or doing over-riding any concern for Betty.

Betty gave Stephen a quick kiss and when he moved to walk with her, she shook her head and said, "We'd better not be seen together. That little bitch of a sister might tell Mum."

"Okay, see you later then," Stephen replied, taking out his glasses and putting them on. Betty nodded and went hurrying off across the lawn.

Graham stood with Stephen and watched, noting now that the party was in fact over. Most of the food vans and trailers were gone and people were moving about obviously packing up and cleaning up.

"We'd better go over there too and help clean up," he suggested.

Stephen gave a grunt in reply but began walking with Graham. The two boys went slowly, and Graham said, "Sorry Steve. I didn't know you were there."

"That was obvious," Stephen replied, giving a short laugh. "But as you said, we are even now. Besides, it might have been for the best or Betty might have gotten into trouble."

"Yes, from you, if not from her dad!" Graham said in a voice laden with sarcastic jealousy. Once again, he envied Stephen his social skills.

Stephen snorted and gave another short laugh, but Graham suspected he was actually annoyed and probably very frustrated.

I know I would be, he thought.

As they made their way across the lawn two more cars drove off and as more of the park came into sight Graham was even more surprised. The area was now almost deserted. The jumping castle had been deflated and was being rolled up and the merry-go-round was in the process of being dismantled. Now the scattered litter of papers and rubbish on the lawn gave the place an untidy appearance under the glow of the strings of party lights.

It all gave Graham a feeling of anxiety that he had missed something important while he had been brooding along the creek. He saw Betty calling her sister off the old steam locomotive and watched them go hurrying off towards their home.

Now where is Carol? Graham wondered, looking anxiously in all directions.

To his dismay, neither she nor her brother or sister or parents were to be seen. *Have they gone home already?* he wondered. In fact the only person he could see that he recognised was Declin. He was helping a couple of other workmen to clean up. A spurt of jealous anger surged through Graham. *But at least he's not with Carol,* he thought.

The two boys stopped at the bitumen ring road. Stephen also looked around. "What do we do now?" he said.

That was what Graham was wondering. One option was to go over to Carol's house, and he looked that way and then felt his stomach turn over with anxiety. How would he be received if he did? It was a worry.

To his embarrassment, Stephen added to his indecision by saying, "Have you cashed your chips with Carol then?"

Graham shrugged. "Don't know. She just told me to take a walk and to calm down," he replied.

"Yeah, she wasn't happy when you stood up to that git Declin," Stephen replied, gesturing towards where Declin was working.

"Yeah, she was pretty annoyed," Graham agreed. Then he gritted his teeth and clenched his fists as a spasm of jealous anger went through him. "I'd like to punch his lights in," he added.

"That wouldn't help," Stephen said. "Come on, let's go and get our gear and find somewhere to spend the night."

Graham still wanted to seek out Carol to talk to her, to try to find out where he stood, but he felt too embarrassed and defeated to say so. Instead, he agreed and walked with Stephen. The two boys walked across to the front gate of Carol's yard, Graham's eyes all the while scanning the house hopefully. There were lights on inside, but the front door was closed and he saw no sign of anyone.

Nor did he have the courage to go up the stairs and knock on the door. Instead, he turned right and looked for his gear. He saw that his pack, webbing, and bag were all just there beside the garden bed and so were Stephen's. Feeling bad about himself for not being more assertive, he picked up his webbing and swung it on. Then he swung on his pack and picked up his civvie bag. Stephen did likewise. As he did, Graham kept glancing up at the house, hoping to see someone, but paradoxically not wanting to be seen. Now he just felt like slinking away into the darkness.

And that is what they did. After moving back through the gate, Graham led the way to the left. With the camping gear on he felt quite self-conscious, and he glanced across to where Declin was working, hoping he would not notice them. To his ashamed relief, Declin had his back them and was busy rolling up a rope.

But where to go? The park was out of the question and anywhere around the houses was unsuitable. Still puzzling over where to go, he led the way in silence back across the lawn between Carol's house and the mill.

When they reached the gravel road they stopped and looked both ways. "Where to?" Stephen queried.

That put Graham on the spot and his mind raced. To his own embarrassment he knew he had been secretly hoping to be invited to bunk down at Carol's but beyond that he had not thought about where to sleep.

Yes, where? he thought anxiously.

Chapter 32

STUNNED

Graham's first thought was to camp somewhere along the gravel road or the creek bank, but as he turned that way and began walking he considered both areas and decided they would not do.

"Somewhere up the creek past that bridge," he said.

"Bloody hell!" Stephen grumbled. "That far!"

"Sorry, but there isn't anywhere closer. If we camp along here a mill vehicle might come along and tell us to pack up and bugger off," Graham retorted.

"Or we might get run over by a cane harvester!" Stephen chuckled.

The two boys trudged along past the bagasse heaps and loading hopper, continually looking towards the mill. Even though the buildings were a hundred paces away, Graham felt very exposed and oddly embarrassed as they crossed from each line of shadow from one mango tree to the next. For reasons he could not explain, he hoped nobody would notice them walking past. At that moment he just wanted to be inconspicuous.

The boys walked mostly in silence. Graham began to perspire and wished he was wearing his bush clothes rather than his good civvies. At 9:25pm they arrived at the end of the bridge and that forced another decision from Graham, to go on along this bank or cross over?

A thoughtful study of the road and rail lines leading north between the creek and a cane field decided him to cross. The cane field on the mill side of the creek had not yet been harvested and he had images of snakes slithering out of the long grass along the creek and into the sugar cane.

So he led the way across, stopping to look down in the middle. As they stood there, Graham had some sharp memories of his dark broodings only an hour or so before. To end that he resumed walking. On the other side he again had to choose. The road and rail line curved sharply and went up the long slope with newly harvested cane fields on either side. On the right a dirt vehicle track went along the top of the creek bank with the open cane field on the left.

"I doubt if there'll be any traffic during the night," he said.

Stephen laughed and made roaring engine noises and then a squishing, grinding sound. Graham had to laugh but he was really feeling so wretched and worn out that he was not in the mood for Stephen's black humour.

Walking along the dirt track was not all that pleasant and Graham began to fret that he had made a mistake. He was also scared of snakes. All along the way were sticks of sugar cane lying on the track and he kept staring at them in the starlight to see if they were slithering reptiles or not.

But then his luck changed. They came to where a tree grew beside the creek bank and the area under it was bare earth from vehicles being parked or turned. Next to it the field was just furrows of freshly turned bare earth.

"This will do I reckon," he said.

Stephen agreed and the boys dropped their bags and shrugged off packs and webbing. "I'm going to change back into my hiking clothes," Stephen said.

He unrolled his ground sheet and sleeping bag and then sat to pull off shoes and to change. Graham did likewise, turning his back out of modesty. Now he was thankful he had packed a spare shirt as the one he had worn during the day was still damp with sweat and smelly. That stayed in its plastic bag.

Having changed, Graham felt more comfortable and relaxed. He sat down on his bedding and thought about what to do next. By the time they were both changed it was nearly 10:20pm. Stephen stared up at the sky and indicated the low clouds.

"What if it rains?" he queried.

Graham was too dejected to care. "Let it," he replied grumpily. "I'm not trying to put up a hutchie. I will just pull mine over me if it does rain."

Stephen nodded and then began to unpack his webbing. "I'm going to have a cup of hot chocolate," he commented.

"Someone might see our fire," Graham suggested.

Stephen laughed and made a big show of looking in all directions into the darkness. "Oh yeah? Who?"

Graham could only shrug and feel silly. He decided he also needed a lift, so he dug out his hexamine stove, mess tins, matches and began heating water. He had Milo and sugar premixed in a plastic bottle and this went into his cup canteen, and he added the hot water and then sweetened condensed milk from a tube. The result was a very sweet, warm drink that did a lot to lift his spirits.

Stephen left his hexamine burning and sipped at his hot chocolate. "I wonder how the explorers are faring up on the mountain?" he commented, gesturing towards the dark bulk on the other side of the fields.

Graham experienced a twinge of regret at that. He felt bad about leaving his friends and part of him wished he had stayed up there with them. For a few minutes the boys discussed their friends and their expedition.

Stephen grinned. "At least Willy has got Marjorie with him if it gets really cold, and Andrew can snuggle up to Tina."

At the mention of Tina, Graham felt a sharp stab of hurt and was reminded of his failed attempt to win her affection. To hide this he shook his head. "Don't think so. Tina won't allow any hanky-panky," he replied.

Stephen looked thoughtful and then nodded. "Suppose so, and Andrew won't misbehave with Carmen there."

"Andrew wouldn't misbehave anyway. He's too bloody honourable!"

"Oooh! Do I detect the sharp edge of jealousy there?" Stephen replied, grinning so that his teeth showed white in the firelight.

For a few seconds Graham felt really hurt. "Don't be a bugger, Steve!"

Stephen looked contrite. "Yeah, sorry mate. But if you weren't so bloody honourable yourself you could lay the sheilas in rows. They really go for you, yer know."

It took a few seconds for Graham to decide that now it was Stephen being jealous, he presumed because he thought he was better looking. But all he could do was shrug as he knew that even if what his friend said was true, he could not stop being himself. He knew his conscience and character would be his guide.

To his relief, Stephen changed the subject and the friends finished their supper with a few biscuits and then prepared for bed. As part of this, Graham walked back 50 paces along the dirt track to do a pee. As he did, he stood on the starlight and stared at where the lights of the mill just showed through the trees and wondered if he had any chance of recovering his relationship with Carol.

And do I want to? he thought.

Sadly he decided he needed to find a way to end the relationship with the minimum fuss and hurt to both of them.

* * *

Back at the campsite, both boys lay down and the conversation lapsed. Graham rolled on his side to avoid talking but his mind stayed active. For the next few hours he tried to come up with the right wording to say what needed to be said.

Eventually he fell into a fitful sleep, woken by a few raindrops, which got him muttering swear words but which thankfully did not develop into a proper shower of rain. There was a bad dream as well in which he found himself trying to escape from something, or was it someone, inside the sugar mill at night. He kept hurrying between vast machines and in and out of areas of light while being terrified of what might be lurking in the numerous patches of shadow. He ended up among the huge distillation vats and then trapped out on a steel deck high above the milling train with steam hissing and IT coming to get him.

He woke to find a blue sky above and himself half off his groundsheet, his arms and half his sleeping bag in the dust beside it. His eyes felt gummy with sleep and he had a dry mouth and a headache. A check of his watch told him it was just after 6:30am, which surprised him as he hadn't meant to sleep in. Looking up he saw that the sun was already shining on all the upper slopes of the mountains.

We should have got up an hour ago, he thought.

Groaning and feeling washed out, he rolled over and got up. Stephen opened a bleary eye to study him and to question the time.

"Do we need to get up so early? What's the time?"

Graham told him and then added, "Besides, we don't want Farmer Brown to come along and plough us in."

"Or kick our arses!" Stephen added, also moving to get out of his sleeping bag. As he did, he asked, "What are you planning to do today?"

"I want to go back to Carol's," Graham replied.

Stephen made a face. "Don't like your chances," he commented.

Which was how Graham felt but he stubbornly wanted to persevere. He did not tell Stephen that he had spent half the night awake planning how to end things with Carol.

"What do you want to do?"

"I'll come with you," Stephen answered. "We might get to meet up with Betty."

"You don't want to go up the mountain?"

Stephen sat up and shook his head. "Nah! Anyway, we'd look a right pair of nongs if we slogged all the way up and missed them and found they'd gone down another ridge. Nah, I reckon I rather try to climb Betty's twin peaks."

Graham had to smile and thought that Stephen probably had a good chance of achieving that ambition. So both boys got up and went off to relieve themselves and then to pack up and have breakfast. Graham always enjoyed field cooking and his mood lifted a bit as he ate. Afterwards he heated more water and carefully shaved, kneeling over his mess tin to soap his face and apply the safety razor.

"You that hopeful?" Stephen queried as he watched him combing his hair afterwards.

"Not really," Graham replied.

He didn't want to admit he had actually been driven by his youthful soldierly pride of always doing his morning routine properly and looking his best. And he did feel better.

That American admiral is right, always make your bed first thing, he told himself.

By 8am Graham was packed up and ready. Then he had to wait while Stephen went off to do a morning crap. While he did, Graham sat on his pack staring up at the jungle-covered mountain. The sound of a train moving towards the mill came to him. For a few seconds he thought it was on their side of the creek, but it wasn't. It went rattling past a few hundred metres away on the other side.

A few minutes later, Stephen returned and bent to pack his webbing. Groaning and feeling stiff and sore Graham stood and swung on his webbing and pack. Stephen did likewise and the two boys began walking at 8:20am. As they did, the sound of another train came to them, the loud blaring of its air horn giving warning. This time it came rumbling across the bridge and went past a hundred metres to their right, its diesel engine roaring as it pulled a train of empty cane bins up the long slope and then over the top and out of sight. To Graham's relief, the train crew did not even appear to be looking in their direction.

A few minutes later the boys reached the bridge. This time Stephen looked carefully in both directions before walking onto it. Graham shook his head.

"There won't be another train for quite a while. It's a single line track," he said.

"Doesn't matter. I don't fancy jumping off this bridge into water that deep with my pack and webbing on," Stephen replied.

Graham looked down and again noted how deep the water was at that point. "We will get plenty of warning. The loco will blow it's horn," he answered.

Stephen pointed back, "There is a siding back up there on top of the rise and another train could pass that one there."

"Maybe," Graham agreed, also glancing back over his shoulder. Then he grinned, "Remember when we had to jump off the Blackwater Creek Bridge up near Koah a few years ago?"

"My word yes! That was bit of a thrill," Stephen agreed.

The reminiscing over the incident when a train had caught them in the middle of a long and high rail bridge on that expedition carried the two boys across to the other side and along the gravel road in the shade of the mango trees until they were past the Locomotive Workshops.

By then Graham was getting very anxious and he was also aware he was sweating. He did not want that. He wanted to be fresh and not smell while he was talking to Carol. And that raised again the issue of what he would say.

But when to talk to her? And where? He fretted. There seemed to be no other option but to go to her house and ask to see her.

"I hope we aren't too early," he said as they went past the sugar loader.

Stephen snorted scornfully. "It's getting on towards 9 o'clock. They will be out of bed."

So, despite his misgivings and the butterflies in the stomach, Graham led the way to her front gate. Here he swung off pack and webbing and placed them and his civvie bag just inside on the lawn. There were no sounds from inside the house, but the front door was now open.

Gulping with anxiety, Graham took several deep breaths and made his way up the front stairs. He could see no-one on the front veranda or in the hallway and he hesitated and listened for a moment before plucking up the courage to knock.

He heard footsteps in the next room and Kirsty's head appeared around the door frame. To Graham's surprise, her eyes went wide and she looked scared and at once hurried back towards the kitchen.

"Mum! Mum, he's here!" she called.

Kirsty vanished out of sight and Graham heard the mutter of voices. He was mystified by her reaction. *What's going on? What has Carol said?* he wondered.

But having made the move he now stood and waited, his anxiety growing by the second. From the kitchen she distinctly heard Carol's mother say, "Yes, here, at the front door... Yes, okay."

A moment later, Carol's mother hurried along the hallway. "Yes, what do you want?" she asked.

To add to Graham's concern he noted that her face was anything but friendly and that she had her mobile phone in her hand.

"I... I just wanted to talk to Carol," Graham managed to say.

"Well she doesn't want to talk to you. But her father does so you just wait downstairs please," Carol's mother replied.

That alarmed Graham but also puzzled him. *I'm in trouble!* he thought.

Immediately his guilty conscience began to dredge up possible things he had done wrong. Top of his list was swimming naked with the girls and his insides began to churn with anxiety as he turned and made his way back down the stairs.

Stephen gave him a quizzical grin. "What's the matter?"

Graham felt his stomach turn over with fear and he had to swallow before replying. "Carol's father wants to speak to me," he said.

Stephen at once looked concerned. "Do you know what for?" he asked, glancing up at where Carol's mother stood at the front door.

Graham shook his head and had to fight down a swirl of nausea as the fear built. "Don't know. She didn't say. Must be about skinny dipping. I haven't done anything else," he croaked.

It took him an effort to speak without a tremor in his voice. To his shame he began to feel dizzy, and he began to sweat. He had to consciously stop himself from looking scared.

From up inside the house Graham heard the patter of running footsteps and then Kirsty squeaking but he could not hear what she was saying. He thought, *Carol is here. Kirsty is telling her.*

Graham looked up at Carol's mother but the hard and unfriendly look on her face dismayed him even more. His gaze ran along the wooden louvres at the front of the veranda. He was hoping to see Carol or Kirsty but there was no sign of them. But something was obviously seriously wrong, and his concern grew by the second. For a few moments he considered just walking away but that seemed to be such a cowardly act he got all stubborn.

Turning to Stephen, he said, "You don't have to stay here, Steve. It doesn't concern you."

Stephen shook his head. "If you are in trouble I am staying. I was there too, remember," he said.

Graham was touched by his loyalty and again tried to persuade him to leave. But then he noticed Mr Battersby hurrying across the lawn from the Mill Office. "Here he comes. We'll soon know what's up," he said.

He then had to fight down a sudden impulse to flee. Not knowing what the problem was just made it worse.

Mr Battersby arrived at the run, mobile phone in hand and panting for breath. Graham stood his ground and forced himself to look calm. "Hello, Mr Battersby. What's the problem?" he managed to say.

Mr Battersby came to a panting stop in the gateway and stared at him. "You boys just wait here. The police want to speak to you," he said.

"The police!" Graham cried, stunned by the statement. It then came to him that Mr Battersby was standing so as to block any move to leave through the gateway. It flashed through Graham's mind how futile that was as he and Stephen could always just run away around the house. But as quickly as the idea crossed his mind, it was dismissed. As the initial shock wore off, his mind began to search for a reason.

Stephen had obviously thought the same thing as he now stood defiantly and said, "Why? We haven't done anything."

Graham glanced at him, and the idea formed that perhaps Betty's father had called the police. In his own mind he felt sure that Carol's father knew nothing about him and Carol swimming naked.

He is not acting like an angry father who is protecting his daughter.

Mr Battersby pressed his lips together and shook his head and did not answer. That stung Stephen, who frowned and snapped angrily, "Why do the police want us? What are we supposed to have done?"

Yes, Graham thought, *what are we supposed to have done?*

Chapter 33

SHATTERED

Shocked but intrigued Graham stood there, his whole body now seeming to squirm with tension as his mind raced through all the possibilities he could think of. But despite his guilty mind dredging up everything he thought might be worthy of the police taking an interest, he could not think what the reason might be. And believing himself to be innocent he made no attempt to move. To his relief, Stephen stayed beside him.

That Stephen was angrier and more worried was obvious by his aggressive stance and his truculent tone. He turned his back on Mr Battersby and glared at Graham.

"What is he talking about? What are we supposed to have done?"

Graham shook his head. "I have no idea," he replied. He met Mr Battersby's eyes and could tell the man was looking very uneasy. "But I intend to find out," he added.

A few tense minutes passed, the players in the little tableau all remaining in their places. Graham wiped away sweat that started to trickle down his face into his eyes and tried to keep his emotions under control. He realised they were both standing in the blazing morning sun and briefly considered moving into the shade. But seeing the worried look on Mr Battersby's face kept him rooted to the spot.

And he found that not knowing made it worse! He started to hyperventilate from anxiety and had to grit his teeth and hold his hands tightly by his side while bringing his breathing back under control.

What are we supposed to have done? Did Steve do something last night and not tell me? he wondered.

As he stood there, Graham experienced a series of vivid flashbacks to an incident at the start of the year when he and Stephen had been accused of murdering a boy, the brother of Stephen's then girlfriend. On that occasion, Stephen had managed to avoid being arrested by running away and he had phoned Graham who had joined him during the night. That had been the start of a gruelling and terrifying night march over the mountains and even more terrifying encounters with some very dangerous men before they had been able to persuade the police of their innocence.

Should we be taking to the jungle? Graham wondered, again meeting Stephen's worried gaze. But having no idea why the police wanted them, he decided that such an action would just make them look even more guilty. *And if it's just over the girls then I will take my medicine.*

Then the sound of a police siren in the distance sent his anxiety sharply up. His heart seemed to skip several beats and he felt fear grip his chest and throat. As the siren's strident wail rose and fell and came rapidly closer, so his emotions rose with it until he reached the verge of panic. He found he was trembling and gasping deep breaths.

Once again, he considered running while there was a chance, but again he stubbornly stayed as the police car raced into view from the town. It turned onto the ring road so sharply it almost went into a broadside skid, and the urgency of its movement added to Graham's concern. Through eyes narrowing with fear he watched the car pull in and skid to a stop on the grass in front of the house. Out of it climbed two uniformed officers, a female sergeant and a male senior constable.

Relief showed on Mr Battersby's face, and he hurried over to meet the police officers, pointing towards Graham and Stephen as he did.

Bloody hell! He meant it! Graham thought, disbelief conflicting with what he was seeing. *But what are we supposed to have done?*

The female sergeant, a thin faced blonde, spoke briefly to Mr Battersby and then moved in through the gate. The male senior constable, a big, burly fellow Graham had no wish to tangle with, followed.

The sergeant looked at him. "Graham Kirk?"

"Yes ma'am," Graham replied politely.

"You are under arrest," she said. She then gave the legal warning that Graham had heard a hundred times on TV cop shows.

Once again, Graham was stunned. "Arrest! What for?" he cried.

"Assault occasioning grievous bodily harm," the sergeant replied, moving to take out her handcuffs as she did.

Graham could only stand and gape, his mouth hanging open in surprise. "Assault! What? Who?"

"You are named as having bashed a man named Declin Riley," the sergeant said. "Now put your hands behind your back."

"Declin!" Graham cried in astonishment. "I did not!"

He was so stunned he just did as he was told. The solid feel of the handcuffs snapping shut just seemed to add to the unreality of it all. As he turned to face the police officers, his mind raced.

"I never touched him! When did he say this was supposed to happen?"

The sergeant gave him a hard look. "He didn't say. He's in hospital in a coma. He has been so badly bashed he may not live," she said.

Graham was appalled. "But... but I didn't touch him. When did this happen?"

"Last night. Between about 8 and 9 o'clock. Where were you between 8 and 9?"

Graham felt the fear rising like a fog to fuddle his brain. "Here, at the Christmas Party," he said.

"We were told you were not here, that you had walked off into the night," the sergeant replied.

To Graham it felt like a black pit had suddenly opened up at his feet. "I... yes. I went for a walk along that road behind the mill."

"Why was that?"

"My... er... a girl I was with suggested I go and calm down," Graham replied. Now he was blushing, not wanting his social failures publicised.

"What girl was that?" the sergeant asked.

"Carol, Mr Battersby's daughter," Graham answered, glancing at him as he did and getting a very frosty stare in return.

"And why did she suggest you go and calm down?"

"Because... because I was angry," Graham replied.

"Because you just had a fight with Declin Riley?" the sergeant asked.

Graham felt ill. "It wasn't a fight. We just shouted at each other and put our fists up. There weren't any punches thrown!" he cried. He was starting to feel trapped and desperate now.

"Can anyone vouch for you during those times. Did anyone see you walking?" the sergeant asked.

Graham shook his head but then remembered stumbling over Stephen and Betty. He was about to say so when he realised that would probably drop his friend in it. So he hesitated, trying to choose the right words, and knew he shouldn't have.

He said, "I met Steve here when I was just coming back across the lawn." He indicated which lawn by a jerk of his head.

The sergeant now turned to Stephen and Graham noted that the senior constable had positioned himself close behind him. Stephen looked anxious but also angry.

The sergeant stared at him, then said, "Are you Stephen Bell?"

"Yes," Stephen replied

The sergeant nodded to the senior constable. "Stephen Bell, I am arresting you for assault occasioning grievous bodily harm. Cuff him."

For a moment Graham thought Stephen was going to resist but then he shrugged and put his hands behind his back.

"We didn't do anything. We haven't beaten anyone up."

"We have several witness reports naming you," the sergeant commented.

"Oh who?" Stephen cried. He was obviously angry and starting to get upset.

Graham felt sorry for him. Stephen had been in serious trouble with the police a few times over the last couple of years and he knew his parents would be very unhappy about yet another incident.

"But we are innocent! We didn't do it!" he cried.

At that moment Carol spoke. She was upstairs, and when Graham jerked his head around he could see her eyes behind the louvres.

She called, "We were told that you did! Oh Graham! How could you?"

"Carol, I didn't!" Graham cried, his anxiety now causing his eyes to mist with tears.

"You did! People saw you! Oh, I hate you! I never want to see you again!" Carol screamed, her voice then breaking into sobs.

Graham was aghast. He shook his head but now had tears starting and the embarrassment added to his emotional turmoil. The sergeant began urging him towards the gateway.

And there was then more hurt. As Graham was led through the gateway, Mr Battersby hissed at him, "And don't you ever speak to my daughter again! You keep away from her, even at school, you hear!"

That put the final seal on Graham's defeat. He felt absolutely shattered emotionally and made no resistance while he was placed in the back of the police car. It was a classic 'Paddy Wagon' type with a cage on the back and that somehow made it worse. He felt so embarrassed he just wanted to curl up and hide.

Stephen joined him and that helped him get control as he did not want to be a disgrace in front of his mate. The back door was slammed shut and a latch clanged into place. There was then a short delay while their gear was collected and placed in the back part of the cab.

Graham heard the police talking to the Battersbys but not what they were saying. Then the car started up and began moving. After getting as comfortable as he could Graham looked across at Stephen.

"Sorry, Steve. Honestly, I haven't done it. I have no idea what they are talking about or who these witnesses might be," he said.

Stephen was looking both angry and upset. He nodded and shook his head. "My oldies will ground me for life if I am in trouble again," he replied.

"But who? Why?" Graham said.

He bent to look out through the small, barred window and saw that they had just passed the Caster Hotel. Images of Declin there at various times flitted across his mind and he tried to hard to think when he was supposed to have beaten Declin up.

Stephen had the same thoughts, as he said, "So if you didn't bash this Declin fella up, who did? And why? And why are we being blamed?"

"Framed," Graham replied.

"Yes, but who by? And why?" Stephen said. He then leaned closer and used his facial expressions and eyes to indicate he thought the cage might be wired for sound recording. Then he whispered, "Graham, don't mention Betty please."

"I won't," Graham replied. "I nearly did before but then realised that might drop you right in the poo."

Stephen nodded and gave a rueful grin. "Thanks."

"Do you think Betty's dad had anything to do with this?"

Stephen shook his head. "Nah! He wouldn't call the cops. He'd just re-arrange my face."

Graham thought that was probable and he now sat and tried to think of a way out of the trouble. But what made it hard to think straight were those emotionally shattering words from Carol and her father.

I have really lost! How can I retrieve the situation? he thought gloomily. Then even more dismaying thoughts crossed his mind. *If I can't prove I am innocent Captain Conkey might not want me as CSM next year,* he decided. From which came the horrible possibility of him being discharged from the Cadets in disgrace. *And if I get convicted of a criminal offence and go to jail, I won't ever get to be an officer in the army. I won't even be able to enlist as a soldier!*

Those thoughts sent his emotions into a black pit of despair, and he began to gloomily brood over the future. He knew he had never felt so shattered in his life. And he also knew that there were many humiliations and embarrassments likely to come.

Starting with having to face Mum! he thought unhappily.

With such depressing thoughts fogging his mind, Graham found the drive to Cairns a miserable experience and several times tears prickled. Only his pride held them in check.

And a sense of unreality. *This can't be true! This isn't really happening!* he thought. But the hardness of the hand cuffs and smooth, cool metal of the cage told him it was.

Oh, how can I get out of this mess? he fretted.

* * *

They were taken to Cairns Police Station and escorted through to where a bored senior sergeant had them processed, their pockets emptied and so on. Next was the humiliating experience of being checked by a doctor. That required him to strip to his underwear with other people present.

The doctor shook his head. "No signs of any bruising or contusions," he said to the plain clothes policeman who was also in the room.

After getting dressed, Graham had a sample of his DNA taken and then his fingerprints. He was taken back out to wait while Stephen underwent the same ordeal. They were then taken out along a corridor and the next of the really hurtful experiences occurred. His mother was waiting, looking very anxious and upset.

"I didn't do anything! I don't know what is going on!" he cried.

Then his eyes locked with those of Stephen's father and he felt even worse. Both of Stephen's parents gave him a hurt, accusatory look, as though they blamed him for getting their son into trouble.

At that point they were separated, Graham and his mother being placed in one interrogation room and Stephen and his parents in another. A grumpy looking male detective sergeant and another officer whose rank and name Graham did not get then joined them, along with a man who was introduced as the Duty Solicitor.

Hearing that really hammered home the seriousness of the situation to Graham and he felt he had fallen into a pit of despair. It took all his efforts not to break down and blubber. There then followed over an hour of questioning, which Graham did his best to answer. His only deviation from the truth, and he was ready for it this time, was in not mentioning Betty when he described meeting Stephen on his return to the party.

There was then a break which his mother insisted on. During it Graham was escorted to a toilet and then given a drink of water. By then he felt wrung out and was feeling totally shattered. But it was over Carol as much as the legal stuff. And through it all he maintained his innocence and was baffled by what was going on.

"Why have I been named?" he demanded to know, tiredness adding anger to his fear and frustration.

"Some of the mill workers saw two boys attacking someone. They came out to stop it and the boys ran away towards the site of the Christmas Party. The workers then found Declin Riley and called the ambulance," replied the DS.

Graham was totally puzzled. "What workers? I didn't see any."

The DS did not reply, but asked, "How do you know Declin Riley?"

"He likes Carol and he doesn't like me," Graham replied.

He then had to explain the rivalry and the times when he had met or seen Declin. But none of that helped make clear who had bashed him and why. "Anyway, how is he?" Graham asked.

"In a serious condition in hospital. If he dies you will be looking at a murder charge," the DS replied grimly.

Graham's mother sobbed and looked aghast and Graham was appalled. "But I didn't hit him! I didn't even see him after we had our argument."

Once again, he was questioned on every detail and Graham was pleased to note that the detectives were looking as frustrated and baffled as he felt. By then the sharp edge of his fear had worn off and he was getting irritated and angry. Which led him to being foolish. When he was asked to sign a transcript of the interview, he made a point of reading and then used the pen to make several corrections to the spelling and grammar.

The DS frowned. "What are you doing?" he demanded to know.

"If you are going to hang me then at least get someone who paid attention in school!" Graham retorted.

"Don't be a little smart-arse kid!" snapped the DS.

That got both Graham's mother and the solicitor involved. Graham's mother was also very worried, and she cried angrily that the police could make sure everything was done correctly.

Another hour was taken up with Graham writing a statement which was then checked over by the solicitor and his mother. The solicitor made a couple of corrections to it and gave him a wry smile.

"We don't want the pot calling the kettle black," he said. Graham could only blush.

By then Graham was expecting to be formally charged and was swallowing with anxiety and that thought sent his spirits plummeting again. But, to his intense relief, the DS said that he was a suspect and that he could go but must not leave town.

"We will be doing further investigations," he said.

Relief gave way to anger. "That's because you haven't got any evidence against me!" Graham cried. "And you won't find any because I didn't do it!"

"We will see. Now, this is a formal caution," the DS replied frostily.

He then warned Graham not to try to interfere with witnesses and not to leave town. His mother was then asked him to come in again the following morning so he could sign a typed copy of his statement.

Then it was home. Once outside Graham felt very conspicuous and felt sure all the people in the street could tell he was in trouble with the police. But then he realised they weren't even glancing at him. He wanted to speak to Stephen but there was no sign of him.

There was then the embarrassment and stress of explaining to his brother and sister why he had been arrested. It was mid-afternoon by then and he felt exhausted. After some afternoon refreshments he was able to escape from his sibling's curiosity and went to lie on his bed, where he promptly burst into tears as the whole situation overwhelmed him.

Black despair engulfed him. *Oh how do I get out of this? What will I do if I can't? If I go to prison my whole life will be wrecked. I won't be able to join the army and I will never get to be an officer, not even a Cadet Under-Officer. And I've lost Carol too!*

It all seemed so black and hopeless that all he could do was lie there and sob.

Chapter 34

BLACK DESPAIR

Graham's whole being felt like it was gripped by powerful and evil forces beyond his control. To him it felt like a living nightmare. For the next few hours he lay there, self-pity and doubt adding to his deepening sense of depression.

His mother insisted that he get up for the evening meal and, although he said he did not feel like anything, he did eat. During the meal, Alex and Kylie both wanted to know what had happened, but his mother told them only the outline and then insisted they stop asking.

"And you can go and make sure your homework is all done!" she ordered as they got up at the end of the meal.

Graham was left with his mother, and she gave him a sorrowful look and shook her head. "Now let's talk to your father," she said.

That was another ordeal Graham had been dreading and he suddenly felt so nauseous he became worried he might bring his food straight back up. But there was no avoiding it. His mother connected through the radio telephone and then gave her father the outline of the problem.

That all made Graham squirm with shame as he knew hundreds of people who knew the family could listen in. *Will be listening in,* he told himself as he burned with embarrassment.

His father then questioned him. Graham gave his version of what had happened and again insisted he was innocent. "I didn't do it dad! I haven't had a fight with anyone," he insisted.

"Then you have somehow made some bad enemies, son. If you have been set up there has to be a powerful reason for it," his father replied.

But who? Graham puzzled. *And why?*

That ordeal over, Graham was allowed to go to his room while his parents continued to talk. Once again, Graham threw himself on the bed and wept. His mother came to comfort him ten minutes later and he slowly calmed down. Then they discussed his father's theory but that was no help. He could not think of anyone who might dislike him so much they would go to such lengths.

His mother looked grim. "It may not be someone you know. It might be someone who has it in for this Declin fellow and you and Stephen were just selected to take the blame. How well do you know this Declin?"

Graham shook his head. "Not well at all. I told you, he likes Carol and we have only seen each other a few times."

"Is it rivalry over the girl?" his mother queried.

"You mean is there another person who also admires her?" Graham asked, puzzled.

His mother frowned, then shrugged. "I don't know, but when girls are involved males do some very irrational things," she replied.

That got Graham blushing again as nameless feelings of guilt pulsed through him. But he was still at a loss to explain how it had all come about. His mother gave him a hug and said, "Then we must prove you are innocent."

"But how?"

His mother shook her head. "I'm not sure, but we are going to see a lawyer tomorrow. Now you try to relax and don't get to upset. It isn't the end of the world."

She went away and Graham lay back. A tear trickled down his left cheek. *I wish it was!* he thought. It all looked so black and hopeless that he became even more dejected.

He suffered a long, unhappy night. He hardly slept and when he did the horrible sugar mill nightmare kept recurring. No matter which way he ran he could not find his way out from among the big machines and he was high up and in danger of falling. And when he was awake, he brooded. Black thoughts crept in: of being an utter failure, of being thrown out of Cadets, of prison, well, juvenile detention anyway, and of having to endure, however briefly, the hurt and pitying looks of his friends and classmates.

Carol's parting words burned into his mind, making him feel utterly detected and worthless. '*I never want to see you again!*' *And she didn't even believe me.* That hurt just as much. It made him sure the relationship was truly over and he could not think of any ploy or tactic to retrieve it.

And he wasn't sure he wanted to. The gloomy thoughts of the previous night returned, that they weren't suited and that he didn't really love her.

* * *

At least he did not have to face up to Carol, or to his friends or classmates when Monday morning finally dawned. His mother was adamant he was not going to school.

"We are seeing a lawyer and then going to the police station," she said.

"What will you tell the school?" Graham asked.

"I will tell the principal the truth," his mother replied.

"What about Captain Conkey?" Graham asked.

That was bothering him a lot more. Now he explained to her his fears of being thrown out of the Cadets, and of not being able to join the army. During that he began to cry, to his great embarrassment.

His mother was very understanding and comforting. "I am sure it won't come to that. Now calm down and come and have breakfast."

"Don't want any!" Graham sobbed, more tears trickling out.

"Yes you do! And first you will go and have a shower and shave. Even if you think you are going to stand in front of a firing squad you can make your parents proud and face up to it like a man. Your self-respect is involved," she snapped.

"Yes Mum."

Graham blushed and sniffled and then did as he was told, ashamed that he had given way like that. And his mother was right. He did feel much better after the shower and shave and dressed in clean clothes.

"And do what that American admiral you are always quoting says," she added. "Go and make your bed."

So Graham obeyed. He then said goodbye to Alex and Kylie, both of whom appeared sympathetic. Kylie was the more genuine. She gave him a little kiss.

"Chin up!" she said. "We believe you and still love you."

"I suppose you will tell Margaret?"

"Of course! She has a right to know. She loves you, you bonehead!" Kylie replied.

Then she was gone. Graham did not know how to feel about that, a mixture of gladness and sadness mixed with shame at hurting her. Anxiety over Declin's wellbeing had been gnawing at Graham all night and he now asked his mother to find out if he was still alive. Luckily, she had a number at the police station that she could call and was able to report that Declin was still in a critical condition in a coma.

At least he hasn't died! Graham told himself. The idea of being charged with murder filled him with horror.

It was a long, unpleasant, and tiring day. But while being sobering and serious it was also very instructive into the real world. Graham felt quite small and somewhat intimidated by the police procedures but was impressed by their professionalism and manner. The lawyers also impressed him, but he was concerned when he learned what it was going to cost his parents.

Mum and Dad must really love me if they are prepared to pay that much! he thought.

There followed some very intense and sometimes awkward questions. When they got home it was after school had finished and he had to face another test he was hoping to avoid: Margaret was there.

It was clear to him that she would have loved to rush over and throw her arms around him, but she managed to restrain herself. All she did was give him a friendly but anxious smile and wish him well. To his relief, she did not question him but went off to Kylie's room with her.

Later, when Margaret came to say goodbye before going home, she revealed her emotions a bit more. For a few seconds she stood looking at him and then her eyes filled with tears, and she stepped forward and put her arms around his neck. As she kissed him on the forehead she whispered in a husky, quavering voice, "Good luck! Oooh!"

Then she fled as more tears came. Kylie went out with her to see her off, giving Graham a pursed-lipped look of disapproval as she did.

And Graham did feel bad about how he was treating Margaret, but also felt uplifted by her obvious care and concern. That helped him later in the night when he woke from another nightmare and sank into another pit of black despair over his possible fate.

For hours he lay in the darkness, brooding over what had gone wrong and of what might get even worse in the future. Once again, he became so absorbed by his own misery that niggling thoughts of suicide crept in.

It was the memory of Margaret's kiss that helped him. *She loves me and if I... if I... if I did anything it would absolutely shatter her.*

Slowly he reasoned his way back to a more balanced view, knowing that his mother loved him and would be destroyed if he committed suicide.

And Kylie.

* * *

Dawn came, emotionally bleak but hot and tropical. Now Graham began to nerve himself for more embarrassment and possible humiliation. His mother had said he was to go to school and that meant possibly awkward questions. It also meant he would have to face Captain Conkey. An anguished feeling that he had somehow let Captain Conkey down assailed him.

And I will see Carol too, he thought.

That was an ordeal he dreaded. But despite his nervous anxiety he made himself get up and shower and shave and then dress with more care than usual. As he combed his hair, Graham's studied his appearance in the mirror and was shocked. He looked exhausted and had dark rings under his eyes.

The strain must be wearing me down, he mused. Then he shrugged. *I will just have to put a bold face on it until the axe falls,* he told himself.

He even made a point of making his bed without being reminded. Then he forced himself to eat a big breakfast, all the while enduring the querying gaze of Alex and Kylie.

He also made a point of getting his mother to find out what Declin's condition was. To his relief, he learned that Declin was still alive, unconscious and still in a serious condition.

"If only he can wake up," Graham said. "Then he can tell the police it wasn't us who hit him."

His mother looked thoughtful. "Maybe. We hope so. But he may not have seen who hit him," she replied.

That was a sobering prospect and added to Graham's gloom.

School was another of those emotionally buffeting experiences that also taught him some hard life lessons. The main one was that he wasn't the focus of the universe. To his surprise, and even annoyance, he discovered when he walked in that no-one was taking any particular notice of him and when he said hello to classmates they answered in a way that made it clear they knew nothing about his predicament.

Having placed his bag outside his classroom he took several deep breaths and at once set off for Captain Conkey's staff room. *Get it over with!* he told himself.

So, bracing back his shoulders after taking several deep breaths, he knocked on the door. Luckily, Captain Conkey was at his desk and immediately put down his pen and came to the door.

"Yes Graham?"

"You know I am in trouble, sir?"

"Yes. Your mother phoned me. Don't tell me the details if you aren't allowed to, you know, for legal reasons, or if you don't want to," Captain Conkey replied.

Graham was very touched by the concern and support in the teacher's voice and for a moment emotion threatened to choke him up. Mastering it with a swallow he nodded.

"Thank you, sir. I just wanted to say that Stephen and I are innocent. We have no idea who bashed the victim."

"But it is a serious charge?"

"Yes sir. Sir, am I allowed to attend Cadets?"

"Yes, but it might be a bit awkward for you if the others know."

"I'll be alright sir. And sir... what about... about the Promotion Course?"

To Graham's dismay, Captain Conkey shook his head. "I can't make any promises there. We will have to see what the court says," he replied.

Graham had been expecting that, but it was still a bitter pill and he had to blink back tears. So upset was he that he did not trust himself to speak, and he nodded and quickly left.

Making his way downstairs he sought out his friends. As he did, he looked anxiously in all directions for Carol. To his mingled relief and regret he did not see her, but he found Peter and Roger sitting in their usual place. Willy and Stick were also there. There was no sign of Stephen. Peter moved along the seat to make room for him.

"What happened? Tell us the story," Peter demanded as soon as he was seated.

Graham shook his head and felt misery well up. "Sorry. We are not allowed to talk about it to anyone. Please don't ask."

"Who said?" Stick asked.

"The police. Drop the subject, please," Graham replied.

To change the subject, Peter described the search for the aircraft wreck, with the others adding details. This included a lot of moaning about the rain, the leeches, the wait-a-while and so on.

"Are you going to go up there and have another look?" Graham asked.

Peter looked doubtful and shook his head. When Graham looked at Willy, he gave an emphatic shake of the head.

"No thanks. I've had enough jungle to last me for quite a while."

That at least caused some laughing and the mood slowly improved. The conversation shifted to rumours about what the Year 12s were planning to do on their last day at school. Over the last few years a tradition had grown up of the seniors doing something unusual on their last day. This time the rumour was that they would be setting electric wires to all the urinals so that when boys went to do a pee they would get an electric shock. Peter dismissed the story as not being technically feasible.

Graham knew that Peter usually got top marks in subjects like science but he still wasn't convinced it could not be done. Stick thought it was a great rumour and went off to tell some of the Year 8s.

Then it was time for classes. There were still two weeks of school to go for the Year 10s and Graham was not looking forward to them at all.

Complete waste of time! he thought. *We have done our exams and all the teachers will do is go over all our mistakes in the tests and carry on about how we need to do better for next year.*

In this he was not wrong, the situation made worse by the fact that the Year 12s would finish at the end of that week and the Year 10s and 11s at the end of the following. One of the approved school trips in the week after that was the army cadet's annual promotion courses. To Graham that now figured as a major worry. He began mentally preparing himself for not going and for being discharged from the Cadets in disgrace.

Now the exams were over the school reverted to its normal timetable of six periods each day. Graham went to his first class and sat there silently brooding. The seat next to him was empty as Stephen had not yet returned. That depressed him more. With the prospect of legal disaster looking Graham began to think through his options.

If I don't get to go on the warrant officers course I may as well just leave Cadets anyway, he thought.

During that first period, Graham was informed of his exam results in English. He had done well, a 'B', better than he usually got. And, as he had predicted, the class then began to laboriously dissect the test questions, plus do similar questions to ensure they now got the message and understood.

During the break between periods Willy came along the veranda on his way to another class. "G'day Graham," he said. "Is there any change to that bloke Declin's condition?"

Graham shook his head and muttered, "No." Then he had to turn and walk quickly away to hide the tears that sprang to the corners of his eyes.

In second period, he learned that he had achieved a Very High in History. That pleased him but he had been reasonably sure he would get a good result so wasn't all that surprised.

I need V.Hs or 'Highs' in all my subjects right through Year 11 and 12 to be sure of being accepted by the Army to be an officer, he reminded himself. Then he was plunged into gloom that was close to despair when he remembered that he might never make that ambition if he was convicted of a crime. *If that Declin dies, I could be in prison for life!*

Once again, life seemed to be an uphill struggle and his spirits dropped. And old memories did not help. He thought back to two years before, when he had learned that he could never be a naval officer because of his eyesight.

I was ready to commit suicide then, he remembered.

He and Andrew had been diving at Green Island and in a 'fit of the dejections' he had told Andrew he didn't want to live anymore and that he was going to end it all. Graham shuddered at the memory. He had been going to just going swim out into deep water and let himself drown.

But Andrew talked me out of it. Then we were in that plane crash on the way home and we ended up in the sea for eighteen hours.

More memories came and he relived that grim ordeal. The pilot of the float plane had been badly hurt and the other passenger had been Graham's paraplegic friend, Ken. Andrew had helped get them both out and then Graham found himself struggling to keep Ken alive. Several times Graham had said he wanted to give up but each time he had changed his mind because he knew he had to stay alive to save his friend.

And then Captain Conkey and Warrant Officer Howley made me join the Cadets and that has given me real hope, he mused, as a flow of positive memories, of challenges met and overcome, crossed his mind.

He gave a grim smile. *I will just have to fight this and try to win.*

* * *

During 'Little Lunch' Graham sat with his friends. He was too upset to take part in the conversations and was irritated and annoyed by Noddy Parker's silly jokes and clowning. Instead, he kept looking around for a glimpse of Carol. He did not see her, but he did note several girls standing with their heads turned in his direction. By the way they looked away and whispered and then back again, he had the unpleasant suspicion that they were talking about him.

Carol has probably told them, he thought. And it was obvious she did not believe he was innocent.

Later in the day, during the break between Periods 3 and 4 when classes were moving from one room to another, Graham got direct confirmation of his worries. He was walking with his class across the pathway beside the quadrangle, straggling as was usual. From the other direction came another Year 10 class, Carol's. Graham saw Carol hurrying towards them, a bundle of books clutched tightly across her front. Suddenly she saw him. Their eyes met for a moment and her face appeared to freeze. Then she turned abruptly and almost scurried back the way she had come. Within seconds she vanished through a ground floor doorway.

Seeing Carol's reaction sent Graham's hopes plunging even deeper. Again bleak despair swamped his whole being. For pride's sake he had to hold back his tears to grin at Peter as he passed and then he gritted his teeth and had to stifle the sobs that were starting to make his chest heave.

During fifth period, Maths B with Mr Ritter, Graham sat alone, deep in despair and so miserable he felt like bursting into tears. The only time he smiled was at one of Mr Ritter's witticisms when he said to Vincent (the class clown), "Vincent, Maths B is fun, not funny!"

Then, ten minutes into the class and just as Mr Ritter was starting to analyse an exam question on equal angles on a square grid a Year 11 girl appeared at the door and knocked.

Mr Ritter turned. "Yes?"

"Excuse me sir, if Graham Kirk is in this room he is to go to the office immediately."

Mr Ritter turned to Graham and raised an eyebrow. "Off you go, Kirk, office!"

Oh no! Graham thought, dread clutching at his heart. *What has gone wrong now?*

Chapter 35

TERROR

Declin could hear the voices and it was only very slowly, and as though through a thick fog, that he could understand the words. And it was only much later that he could recognise the voices of the speakers. But, to his horror, he found he could not move. He could not turn his head or open his eyes and could not even open his mouth to speak. And he knew he desperately wanted to.

That is Carol I can hear. She is with her mother. I must tell her what happened!

"Come on, Bub, there's nothing you can do," said Carol's mother.

"I could sit with him."

That was Carol! Does she care about me that much?

Declin strained, seemingly with every muscle, but he could not wrench his eyes open and his lips would not form words. He tried again. It felt like he was heaving mightily but obviously nothing moved.

Am I paralysed? Where am I? What has happened to me?

Fear began to build, fear of the unknown and a sort of numb anxiety about the future.

Carol's mother spoke again. "You cannot! You are going to school. Now come on!"

"Mum! But... but I don't want to," Carol replied.

"Well, too bad. You are going to school and that's that!"

Declin heard their voices recede away from him. But the words had cheered him as well as puzzled him. *Carol does like me. She's noticed me! But what was she talking about? Did I have a fight with that cadet Graham?*

He remembered the scene at the Christmas Party, but he could not remember any incident involving Graham or his friend after that. But what he did remember was walking home after helping with the clean-up.

I was just passing the pub when I heard something... rapid footsteps was it? And I was turning to look when someone stepped out of the shadows and hit me, he remembered.

But who had hit him and what with he did not know. But now his head began to throb, and he again tried to move and found he could not.

More voices. Then distinctly he heard the word 'doctor'. People fussed around him, adjusting things, touching him.

Am I in hospital? But where?

With that knowledge came more fear. He began to again wonder if he was so badly injured that he was paralysed. Now he became conscious of tubes across his face and body and of a thing gripping his right forefinger. A machine beeped faintly and the image of a hospital room formed.

In hospital for sure. Oh God! Am I now one of those vegetables? Will I never be able to walk again?

Now the fear surged and built into terror. He began to strain and gasp. Hands touched him and he heard a female's soothing voice telling him to relax. But still Declin could not speak or move.

For quite a few minutes he struggled to open his eyes and to move but then slumped back in terrified defeat.

* * *

Declin realised he must have lapsed back into sleep, or unconsciousness, as now he could hear different people speaking. The voice was familiar but at first he could not recognise it.

Then he distinctly heard the person, a man, say, "Why don't I just turn off this machine and shut him up for good?"

"Good idea, but not now. People will remember us visiting and be suspicious," replied another man.

Then real terror coursed through Declin. *Rossiter! And that is that weasel, Dennis, suggesting he switch off my life support machine. They mean to murder me!*

It was ghastly. The awareness that he was unable to move or even call for help while his enemies plotted his death came as a stunning wash of fear. Once again, Declin strained to make his muscles obey his command.

Dennis spoke again, grumbling, "That stupid Marvin should have hit him harder or finished him off. Then we wouldn't have had to make up that story about those kids doing it."

"Yeah, well, Marvin said someone came out of the pub and saw him, so he scarpered," Rossiter replied.

"So what do we do now?" Dennis queried.

"This caper at the mill is nearly up. We need to cover our tracks. Next move is to get ourselves a hostage and lay another false trail."

"How?"

"We kidnap the boss's daughter and do things to her so that it looks like those boys did it," Rossiter explained.

Another pulse of a completely different type of fear swamped Declin's emotions. *Carol! They are going to snatch her and do things to her!*

But the next part of the conversation moved his whole being to frantic near panic.

Dennis said, "But she'll tell them it was us."

"No she won't. They will find her naked body in the creek down at their little secret swimming hole," Rossiter replied.

"We can have a bit of fun first though?" Dennis queried, his tone of voice indicating none of the revulsion Declin was experiencing.

Ghastly images flashed across the screen of Declin's mind of beautiful Carol, naked and being defiled and then being strangled and cast into the creek. Fear for her safety now seemed to consume his whole being and again he struggled to speak.

"When?" Dennis queried.

"This afternoon, before we go on shift."

Dennis spoke again, close beside Declin's left ear. "Sounds risky. I could maybe just bump this plug here so the power stops for a while."

Declin realised he could see Dennis. Through a misty haze he also saw Rossiter standing beside his bed. Terror battled with determination, and he forced his eyes to focus and found he could move his head. As he did, he heard approaching footsteps and saw Rossiter turn to look.

Rossiter then turned back to him and smiled. "Oh hello, Declin me boy! Awake are ye?"

Declin tried to croak a reply but found he was still constricted and could only croak. The tubes in his mouth did not help. Out of the corner of his eye he saw a female nurse enter the room.

"Who are you? It isn't visiting hours," the nurse snapped.

"We are just work mates at the mill," Rossiter replied. "He's awake at least."

"Awake, is he?" cried the nurse. She put down the tray she was carrying and went hurrying out.

Rossiter leaned forward and patted Declin's upper body. "Well, here's to yer quick recovery boyo!" Then he leaned closer. "Now listen shitface, you were lucky this time. Yer won't be next time. This is the deal; we need that mill brought to a grinding halt for hours. Now this time don't disappoint us, or you and your family will die. And just to give you some extra incentive to co-operate we will take your little girlfriend prisoner. If you want to keep her safe, crash the mill. And don't dob us. Don't go to the cops or she dies! And it will be a horrible death, and before she dies we will entertain ourselves and leave clues to show you raped her. Get it?"

Rossiter then turned and hurried out. Dennis gave a horrible, leering grin and followed. Declin was left gasping and trembling, utterly appalled at what he had just heard.

Oh my God! Carol! How can I save her?

Suddenly the room was full of medical people and they went to work checking and testing. A doctor, Declin presumed, leaned close and looked into his eyes.

"Awake then? How do you feel?"

Declin struggled to speak, desperate to tell them to save Carol. But he just ended up gasping for breath and they had to calm him and give him oxygen. After a few minutes he was able to breathe normally. Then medical checks and tests kept them busy for at least twenty minutes. During the whole of that time Declin's mind raced.

How can I save Carol? How do I keep her safe? He had no doubt that Rossiter had meant what he said. *They must have given me a sedative,* he thought as he realised he was drowsy and slipping off to sleep. *No! No! I must get up. I must save Carol!*

But he could not make his limbs or vocal cords work. Despite struggling he slid into oblivion, even more of a terrifying nightmare than dreaming.

This was real.

* * *

Sometime later he came to and found a nurse sitting looking at him. "Awake again, are you?" she said, smiling sweetly as she did. "That wasn't a very long sleep."

Awareness flooded into Declin and with it came the feeling of dread. *I must save Carol,* he thought. But how? *They said don't call the police or she dies.*

That fear paralysed his will for a while, but his mind kept working. "What time is it?" he asked. Only then did it dawn on him that he was able to speak again.

The nurse glanced at the watch pinned to her blouse. "Just after one."

"And what time did I first wake up?"

"About an hour ago. Now you just relax," she replied.

They can't have kidnapped Carol yet. She will still be at school, Declin reasoned.

He swallowed and then, knowing it might mean his death, he croaked, "Please, call the police. It is terribly important."

The nurse gave him a smile and shook her head. "First the doctor. You've had a couple of nasty hits on the head."

"Police!" Declin croaked. But she went and got the doctor.

The doctor did more tests and the whole time Declin fretted. "I must get up! I have to call the police," he cried.

"You have suffered a very serious head injury. I am amazed you are awake at all. You need complete rest," the doctor replied.

"What happened?" Declin queried.

The doctor stared at him. "You don't remember?"

"I remember a person stepping out of the shadows and hitting me, that's all," Declin replied.

"Yes, at least three times, with a blunt instrument, probably a wrench or something," the doctor replied. "He hit you very hard. There are some hairline fractures in your skull. You are extremely lucky to be alive."

"That was Marvin," Declin replied, remembering what Rossiter had said.

"Marvin? Is he one of those boys who have been arrested for it?" the doctor asked.

"What boys? It wasn't any boys. It was a big thug of a man who works at the mill, he and his mates Rossiter and Dennis. You must get me the police," Declin cried.

"We were told it was two boys," the doctor replied, frowning.

Declin shook his head and instantly regretted that as piercing pain stabbed through his skull. "Aaagh! No! Do you mean Graham and Steve?"

The doctor shook his head. "Don't know their names."

"It wasn't them. You must call the police. Those men are planning to kidnap Carol and use her as a hostage and will kill her," Declin cried.

"What men? Who is Carol?" the doctor asked, now looking concerned while glancing at the hovering nurse.

"The two men who visited me an hour ago: Rossiter and Dennis. The girl is the Mill Engineer's daughter Carol," Declin explained. He began to take deep breaths and had trouble keeping his eyes open as waves of pain and nausea engulfed him. "Call the police, please!"

"Yes, in a minute. Let me attend to you first," the doctor replied.

He moved to check the drip that Declin now saw was connected to a catheter in the back of his right hand. "Don't put me back to sleep! Get the police!" Declin cried in alarm.

Suddenly terrified that he would not be in time to save Carol he moved to sit up, ignoring the stabs of pain that speared through his head.

The doctor was alarmed. "You must relax! You must lie down and rest!"

"Get the police!" Declin shouted.

"We will, now relax," the doctor replied. "Just let me do this."

Declin forced himself to sit up. "No! I want to go!" he shouted, fear for Carol overcoming his normal shyness.

"Well you can't!" the doctor replied, moving to push him down again.

Declin thrust his arm away. "Can't? Who are you to tell me what I can and can't do?" he retorted angrily. Something he had heard came to him and he used it. "You have no legal authority to tell me what to do. I want to see the police! Now take this thing out of my hand."

Declin moved to pull the catheter out, but both the doctor and nurse restrained him.

"Stop! You will harm yourself!" the doctor warned.

Declin knew he was not thinking straight but his entire focus now was on keeping Carol safe. *She won't be at home. She will be at school,* he thought.

"Get me a phone please," he requested.

To appease the medicos he lay back and appeared to relax. The doctor made a few more notes and then moved to near the door and spoke to the nurse in a low voice. She then moved quickly away along the corridor. The doctor came back and smiled.

"Okay, you can relax now. We will do that."

Declin felt a stab of worry. "I want the police to come here so I can talk to them," he replied.

"Yes, alright."

"I mean right now! This is urgent," Declin insisted. Now that he had made the decision, he felt consumed by anxiety.

The doctor looked annoyed. "The nurse has gone to call them. You just relax till they arrive. Now I have to go and complete my rounds of the other patients." With that he left and went into the next room.

Declin lay back but could not relax. His whole being felt agitated, and apprehension built up until he was breathing fast, as though he had run a race. With an effort he calmed himself. His eyes continually flicking to the door. Minutes ticked past but no-one came to tell him the police were coming.

Did the nurse call? Are they on their way? he fretted.

More minutes passed and then began to blur as his anxiety grew again. Not having a watch made it worse.

Oh, what can I do? How can I deal with people like Rossiter? With a whole gang of them? he thought.

Anguish gripped him and he sat there and sobbed. He had never felt so helpless or so frightened in his life. Saving Carol now loomed as the most important thing and dominated all his thoughts.

She should be safe at the moment, he reasoned. *She is at school, and they can't easily get at her there. But she must not go home.*

Then another worrying thought came to him. *Carol must be warned, and her parents.*

But how? He had no phone and no money and the hospital had refused to let him make personal calls.

"Oooh!" he cried, gritting his teeth and clenching his fists.

His head throbbed and he knew he was possibly causing harm, but he did not care. He had now accepted that the gang would probably kill him because he had gone to the police.

But I must keep Carol safe until the gang is arrested. Then the idea floated through the pain. *She is at school. That's only a couple of blocks away. I will go there and warn her and warn the school.*

* * *

Having decided on his course of action, he was gripped by a sense of compelling urgency.

Ignoring the chest pains and the sore muscles and headache, he went to the bedside locker and opened it. To his enormous relief he saw his own clothes. Quickly he pulled them out. With a gasp of determination he wrenched the catheter out of his hand, leaving the tape adhering. A trickle of blood showed but he didn't care. The room had its own shower room, so he hurried in there and, with trembling fingers, began to unbutton the hospital pyjamas.

As he did, Declin glanced in the mirror above the washbasin and was so shocked by what he saw that he stopped and gaped. His whole face looked bruised, and he had an absorbent bandage covering the right temple and another on his forehead. There were dark rings around both eyes, and they looked bloodshot. Then he realised that there was a wound on the back of his head. By bending forward he was able to just see that some of his hair had been cut or shaved off and a line of sutures showed amid the brown blotches of antiseptic.

Bloody hell, I look a wreck! he thought.

But then anxiety drove home back into action and in a couple of minutes he was dressed in his own clothes. For a few moments he studied himself in the mirror, facing his fear and summoning up his courage. For another few seconds he listened at the bathroom door, not wanting to encounter a nurse and have another argument.

Then he opened the door and hurried across to the bed and pulled on socks and joggers. By then he was feeling so scared he was hyperventilating. As he laced up his shoes, he kept glancing to the door in case someone returned.

Have they called the police? he fretted.

Taking a deep breath he steadied himself on the bedframe for a moment then walked to the door. There was no sound of anyone outside, so he opened it and looked out. Still nobody.

Where did they go? Declin wondered glancing both ways along the corridor.

The corridor was empty, so he started walking along it. He wasn't sure which way to go but felt so driven that he just went.

As he walked past the next room, her heard voices inside and thought they sounded like the doctor and nurse. Three rooms along was a nurse's station but there was no one there either. Declin stopped, his head spinning. Again he leaned on the counter to keep his balance and to allow his senses. For a moment he eyed the telephone and considered using it but then decided not to.

I don't know the school's number and it will just waste time finding out. I can be there by the time I do all that.

So he staggered along the corridor. At any moment he expected to be challenged by one of the staff, but he met no-one and was soon out in the main part of the hospital. Luck helped. He found an evacuation diagram and was able to work out which way to go. Now he started passing people, some of whom gave him curious or frowning looks. But, to his intense relief, none of them asked him what he was doing.

Three minutes later he was out on the footpath at the front entrance to the hospital. Now he knew which way to go, and he turned right and set off along the street. His memory of making his way to watch the Cadet Passing-Out Parade made it easy, but his physical condition did not. Several times he felt so giddy he had to stop, and his vision kept blurring. He also found he was stumbling and gasping for breath. Several times he had to stop and cling to a fence, earning more curious looks from passers-by and people in passing cars.

It took him fifteen minutes to walk to the high school. By the time he got there he was feeling quite ill and was sweating profusely. It was very hot walking in the tropical sun, especially without a hat. Blinking perspiration from his eyes he stopped at the main entrance.

He found it a relief to walk in out of the bright sunlight but then had to stop and look around in the shadows as he was unsure of where to go. Noting a flight of stairs and a sign indicating the school office, he moved over and steadied himself on the balustrade. Another wave of giddiness caused another gasping pause. Then he set himself to climb the stairs.

Arriving panting at the landing, Declin again stopped. A wave of blackness swept over him and he clung to the railing. When his blurred vision cleared, he saw that the door to the left was the principal's. A door and counter on the right was the Admin. Directly in front was a long bench seat and two grubby little boys in school uniform sat on it. Both gave him curious stares and Declin gave a wry smile.

A lady was giving him a raised-eyebrow, concerned look from behind the counter so he walked across, stumbling slightly as he did.

"Yes sir?" she said.

"I need to see the principal please. It is very urgent," Declin croaked, grabbing hold of the counter as he began to sway.

The lady's concern grew to a frown, and she picked up a telephone and rang a number, all the while watching him. Declin felt bad about that. *I must look a worrying sight,* he thought. *She will be thinking she's got a madman here.*

A grey-haired man dressed in long grey trousers and white shirt and tie appeared through the doorway a moment later, immediately followed by an even larger man.

"I am the principal, Mr Croswell. This is the Deputy Principal Mr Fitzgerald. How can we help you, sir?"

Declin introduced himself and saw both their eyebrows go up as they clearly recognised his name. "I am the man who was bashed at the Caster Mill on Sunday evening. Two of your students have been accused of doing it. I can tell you they did not. But that is not why I am here. I am worried about another of your students, Carol Battersby. I believe she is one of your students?"

The principal shook his head. "I am sorry, sir, but we cannot give out information on any of our students. But if you give us a message, we can try to make sure it reaches the person or persons involved."

That came as a shock to Declin and for a moment baffled him. He again reeled and reached back to grip the counter. Declin saw the deputy principal move away. He spoke to the two boys and they hurried off, casting more curious glances at Declin. He also saw the principal give the lady behind the counter a look and a nod and he heard her move away.

Declin took a deep breath and gasped, "Yes please. It is very urgent. She may be in great danger. You must get the police at once."

At the mention of the police both men looked both concerned and relieved at the same moment. The principal gave another look to the lady in the office. Declin heard her start talking on a telephone.

The deputy returned and said, "Would you please come into our office so you can sit down out of sight of any students. You look a bit of a sight."

"Yes. Sorry. I came straight from the hospital," Declin answered. He allowed himself to be guided across into the other room where he was able to lower himself into an armchair.

"Now, what is this about a girl being in danger?" the principal queried.

Declin quickly told his story. By now he was feeling that he had made a mistake by not waiting for the police at the hospital and it took an effort to speak clearly. As he described what he knew, he saw looks of concern grow almost to alarm on their faces.

The principal listened intently, then said, "Just wait here please. I will just check something."

He stood up and left the room and the deputy asked Declin how he was feeling and got him a glass of water. A few minutes later the principal returned, looking even more concerned.

"Mrs Battersby has picked Carol up at lunch time and taken her home. She was feeling sick," he said.

It took a moment for this information to sink in. When it did, Declin was aghast. "She must not go home! It's not safe! Those men will be there. Oh, you must warn her. Please ring her at once!" Declin cried.

The principal picked up the phone on his desk and called the office and asked for the Battersby's home number and rang it. There was no answer. Her mobile was tried but the response was an out-of-service reply. A message was left.

Declin became more and more agitated. "Call her dad at the mill," he suggested.

He gave them the number. The mill office was rung and he heard the office girl Marlene answer. She said that Mr Battersby was out inspecting work on a rail bridge. She promised to tell him as soon as he came back.

Declin was even more concerned. "Get the people in the office to get Mrs Boothby and Carol to come to the office for safety," he called.

That was done but still Declin wasn't satisfied. Glancing at the clock he saw it was almost 2pm. "Rossiter and his mate have had time to drive back there by now. Please tell them to hurry and then to call the police," he croaked.

"Here, more water," the deputy said. "Please relax, Mr Riley. The police are on their way, and we have passed the message on to the mill office."

Declin took the glass and quaffed most of it, then sat back. "Could I also take the opportunity to say sorry to Graham Kirk and Stephen Bell? I did not accuse them and they did not bash me. It was Rossiter's mate, Marvin. I would like to apologise to them."

The principal and deputy exchanged looks and the deputy got up and left the room. More minutes ticked by. The clock on the wall showed 2:05pm.

Oh come on! Where are the police? Oh hurry up! Declin fretted.

The deputy returned. Looming over Declin, he said, "I have called Mrs Kirk and she has agreed you can meet so I have sent for Graham. Stephen Bell is not at school."

Declin nodded and looked towards the door. Inside he was boiling with impatience mixed with dread.

I must save Carol! he thought.

Chapter 36

HURRY!

As Graham made his way to the office he was puzzled. In his mind he turned over what school incident he might have been involved in that would merit the attention of the office, but he could not think of any.

What did worry him was the notion that it might have to do with the police and Declin. So when he saw Declin sitting in the principal's office he was not surprised. There was a flash of anxiety that Declin was going to accuse him or even hit him. But a glance at the man's battered and bruised face, red eyes sunk in dark rings, and bandages on forehead and temple, and he dismissed the notion. Now intensely alert and curious, he was told by Mr Croswell to have a seat.

Mr Croswell gestured towards Declin, and said, "I believe you know Mr Riley? He has something to tell you."

Graham nodded and warily met Declin's eye. "Yes sir."

Declin sat forward then winced and put his hand to his head. "Aargh! Sorry. Yes, I want to say I apologise for all the trouble you and your friend are in."

Graham nodded, unsure what was really going on. Declin licked his lips and looked quite upset. "I hear you and Stephen have been arrested for bashing me?"

"Yes, we have," Graham replied, emotion making it difficult to keep his face composed.

Declin nodded and then went on. "I was bashed by a man named Marvin. I don't know his last name. He works at the mill and he and a couple of men named Rossiter and Dennis are trying to stop the mill."

That surprised Graham. "Stop the mill? Why?"

"I don't know, but I believe they have murdered a couple of workers and are intimidating others to cause sabotage to the mill," Declin replied.

Mr Croswell interrupted. "Do the police know this?"

Declin shook his head and looked miserable. "No sir. I... I... I've been too scared to tell them. They have threatened me a couple of times."

"So why are you telling us now?" Mr Fitzgerald queried.

"Because I overheard them planning to take Carol... Carol Battersby, the Chief Engineer's daughter, as a hostage and… and..." He broke down and began to sob.

Graham was shocked. *Going to kidnap Carol! We must stop that.*

Mr Croswell frowned. "When did you hear this?"

Declin shuddered and did not answer for a few seconds. "While I was in hospital. I had been unconscious and when I woke up I could not move. I could not even speak, and I was scared. Rossiter and Dennis were there, and Dennis suggested that he switch off my life support machine. I... I..."

He began to sob again. Then he took several deep breaths and wiped his eyes. "Sorry," he croaked. "I thought I was going to die. Anyway, while I was lying there, I heard them talk about kidnapping Carol. I woke up and they threatened me and said that... that... that they would (sob) would do horrible things to her and then kill her if I didn't do what they say."

Graham was aghast. The look on Declin's face made him believe what he was hearing. *The poor bugger looks absolutely haunted,* he thought.

Mr Croswell reached forward and picked up the phone on his desk. "This is extremely serious. I will see if I can hurry the police up."

While the principal made his call, Graham turned to Mr Fitzgerald. "Sir, you need to get Carol here right now to make sure she is safe."

Mr Fitzgerald looked grim. "We have tried. She has been taken home by her mother."

"Oh that's not safe!" Graham cried. "Phone her and get her to go to the mill office and get the police to go there."

Declin shook his head. "We've tried all that. She is not answering the phone and her father is out on some job repairing a railway bridge."

"They might already have her," Graham said, voicing the fear that sprang into his mind.

Declin looked shocked. His face went all pasty white and he looked ready to burst into tears. "Oh what can we do?" he cried.

Mr Croswell put down the phone and turned to them. "The police are on their way."

Declin turned pleading eyes to him. "Sir, please try to contact Mrs Battersby or Carol's dad again. We must be sure that Carol is safe."

Mr Croswell did so and had only just finished when the office lady appeared at the door with two men in plain clothes who could only be policemen. They were introduced as Inspector Mallory and Detective Sergeant Winter.

Declin at once began to explain and when the detectives wanted to ask their own questions and record it all he began to get agitated. "This is an emergency! Carol might be in great danger. We need to hurry!"

"We will pass this information on to the Innisfail station. It is in their area, and they will send people to deal with it," the DI replied.

"Can you take me there now?" Declin asked.

To Graham, he looked very disturbed and wild-eyed.

The DI shook his head. "Sorry sir, no. We can take you back to the hospital which is where we expected to find you."

"Sorry," Declin replied. "But I just had to make sure Carol was safe, and she isn't! Those men might still get her. We must go there."

The DI frowned. "We would prefer you to go to the hospital. If not, then come to the station with us so we can get this all down as signed statements."

"Am I under arrest?" Declin queried.

"No, of course not! You are the victim here," the DI replied. He then turned to Graham. "And, after what Mr Riley has told us, you no longer have to worry about any charges being pressed, young Kirk."

"Thank you, sir," Graham mumbled. He knew he should feel relieved but anxiety about Carol was now gnawing at him.

Mr Croswell turned to him. "Thank you, Graham. You can go back to class now. I will phone your mother in a few minutes to let her know you are no longer in trouble."

"Yes, sir. Thank you, sir. Er… can I speak to Mr Riley privately for a minute please?"

"Yes. I think we are all done here now," Mr Croswell replied. He stood up and ushered them all to the door.

Outside in the lobby, Graham stood to one side while the policemen again tried to persuade Declin to accept a lift back to the hospital. He also declined to go to the station.

"I will make a full statement when I am sure Carol is safe," he insisted. "Now please phone the Innisfail police and get them to Caster as quickly as possible."

The DI did not look happy but nodded. "I will. I will phone while we are driving. We have to get to another situation. We will be in touch. Come on Winter, we need to get out to Redlynch ASAP." With that he and the DS turned and hurried down the front stairs.

Mr Croswell made his way into the main office and Mr Fitzgerald glanced at Graham, then headed off along the veranda.

Declin turned to Graham. "Yes, what did you want?"

"First I want to say thanks for having the guts to say what you did," Graham said, thrusting out his hand.

Declin took it after a moment's hesitation. "That's alright. It wasn't right for innocent people to be blamed by those thugs."

"And I want to tell you that I think anything between Carol and me is over," Graham added. That hurt a bit, but he felt better for saying it.

"Thanks," Declin replied. "But I don't like my chances. I think her dad will just sack me and warn me off because of my age. But that doesn't matter. I must make sure Carol is safe."

"Didn't the policemen say they would get the Innisfail police to deal with this?" Graham queried.

"Yes, but he hadn't made the phone call before he left, and it could take hours. Carol went home at lunch time, and I couldn't get her mother or father and only left a message at the mill office. I have no idea if they received it."

"So how can you make sure Carol is safe?" Graham queried. He felt sorry for Declin but also very anxious about Carol.

"I am going to go back to Caster right now," Declin cried.

"Not back to the hospital?" Graham asked, worried about how ill and unsteady on his feet Declin looked.

Declin shook his head emphatically. "No! I need to hurry." With that he turned and started down the stairs. As he did, he stumbled, and Graham only just grabbed him in time to stop a potentially serious fall.

"You need to go to the hospital," he said, steadying him and then holding him up.

"No! I must go! Have you got any money?" Declin asked. He gripped the balustrade and began to carefully make his way down the stairs.

"How much? What for?" Graham queried. He had some money but was intrigued.

"For a taxi. I don't have a car," Declin replied.

They were at the bottom of the stairs by then and Graham held him up as he hobbled across to the open doorway. Declin stopped to lean on the doorframe. He was gasping and clearly unwell.

"I have a bit," Graham explained, "But not enough for that."

"What about a bus?" Declin asked. He stepped out onto the footpath and looked along the street.

His determination and sincerity touched Graham. "I can manage that," he agreed. He began to feel in his pocket.

Suddenly Declin gasped and pointed. "A bus! Here comes a bus! Where is the nearest bus stop?"

Graham glanced along the street and glimpsed an approaching bus. "There, right at the front of the school," he replied. He signalled the bus driver and began urging Declin towards the nearby bus stop sign.

To his relief, the bus squealed to a stop and the door hissed open. Graham held Declin tightly by the arm and half lifted him up onto the step at the door of the bus. Declin grabbed the handrails and heaved himself up. The bus driver frowned when he took in Declin's condition and Graham's school uniform.

"Where to?"

"The bus depot please," Graham replied, fumbling out some coins.

"How many?"

Graham had not really thought of going to Caster but now concern for Carol came to dominate. "Two please."

The driver looked doubtful and for a moment Graham feared he might challenge him, but then he shrugged and took the money. By then Declin had swung himself up into the first empty seat. Graham moved to sit next to him in the aisle seat.

Declin frowned and looked at him. "Thanks, but won't you get into trouble for leaving school?"

"Possibly," Graham replied, shrugging. He glanced at his watch and saw that it was 2:45pm. "Only another fifteen minutes. I doubt if they will realise I have gone before school ends."

Declin nodded and sat back, simultaneously sighing with relief and groaning. Graham realised that Declin was shuddering and breathing very fast and he looked at him anxiously but as Declin had closed his eyes he did not speak.

I hope he doesn't die on me! he thought anxiously.

* * *

As the bus went on along the street, Graham began to have doubts. First was worry about how long it might all take. He calculated quickly that it might take an hour or so to get there and another hour or so to get back, if there was a bus. How long he might be there he couldn't decide.

That might mean six or seven o'clock tonight. I don't want Mum all worried. I will call from Caster, he rationalised.

From then on, he began to fret about how slow the bus was going, his agitation rising at every stop. To him it seemed to take hours to reach the bus depot but was, in fact, only about twenty minutes. As soon as the bus pulled to a stop, he stood up and helped Declin to get out. Declin looked awful and the expression 'Death warmed up' flitted across Graham's mind.

But time was pressing, so he urged him to stagger over to the booking office to buy two tickets to Caster. As luck would have it, he had just enough money and there was a coach leaving in five minutes. They just had time for a quick toilet break before hurrying out to the coach. The driver was standing next to it looking impatient and obviously ready to close the storage bins. He also frowned when he saw Declin but did not stop them getting on once they had shown him their tickets.

This time Declin slumped into a seat and was asleep even before the coach pulled out. Graham sat next to him, anxiously monitoring his breathing and hoping he wasn't going to die or need emergency medical treatment. When Declin settled to regular breathing and a relaxed facial expression, he felt easier.

But it was tension all the way. The whole hour-long journey was nail-biting for Graham. There was fear of not getting there in time. But there was also anxiety about how Carol and her family might receive him. That kept him in a state of tension the whole way.

After what seemed for ever, Graham saw the chimneys of the mill in the distance over the cane fields. Normally he enjoyed watching the various aspects of the sugar industry, but now he barely noticed the cane harvesters at work or even the sugar trains. It was just a relief to know that they had arrived.

But of course they hadn't! They were only at that part of the town astride the Bruce Highway. Graham shook Declin awake as the coach rounded the last bend. For a few moments, Graham wondered if Declin was too ill to do anything but he blinked, shook himself and took in where they were. As the coach pulled to a stop at the petrol station, he urged Graham to get up.

"We need to hurry," he said. "What time is it?"

Graham was in the act of standing up and had to steady himself on the back of the seat to look at his watch. He was dismayed to note that it was 4:20pm. All he could do was nod and quickly make his way along the aisle and down off the coach. Declin followed more slowly, his teeth gritted and using both hands to keep his footing. As he stepped down and let go, Declin actually staggered. Graham reached out and grabbed him.

"You alright to walk?" he asked, at the same time thinking what he would do if Declin collapsed.

He kept a tight grip on Declin's left arm and moved him away from the coach as the door hissed shut and the coach roared into movement.

Declin croaked a reply and when Graham glanced at him his dismay increased. Declin had a fierce, haggard and desperate look on his face and there was a wild, anxious look in his eyes. He was not even glancing at Graham as he spoke but was focused on the distant mill.

Crossing the highway was a bit of a challenge and Graham feared Declin would stumble and get run over by one of the many cars and heavy trucks flashing by. But they made it safely and then across the narrow-gauge railway to the footpath in front of the shops.

Looking along that main street caused Graham more dismay. It looked a dishearteningly long way. The trees at the park and the mill appeared very small and far away. But Declin just kept staring that way and set off walking, almost striding along. Graham had to almost run to keep up, Declin walking on his right.

"Slow down, Declin! You'll blow a valve or something," Graham cried.

Declin gave his head a determined shake and a look of almost savage intensity formed on his face. "No! We must hurry! I have to be sure Carol is safe," he cried.

So they hurried on along the street, both sweating in the afternoon heat. For part of the way the shop awnings gave them some shade, but the only real relief came when the direct sunlight was blocked by clouds building up over the mountains ahead of them.

As they passed the hotel Graham looked in, partly to check if the men were in the bar but also hoping for a glimpse of the Irish barmaid. He also had the thought to go and use a telephone to tell his mother where he was and to check if the police had warned Carol and her mother. But when he suggested this to Declin he just shook his head, grunted and strode on.

To Graham's relief, there was no sign of the men in the hotel bar. But Declin was not looking good. By the time they were past the shop, his skin had gone a very pale colour and his eyes looked sunken in dark rings. Once again, Graham feared he might just collapse.

Then it was out into sunlight again, the shafts of the sunbeams lancing straight into their faces. Graham just squinted but he noticed that Declin was really having trouble. Declin put his hand up to shield his eyes and kept looking sideways to avoid the obvious pain from the light.

Thus he was looking left across Graham's front when he suddenly gasped, grabbed at Graham and pointed left. They were almost at the end of the houses by then and Graham looked and glimpsed a dirty brown, light truck with dog cages on the back. The vehicle was travelling in the same direction along the gravel road behind the houses and vanished from view behind the last house.

Declin's grip tightened and a look of anguish crossed his face. "Rossiter! He and Dennis and Marvin. Oh quick, we must hurry!"

He broke into a shambling run and Graham did the same. They ran along the grass footpath and reached the open space of the main railway just in time to see Rossiter's vehicle roar across the level crossing without stopping. It went racing off out of sight behind the Mill Manager's house.

Declin was aghast. "Oh they are going to Carol's! Oh quick! We must save her!"

He started running even faster.

Chapter 37

RUN!

Graham ran as fast as he could, all the while glancing towards Carol's house and then across at Declin who was pushing himself to keep up, despite obvious pain. They crossed the main railway without even glancing sideways. Having the sun in their eyes did not help, but thankfully they ran into the shade of the big trees in the park.

The mill office and sugar mill were now only a couple of hundred metres ahead and Graham flicked a glance at the old steam locomotive. He was hoping to see people, particularly police, but there were none in sight. Nor were any police vehicles in evidence. Gasping and sweating, the pair ran across to the lawn in front of the Mill Manager's house.

Graham wasn't at all sure that the vehicle had stopped at Carol's house, but he was determined to find out. What he would then do he had not thought about and his apprehension about Carol kept him running. At each running step his gaze flicked from the front of her house to each bit of the side yard as it came into view.

With each pace he got to see more of the yard of Carol's house, and he noted that the front vehicle gate was open. Then he saw what he had been dreading and his chest tightened with fear. The men's vehicle was parked in the backyard. It had obviously come in through the back gate.

"There it is!" he croaked, pointing.

But there were no people in sight. As they hurried along the foot path, Graham again wondered what to do. *Go and check or run to the mill office?* he thought. But going to the mill wasn't a strong idea and his emotions over-rode caution.

Pointing in the vehicle gate Graham cried, "You go round the back. I'll go in the front."

Graham pounded in through the small gate and along the concrete path to the front steps. The steps he barely noticed as he raced up, touching the railings a couple of times. Out of the corner of his eye, he noted Declin vanish along the side of the house.

The front door was open, and Graham just charged in. He was now so wound up with anxiety that the social niceties did not occur to him. But the sudden transition from bright sunlight to semi-darkness gave him pause. For a second, he stopped to look left and right.

And then a scream caused him to jerk his head to stare along the hallway, a girl's scream, Carol's! At almost the same moment, a large man appeared in silhouette against the back door. And the man was carrying a violently struggling Carol, still dressed in her school uniform. Even as Graham's brain registered what he was seeing, he saw the man, Marvin he recognised, strike Carol hard on the side of the head. Her screams ended abruptly.

At that moment there were loud and angry voices from downstairs to the left. Declin began shouting, "Carol! Carol! Are you alright?"

Marvin went through the back door and out into the sunlight, Carol's head lolling over his shoulder as he did. The man went down the backstairs as Graham began running. With no thought but saving Carol, he raced along the darkened hallway and through the kitchen, arriving at the back door as Marvin reached the bottom of the steps.

There, only a few metres below, was Carol in the gip of the brute! Graham did not hesitate. He launched himself down the stairs in one gigantic leap. It was something he had done at home many times when trying to catch or outrun his brother or sister, but now he was in deadly earnest and did not even pause to consider consequences. Except he understood instinctively that his attack had to be serious. So he went feet first, touching the railings just once to maintain balance.

Thud!

Graham's leather school shoes thudded hard into Marvin's back, right between the shoulder blades. The man had just started to turn to glance over his shoulder but was way too late, as 75kgs of angry youth with the flying momentum flattened him. He went down with a gasp as the air was driven out of him by the force of the blow. Graham, Carol, and Marvin went tumbling in a heap on the back lawn.

Now Graham was scared. On the way down he had glimpsed Rossiter and Dennis attacking Declin, punching at him and knocking him down.

I have to get Carol to safety, Graham thought.

Fear of Marvin grappling with him had Graham rolling clear across the grass and then scrambling to his feet instantly. Carol had also rolled clear, and Marvin lay gasping and twitching. As Graham scrambled to his feet, he saw Rossiter kick at Declin, then turn in astonishment to gape at him. Again Graham acted instantly and without conscious thought, or maybe it was conscious, but he only articulated it as he acted?

Realising Rossiter was the more dangerous, Graham rushed at him and pushed. Rossiter tried to fend him off and punch him but then he stepped back in attempt to keep his balance. Instead, he tripped backwards over Declin. As Rossiter fell, Graham glanced at Dennis, who had also been kicking at Declin. A look of astonished alarm formed on Dennis's face and he hastily scuttled back, running into the side of the parked vehicle as he did.

Graham knew he had only seconds to get away and reasoned that he must leave Declin to his fate if he was to save Carol. So he turned and ran to her, grabbing her by her left arm and hauling her to her feet. She stared at him through half unfocussed eyes, puzzlement in her expression. By the way her eyes were rolling, Graham deduced she was half stunned.

"Get up Carol! Run!" he cried.

By then Rossiter had rolled sideways and was struggling to his feet, mouthing obscenities as he did. "Grab the little bastard, Marvin!" he shouted.

But Marvin was still winded and was making ghastly sucking and croaking noises as he writhed on the lawn. Graham hauled Carol away out of his reach and then steadied her.

"Come on, Carol, run!" he again cried.

Rossiter went to lunge at them, but Declin suddenly grabbed his ankles and tripped him again. "Run Carol! Run! Graham, get her away!" Declin cried.

Rossiter began to struggle and then, with one foot free, to kick at Declin's face and upper body. But Declin clung grimly on and Graham was able to get Carol walking and then urged her into a tottering run.

His objective was the mill office, but to get clear of the men he had to run away from it and that took them out the back gate and onto the gravel road. As he and Carol turned right on the gravel road, Graham kept glancing back to check for pursuit and ahead to his right to see how far it was to the mill and mill office.

It was Declin's courage that had given them time. Graham saw that and was grateful. He saw Declin cling desperately to Rossiter's leg while both Rossiter and Dennis kicked at him.

Rossiter then grabbed at Dennis and shouted, "Get after them, you bloody drongo! Don't let them get to the mill. Go!"

Dennis hesitated, gave Declin another kick which caused his head to flick back and his eyes to roll up, then started running after them. Rossiter added another savage kick and Declin slumped and let go. Then Rossiter also started running, but the other way, out of sight towards the front of the house. By then Marvin was starting to sit up and was holding his chest and gasping.

Oh bloody hell! We are in trouble! Graham thought.

He suspected that Rossiter was racing to cut them off, and he was not wrong. As he and Carol reached the corner of the back fence and he could see across the expanse of lawn to the mill office, Rossiter appeared at the front fence, already between them and the mill.

For a few running paces Graham dithered, trying to decide whether to go back or go on. The notion of running back to the other houses or even to the town flickered across his mind, but a backwards glance showed Dennis 50 paces behind and a very angry Marvin getting to his feet and lumbering after them. The only way that seemed to be open to them was on along the gravel road and then somehow across to the mill further along.

But can we outrun Rossiter and Dennis? Graham wondered.

He was sure he could outrun Marvin. But could Carol? He glanced at her and she seemed to be running alright, driven by fear.

She met his gaze and gasped, "Who are these men? What do they want?"

"They want to kidnap you and take you as a hostage. They are the men who bashed Declin," Graham gasped back.

"Declin?" she queried.

"Not now. Save your breath. Run. We have to try to get to the mill somehow. Don't let them catch you," Graham answered.

It was on the tip of his tongue to warn her that the men planned both rape and murder, but he could not bring himself to say it to here.

"Hostage? What for?" Carol asked, her head turning to look at Rossiter and then behind her.

"Save your breath. Declin can tell you," Graham retorted.

If he lives! He thought, remembering the brutal kicking he had just witnessed. *And if we can get away from these blokes!*

He looked hopefully towards the mill offices and mill, but there was nobody in sight. He began to debate whether the loss of wind from shouting for help might lose them the race.

That was the real issue. Rossiter was now about 50 paces on their right, squarely between them and the mill. Dennis and Marvin were both following them along the gravel road, Marvin obviously labouring and much slower.

Rossiter suddenly stopped and pointed back. "Dennis, go back and get our vehicle, quick! Marvin, go and get your truck from the car park and come back and get Riley. Put him with O'Malley and then join us."

"With O'Malley?" Marvin queried in a gasping, wheezing voice.

"Yes, you lumbering idiot! To stop him talking as well. Now run!" Rossiter screamed angrily. He then resumed running, having fallen back 25 metres.

But he was still closer to the mill than Graham and Carol. By then they were approaching the bagasse heaps and had to run across the spur line of the 3'6" railway.

"Don't twist your ankle," Graham cautioned as they did.

As they approached the loading hoppers, Graham began to feel the first niggling doubts as he was fast running out of puff and he could see that Carol was as well. The beginnings of a stitch started to niggle in his left side. Still no workers visible! He began to put his hopes on the rail workshops which he could see ahead.

They were now at the point where the tram line curved around from the mill back past the rail workshops. At that moment there were only a few empty cane bins standing on that section of track, and Graham could clearly see the tippler at work.

There must be people there, and at the control room. It is just up there, he thought.

But Rossiter had caught up and was still between them and the mill. He began leaping across the curving rails and then running along beside the tracks that the empty bins were marshalled on. To Graham's dismay, he noted at least four lines of empty cane bins standing on railway tracks waiting to be taken away.

Rossiter is going to keep us on the wrong side of all these trains, Graham deduced.

And there was no-one in the workshops. He and Carol did not dare slow and go in as Rossiter was angling closer and actually ran past the other side of the workshop buildings and then the other side of the nearest line of cane bins. Despair began to grip Graham as he was now gasping and so was Carol. The distress was very clear on her face, and she was gripping her right side as a stitch hit her. It was obvious to him that they could not run much further. He began to consider turning to fight while Carol made a run for the Control Room.

They were now past the rail workshops and approaching the end of a train parked on the outside track. It was obviously ready to go as it had one of the yellow brake wagons attached at the back end. But it would be between them and the mill!

Do I turn and fight now? Graham wondered.

He glanced at Rossiter and then looked around to see if there was something he could use as a weapon. And then suddenly Rossiter went down, tripping on something amid the scatter of weeds.

At the same moment, the blare of a diesel locomotive's air horn jerked Graham to look ahead. *A train! There will be people in the cab,* he thought.

With that in mind he pushed himself to keep going. But Carol was slowing so he reached out and grabbed her hand and began to pull her along. She gave him a terrified and anguished look and he knew they could not keep it up much longer.

Then his hopes went down even more. The train jerked into motion and began moving away from them, and Rossiter was up and running after them!

Seeing that yellow brake wagon start rolling away was almost the last straw, but then Graham decided that it was going so slowly that they had a chance to catching up. He swerved out across the gravel road near where their secret track went down through the long grass, looking to see if he could see the men in the locomotive's cab. But there was sign of a head poking out of the window and the loco was at least a hundred metres away or more.

They caught up with the yellow brake wagon and passed it and Graham screwed up his determination against the pain that was now stabbing through his middle. His heart felt ready to burst and he was sucking in great gulping gasps. Then Carol stumbled and it was only with difficulty he managed to catch her and keep her on her feet.

Oh God! We aren't going to make it! Oh, what can I do?

But he managed to force himself to keep running. A fearful glance over his shoulder showed Rossiter was also gasping and sweating but was again less than 50 paces behind and now out on the gravel road.

Then the train increased speed so that the little wheels were all squeaking and the metal bits clanking and rattling. And it was going faster than they were! The yellow brake wagon rolled up alongside and Graham began to despair, until an idea came to him. The brake van was just a flat wagon with various boxes and uprights on it.

We can get onto that, he thought.

Pointing to the brake wagon, he yelled at Carol, "Get on!"

She looked at him with a puzzled look. That exasperated him. "Get on! We can't keep running," he said.

He angled across the road and saw her nod. His fear now was that she would misjudge or stumble and fall and he knew that would be the end as Rossiter was even closer, his rasping breaths clearly audible. But with a nimbleness she later explained came from gymnastics and dancing, she skipped gracefully aboard and grabbed at the machinery.

Graham followed, and he nearly did trip. He certainly banged his right ankle on something and then whacked his face on an upright. But he managed to grab hold and hauled his feet up. As soon as he did, he wriggled around so as to face Rossiter, ready to fight him off.

But it wasn't necessary. The train was still picking up speed and it became obvious that Rossiter could not catch it up. He tried, pushing himself in a sprint that brought a grimace of pain to his face, but he couldn't. Swearing and cursing he slowed to a walk, shaking his fists and sucking in great gulps of air.

"Safe!" Graham croaked, his vision going blurry and his eyes stinging as sweat trickled down into them.

And then he wished he hadn't said that because a vehicle was roaring along the gravel road after them, Dennis driving the crook's vehicle!

With a sinking heart Graham clung to an upright with a rotating orange light on it and stared back. To his dismay, he saw the vehicle shudder to a stop beside Rossiter. Rossiter immediately scrambled in and even before he had closed his door the vehicle leapt forward.

Oh bloody hell! Graham thought.

Despair mingled with anger. To be so close to escaping and then to fail! He glanced towards the mill, which was now diagonally behind them. It was getting further away with every second. Worse still, the rail marshalling yard was between them and there were now multiple lines of parked cane bins in the way.

Gasping with desperation and fear, Graham twisted to look ahead, and got another shock! The train was curving to the left and the locomotive was even then halfway across the bridge.

There was a man visible in the cab and Graham scrambled to his feet and clung to the stanchion with the flashing light and waved frantically. Carol clung on and alternately looked ahead and back, her face a mask of anxiety.

But it wasn't all bad news. Graham glanced back and saw that the crook's vehicle had caught them up, but it was obvious the men could not immediately get at them.

We still have a chance! Graham thought.

In his desperation, crazy ideas began to flit across his mind: jump off and run through the rows of parked bins to the mill; jump off as the train crossed the bridge and try to hide in all the weeds and long grass along the creek bank.

By then the brake wagon was rumbling across the bridge and Graham looked down and immediately abandoned the idea. Not only was it a long way down, and he doubted his own courage to make such a jump, let alone Carol's, but he saw that the crooks could just stop and immediately follow.

And we can never push through that long grass faster than someone chasing us. It was also obvious that they would leave such clear tracks that hiding was not really an option.

As the train rattled and rumbled across the bridge, the crook's vehicle just followed, Rossiter and Dennis glaring malevolently at them as it did. Graham met Rossiter's gaze and felt his stomach turn over with dread.

Oh, how can we get out of this? he fretted.

And then the train was off the bridge and clanking its way slowly up the long slope beyond. As the rail line diverged from the dirt road, the crook's vehicle raced up alongside on the left and Graham braced himself for the fight of his life. He sensed that it would be to the death and his body quivered as adrenalin coursed through it.

Oh, how can we escape?

Chapter 38

DESPERATION

The crook's vehicle was roaring and bouncing along the rough dirt track only a few metres to Graham's left. Dennis was grinning at him and Rossiter glaring hate. Dennis shouted loudly, swearing, and making crude gestures but Rossiter was shaking his fist while clinging on with one hand. Graham tensed ready to repel boarders, sickeningly conscious that he had only his bare hands and shoes as weapons. A quick glance around the yellow brake wagon revealed nothing loose that he could use as a club or poker.

Dennis and Rossiter began shouting for him and Carol to jump off, but Graham shook his head. Fear kept him clinging on tightly and there was no way he would do what they said. Another glance around showed him that they were now in the middle of a wide area of newly harvested or freshly planted cane, neither of which offered any cover for hiding.

Then he noted Rossiter frowning and it came to Graham that the man was baffled. *He is on the left side of the vehicle and can't attempt a jump from there,* he reasoned. And then he deduced that Rossiter was not game to try to climb out onto the back of the moving vehicle. *Particularly while it is bucking like it is on the rough ground.*

Rossiter looked around then swore before pointing ahead. Dennis nodded and hunched to grip the steering wheel. The vehicle suddenly leapt ahead, accelerating away at nearly twice the speed.

"What the hell are they doing?" Graham asked himself as the vehicle quickly drew ahead along beside the now slowly moving train.

Then the answer came to him, along with a stomach-sickening swirl of bile. *They are going to stop the train! They are going to catch up with the engine to tell the driver to stop.*

Graham again stared wildly around, seeking a way of escape. But he saw that the train was now half a kilometre from the creek and in the middle of bare, open fields on the long rise. To the left, the jungle-covered slopes of the Graham Range towered up but the nearest trees were even further away. Graham began to sweat as desperation gripped him.

Then the brake wagon clanked over a set of points and the sound made Graham glance down. He saw that they now had a siding on their right and even as that registered in his brain, they began passing a line of cane bins parked on it. The bins were full of freshly cut cane and he knew they had been parked there to wait for a locomotive to haul them to the mill.

By then the train was on the crest of the rise and going very slowly, but Graham knew it would speed up as it went down the other side. A glance showed the dust of the crook's vehicle well up near the engine and he almost vomited from fear as he struggled to come up with a plan. He glanced down at Carol and saw she was looking haggard and distraught, and he experienced a momentary wash of shame at having failed her.

Their eyes met and she wailed, "What will we do?"

In that instant a desperate plan came to him. He had been considering jumping off and running for the cover of the creek but now another idea came to him.

"Get off!" he shouted, reaching down to grab at her.

For a few seconds she resisted him but then she nodded and scrambled to her feet. For a few moments she stared down and hesitated and Graham was about to push her when she jumped. She did it nimbly and gracefully and managed to stay on her feet, running to match the speed of the train.

Graham followed and immediately stumbled and fell flat on his face. His elbow struck the steel rail and his head took a knock, but he was too focused to care. Rolling over, he sprang up and started running back.

"Get on that end cane bin," he shouted, pointing to it as he passed.

He was so desperate he was almost in a fluster. He knew his plan was an all-or-nothing gamble, but each step was clear in his mind. By now the yellow brake wagon was receding down the far side of the hill and he knew they could never catch it up. Driven by fear he sprinted to the set of points 25 metres away, hoping that the lever was not locked in some way. To his relief, it was not. It appeared to be just the usual point lever with its counter-balance weight, and he grabbed the handle and heaved it across. To his intense relief, he heard and saw the points click across.

"Now, can we get the bins rolling?" he gasped as he set off sprinting back to where Carol stood beside the last bin. "Get on!" he shouted again, gesturing frantically for her to climb up.

But she didn't. Instead she gabbled at him, wanting to know what he was doing. Graham ignored her, his eyes questing under the wheels for the chocks or brakes he knew must be there. It was a wooden chock, jammed in under the last wheel. Knowing he must use every ounce of his strength Graham hurled himself at the bin and threw his weight against it, pushing for all he was worth. It was just enough. The bin moved a fraction and he kicked frantically at the chock. Carol saw what he was doing and also added her weight. To his relief, the baulk of wood fell away inside the rails and then the sheer mass of the loaded bins took over.

Even as the satisfaction surged through Graham, he realised he had unleashed a monster. The bin rolled immediately back, almost snagging and trapping his shoe (and the foot inside it!). Just in time he wrenched it clear but by then the bin had started to roll. Stumbling for a few steps, Graham spun round and grabbed the wire mesh side of the bin.

"Push!" he shouted.

Throwing his weight against the uphill corner of the bin, he leaned hard on it and scrabbled with his shoes to get a grip. Luckily, they encountered the timber sleepers and he was able to get a good purchase. Carol saw what he was doing and ran to the side of the wire mesh bin and also began to push.

For a few seconds Graham feared he had miscalculated. The small steel wheels only moved a fraction and the couplings strained and clinked. But the bins barely moved.

"Oh push!" Graham groaned, leaning forward and straining until he felt his heart might burst.

And then the bins began rolling. Graham found himself running along beside them, whooping with delight and relief. Then he realised they were starting to pick up speed.

"Quick! Get on before they go too fast," he called.

This time Carol did as she was bid, springing up and vanishing in between the first and second bins to stand on the couplings. Graham ran along with his fingers in the wire mesh, trying to judge what to grab on to and when to jump. Then the bin swerved towards him as the rails slewed it across into the points and he found himself dancing on the tops of the steel rails as he tried to avoid tripping or getting his foot caught.

To avoid tripping, he sprang up and clawed his way up the side of the bin, ignoring the pain of the wire cutting into his hands. He found himself kneeling on top of the newly cut cane billets, gasping as though he run another kilometre. Then the bin lurched back the other way is it swung onto the main line and Graham went tumbling on the billets. Only by clinging grimly to the steel rail on the top did he avoid being tumbled off.

The billets hurt and smelt of sugar and molasses, but he ignored the stickiness and odours and hauled himself to his knees. It took him a moment to orient himself and then he looked down and saw Carol's anxious face looking up from between the bins. He gave her what he hoped was a confident grin and then stared back along the line, fearful of what he had now started.

He saw that the line of loaded cane bins numbered only ten or a dozen. He could not be sure and did not waste time trying to count them. It was enough for him that the bins were now rolling down the slope back towards the creek. Raising his eyes he scanned the crest of the rise, searching for the crooks. To his relief, there was no sign of them or their vehicle. The train they had been on had also vanished down the other side of the rise.

Maybe we have pulled it off? Graham wondered, hope returning.

But then the jerking, rocking sensations from the moving bin brought other concerns. Graham looked around and was astonished at how fast they were now moving. The bins were now rolling down the long slope at what he judged was an alarming speed. It dawned on him that the loose bins were picking up speed with every second; that it was already dangerous to try to jump off.

Oh bloody hell! What have I done? If we try to jump off, we could break a leg or a back or something, he thought.

His alarm must have transmitted itself to Carol as she looked fearfully around. "Should we get off?" she cried.

Graham shook his head. "Too dangerous," he called back.

In fact, the bins were now lurching so wildly that he found he was in danger of being flung off and he had to lie low and cling on. Carol was also in danger and twice lost her footing and had to take a grip on the top rail. She was plainly in danger of slipping and falling down under the wheels.

"Climb up here," Graham shouted, necessitated by the need to make himself heard above the grinding of the steel wheels on the steel rails and the rattling, clanging, and clanking of numerous small metal fastenings, catches, and couplings.

Carol scrambled up and crouched next to him, looking fearfully around as she did. "Can you stop this?" she queried.

By then the bins were racing down the long slope so fast that it dawned on Graham that they were probably in mortal danger if they derailed. That got him looking over his shoulder, blinking into the rushing wind of their progress. He saw that the railway curved to the left as it approached the bridge and he wondered if the bins might derail on the bend.

Then, into his mind, came the images of the previous train crashes he had seen at the bridge, the piles of twisted wagons and spills of cane billets in the water.

If we get caught in a crash like that we could be drowned, even if we aren't crushed or mangled in the smash, he thought.

But before he could properly consider this, his heart gave another lurch of alarm. Into view behind the bins appeared the crook's vehicle!

The vehicle came racing up over the crest of the rise, trailing dust and visibly bouncing and rocking on the rough track. Once again, Graham felt sick with apprehension and could do nothing but hang on and look around in desperate hope. Both Rossiter's and Dennis's faces were visible as the vehicle rapidly caught them up. They both looked furiously angry and that at least gave Graham a spurt of satisfaction.

Within a minute, the vehicle was again racing close alongside, and this time Graham wondered if Rossiter might try to jump across, his door being only a few metres away. But although his head turned to look at the wagons and then ahead and then back at the train, he obviously thought it too risky.

Graham could only agree. By then the group of bins was racing down the slope at a truly alarming speed and Graham began to fear the wildly rocking and rattling bins might derail at any moment. He eyed the rapidly approaching bend and remembered it to be quite sharp.

Will these things derail on the bend? he worried.

"Yes, they will!" he muttered, fear coursing through him.

Which meant he and Carol needed to brace themselves for disaster!

Graham scrambled around to face the way they are going. "Carol, get up ready to jump," he shouted. "This thing is going to come off the rails at the bend. We need to jump clear or we will be crushed."

Even as he said this, he noted that the bins were entering the curve, jerking and swerving to the left, their little steel wheels shrieking and squealing against the inside of the right hand rail. The bin began to tilt to the right and shudder as centrifugal force took an invisible grip.

The vehicle was now roaring along almost right beside them, and Graham saw Rossiter pointing and yelling. A piece of grass smacked into Graham's left eye, and he blinked and tried to rub it out as he rose to a half crouch.

We will really have to jump a long way to be sure of getting clear.

And he knew it would hurt. Fear of the probable injuries began to paralyse him, and he found he was clinging on grimly and gaping. Dust and grass blew into his face and mouth, and he spat and coughed. A glance behind added to his fear. He saw that the whole line of bins was bouncing, rocking, and jerking but not in any concerted way. Each bin was moving independently, and they were stirring up their own dust cloud filled with grass and leaves. Loose cane billets were being bounced out and the whole mass of them looked to be seething.

And then Graham gasped. The bin third of fourth from the back leapt higher than the others and then landed heavily at an odd angle. A shrill, metallic shrieking began to fill the air and sparks flew up. The bins behind it began to jerk wildly.

It has derailed! Oh bloody hell! We are going to crash, he thought.

He looked ahead in desperate hope. The bins were now rattling into the bend. Through eyes watering from dust and grass debris, Graham saw the bridge come into view and noted that what he remembered was right, the last part of the curve was very tight. Suddenly, he saw the sunlight reflect off the water in the creek and he knew what they must try to do.

Turning to an equally terrified Carol, he shouted in her ear. "We have to jump into the creek. But really spring out or a wagon might land on top of you and crush you."

She nodded but looked so frightened that he wasn't sure if she could act. He was dimly aware that the bins were now shuddering violently and leaning far over as they screeched around the curve. From behind came terrible clanging and grating noises. He noted that the crook's vehicle had pulled up in a swirl of dust as the road and railway converged to cross the bridge.

But the men were the least of his worries. Now all his thoughts were focused on surviving what looked like a certain train wreck. And even as he hoped it wouldn't happen, it did.

Graham felt the bin heave and tip beneath and his feet and he found himself looking down into the water at the end of the bridge. The bin began to topple away from under him and in a desperate bid for survival he used his leg muscles to spring outwards.

"Jump!" he screamed.

Fear made him keep screaming as he plummeted. It seemed a terrifyingly long way down, but he knew it was only ten metres or so. But it was not the fall into the water he was afraid of. It was the wagons behind landing on him. Somehow, he managed to bring his feet down and under control and his arms to his front before he struck the water.

There was a stinging splash that left him partly winded and wholly terrified. The force of the drop took him deep, but that was expected. He had actually been worried it might not be deep enough. As soon as he was underwater, he opened his eyes despite the bubbles and blurriness. As he went down, he was aware of dark shadows above him and he cringed. They were from the next few wagons also derailing and tipping over. Amid the bubbles and swirling currents, Graham was aware of his shoes hitting the sandy bottom and of his arms doing a frantic breaststroke. They became his main means of propulsion when he discovered that he could not get an efficient upward thrust with his feet because of his shoes.

Get away! Get away! his mind cried.

Something big struck the backs of his legs and scraped down his calves but he flicked them up and kept swimming. Suddenly he was engulfed in a dark mass of hundreds of cane billets. Some struck his back and head and then his face and body as he swam through them. Now what he had feared was actually happening, the wagons were coming down to splash into the water above him!

A big shadow to his right made him glance that way and his heart went into a desperate overdrive. A huge mass of cane billets was falling through the water, followed by the steel shape of a bin. And under them was Carol!

Now past experience paid off. Graham was a very good underwater swimmer and very confident in the water and he instantly decided to risk being trapped. Changing direction he swam the few strokes into the mass of falling billets and grabbed at Carol's hair. By luck more than skill, his fingers twined in her hair and he took a tight grip and began swimming for all he was worth.

It was enough. Within a few strokes they were clear of the falling objects and skimming across a clear, sandy bottom. Carol reached up and began to claw at his fingers, so Graham let go. Glancing up he decided it was safe, so he headed up. As soon as he broke surface, he took a huge breath and then blinked and looked back. To his enormous relief, Carol broke surface beside him and also stared back.

What he saw caused him to shake his head. He and Carol were now about 20 or 30 metres downstream of the timber trestles holding up the bridge. In the water between them and the pilings were a jumbled heap of cane bins, the last one still settling and spilling its load of billets as it did. Waves were washing outwards, and small objects were still falling. The surface of the water was now a huge matt of floating cane billets.

Then Graham looked up and saw that one of the bins was jammed sideways across the bridge and that its cargo of cut cane had all spiled forward across the decking. Two more bins had run into that one and were standing at odd angles. Stopped just on the bridge behind them was the crook's vehicle. Dennis was gaping at the wreckage open-mouthed.

Rossiter appeared at the front of the crook's vehicle. He climbed up onto its bull bar and stared at the wreckage blocking the bridge. Then he looked down and immediately saw him and Carol. Rossiter pointed and shouted and ran back around the other side of the vehicle and back off the bridge out of sight. His shouts got Dennis to look down and he then climbed out and followed.

Rossiter is going to try to catch us by coming down through the long grass on the creek bank, Graham thought. That got him studying the vegetation and he saw that it was a thick tangle of very long grass and lantana and other bushes. *He won't find that easy,* he decided, having several times pushed through similar tangles.

Then he turned and looked at the other bank, thinking to swim to it and climb up. But it was also a thick tangle of weeds, guinea grass and bushes. *It will take forever to force a path up through that,* he thought.

Once again, it came to him that any pursuer would be able to follow their path much faster than they could make it. From that came the notion to use a track but his urgently scanning and dust filled eyes could not see any sign of one. But downstream to his right, about 75 metres away, was the big tree at the secret swimming pool.

"Swim down to your pool," he croaked to Carol.

She glanced at him and nodded and immediately began swimming in that direction with a smooth over-arm crawl. Graham set out to try to keep up with her but quickly discovered that she was an even better swimmer than he was. He also discovered that with his shoes hampering his feet he was making very little effective distance for a huge effort.

He was very reluctant to part with his shoes, suspecting that they might be even more important when running but there seemed to be no option if he was to reach the shore at all. So he paused, put his head under the water and drew his feet up one at a time and quickly pulled off both shoes, then peeled off the socks. Then he resumed swimming and was at once rewarded by being able to swim properly.

But he also quickly decided that the overarm stroke was not the best one to cover the distance and changed to a side stroke that allowed him to keep his head clear of the water. Not only did that help him breathe but he was able to look back to check on Rossiter's progress.

Within half a minute he saw Rossiter. The man was attempting to push through the thick tangle and could be heard cursing and swearing as he did. Then Rossiter saw Graham and Carol swimming and swore even louder. He turned and vanished back out of sight.

What's he doing now? Graham worried.

He had an idea he did not want to voice. But he was right. Half a minute later, Rossiter re-appeared at the vehicle and started clambering over the wreckage of the cane bins on the bridge. Dennis followed him.

"He's going to try to cut us off again!" Graham shouted. It was a sickening thought and got his heart hammering again.

Carol glanced back and Graham pointed to the bridge. "Swim, Carol! Swim! They are going across the bridge. We must beat them to it."

Carol grasped the situation immediately and again began swimming like a champion. Graham put his head down and pushed himself. But the burst of speed only lasted half a minute before he had to revert to the side stroke to get enough air. As he did, he saw Rossiter scrambling over the huge pile of loose billets blocking the decking. Dennis was clambering over the twisted bins like a gangly spider.

Swivelling his head around to look downstream, Graham measured his progress and was again dismayed. He and Carol had only covered about half the distance.

This is going to be bloody close! he decided.

Chapter 39

LIFE AND DEATH RACE

"Swim Carol, swim!" Graham croaked, half-choking as water got into his throat as he did.

She nodded and struck out. Graham followed, hampered by his wet clothes and by muscles that did not seem to want to work properly. To add to his dismay he felt himself weakening.

Glancing back, he saw Rossiter spring off the pile of billets and go running out of sight along the bridge. Dennis scrambled off the loose billets and followed. Spurred by desperation, Graham swam. But it was tiring and slow and Carol drew quickly ahead. Only by exerting himself to his utmost could Graham keep going.

But then he realised he was approaching the big tree and the sight of the rope swing hanging down spurred him to a last effort. Then he was under the tree and there was the beach and Carol wading up out of the water near the end of the track.

To Graham's concern, she stopped and looked back and called to him. Graham cleared his throat and croaked back.

"Carol, run! Don't wait for me! Get to the mill. Go!"

But she did wait and even waded in to grab his arm as his feet touched bottom. But Graham found his feet felt like they were made of lead, and he staggered up into the shallows on legs that felt as though they were made of rubber. To add to his dismay, he found his vision blurred and he had trouble keeping his balance. His heart hammered as though it would burst. His breath came in great sucking gulps.

Blinking and gasping, he shook his head and again croaked at Carol. "Run, Carol! Get to the mill! I will delay them or I can hide. Go!"

"No! We both go. Come on!" Carol replied, gripping his arm tightly and holding him up.

"Run!"

"No! Keep walking," Carol gasped, also taking huge gulps of air.

By then Graham was out of the water and on the beach at the end of the track. "Okay, go first," he gasped, gesturing to get her moving.

To his relief, she let go and started up the track through the long grass, glancing back every couple of paces to see how he was coping. Somehow Graham got his legs moving, the sand rough and gritty under his bare feet. Still sucking in huge breaths, he plodded slowly up the slope. Ahead of him, Carol hurried up the track through the long grass and he noted that at some stage she had also discarded her shoes and socks.

It was only about 30 metres diagonally and perhaps 10 vertically, but to Graham that slope now loomed like an Everest. He focused his eyes on Carol's back and tried to stay with her but again she drew ahead. It seemed that the swim had completely drained him of energy, but his fitness began to reassert itself and his vision came back into focus.

Gasping and filled with dread, Graham reached the top of the path and staggered out onto the gravel road. There was the mill! It was still several hundred metres away, but safety was in sight! But a glance to his left sent stabs of terror through him. Rossiter! And Dennis. Both crooks were running towards them from the bridge and were only about 50 paces away!

Carol saw them and immediately broke into a frantic sprint. Spurred by intense fear, Graham also found the strength to run. But Carol had started running directly away from the men, going back along the gravel road.

"The mill, Carol! Run to the mill!" Graham gasped.

And already he was regretting not having his shoes as the gravel was hard on his bare feet. And things got instantly worse as he swerved to follow Carol across the first railway line. There were prickles and the ballast was composed of sharp little stones.

Blue metal, Graham thought, eyeing the crushed rock which supported the railway lines.

There were two railway lines with nothing on them but then there were four or five parallel lines on which seemingly endless rows of empty cane bins were parked. Beyond that were lines with rows of full bins and then the mill. At first Carol turned and ran along beside the first row or empty bins, as that still took them towards the main part of the mill.

Graham pounded after her, ignoring the hurt his soles were now suffering as he could hear the men's boots thudding behind. A frightened glance back showed Rossiter to be only about 40 metres behind.

Rossiter noticed his glance as he yelled, "Stop you bloody kids, stop! We just want to talk to you."

Pig's bum! Graham thought.

At the very least he expected a severe bashing, and Declin's warning as to the men's real intent spurred him to keep running. But Carol was audibly gasping, and Graham knew he could not keep it up much longer either. He began to again contemplate fighting, knowing with sick certainty that he would be no match for a fit, grown man with murderous intent.

Then Graham looked ahead, hoping to see people at the railway workshop. Instead, his blurring vision focused on Marvin. The man was doing something between a light truck and a large, low brick storage tank which Graham thought held molasses. At that moment, Marvin lifted his head and looked in their direction and he gaped and straightened up.

Bugger! Graham thought. "Carol, Marvin's ahead. Go left, go between the wagons."

No sooner had he said this than Rossiter's voice came from close behind. "Marvin! Marvin you great lump! Cut them off! Don't let them reach the mill."

To Graham's horror, he saw Marvin drop what he was holding and start running across to where the railway lines curved back out of the unloading area and tippler.

"Oh God!" Graham gasped, dread rising to clutch at his wheezing chest.

But Carol had seen the danger too and acted. She skidded to a stop and nimbly hopped through the gap between two empty bins. Graham followed, having to pause and wait while she clambered through, and hotly conscious that Rossiter was now only about 30 metres back. Graham sprang up onto the couplings and then jumped out onto the gritty ground beyond.

Carol had again turned aright and kept running, the main part of the mill now looming up a couple of hundred metres ahead.

"Go left Carol, aim for the Control Room," Graham croaked, hoping there should be people there and at the tippler where they unload.

He saw Carol nod as she ran. Twenty paces further on again she stopped and went to clamber through. As he reached her, Graham heard Rossiter jump down after climbing between the wagons and a glance told him that gap had closed to only about 20 metres. Rather than delay while waiting for Carol, Graham ran on to the gap between the next two wagons and went scrambling through there. He knew that every second was now vital.

As he jumped down, Graham almost collided with Carol. She was gasping and her chest heaving and her eyes rolling. She cast him a despairing glance but kept on running. Graham followed. To him it had become like a nightmare in which the curving lines of bins just went on and on and no matter how hard he ran he could not seem to find a way out. But a tiny corner of his rational brain told him there were ways out and they just had to keep going.

But there was Marvin. The man was about a hundred metres ahead, standing between the now curving rails and blocking the direct route to the main part of the mill. Carol gave a cry of fear and immediately turned left and sprang up between the next row of bins. Once again, Graham did not wait those extra seconds for her to get out of the way but ran to the next gap, hotly aware that Rossiter's boots were thudding close behind.

This time as Graham landed, hurting his feet on what felt like broken glass and prickles, he saw that Carol had immediately made her way through between the next line of parked bins. Graham glimpsed her back as she went through. But he also heard Rossiter close behind and he began to sob with fear.

I'm not going to make this, he thought.

Forcing himself to keep going, he sprang up between two bins and then leapt out. As he landed, he glanced to his right and got a glimpse of Marvin lumbering across the gap towards the mill. Behind him he heard a gasping and swearing Rossiter skid to a stop then spring onto the couplings he had just vacated.

Again sheer fear was the spur, and Graham ignored the burs and sharp stones and ran across to jump up between the empty wagons in the next row. His haste was almost his undoing as his bare feet slipped on greasy steel and he slid down to land awkwardly on the rough wooden sleepers between the rails. The rail almost tripped him, and he stubbed his toe as he propelled himself out beyond that line of wagons and through to the next.

As Graham ran across to the next line of empty wagons, he heard Rossiter spring up onto the couplings of the one he had just left and a spurt of fear stabbed through him. It was obvious that Rossiter was faster and stronger and that he was catching up. A terrified glance suggested a gap of only 10 paces!

And they were now so close! The closest part of the buildings looked to be only a hundred metres. Graham found himself in a more open strip of sandy ground, a vehicle track in fact, separating the rows of empty bins from the lines of ones loaded with newly cut cane. There were at least three or four rows of these. They curved in to sets of points that led to a single line which went into the unloading tippler.

Carol had begun running that way as the lines curved towards where they wanted to go. The Control Room was clear to see above the loaded bins. Graham turned and followed, a severe stitch now sending agonising stabs of pain through his left side. Marvin was somewhere in that direction, but Graham decided they would be safe if they got there, anywhere where there were other people! Another noise behind him made him glance that way and he saw Dennis go scrambling in between two loaded cane bins. And Rossiter was almost within arm's reach!

Racing as fast as he could push his pain-wracked body, Graham ran on, Carol just managing to keep ahead. Then Marvin again appeared between them and the mill. Carol immediately turned to her left and sprang across between the loaded bins. Graham was by now almost frantic with anxiety. He reached out and grasped the corner of the wire bin and swung himself around into the gap behind her.

In an instant he made a desperate decision, one that made him choke up with dread. As he scrambled across with Rossiter actually touching his shirt as he snatched out, Graham's eyes noted a piece of rusty steel lying beside the rails. It was about 30cm long and had holes in it and he recognised it as a fishplate for fastening rails together. But it was also a potential weapon, and as he jumped down he scooped it up and stepped out of sight behind the bin full of cane billets.

Sobbing with exhaustion and fear he swung the steel piece back and as Rossiter came jumping down between the wagons Graham struck with it. Rossiter saw it coming and tried to put a hand up to save himself. But he wasn't quick enough, and the end of the steel struck him hard in the face. He let out a ghastly cry of pain and fell down to sprawl on the sand.

Graham stared at the man, aghast at what he had done. *Oh my God! Have I killed him?* he thought.

Then he saw Rossiter reach up with both hands to grab at his face, to cover his left eye. The guilty thought that he had somehow mangled Rossiter's eye then assailed Graham. Appalled at the enormity of causing such harm, he dropped the piece of steel and stood trembling.

But the appearance of Dennis jumping down 20 metres away, and then Carol's voice, got him moving. He saw Dennis's eyes open with alarm and then he swore and began running towards him. Graham turned in a stagger, now completely out of breath and gasping on his last legs.

Behind him he heard Rossiter groan and then swear. Then the man bellowed, "You little bastard! I'll kill you for that!"

A terrified glance showed Dennis helping Rossiter to his feet. Rossiter was holding his face and blood was streaming down the left side. To Graham's mingled relief and concern, he saw that Rossiter's left eye was blinking as blood trickled down from a gash in his forehead and eyebrow. But the man was now really enraged, and he began staggering after him.

He shook Dennis off and shouted, "Get after them, Dennis, you bloody drongo! Catch them! Don't let them get to the bloody mill!"

A wide-eyed and terrified Carol went scrambling across between yet another line of loaded wagons and Graham, after one more frightened glance towards Rossiter and Dennis, went after her. He glimpsed Dennis moving as he did. On the other side was one last line of loaded wagons. The aroma of cut sugar cane making the air thick and choking. As Graham jumped down, he saw Dennis do likewise, so he just ran across to that last line of wagons and scrambled through, his chest wheezing and the breath hot and rasping in his throat.

Graham turned right and ran toward the closest buildings of the mill. On his left was a bitumen road, several small sheds, which he ignored, and then the open lawn extending across to the ring road and workers' houses. Ahead was the Control Room up on its steel scaffolding, steel steps leading up to it. And the unloader was on the right and working. Even as Graham resumed running, the whole train of wagons beside him suddenly lurched forward and two more bins were unhooked by the automatic decoupler and drawn into the huge rotating structure.

Now only 50 metres... 40 metres... 30 metres... 20 metres... 10...

Graham was now so winded he could barely stagger, hunched over from the pain of a stitch and gasping, fearing he might have a heart attack it was thumping so hard. His vision kept blurring, but he noted Carol almost at the steps and he struggled to focus, looking for people. But into his vision appeared a grinning Marvin. The man was at the far end of the tippler and moving to cut Carol off from the steps leading up to the Control Room.

Where are the men who should be working here? Graham thought.

He tried to call for help but could only gasp and wheeze.

We're done for. It's over!

* * *

Carol tried to step aside but Marvin mirrored her and blocked her again. He was leering and taunting and the sight of him suddenly sparked fierce anger in Graham. He dashed forward, just as Dennis arrived from the other direction. Carol tried to reach the bottom of the steps before Marvin but was baffled. Graham saw her head shaking and she cried out telling him to get out of her way.

But Marvin didn't and Carol turned to run back towards Graham. From behind him came Rossiter's voice, shouting above the roar and grind of machinery as the tippler suddenly rotated.

"Grab her! Don't let her past," he ordered.

Marvin lunged forward and grabbed Carol. Shock appeared on her face, then outrage, and then fear. She screamed, then screamed again. But her screams were lost in the noise of the double loads of cane billets cascading down into the steel pit with a thundering roar.

Driven by a mixture of anger and fear, Graham pushed himself to run those last few paces. Marvin saw him coming but obviously misunderstood his intentions. Instead of trying to get past him Graham crashed into him and Carol, his fist driving forward into Marvin's face. The knuckles took the brute squarely on the nose and Graham had the momentary satisfaction of seeing blood spurt.

But he was partly successful as Marvin let go of Carol. Graham wanted her to flee up the steps, but as she tried to get away Marvin's huge hand shot out and slapped her, knocking her to the steel decking. Then he swung a backhander which Graham could only partly avoid. It hit the left side of his face and sent him reeling back. As he struggled to regain his sense and footing, he was half-deafened by the noises of the tippler rotating to place the now empty bins the right way up.

There were running footsteps behind him, and Graham knew it was Dennis. Unable to run any more, Graham stopped near the end of the tippler and turned to face his attacker. A terrible feeling of failure gripped him, but he resolved to fight to the bitter end. Dennis skidded to a stop and behind him appeared an enraged Rossiter, his face a horrible bloody mask.

Graham gritted his teeth and clenched his fists. Beside him he was dimly aware that the conveyor belt down in the pit had begun moving the piles of cane billets towards the slashers. The noise was disorienting and distracting. To add to the problem, the two empty wagons lurched into motion and were drawn forward.

Rossiter raced in, fists flailing. As he did, he snarled, "Grab the little shit! Chuck him in. Marvin, throw her in as well."

Graham lashed out but Rossiter ignored the punches and grappled with him, gripping him around the chest. His angry, hate- and blood-filled eyes appeared close to Graham's face, and he sensed this was a fight to the death. Struggling desperately, he lashed out and tied to break free. But Dennis now moved in and took hold of his right wrist and Graham found himself unable to run or punch. Fear surged as the implication of what Rossiter had said suddenly sank in.

The pit!

Graham was aghast. There it was beside him, the cane billets already being moved up into the revolving steel knives to be slashed into fibres.

"No!" he cried as he felt himself lifted.

To his utter horror, he found his feet off the deck and the steel safety railings in the middle of his back. Desperately he tried to cling on, but Dennis banged at the fingers of his right hand and Rossiter wrenched the fingers of his left away from where Graham had taken a grip on his clothing. In desperation, Graham jerked and twisted and tried to kick. But to no avail. He was firmly gripped.

As he was lifted up and over the railings, Graham found himself staring down into the vibrating, moving piles of cane billets and his eyes suddenly focused on the revolving blades at the top end of the pit.

No! his mind cried. *No!*

And then his emotions got another cruel twist as he saw a screaming Carol plummet down to sprawl on the moving cane.

We are dead! he thought.

Chapter 40

COURAGE

Declin knew he was hurting. He also knew he needed to move.

Carol is in danger! he thought. His senses swam and he battled to stay conscious. *Where am I? What's going on?*

He had to blink and then use will power to keep his eyes open. His vision was blurred and he hurt all over. Dimly he noted that he was being gripped under the armpits by a man. Then he was dropped and more stabs of pain lanced through him. That woke him up and he saw the person standing over him.

Who is he? What's happening? Declin wondered, more darts of pain jolting his thoughts.

Sudden memory of fighting with Rossiter and Dennis flooded into his consciousness, and awareness of them hitting and kicking him. Then he saw that the man standing over him was Marvin and fear in almost paralysing strength surged through him.

I must move! I must get away! I must save Carol!

But what was going on? Declin blinked and tried to focus his eyes as he looked up. He was just trying to summon the strength and will to fight Marvin when, to his surprise, the man just turned and ran away.

Wha... What the hell?

Declin realised he was lying on the dirt beside a vehicle at the bottom of a steel ladder. His gaze travelled up the ladder and he recognised the old brick molasses tank.

What am I doing here? How did I get here? And where is Marvin going?

Then another distant voice penetrated his consciousness, that bloody Graham's. "Go left Carol, aim for the Control Room," he called.

Declin's head jerked around and he rolled onto his front, an action he instantly regretted as it hurt so much. He found himself blinking in the glare and staring across rows of railway lines into the marshalling yards. And there was Carol!

As though through a telescope, Declin clearly saw her scramble across from one line of parked cane bins to another, followed by that bloody Graham. They were over a hundred metres away and appeared to be scrambling across through the lines of parked wagons with desperate haste.

Then Rossiter and Dennis appeared, clearly chasing them. Instantly Declin understood: Carol and Graham were trying to get to the safety of the mill and they were being chased by Rossiter and Dennis.

And that brute, Marvin! Where is he?

Declin ignored the pain and the bout of nausea that followed and pushed himself to his hands and knees. For a few seconds he was swamped by a bout of dizziness and his vision blurred, but then he shook his head and forced his eyes to focus. There was Marvin, lumbering across the rail tracks where they curved back out of the unloading tippler.

"Marvin is trying to cut them off," Declin murmured.

Reaching up he gripped the truck beside him and hauled himself to his feet. A terrible feeling of dread now gripped him, and he felt an intense urge to run to Carol's aid. But again he was swamped by nausea and his stomach heaved and he bent forward as a trickle of vomit and bile spread down his front and onto the dust.

Wiping his mouth and then using his sleeve to wipe his watering eyes he straightened up, his will power kicking in.

"Get moving man! She needs you. Move!" he told himself.

Declin set off on legs that felt like rubber, staggering and stumbling after Marvin. Twice he tripped and fell and each time it seemed to take a massive effort to get back upright. Each time he stood for a few seconds swaying and teetering before gritting his teeth and staggering on. Each step took an effort, and his vision came and went in waves of clarity and blackness.

Ahead of him he saw Marvin clamber through the line of empty bins on the mill side of the tippler and that spurred Declin to keep going. He could hear shouts and then, to his horror, he heard Carol scream, the scream mostly drowned out by the roar and rattle of two bins emptying into the pit.

Marvin has got her! Declin thought.

The need to save her spurred him to greater efforts and he forced himself to go faster. He reached the line of empty bins just as the next two bins were uncoupled and rotated. Quickly, he clambered across between two of them. It was knowing how it all worked that saved Declin from a nasty accident as he was ready when the machinery jerked the line of empty bins forward to allow space for the two newly emptied bins to be recoupled.

As Declin regained his footing in under the gantry at the end of the tippler, he saw the three crooks wrestling with Carol and Graham. To his dismay, he saw that Marvin had hold of Carol. Then dismay turned to horror as he saw Marvin swing Carol up and toss her over the steel safety railings into the pit. Carol screamed as she fell, the sound chilling Declin but sparking him to instant and violent action.

Rushing forward he leapt to the 'Stop' button on the steel post beside the tippler. Slamming it in, he looked around. *Where the hell are the men who should be on duty here?* he wondered.

Then it came to him: Rossiter and Marvin were one of the usual crews. And there was Rossiter. He and Dennis were struggling with Graham and even as Declin shouted to stop, they hoisted him up and tossed him down onto the piles of cane billets in the pit.

But the machinery had all shuddered to a stop and Declin moved to look down. Carol was lying there writhing on the pile of billets and for a horrible moment Declin wondered if the fall had broken her back. Graham was rolling over and trying to get to his hands and knees on the unstable pile.

And then Declin realised his peril. Rossiter rushed over and grabbed him.

"Chuck this interfering mongrel in too!" he shouted.

Declin was swamped by dread and struggled violently, yelling at the top of his voice as he did. "Help! Help! Save me! Help!"

But Marvin had turned and there was Dennis as well, grabbing at him. Declin redoubled his frantic efforts to break free but was punched and almost lost consciousness. Now desperate to break free, he lashed out with fists and feet and that drove both Marvin and Dennis back a pace or two. But Rossiter punched him again in the head and he found himself falling.

Declin fell hard on the concrete floor beside the pit and Rossiter began to kick at him, hard, savage kicks into his chest and stomach. Declin twitched and kicked back in a frantic attempt to survive. Then suddenly, Rossiter was sprawling on top of him and squirming violently.

Through a bloodshot and rapidly watering eye, Declin saw that Dennis had got in the way while also trying to kick, tripping his boss and causing him to fall.

Rossiter rolled onto his back and lashed out at Dennis with his boots, driving him back. But he had taken his focus off Declin, who now pushed hard to get out from under the man. And suddenly he was free, and Rossiter was also down in the pit. He had slid through under the second rail. He landed heavily and rolled sideways, knocking Carol over as he did. She fell backwards, tumbling against Graham.

Swearing and enraged, Rossiter scrabbled to regain his footing and managed to get to his feet. He glared and spat hate and his hands became claws and he took a step towards Declin.

"I'll kill you, you interfering little bastard!" he snarled.

At that moment the machinery restarted. The conveyer belt resumed moving with a sharp jerk and the knives resumed rotating. Rossiter was caught off balance and went stumbling backwards down the unstable pile of billets. With a gasp of annoyance he fell backwards down the slope, to slide headfirst into those flashing steel cutters!

Declin stared aghast as Rossiter's head suddenly blossomed scarlet and then vanished in a red spray. His scream was cut off instantly. The whole mass of billets and Rossiter's body began moving towards the slashers.

Looking up, Declin saw that Marvin had run to the control buttons and had obviously pressed the 'Start' button. He was now looking back over his shoulder, his face a mask of surprise and dismay as he realised his boss was being mangled down in the pit.

And Carol would be next! And Graham. He was frantically trying to regain his feet and looking for a way up. The next two full cane bins began rumbling into position.

"Move!" Declin ordered.

The order was to himself, but to his relief and surprise both Marvin and Dennis acted on it. Aghast at what he had done, Marvin took one more look and fled into the interior of the mill. Dennis turned to run the other way but ran into several workers and Mr Battersby who had appeared at the bottom of the steps.

In a supreme effort of mind over physical weakness, Declin forced his battered body across to the controls. Once again, he slammed the

'Stop' button. And just in time! Carol was clawing her way desperately across the moving pile but was less than a metre from the slashers!

To Declin's intense relief, the machinery shuddered to a stop. For a few seconds he clung to the post and then blackness engulfed him.

* * *

Graham stared at the bloody horror that was Rossiter. His whole body trembled as the shock and relief took hold. He had seen a man fall into a wood chipping machine when rescuing Willy Williams a few months before, but this seemed much worse. Shaking his head with disbelief and reaction, he looked away.

Carol was also staring aghast at what was left of Rossiter, but then her father called and she looked up. So did Graham. Mr Battersby was standing with a group of workers and he was calling for them to climb out. Carol tried, but the pile of cane billets kept sliding and moving and she could not reach. Despite reaching up with her arms above her head, she was still out of reach of the helping hands. Graham immediately slithered and scrambled over to her, also driven by fear of the machine.

With an effort he controlled his urge to spring up and get lifted out of that death pit by the waiting hands. Instead, he swallowed and knelt against the concrete side. Remembering how he had seen soldiers go over an obstacle course, he knelt with one knee forward so that the right thigh was horizontal.

He gestured to his knee and called to Carol, "Step on my thigh and then up onto my shoulders and I will lift you up."

It took a few moments and a repeat of the instructions before she understood and did as she was told. As soon as she had lifted herself up onto his shoulder, Graham called for her to put her arms up against the wall and then he stood up. That took a real effort as his leg muscles were all shaking and he felt terribly weak. But it worked. Carol was boosted right up and the men were able to reach down to grab her wrists. Suddenly the weight came off as she was whisked up and out.

Then it was Graham's turn and to his dismay he could not jump high enough. He had to wait until a rope was found, a short length of old but thick rope. He was drawn up and then grabbed by strong hands and lifted up and over the steel safety railing. It was such a relief to be out of that place that his whole body began to tremble as he was lowered to the concrete floor.

Unable to stand, Graham was lowered to a sitting position, leaning with his back against a steel post. A workman with a First Aid kit knelt to check him over. The shock then hit him. His lips quivered and he began to sob and shiver. Another worker knelt and began to wipe Graham's face and arms with a cool damp cloth.

The First Aider patted his shoulder. "You will be alright kid. You are safe now."

For a couple of minutes Graham could do nothing but sit and shake. His breath came in huge gulps and they had to caution him not to hyperventilate. Slowly he calmed down and he was able to look around.

And what he saw dismayed and annoyed him. More workers had arrived and another First Aid team. But when they parted, Graham got a glimpse of a weeping Carol kneeling and hugging Declin to her bosom.

A spurt of jealousy assailed him. Anger and reaction all boiled up and Graham tried to hoist himself to his feet. He felt hurt and angry, but that emotion was exacerbated by the knowledge that he was being unfair, that in fact Declin had saved their lives. But the workers held Graham down and told him to relax and suddenly that was all he could do. The energy and emotion just drained out of him and he sat there shaking his head and trembling.

With his emotions in a swirl of confusion, Graham watched as Carol was eased away and then hurried out by her father and another worker. Then Declin was placed on a stretcher and carried away. The First Aider with Graham then asked if he was okay to walk.

Graham nodded but when they hoisted him up, he winced as he realised just how much his feet hurt. "I've got a few prickles and cuts in my feet," he explained.

"We'll get you to the Sick Room at the office and fix you up," the First Aider replied.

So, helped by a worker on each side, Graham limped and hobbled around and onto the lawn. There were more people there, managers and office staff and workers.

Halfway across the lawn, Declin's stretcher was halted in the shade of a tree beside an ambulance that had just arrived and parked on the grass. The paramedics hurried over to assess Declin. Graham and his helpers stopped nearby at his request. As Graham stood there waiting, he saw Carol move from her father's side to stand beside Declin as he was lifted across onto the wheeled stretcher from the ambulance. She then took his hand and began to tenderly stroke his forehead.

That hurt a bit too, but Graham just shrugged. Moving free of his helpers he hobbled over to Declin. He gave a wry smile and held out his hand.

"Thanks Declin. You saved our lives," he said.

Declin met his eyes and nodded then held out his hand. They shook. As they did, a police car skidded to a stop nearby and two policemen climbed out. Graham saw that it was the same two that had arrested him.

"What the hell's going on?" queried the female sergeant.

"There's been another accident. There's a body in the tippler pit," replied Mr Battersby, pointing in that direction. "And two of my fellows are holding a man."

The police sergeant nodded and pointed. "Off you go, constable. Secure the area. Now, do we have any witnesses this time?"

Mr Battersby pointed to Declin and Carol and then to Graham. "Yes. My daughter and Mr Riley here and this boy."

The police sergeant glanced at Declin and then at Graham. Then she frowned and looked harder.

"Aren't you the boy we arrested on Sunday?"

Graham felt his stomach give a sickening lurch. "Yes ma'am," he croaked.

The police sergeant then turned to Declin. "Riley? Aren't you the man who was bashed and taken to hospital Sunday morning?"

"Yes sergeant."

"So what's going on? Has Kirk assaulted you again?" the sergeant queried, plainly puzzled.

"No sergeant. He came with me. He didn't assault me and put me in hospital. That was Rossiter and Marvin. They tried to kill me and then obviously spread the story that Graham and his friend, Stephen, had done it."

"So Kirk here did not attack you?"

"No sergeant. Neither did his friend, Stephen," Declin answered.

"But why would those men bash you?" the police sergeant asked, now taking out her notebook and pen.

"Because I wouldn't stop the mill when they said and because I saw Rossiter murder Mr Henley," Declin replied.

The mill manager now spoke. "Stop the mill? Why would they want you to do that?"

"Because that was what they were doing. They were sabotaging the mill to make it stop."

Astonishment showed on the manager's face. "But why?"

Declin could only shrug. "I don't know. I just know that was what they were trying to do," he replied.

"So if you knew, why didn't you tell us?" the manager snapped.

Declin blushed and looked down. "Because I was scared. Because they threatened to kill me and my family," he answered.

"Can you prove any of this?" the police sergeant asked.

Declin nodded. "Yes. I have a video. I took it out of the CCTV when Mr Henley was killed."

That comment earned Declin some hard looks from the managers and Graham felt sorry for him.

He might lose his job for doing that, he thought.

There was some discussion and then the sergeant said, "You were in hospital this morning and then went to the high school. What are you doing here?"

Declin answered. "We came here to make sure Carol was safe."

At that he looked up and she gave him a loving look and squeezed his hand.

"So what happened?" the sergeant queried.

Graham answered that. He described how they had gone to Carol's and found the men kidnapping her, the fight and then running. He went on to describe how he and Carol had climbed onto the back of the train and then how Rossiter and Dennis had followed in their vehicle. The story of the chase across the bridge and up onto the next rise held everyone's attention.

But then Graham hesitated, realising the next bit could get him into real trouble. However, there seemed nothing for it but to go on, so he described how he and Carol had set the bins full of cane rolling. As he said this, he saw furrowed brows on the manager and some of the staff.

"We had nowhere else to go. Sorry, but we crashed your train."

"Crashed the train?" cried the manager, anger blooming.

"Into the creek," Graham answered, nodding and bracing for more trouble. "Sorry, we were desperate. We were sure the men were trying to kill us."

"Kill you! Why would they do that?" the police sergeant asked.

Carol answered. "Because we knew... know too much," she said.

"So what happened then?" Mr Battersby queried.

"We went into the creek when the bins derailed," Graham explained. "So we had to swim. Then we ran here to the mill."

Mr Battersby nodded. "Yes, we saw that on CCTV but didn't know what was really happening."

Graham remembered being in that pit with the slashers going and the next two full bins starting to be hauled overhead to empty and he shuddered. Anger flared.

"You could have come down to help!"

"We thought there were men here on duty," Mr Battersby replied defensively. "We didn't realise that Rossiter and Marvin were two of the men chasing you. But when we saw the fighting at the tippler we came down."

One of the workers nodded. "But not in time. You did a great job at saving them, Declin. If you hadn't hit that stop button they would have been... er... history."

Again Graham was assailed by searing flashbacks. "Yes, thanks Declin. You arrived just in time," he said.

Carol hugged Declin and then said, "What happened to you Declin? How did you know where we were?"

Declin frowned and shook his head, wincing at some pain. "I... I don't know. They knocked me out at your place and when I came to Marvin was holding me between his truck and the molasses tank. He then ran off and I followed. I have no idea how I got there or what he was doing."

At that Carol went pale and in a hoarse whisper said, "O'Malley."

"What?" Declin asked.

"O'Malley. As we were running away, I heard Rossiter call to Marvin to get his truck. 'Put Riley with O'Malley'," he said.

The police sergeant frowned. "Who's O'Malley?"

Mr Battersby answered. "One of the workers. He didn't turn up for work one day, so we assumed he had just left."

Graham had been listening and he remembered Rossiter calling to Marvin. Suddenly a chill of dread gripped the back of his skull and neck, and he came out in goose bumps.

"He will be in the molasses tank," he croaked. The police sergeant looked at him. "I am guessing that Rossiter murdered him and that they put his body in the molasses tank. Marvin was going to put Declin there as well."

"Oh my God!" cried the manager, looking suddenly ill.

"Bloody hell!" agreed the police sergeant. Carol looked aghast and Declin looked very pale and thoughtful.

One of the paramedics now interrupted. "Sorry, sergeant, but we need to get Mr Riley to hospital. He needs some scans and checks."

The sergeant nodded and turned to Carol and Graham. "What about this pair? Do either of you need a doctor?"

Carol shook her head but the First Aider pointed to Graham. "This young fella looks like he's had a few knocks and scratches. He should."

The police sergeant agreed. "You go in the ambulance, young Kirk. We will catch up with you later."

"Which hospital?" Graham asked, fearing the ambulance might go to the Innisfail Hospital.

"Cairns."

"Can I go home afterwards?" Graham asked the sergeant.

"Yes, we have your address. Now that we know you didn't assault Mr Riley, you aren't under arrest."

* * *

Graham's last view of Carol was when her mother arrived and she and her father stood in a weeping huddle. The back doors were then closed and the ambulance set off. Declin was wired up to various machines and a catheter and drip inserted. Only then did the paramedic turn his attention to Graham, cleaning his cuts and scratches with antiseptic wipes.

The next few hours were painful, both physically and emotionally. The burrs and cuts in his feet were attended to and when they got to the hospital he had to sit and wait before a doctor checked him over. His ripped shirt went in the bin, so he had to sit in just his shorts. With no shirt or shoes he felt very self-conscious. When he came out, he found his mother waiting, her face a mixture of concern, love and exasperation.

"What have you been up to this time?" she demanded, but when she learned the full story she was very proud of him and said so.

At home, Graham was able to soak in a hot bath and then lie in bed. His big brother Alex was plainly jealous and sister Kylie was thrilled and said he was 'a real knight in shining armour'.

To Graham's annoyance, she was also obviously pleased that his 'affair' with Carol was evidently over and she again pressed Margaret's case, but only subtly. Margaret achieved more just by being her gentle, caring self when he saw her next.

Graham insisted on going to school the following day, primarily to go to Army Cadets and to see Captain Conkey. Captain Conkey already knew the outline and a check with the HQ confirmed that Graham was no longer suspended and that he could attend the Warrant Officers Course in December.

Carol wasn't at school that day, but when she did return the following Thursday she was friendly but distant. Graham learned from Rosemary that Mr Battersby had agreed that Declin could be friends with Carol and that she and Declin were happy together.

"Declin is a real gentleman and has promised to wait until she is old enough before he takes her out," Rosemary said.

Which made Graham grunt and be grumpy, and for the rest of his life, whenever he smelt or tasted brown sugar or molasses Graham experienced a series of searing flashbacks, half erotic, half traumatic. But he still liked sugar mills and sugar trains.

And he did not get into trouble for wrecking the cane bins. Marvin and Dennis both went to jail for murder, and during the trial it came out that they were employed by a businessman, a real estate agent who wanted the mill closed so he could buy up the land to subdivide it. The trial also found that Rossiter and his cronies were responsible for at least four murders (O'Malley was in the molasses tank, and the fall from the chimney was no accident, nor was the electrocution or Mr Henley's fall into the slashers). Declin kept his job and even got promoted.

Graham completed his Warrant Officers Course and became CSM, and almost immediately found himself involved in another adventure.

Enjoy more C.R. Cummings stories

The Air Cadets

The Navy Cadets

The Army Cadets